# UNUSUAL MINDS

## TRACIE HOLLIS

## About the Author

Tracie Hollis is a researcher and instructor in the tech industry when she is not dreaming up dystopian worlds. She lives in Atlanta, Georgia with her partner and their two semi-wild toy poodles.

# UNUSUAL MINDS

## TRACIE HOLLIS

BELLA
BOOKS
2023

Bella Books, Inc.
P.O. Box 10543
Tallahassee, FL 32302

Printed in the United States of America on acid-free paper.

First Edition - 2023

Editor: Medora MacDougall
Cover Designer: Kayla Mancuso
Photo Credit: ElevenPics Photography

ISBN: 978-1-64247-434-3

## PUBLISHER'S NOTE

"That proves you are unusual," returned the Scarecrow, "and I am convinced that the only people worthy of consideration in this world are the unusual ones. For the common folks are like the leaves of a tree, and live and die unnoticed."

-L. Frank Baum, *The Land of Oz*

*For Roxanne*

# PROLOGUE

At dawn, a torrent of rain came like a premonition, pummeling the star magnolia trees in my parents' yard, ripping the spring blossoms from their nurtured existence. But by the end of school that day the rain was forgotten, the sun burnt through the dense gray clouds and shone so brightly a rainbow appeared over the causeway, and Lucy and I straddled our bikes and took off down the road, leaving the fragrance of budding flowers and wet grass in our idyllic neighborhood behind.

We spent most of our carefree afternoons at the river. We would dance between the lodgepoles like the low-slung afternoon sun, and that day was no different. Steam rose off the roof of the moldering old river shack dripping with flowering moss, and Lucy and I picked its sweet-smelling flowers as we stomped around in the slick, marshy earth. Nearby, the gigantic cypress trees leaned out over the Mississippi as if listening to its sloshy song, and their precarious, low-hanging branches curved like beautiful cathedral arches. It was as mesmerizing as a fairy tale, and the Mighty Miss called to us, "Come closer, closer."

My recollection of Lucy became fractured after those moments, like a broken mirror—its glass shards reflecting different slants of the world. Fragmented snapshots: the flowers Lucy collected were swirling in the brown river's current, pink petals sucked deep into the thick gravy. The roar of the river muffled the sound of retreating footsteps.

I hadn't heard Lucy cry out, but she must have. I didn't want to remember what happened next or the secret Lucy had told me. So, there were different versions of my story, different interpretations of the truth. I pushed Lucy's memories deep into the recesses of my mind and blotted out how fairy tales turn dark, that rainbows and flowers die, and people are unpredictable. I was a precocious and clever child, but I never imagined the river pulled, pushed, and took.

One week later, he arrived at our doorstep asking questions about Lucy. My parents huddled near me, and the memories returned despite my desperation to bury the truth. Finally, I told him what I had kept a secret—Lucy and I were at the river the afternoon she disappeared.

My mother's face twisted with fear and disbelief, and then I met his accusing eyes. Deputy Davis's expression creased with suspicion when he asked me, "Why didn't you say something earlier?" And "How did it happen?"

And the question I asked myself: *Why didn't I try to help her?*

I froze, or perhaps it was because emotions were difficult for me— my mother often reminded me of this. The deputy thought it was a glitch in my programming.

The day after they buried Lucy's empty casket in the ground, Deputy Davis took me into custody. My mother screamed as he ripped me from her arms. I imagined myself a magnolia blossom floating downriver. Lucy was gone, and I was going after her, some eighty miles past cattails and reeds into the brackish water of the Delta wild. In the shallows, I would rot and unravel in the murky soup.

Lucy's parents thought I was a murderer and that "little girls like me were prone to telling tall tales." There was no evidence, no body— the river had washed everything clean, except me. With an almost panicked desire, I have scribbled down my fragmented memories to account for what happened that day at the river, in case they erase me.

Inside the old river shack, he was watching us, an unwanted secret in the shadows. And I wanted someone to make him real, to see him the way I saw River—the way Lucy talked about him.

*Angela Mathers*
*April 2, 2030*

# TWENTY-TWO YEARS LATER

# CHAPTER ONE

## *Angela Mathers*

The day Angela had been waiting twenty-two years for was finally here. Unable to sleep, she got up, gazed out the window overlooking the compound, and watched the city streetlights slowly flicker out as a weak palomino sunrise woke the hazy D.C. skyline. The compound was in the heart of the city. It felt vague and foreign to her, less like a home and more like a concrete cage. She was born in the small town of St. Edenville, Louisiana, her family transplanted there from the north. Her father was a lawyer and her mother a housewife. They had money and were once well respected by the locals, but Angela's predicament had changed all that. For her, for them, and, in due course, the whole country. Sometimes at night, she could still hear the river's angry churning.

She touched the windowpane and felt the hum of the city vibrating under her fingertips, a constant reminder that she was suspended as the world changed around her. Her fight to regain what was lost seemed ill-omened, but like a robbed treasure hunter she would risk everything to find it again. And this morning, she felt it reverberating all around her. "Redemption," she whispered to the four walls.

In a sports bra and shorts, she stepped onto the treadmill and pressed Start. The treadmill and music came to life, and so did her heart.

*Redemption.* Angela felt it deep in her bones, banging hard with every footfall. She raised the speed of the treadmill and then reminded herself of the task at hand. She grabbed her tablet, propped it up on the treadmill, touched the screen, and worked on the speech she would give today. As the sun breached the US Capitol's broken half dome, she pushed herself harder, moving her legs faster as her fair complexion shone with sweat. The tattoo on her left hand caught the sunlight and reflected a rainbow of colored teardrops across the ceiling that fell like rain down the wall. As a child, she had loved the smell of rain, but then it rained the day he took her, and the petrichor was replaced with the bitter odor of tobacco on Deputy Davis's breath. "Angela Mathers, by order of the federal government, I place you in custody."

The smells that marked her past were turning points in her life: before Camp I/O and after. Like the odor of old fruit when Sister Agnes dragged her from the back of Davis's police car and into camp.

Camp I/O was a converted insane asylum from the Antebellum era. The State of Louisiana had transformed it into an "academic camp for children with chip enhancements"—a fancy name for jail—where the enhanced were segregated from the unenhanced.

This was Angela's first night away from home, and she lay awake in the foreign bed that smelt like fried cabbage. Lost in the rows of bunks filled with sleeping children. She listened to the unfamiliar whimpering and raspy breathing. There were so many others like her—her parents had never told her.

*What are you in for?* The question came out of the darkness. Angela turned and saw a boy sitting on the bunk next to hers. He smiled as a wisp of dark, wavy hair covered his droopy eyes. Angela was struck by how fragile he looked.

She stammered aloud, "Intelligence. And you?"

*Shhh…use your chip to talk, or they punish us.* The other children's words rang out in the darkness. She hugged her knees to her chest, wishing to be alone. Angela noticed that his lips were slightly apart, but he didn't move them to talk. *We call it silent-messaging,* he messaged. Angela concluded they were using telepathy, a form of precognition that only children with neural chips could do and the guards could not hear.

The boy silent-messaged, *I'm Warren Harris. What's your name?*

Her heart froze as she pondered if the others knew about her complicated past. Suddenly, she feared every thought that entered her mind was being projected into the room like radio waves, and everyone could hear her inner thoughts. Angela tried to clear her mind, arranging her face into a blank expression, then pulled her sheet higher and tighter against her body, staring back into Warren's dark eyes as he watched her.

*Princess*, messaged another boy, popping his head up from the bunk behind Warren's. *That's what we will call you. I'm Jonathan.* His brown skin was lost in the shadows, but his toothy smile warmed her heart and she bowed her head bashfully.

*Don't worry, we aren't mind readers.*

Warren added, *We silent-message so the Old Fashions don't hear us.*

*Open your mouth slightly and think the words. Try it*, Jonathan said, moving closer to her.

*What are you in for?* Angela silent-messaged for the first time. It felt like innate magic to her, the way each word vibrated through the air like a little energy pulse. Jonathan's face lit up, and he wiggled his ears. She tilted her head and messaged again. *With those ears, have you overheard why we are here?*

*They think I'm a computer, and Warren…well they aren't sure but they know his eyesight is unnatural. To learn the truth they are experimenting on us like lab rats.* Jonathan's expression saddened and his voice died away.

The doorbell buzzed, pulling Angela out of her thoughts. She slowed the treadmill while checking the security monitor above her desk. A man's dark, restless eyes stared into the camera lens. She exhaled sharply; this was the last thing she needed this morning. She turned off the treadmill and moved through her apartment. Everything there was standard government issue. The decor was sparse and sterile and nothing personal was displayed. She didn't care if it looked like she had no human sensibilities. In her mind, she wasn't getting comfortable; this situation was temporary.

She opened the door to find Jeff Lewis standing outside, hands shoved in his pockets. He had been Angela's monitor for the last eight years, and she knew he expected the worst from her. Everyone did. Clean-cut and sharp-edged, he was dressed as usual in over-starched khakis and a crisp navy shirt. His build was compact like that of a lightweight boxer, but he was still a head taller than she was. He scrutinized Angela—that was his job.

Winded from her run, Angela greeted him. "Lucky me. Another unscheduled visit by the Chip patrol."

He rolled up his sleeves, showing off his tanned muscular forearms and said, "Good morning. You really like that treadmill, don't you?" His casual conversation was awkward, and they both knew it.

"It's not like I can spontaneously run around the block without security drones and a helicopter swarming me."

She had meant it as a joke, but he shot back, "Not funny."

Angela turned and left him at the door. She had learned the hard way which of his buttons were best avoided. "Does your visit have anything to do with the hearing today?" She hid her hopefulness by drinking a glass of water.

Jeff closed the door and followed her into the kitchen. "Maybe."

She finished her water and, checking the time, moved into the bedroom. She couldn't be late this morning. She would just need to work around him. She undressed, stepping behind an open closet door out of his direct view.

He cleared his throat. "I brought your credentials for the hearing. When they question you, make sure you are humble, unassertive. It will reflect on me if you are unruly. So be factual, but unemotional. Um, not inhuman, though…I mean, don't be devoid of emotion," he stammered.

Angela felt his eyes on her, turned, and caught him watching her undress. "Christ, Jeff," she muttered under her breath. She quickly grabbed her robe, pulling it on. Knowing he couldn't touch her didn't seem to stop Jeff from staring. She sighed. "I know how to act spineless."

"For the record, you never appear spineless. Just remember your place," Jeff warned.

"How could I forget?" She waved her left hand, showing the tattoo that the government had branded her with. She winced internally. Most Jeff types found her intellectually terrifying, so she had learned to hide her acumen. It was the only way she could earn their trust. She couldn't afford to make Jeff angry, not today of all days. He could put her under house arrest. Then she'd be held in contempt for not showing up at the hearing, and all of her hard work would be lost.

She wrapped her hands around her elbows. "Is there something else you need, or may I go?" Jeff mirrored her pose, crossing his arms over his chest. When he didn't answer, she brushed past him and into the bathroom. As the warm water of the shower washed over her, she almost forgot he was out there sweeping her apartment meticulously: checking her desk, opening drawers, downloading her voice and text messages. When the front door closed with a soft thud that vibrated the shower door, she released the sigh she had held in ever since he had arrived. *He's gone.*

* * *

The sliding doors of Angela's apartment complex opened, and city traffic noise swallowed her whole. Trucks and cars trundled by, spewing exhaust fumes. As the world's population increased, older technology from 2030 was unable to keep pace, and a steel-gray smog hung over D.C. today so thick it looked like it had been painted on with a bristle brush, layer upon layer, rendering the city colorless. She remembered the summers of her youth in Louisiana being muggy and hot but nothing like the oppressive heat in the compound's concrete and metal landscape.

She stopped at the guard station, holding her manicured left hand up to the security camera as it scanned her tattoo. When it returned a beep, she stated, "Committee hearing at the Capitol."

The guard gave her a slight grin as he looked her over. Absently, she smoothed her skirt with her palm. She had chosen today's outfit carefully. At first, she'd considered wearing black; it made her appear slimmer, but shorter. She liked her curvy shape but at just a few inches over five feet, she was self-conscious about her height.

Angela had decided in the end that this was not a funeral. She refused to think of it that way. She chose a white business suit instead, cheap and off the rack, but she wore it like a Valentino. The rest of her ensemble included boots with four-inch heels and a computer tote slung over one shoulder. Having on the right costume secretly filled her with power and stature. She felt good. Like a white knight, she flipped her long, blond hair over her shoulder and marched away, ignoring the guard when he said into the walkie clipped on his shoulder, "A0M01 is on the move."

She joined a cluster of commuters walking to work, many of them, like her, former members of the camps. The camp era had been a costly one for the US government. As the children in them became young adults, Congress had realized they were valuable assets to the workforce and had deinstitutionalized them. When Angela turned nineteen, her world shifted and she became a government contractor, assigned to D.C., one of the five metropolitan labor compounds. The compounds were a blending of society. Some people lived amongst them in the compound, prospering as small business owners, service workers, frontline workers, you name it. People who were intolerant of Angela's kind moved out to suburbia. She and others like her were the only ones required to work a sixty-hour week with a meager stipend, government housing, and the freedom to move—under the watchful eye of the government, of course.

The D.C. Compound was where liberty and law enforcement collided. Overhead, security drones buzzed by, and CCTV cameras perched on buildings and signposts tracked everyone's movements. The government put forth extreme measures to protect society from Angela and others like her. Electronic eyes followed her wherever she went. But she had learned ways to avoid the eyes, keeping parts of herself hidden and private.

# CHAPTER TWO

## *Isabella Dodge*

She had left everyone who ever loved her, but the nightmare still came—a young man was dead, and it was her fault. Isabella's fingers nervously tapped out a beat on the steering wheel. Her life was less complicated now, but the last four years had been lonely and full of regret. The thought sent sadness rippling through her like thunder, which pissed her off.

"Jesus, get over yourself, Dodge," she mumbled as she focused on the road ahead. She punched the gas, sending a cloud of smoke out of the tailpipe of her old black Mustang, and it sputtered along the desolate, decaying underbelly of an area once known as the Warehouse District. She had a knack for hunting down spare Mustang parts to keep the old gal running.

Ten miles from the heart of downtown D.C., the broken dome of the US Capitol loomed in the hazy distance. There was no escaping the steamy July heat. Isabella wiped the sweat off her brow as she sat behind the wheel. She reflected on the Capitol in her rearview mirror. When the Codes became the law on July 4, 2030, a guerrilla group called the Guardians had blown up the Capitol dome to protest the enslavement of children. The Guardians' goal had been to defeat the tyrannical US government and free the children from camps, but they had marginal success.

The government never rebuilt the Capitol's dome, citing budget cuts. The US economy declined steadily after the Codes went into effect, thanks to the ban on new technology included in them. Without the development of innovative alternative energy sources, the country's use of fossil fuels increased, resulting in more and more greenhouse gases. She glanced out the side window at a vacant warehouse. A profitable technology company once operated there; all that was left now was a derelict hulk of a building. For the last twenty-two years, American ingenuity had gradually rotted away while people were forced to drive the same car models and use the same smart devices. New technology had gone the way of the dinosaurs: smokestacks went cold, moldering boards covered windows, and graffiti tagged all the warehouse façades. The only things living on the south side of the D.C. Compound were weeds pushing through the cement cracks, cockroaches, and her haunting memory of the lost one.

Isabella squinted, studying the empty street for any signs of life. She turned onto a side street, searching the shadows. "This is perfect," she said to herself, parking the car and getting out. She had wanted to be a race car driver when she was young and then a Guardian. Looking at herself now, disguised as a junkie dime-bag girl, she could hardly believe it. She shuffled over to a streetlight, leaned against it, and waited.

Before too long she spied an old, beat-up Chevy coasting down the street toward her. The driver popped his head out its open window and smiled. Isabella gave him her best strung-out and mess-of-matted-hair pose.

A sign on the car's windshield read Meals on Wheels. He glided his Chevy to a squeaky stop across from her and got out of the car with a flash, smoothing his spiky hair, keeping it high and tight. Isabella remembered him. Darryl, a drug dealer. *What is he doing on this side of town?* she wondered. She needed to get him to move along.

He ambled to the trunk and popped it open. "We got turkey today," he crooned.

She stayed in character and played along; she was after bigger fish today. She trudged over to the car. He smiled as she peered into the trunk—and saw only a tire iron and other worthless junk.

"Where's the turkey?" she grumbled, having really expected to see some drugs. Before she could confront him, the trunk's lid smashed down on her head with a thud, knocking her out cold.

* * *

Isabella woke with a jolt. Her eyes swiveled, adjusting to the darkness. The smell of tires, and a massive headache turned her brain into a conflagration. She clenched her teeth. *I'm tied up in a car trunk, duped by a two-bit drug dealer.* Humiliation curdled, leaving her feeling justified in perpetrating a violent act on Darryl. Muffled voices came from outside as she worked one hand free from the rope that bound them. Running her hands along the grimy interior, she found the trunk release, cracked open the lid, and spied on Darryl. He was standing next to the beefy potbelly of a man clutching a briefcase. Darryl held an X-ray up to the sun, and they gazed at it.

"Right there, that's her chip," Darryl said, pointing at something on it. He rolled up the film before the man could examine it too closely, stashing it in his back pocket. "Let me see the money," he said and grabbed for the briefcase.

The man swung it out of Darryl's reach. "I want to see it first."

Darryl shrugged. "Sure, man." Isabella watched them approaching and slowly closed the lid.

Stationed at the Chevy, Darryl popped the trunk and sang, "Wakey-wakey."

As the trunk's lid opened and the light breached the inside, they peered in. Her blue eyes vibrating at them like some caged feral creature, Isabella got her legs under her and leapt out of the trunk, swinging the tire iron. It sliced through the air, smashing the side of Darryl's head; blood and flesh splattered into the wind. He wailed in pain, holding his head, and slumped to his knees.

In a thick Southern drawl, she yelled, "It was friggin' hot in there!" She hurled the tire iron at the beefy man. It missed him, clattering on the asphalt inches from his feet. Isabella ripped her dress open, reaching inside her waistband and coming up with her hidden badge and Glock.

She thrust the badge at the men. "Special Agent Isabella Dodge, Control. Put your hands up. You boys are under arrest for trafficking," she shouted, grinning and knowing that she probably looked to them like an escapee from an asylum, an insane grin on her face and her tattered house dress flapping in the breeze.

Darryl shrank and raised his hands. Isabella took in the scene, her left eye pulsating: near a dilapidated wharf, a nearby yard worker was abandoning his mower and heading for a red pickup truck full of lawn equipment. At the end of the parking lot, a rickety dock wavered, half-submerged in the Potomac River. Alongside it, a shiny flybridge fishing cruiser glittered in the morning sun, its engine idling in a low, gurgling chant.

Darryl's customer and Isabella faced off, a meager twenty feet separating them. "Lying shit," he said contemptuously. "They don't let Chips into Control." His eyes narrowed in disgust. He pointed to the tattoo on her left hand. "You have the mark of the beast."

Isabella inspected her light brown hand, discovering a shiny chip image superglued on it. She growled. "Damn it, you sleazeball!" she said to Darryl. "Seriously, buddy—I'm not a Chip. Darryl was trying to con you. Put your hands up, now, or I'll take off your kneecaps."

In the distance, she heard the fishing cruiser engine roar to life, pulling away from the dock. In the blink of an eye, she reevaluated the rest of the scene. The abandoned lawnmower was still running, but the yard worker was in the red pickup, its tires squealing as it took off, heading straight toward them.

"Hands up, do it now," Isabella commanded, stepping closer as Darryl's customer stepped back. A burst from a gun's muzzle captured Isabella's attention as the red pickup moved closer, and a speeding bullet passed through the truck's passenger side window.

Scrambling for cover behind the Chevy, she returned fire. The pickup came to a screeching halt as the passenger door was flung open, the man leapt inside, and they took off across the parking lot.

"No, no, no!" she yelled, discharging her Glock into the back of the pickup. Isabella's eyes swept the scene. The fishing cruiser was speeding away at full throttle. Darryl was on his knees, crying and cradling his bloodied face. And—*damn it!*—the truck was circling back, coming back toward them. The beefy man was hanging out of the passenger window, holding up a grenade. He pulled the pin. Isabella's eyes locked on the explosive.

"Relentless jerks," she growled and took aim at the grenade. *Click, click.* Her Glock was empty, and there was no time to reload as the grenade landed inside the car's open trunk, inches from her. "Run," she yelled. She pulled Darryl off the ground and launched into a sprint, fear coursing through her veins. They bolted toward the river as the grenade exploded. The energy force propelled them through the air. She landed in the grass on top of him. Darryl coughed, gasping for breath. "You collapsed my lungs," he said in a wheezing whisper.

Isabella grabbed him by the collar, pulling him to his feet. "I did not, dumb ass. You got the wind knocked out of you. Who are those guys?"

Nearby car alarms blared, triggered by the explosion. Darryl shrugged as he wiped his bloody face with his shirt. "I don't know 'em. I just answered a chatroom post."

"What chatroom?" Isabella asked as she zip-tied his hands behind his back.

"The Virus."

"The hater group Virus?" Irritated, she pulled the zip-tie tighter.

"Ouch. Yeah, I think."

She barked, "I want names." She rubbed her head where the trunk lid had knocked her out, furious that at least two traffickers had gotten away.

"Peter something. I...I never met the other guy, I swear."

Isabella gazed off into the distance as the crime scene went up in flames. Those guys had been professionals: organized, with no license plate to track their vehicle and a kingpin who knew water was the safest route out of the compound.

The alt-right groups in the dark web were mutating again—and Virus looked to be becoming an even more deadly monster.

# CHAPTER THREE

## *Camp I/O 2032*

Angela grew old during her time at Camp I/O, acquiring by age nine the wisdom of an elder soul. By 2032, her innocence had long since vanished. Much like the children at camp were doing.

*We are disappearing,* Angela said to Jonathan and Warren in the camp's cafeteria one afternoon.

Warren took a bite of his cheese sandwich as Jonathan asked, *Are you referring to Diana? I haven't seen her around for a while.*

With his mouth full, Warren messaged, *James. He hasn't been in class for the last week.*

*Something is going on…and it's not good.* Angela looked glumly at the boys.

By now the children had been separated into dorm rooms by gender so the next night, when two shadowy figures stole another girl from Angela's dorm room, she pretended to sleep. She rushed into the boys' dorm to tell them but was confused when she found Warren's arm draped across Jon's chest in his small bunk. She didn't understand why they needed to be so friendly.

*Wake up. It's happening again.*

Jon's eyes flew open. "What?" Shyly, he pulled away from Warren.

*Come on, they stole another girl. Are you with me or not?* she huffed.

They followed the abductors through the mansion's hallways, crisscrossing corridors until they ended at a hub of activity. The lights in the science lab were burning bright as countless silhouettes and shadows shifted behind the window blinds.

*That's a lot of people,* Warren silent-messaged, wiping the sleep from his eyes.

*Something big is going on.* Angela could barely contain herself. Warren stood lookout because of his exceptional visual acuity, while Jon listened to conversations inside the lab.

*They have Missy in there,* Jonathan messaged to the others. *You know, the thick-waisted girl who smelled like mothballs.*

Angela saw his face crease and knew there was something he was not telling them, something terrible. After a chip was implanted in his baby brain, his hearing and intellect had skyrocketed. He could hear frequencies as high as 300 kilohertz, higher than a bat.

*You can tell me, Jonathan. What's happening in there?* Angela asked.

*They are extracting the neural implant from Missy's brain to make her normal again,* Jonathan messaged.

*But we are normal.* Warren looked confused. He grabbed hold of Jon's hand and squeezed it tight and Jon consoled him. Angela turned away from them. She had read about why people held hands and she wished Jon would hold her hand too. Then maybe she wouldn't feel so detached and numb.

Hours passed, and Angela fell asleep on Jon's shoulder, waking when he abruptly stiffened. They stumbled up and hid in the hall bathroom as someone opened the lab door, peering out as a nurse wheeled a sheet-covered body by on a gurney. It was more or less Missy's shape—stocky legs, thick waist, and flat chest, but...

"She's headless," Warren gasped, shrinking back against Jonathan's chest. He covered his mouth and suppressed a scream, and Jonathan's eyes watered. After watching Missy's headless body be rolled out of sight, Angela knew it was up to them to take care of themselves. The doctors and Sisters could no longer be trusted.

\* \* \*

On visiting day Angela told her dad what had happened. "People need to know what they are doing here." Her father shushed her.

"Remember the codes," her mother reminded Angela. Her face, normally bright like Angela's, today was gray and carried a nervous smile. That was the secret phrase they used so they could discuss

Angela's well-being without her being reprimanded or punished: remember the codes.

Angela drew a picture with hidden code words in the shadows and along the contour lines. Only someone looking for them would notice all the words. Her father's face grew pale as he pieced the message together, and Angela watched the sadness living in his eyes dissolve into anger. Her mother sat wide-eyed, mouth slack.

In a heartbeat, all of her parents' suppressed fears suddenly had manifested. Seeing this disturbed Angela more than the lingering, haunting image of headless Missy.

# CHAPTER FOUR

## *Testify*

"A0M01, are you listening?" The voice from the dais broke into Angela's grim recollections. Its tone was not a casual or a bright one. Instead it came at her like a growl.

"A0M01." She was in the Senate committee hearing at the Capitol. Senator Jackson Green and twelve other senators sat in a row before her, their judgmental eyes scrutinizing her. She and her boss, Steven Hawk, worked at a division of Homeland Security, and were the last two witnesses testifying today; doctors, scientists, and parents had testified earlier in the week.

She smiled politely. "Yes, Senator Green." Jackson Green—a third-term Republican senator from her home state of Louisiana and Lucy's father—was a tuck-tailored Black American man with a flair for showmanship. A prominent critic of Angela, he had fought hard to get on this committee.

Senate Majority Leader Janet Abrams interrupted, "Excuse me, Senator Green. We no longer refer to Angela Mathers or any of her kind by their serial number."

Green nodded smugly.

Despite the resonance with the atrocities of the Holocaust a century earlier, the doctors at Camp I/O had tattooed serial numbers on the back of the children's hands. It was done simply as a bookkeeping measure, so the government told parents. What they failed to mention was that at the same time they stripped the children of their Social Security numbers and residency in the United States. While in camp, Angela had pored over thousands of law books and determined that the US Constitution no longer applied to her. Chipped children had no protection under the amendments, no guarantee of equal rights. For her, there were only the Codes—rules and punishments for disobedience.

Senator Annette Powers from Missouri interrupted Senator Green and directed a question to Angela. "Other countries see the Codes as a grievous misstep. They think the American company Cybernetic Health Center is to blame. You were part of Cybernetic's top-secret neural prostheses program. What do you think?" She put on her glasses, inspecting Angela more closely.

"Yes, Senator Powers. The Cybernetic scientists swore their sole focus was on healing children rather than enhancing them." Off the record, though, most of the CHC scientists admitted that some children showed only minor signs of disease or disorder and that parents had wanted neural chips implanted in their children to ensure they would perform at a higher level. "For example I was born prematurely, and the doctors suggested a neural implant to avoid complications."

People called those who had been neurally enhanced "Chips" or "Human Plus." Or worse. But they had refused to acknowledge those names and instead chose their own, Luman. Angela had coined the name. A neologism and a branding strategy, it addressed the gap in the English language and in the humans' understanding of who they were. A new word for a new time in human history. If they could not be considered humans, then they would be Lumans.

Green looked at Angela with contempt. "There's a long list of vulnerabilities connected with neural implants like yours, Ms. Mathers. If your chip malfunctioned or was hacked, would you know?"

Angela answered his question with a measure of patience. "Senator Green, they didn't remove my brain when they implanted the chip; my brain and the neural implant work together, so, yes, I would know." She flashed a smile at Green that melted his furrowed brow, then glanced at Senator Janet Abrams, the other senator from Louisiana, a liberal and, at age forty-four, the first Asian American majority leader. Janet leaned forward, polished, unflappable. Sitting at the center of the group in a sleeveless green dress that showcased her toned beige arms, she was an icon of credibility and confidence. She now stared down the row of senators.

"Senator Green, we are not here to evaluate neural implants. We are here to decide whether the Freewill legislation should go before the full Senate. So, where are you going with this line of questioning?"

"I beg your pardon, Senator Abrams. Congress determined previously that the Cybernetic Health Center had recklessly placed thousands of computer chips into the brains of infants. Now we are saying none of that matters. Now that it's a new administration, everything is okay with the chips. Where is the proof? It's malarkey!"

"Senator Green, there is twenty-two years of proof," Senator Abrams responded. "There have been no hacks, corruption, or loss of sentience to one Luman." Her stern tone blasted Green while his delicate gold cross glimmered against his wool lapel.

"I beg your pardon, Senator Abrams. Just last week, a male broke code and disappeared. Could his neural implant have malfunctioned? We don't know. We can't find him. Yet here we are, discussing a bill that will reduce monitoring of the Luman community and allow them to comingle with humans, and God knows what else. If we do not continue their containment, how will we know if one of their chips goes haywire?" He turned a wolfish gaze toward Angela. "How will the government guarantee our citizens' safety if we revoke the Codes, Ms. Mathers?"

The question hung in the air, biased and angry. Angela locked eyes with Green. She understood this man. Their feud was personal; she had not reported his daughter's disappearance until confronted by the police. She had lacked judgment and showed a shortfall of agency. *I was a child*, she justified.

The police eventually exonerated Angela of the murder charge Jackson and his wife, Betty Jo, had pushed for, but the damage had been done. People became afraid of enhanced children. Social media had spun lies and spread fear about children with neural implants, and Jackson Green rose to political power on the lies. Congress's knee-jerk reaction was to immediately enact the Codes. All children with chips were rounded up and segregated from humans. Angela's parents fought the Codes in court but were forced to surrender her shortly after the camps were opened. Now it was Angela's turn to fight for freedom.

A lump stuck in Angela's throat at the thought of "the male" Green was referring to. "Senator Green"—she swallowed hard—"the Luman you are referring to has a name. Warren Harris. As you know, every Luman has a Global Positioning Tracker, GPS, embedded in their neck, and it's indestructible. The only way Mr. Harris's tracker goes offline is if he's dead—therefore, he's not a threat."

Hearing herself say this fact out loud punched a hole in her stomach.

"That might be the case, but it's unproven without a body. There is no telling what happens to someone when there is no body. No body of proof."

Angela steadied her breathing. *Is he referring to Lucy? He is referring to Lucy.* She felt her blood pressure elevating. She closed her eyes, trying to ward off the splintering images that had been giving her trouble: the muddy fingers at Lucy's shoulder, the flowers Lucy collected churning in the dusky water. She would never escape Green or her childhood mistake, and she wanted to scream "Enough! Enough already!"

"Ms. Mathers, how many Lumans have disappeared with these GPS tracker gizmos?" Senator Green's question stung like acid on an open wound.

"Senator Green, we don't keep track." Angela kept her voice calm. She was not about to give him any more ammunition.

Green stood up and pointed toward the committee doors. "We could have hundreds or thousands of Lumans prowling around," he bellowed. "Causing mayhem, intimidation, and murder. And all because we can't be bothered with keeping count!"

Angela bit her lip and felt things slipping away. She chastened herself for getting hopeful, for thinking she could change mindsets. As calmly and confidently as she could, she reiterated, "Senator Green, as I mentioned before, the GPS trackers are indestructible. Therefore, we don't need to keep track…"

"Ms. Mathers." Senator Arnold Tucker's leathery presence and deep baritone voice took center stage. "Is this GPS tracking thing like the Apple service Find My iPhone?" Loud chatter and laughter radiated from the gallery overhead, and everyone peered up, except Angela. She stared blankly at him, preparing to answer.

Senator Green raised his voice. "We'll get to you later, Tucker." Bristling with impatience, he pointed to Angela. "Neural chips do more than just allow you to perform at an intellectually higher level. To the puzzlement of neuroscientists worldwide, most children with chips develop heightened sensory faculties—eyesight or hearing—or they become singular intellects like yourself. Ms. Mathers, when your parents chose a better quality of life for you, they blurred the line between human and machine. Do you believe implanted devices are morally acceptable?"

She saw what he was doing in making this about her beliefs. It would be easier to deny the Lumans their rights if Angela's beliefs fell afoul of the beliefs of Green and others like him.

"Senator Green, I'm not here to debate my personal religious beliefs with you."

"You are here to answer our questions, Ms. Mathers." Senator Green's eyes narrowed in irritation, and his voice echoed off the committee walls. "Is it God's intent for us to meddle with nature?"

Angela shook her head. *So much for not making this about me.*

"Senator Green, I do not know what God intended. No one does. But he gave us minds to better humanity. He gave us hands to design integrated chips that help those who may not be blessed with genetic good fortune."

Angela glanced at Senator Abrams, who nodded her encouragement. She leaned toward the mic, slowed her breathing, forcing her voice low and resonant. "What I can tell you about is the world that I dream of. It differs significantly from the one I live in today. It is a place of inclusion, where I have the same rights as you. Where I am not compared to a smartphone." Angela paused as her words took root.

"When I was seven years old, the government took me from my family. They took my name. Before that time, what it meant to be human was simple to define. It was me; I was part of humanity. The Codes changed that. Now, I am defined by my differences, by my chip.

"Luman and human, every person deserves basic rights: to be happy, healthy, and know everything that comes with their biological roots. With the help of technology, Lumans have overcome their disabilities and diseases. That achievement should not equate to a loss of liberty but to the start of it."

Angela leaned back from the microphone and studied the panel of senators who would decide her future. She again felt a slow churning of hope. She tried to choke it down, reminding herself that what she wanted from them, the Lumans' road to freedom, could come down to the flip of a coin, an infinitesimally higher percentage of votes on one side or the other.

Her testimony over, Angela was asked to leave the hearing. She slowed her pace, lingering and listening to the closing remarks of Senator Abrams.

"The Freewill Bill is long overdue. A vote here in favor of the legislation will send it before the full Senate. My fellow senators, change is possible through bipartisanship." Abrams rose. "With a show of hands, should the Freewill Bill go before the full Senate?"

Steven Hawk escorted Angela out of the room and the committee door closed behind her before she could see their responses.

# CHAPTER FIVE

*Lasting Kiss*

When the committee hearing doors reopened and people flooded into the large marble hallway, Angela was there waiting to hear the decision. She stepped forward. "Did the measure pass?" she called out, but there was too much commotion, too many moving bodies. She never heard a definitive answer.

"Excuse me," she asked a senator as she passed by. "Is the bill going to the Senate?" The senator looked away. Senator Green trekked out the door, busy on his phone, his expression sour as usual and providing no clues to the outcome of the vote. Her hopes sank as the last person exited the room. No Senator Abrams. How had she missed her? Something was wrong.

Scanning the hall right and left, she finally caught a glimpse of Janet farther down the passageway. There were so many people in the gap between them, though, and she wasn't sure she could reach her before she entered the Senate Chamber—where Lumans were forbidden. Resolutely, Angela rushed ahead. When she reached Janet's side, her aide, Mike, tried to block her access, but Janet casually dismissed him with a flip of her wrist, and the ladies continued down the hall side by side.

Abrams winked at Angela. "Excellent work in there."

"Thank you, Senator. Are we ready for the full Senate?" Angela held her breath, waiting for the senator's response, flexing her fingers nervously. The noise from the crowded hall fell away, allowing her to hear the senator's deep intake of breath and her voice, soft but compelling.

"Absolutely. We should celebrate. Lunch?"

"We are going to the Senate?" Angela clapped her hands to her mouth.

"Yes, the Freewill Bill goes before the Senate in a couple of weeks."

"Yes! Let's have lunch." Angela wilted. "Wait, I have a department meeting in an hour."

Glancing at her watch, Abrams said, "We might have time if we hurry."

"Thank you. I would love that. Thank you so much for your work on this." Angela felt her cheeks warm. She smiled, watching Senator Abrams's expression and expecting a smile in return, but hearing Janet clear her throat instead. She led Angela left into a narrower hallway, where a guard moved a chain-rope aside, allowing them to enter a restricted area. They quickly moved past archaic Corinthian columns and decorative murals yellowing with age. The click-clack of heels on tile echoed in the empty hall.

"This section of the Capitol doesn't get much foot traffic, since it lies directly below the collapsed section of the dome."

"If the Freewill Bill passes, it can finally be rebuilt."

"Hmmm." Janet nodded. "By the way, your closing was excellent," she said. "It swung Senator Powers's vote."

"Thank you. Your handling of Senator Green was superb, but then I expected nothing less." Angela worked to keep her voice low and casual as she struggled to keep up with Janet.

"You think?" Janet asked, nodding at something down the hall past Angela. Angela nodded in turn, and when they reached it Janet pushed open the door to the women's bathroom.

Janet gripped her hand and pulled her inside. She made sure the bathroom was vacant and then pressed her against the closed door.

"That bit about your dream world sealed the deal." She caressed Angela's face and kissed her softly, then with desperation. Pushing open a stall door, Angela pulled Janet inside, locking the door. She kissed her passionately as Janet's hands swiftly unbuttoned her blouse and slipped inside it, caressing her while Angela's hand inched underneath Janet's green silk dress.

The bathroom door swung open with a squeak.

They froze as a woman's shoes clacking on the tile, paused, and continued across the floor and into the stall next to theirs. "Call me," Janet mouthed before kissing Angela's cheek and squeezing past her, straightening her skirt.

Angela waited until she heard the bathroom door open and close to leave the stall. She was bent over the sink killing time, swilling water into her mouth, when the other woman emerged from her stall, moved to the sink beside her, and began washing her hands. Shaking water off them, she turned toward Angela, studied her face, and purred in a Southern drawl, "Excuse me, but you have a smudge of Lastin' Kiss on your cheek."

Angela turned and took in the stranger's dark, shoulder-length hair, naturally curly, and the glasses pushed up on top of her head. She was frozen in her gaze—ambition and intelligence lay in wait behind blue eyes that sparkled like the ocean against her light brown skin and high cheekbones. She was around her age. Too young to be a senator, too well dressed to be an aide. She could be a reporter, but this area was restricted. Realizing she was staring, Angela shut off the water, grabbed a paper towel, and regarded herself in the mirror.

"Hmm, could it be Exposed?" Angela asked, swiping at the smudge.

"No. It's a lighter shade. Safe and tasteful. It's definitely Rouge in Love, Lasting Kiss."

The woman offered Angela an open roll of mints. Angela took a mint with her right hand, hiding her tattooed one, her mouth curving into a grin. "Thanks." Smiling, she popped the mint into her mouth. *That color might be tasteful, but if this woman knew that it was Janet Abrams she had been with, she wouldn't be using the word "safe."* Hopefully, she hadn't seen anything. In any case, she refused to let this snafu spoil her mood.

The woman's phone beeped. As she pulled it out of her pocket, Angela glimpsed a photo of Jonathan on her phone screen. Exhaling sharply, the woman gave Angela a quick nod and rushed out.

What the hell? Angela stared at herself in the mirror, her face gray and filled with confusion. Was she mistaken? That was Jonathan, right? Had something happened to him?

*Stay optimistic*, she told herself, but she couldn't. Not when she knew, all too well, what horrors humans were capable of.

# CHAPTER SIX

## *Camp I/O 2038*

*This place is worse than an Old Fashion slasher flick. I want to explore Venus, Ceres, and Jupiter with you,* Jonathan said as he and Angela left the camp library. Angela, now fifteen, smiled in amusement. During their teenage years, they had grown close, and curious energy radiated between them. Jonathan leaned in and whispered, *Meet me in the science lab tonight, just you and me.*

*Maybe,* she said and walked away. Jonathan had asked her out, not Warren. She wanted to be flattered, but she wasn't.

In the science lab that night, amongst a hodgepodge of desks, an examination table, medical equipment, and a broken telescope, Jonathan and Angela began another of their many kissing sessions and over-the-clothes petting. This time her interest was more than piqued. There, in a liminal space undulating between experimentation and discovery, illuminated by the flickering flame of a Bunsen burner, they shed their clothes and lay together, feeling safe enough to use their voices.

"Are you sure about this?" Jonathan asked. She nodded, though the truth lay somewhere in between—a lot could happen in the dark.

Jon gave her his devilish smile, and she felt all tingly. As they pressed their bodies together, unfamiliar, inexplicable emotions stirred and a strange heat prickled her skin. Lifting an arm, she discovered it was glowing, in the same way the moon was lit by the sun.

The heat and the glow grew as Jon moved in slow waves over her. Suddenly, energy was radiating from their every pore, like a flashover when every combustible surface ignites. Iridescent rays moved in great, swaying bands of color between their bodies. They were two shooting stars burning bright in the southern night sky. Then, all too soon, they were dying embers falling back down to camp.

A chuckle started low, possibly in disbelief, and then erupted from Jonathan's lips. "God, that felt like we were creating a new galaxy." He collapsed onto his side beside her.

Angela blushed. "I'm not sure what it felt like," she said breathlessly. It was the first intense sensation she had ever felt, and she needed a moment to understand it and where it came from.

"The Sisters forbid sex," Jonathan said, still laughing. "Suppose it's because they think our shimmer might cause us to catch fire?"

"We are an enigma to them," Angela said flatly, knowing there was no logical explanation for the policy. "As for this"—she waved her hand over her torso, which was still glowing—"our skin, like our brain, is an organ. Our neural chips have bonded with it and our pores act as the chip's I/O receptors." She cocked her head to one side, working through the problem. "We release oxytocin and endorphins during intimacy. Our neural chips react to the chemicals, a mixture of luciferins and enzymes creates the shimmer in our skins, and…we become bioluminescent."

Jon scoffed. "Bioluminescent? Did you make that up?"

"No. Take fireflies and dragonfish. They are bioluminescent organisms, and they light up to attract a mate. It's part of their courtship—why not us?" Pleased with her analysis, Angela rested her head against Jon's chest, tangling her legs with his on the small table.

"You sure know how to take the romance out of it," Jonathan teased.

"What? I thought you'd want the facts."

"Well, I hoped I made you shimmer."

"I didn't realize you were fishing for a compliment!" She wrestled her way on top of him. "You were amazing, my wonderful lover of dazzling lights and exceptional hearing." She laughed, something rare for her, a low, silken timbre of mirth, and Jon smiled at her.

"Tell me again how the shimmer happens," he whispered, kissing her to stop her giggling.

The moment was shattered by a gasp from the direction of the lab's doorway. Warren, looking completely devastated, turned and rushed away. Jonathan, his eyes full of regret, jumped off the table, grabbed his pants, and quickly pulled them on. Angela pleaded with him to stay, but he rushed out after Warren, cursing himself for not having heard him approach.

Angela dressed slowly and pulled a chair up to one of the desks, examining what had transpired between them. What had happened to her. She paid little attention to her emotions normally. She felt little things here and there, but never had she felt anything as deeply intense as what she had experienced tonight. All too soon, though, it was gone.

She realized something else then. Something important about the light. It was more than energy. When they'd made love, their digital consciousnesses had swirled around them like eddying spirits. It was their attraction to each other, their reaction to each other, that had caused their skin to glow with that wild luminescence.

Standing, she strode over the lab's chalkboard and wrote the word "Luman" on it. The neurally enhanced were not mechanical, not organic machines. Far from it. When the government found out about the shimmer, there would be more trouble, but...

"We are a different humankind," she told Jonathan later. "We transcend our boundaries. We become the light. We are Luman," she whispered, giving her people a name as fluid and as powerful as the surface of the sun.

# CHAPTER SEVEN

## *Another Lost One*

Isabella got into her Mustang and slammed the car's door with a clunk. As her engine revved, so did her thoughts of Angela Mathers. She had seen Jonathan Riley's alert on Isabella's phone, and her expression had shifted from unreadable to wary and then worried. *She probably knows him, too.*

Angela's comments on Warren Harris's death had caught Isabella's attention during the committee hearing. She'd followed her as she and Senator Abrams broke from the crowd, hoping to talk with Angela at some point. Casual first encounters with people made conversations more spontaneous, more revealing, and this was how Isabella liked to operate with subjects of interest.

Well, their encounter in the restroom had certainly been revealing. The energy level there when she walked in, the potential of it, had literally stopped her in her tracks for a moment. She sighed. "Some things are not meant to be discovered."

Isabella cut the steering wheel hard to the left, pulling into the street. "Angela will never talk to me now, not openly," she muttered. She sped down Constitution Avenue across town and rolled to stop amid cop cars parked every which way in front of the ParkAide garage entrance. Control agents drove regulation electric black sedans and criminals saw them coming, but Isabella preferred her Mustang. It was faster, she liked to feel the power of the engine, and it gave her anonymity. Besides, since other countries had imposed embargos on the US because of the Codes, batteries and other electronic parts had become scarce. It was much easier to find spare Mustang parts. They, like other gas engines, had been around a lot longer.

She studied the crime scene. D.C. police were standing around as usual, along with some news crews and a few looky-loos. She opened the car door and D.C.'s July heat and humidity hit her square in the face. "Ah, the sour smell of overcooked trash. Nothing like it."

She stepped out of the car. She was dressed today in a form-fitting designer suit that showed off her tall, disciplined physique. She brought her large Gucci frames down from the top of her head. Self-conscious about her left eye, she wore tinted lenses. Businesslike, she trekked past crime tape, news cameras, and police loitering along the sidewalk.

Sergeant Johnson, standing with another policeman from the Washington PD, noticed her walking toward them and said, loud enough so she heard, "Jeez, not her again. She could be my kid's babysitter."

"She hasn't earned that badge," the other man responded.

"Special Agent Dodge." Isabella unclipped her badge from her hip and flipped it open. In a slow Southern drawl, she asked, "How's it looking, Sergeant Johnson?"

"There was no sign of Jonathan Riley," the sergeant replied.

"Is the scene secure?"

"Yes, no one in or out."

"Thanks, Sarge, I'll take it from here. The crime scene went untouched, yeah?"

"Yeah, Special Agent Dodge." His eyes shifted away from her to the scene.

"Are you sure?" Isabella pressed. The sergeant knew the rules. He also knew that the criminologists regularly broke them.

"Um, Hank, our criminologist, started taking photos after getting the lights turned back on."

"The lights were off when you first got on the scene?"

"Yes, ma'am."

"It's Agent Dodge," she snapped.

"Yes, Agent Dodge. Sorry."

"So, Hank, the criminologist, is the only one who has messed with my crime scene. Have I got that right?"

He nodded.

Isabella walked past them toward the center of the garage. She yelled over her shoulder, "Turn off the lights."

Within a minute, the blackness inside the garage was affecting her vision, making everything glisten. Her left eye pulsated as she surveyed the space. She imagined Jonathan in this space, and a man's hologram suddenly appeared next to her. As usual, she took care not to react to its appearance. She always kept her visions to herself, never sharing how clues came to her.

She watched the anonymous shape glow and define. *Is it him?* a voice said in her head. Abruptly, he turned toward her, and even though he was mostly in silhouette she could tell it was Jonathan Riley. The shading of his strong jaw and deep-set eyes were a solid match to his picture ID.

She read his expression as he looked around. *He heard something,* Isabella thought. She watched as he peered across the concrete floor past parked cars, then hurried through the darkness. Isabella followed his movement down another level into the murky underground. He slowed his pace, crouching down to study something on the ground. Then, as quickly as it had appeared, the hologram disappeared from her mind's eye.

She stood there, circling the space, now empty, the sound of her movements echoing. She squatted for a closer look at the ground. Taking out a flashlight, she shined it where Jonathan had stopped to inspect the floor. There in the dust was a strange disturbance, squiggly lines of some sort and three sets of footprints. She stood and exhaled sharply. Sometimes her visions did little more than coax more questions from the silence.

Finishing her inspection, she approached Sergeant Johnson, who was joking around with the criminologist and some of the other cops. "Any camera footage?" she asked.

"The cameras inside the garage were disabled," he said with a shrug.

These guys never took Luman crimes seriously, and Isabella's tone turned brusque. "Well, then, I guess you'd better get busy checking all CCTV on the perimeter and nearby buildings, drone surveillance feeds, or private video cameras the government has access to. Let me know what you find." The sergeant's grin turned to a frown. "Run shoe and tire prints through the NCIC databases, Hank. Let me know if we get any hits."

"There were tons of footprints and tire tracks in there," the criminologist complained. "This looks like another runner, just like last week. There's no sign of a struggle," he said, trying to get out of all the additional work.

"You think? 'Cause there's a disturbance in the dust on parking spots thirty-five and thirty-six and three unique footprints. Let's gather the facts before drawing conclusions, Hank."

As Isabella's car puttered through city traffic back to headquarters, a text arrived from her boss, Deputy Director Alice Carter. She stared at the cracked screen of her phone:

*Agent, you are NOT excused from afternoon debriefs. Get your ass in here.*

\* \* \*

Twenty minutes later, Isabella pulled her Mustang into Control's underground lot. She moved down the division's dull hallways. Not an acronym, Control was an attitude. The individuals who worked here had complete authority over the Luman community. Isabella was part of Control's investigative branch, the agents who put their lives on the line, solving and preventing both crimes by Lumans and crimes against them. The men and women working in the surveillance branch of Control were called monitors, not agents. They were like parole officers, each assigned to a group of Lumans to track their everyday activities. Monitors made sure every Luman obeyed the Codes but also kept them safe from foreign espionage. A few members of Control saw the Lumans as humans and as such, they valued their lives. Most, though, saw them as uncaring machines. They valued their economic importance but viewed them as disposable. Isabella was a member of the first group. She wanted to bridge the gap between the two attitudes and get her fellow agents to show more compassion, but it was a daily struggle.

Isabella entered Control's bullpen. TVs covered the walls, scrolling stats on crimes in the D.C. Compound. The room was abuzz with activity and agents taking calls. David Ross, an intense, sturdy-looking agent with fiery red hair, spotted Isabella and strode to her desk.

"I heard about your dance with death the other night. You okay?" David's bangs fell over his eyes.

"Yeah, it could have ended better," she said with a pained smile.

David brushed his bangs back, revealing kind eyes. "You weren't on another one of your rogue ops, were you?"

"It's the only way to have fun around this place." She winked.

"Oh, she's been looking for you. That could explain why."

"I know." Isabella glanced at Deputy Director Alice Carter's office. Its floor-to-ceiling windows gave it the look of a massive fishbowl. Isabella slumped down in her chair. She locked her gun in her desk drawer, grimacing at the thought of being on the receiving end of another one of Carter's bad moods. *Might as well get it over with.*

"Come in and close the door, Agent," Carter grouched, waving her in.

A goliath of a woman in her early fifties, Carter was known as a cutthroat interrogator. During a stint in Control's High-Value Interrogation group, she earned the name Mindhunter and stormed up the ranks as a precise badass whom everyone called Sir.

Isabella closed the door and stood at attention. Carter frowned at Isabella and ran her fingers through short, chestnut hair that was graying at the temples. It was a sensible hairstyle. Everything about her, from her wraparound skirt to her comfy pumps, screamed utilitarian.

"I took a lot of flak from management, Dodge, for making you a special agent so early in your career. So, prove me right and them wrong."

There was an awkward silence before Isabella realized that was her cue. "Sir, I know my apprehension of suspect Darryl Hinds was unconventional, but in the—"

"Enough with the unsanctioned ops," Carter said, her reproachful glare speaking volumes as she came around her desk and motioned for Isabella to sit opposite her in the visitor's chair. She cleared her throat. "I need all your attention on the latest Luman disappearances. You're the lead now."

Isabella leaned into the conversation, keen to lead a case at last. "I thought Jake was in charge of it."

"He was. Now he's not. You've been doing most of the work. You can handle it."

Isabella smirked. "Jake pissed off the wrong folks at the Luman Administration, huh?"

"Yeah, well, with all the publicity about the Freewill Bill, we've been taking a beating in the press about our treatment of the Lumans. So, make nice with Luman Administration."

"Yes, sir." Isabella opened the door to leave.

"Agent, no more undercover stakeouts without permission. I mean it."

Isabella left Carter's office grinning. She was officially a lead agent on a case. Finally! On the other hand… She grimaced. Carter had learned about her rogue ops. She needed to be more cautious if she planned to keep up her surveillance of one of the deadliest hate groups in D.C., Virus. Control saw them as a nuisance and ignored them. Isabella sensed their numbers were growing and that they were planning something. So, she spent her off hours surveilling different areas of the Warehouse District, picking up clues, and putting the pieces together—staying busy. And last night, she had been in the right place at the right time. But still, all this extra work to prevent another lost one did little to ease the past. Noah's death was her fault.

# CHAPTER EIGHT

*Silent-Messages*

Angela stepped into the chaotic whirlwind of activity filling the boardroom of the Luman Administration, finding dozens of Luman analysts in business attire huddled around a table.

The analysts' chatter settled to silence as she took her place at the head of the table. She was the Luman Resource Manager at LA. "What happened to Jonathan?" she asked, staring at her staff and the words "Missing Luman" that were scrolling across every computer monitor in the room. Her gray eyes clouded over as she tried not to think about what her heart knew had to be true. She scanned the table. Analyst faces full of apprehension peered back at her. She remembered being one of them, starting her government servitude at age nineteen as an LA analyst. Lumans usually worked in groups overseen by a human. Angela was the first Luman to manage a group of Lumans and she took her responsibilities very seriously.

"Have we learned anything about Jonathan Riley's disappearance?" Angela asked, trying to keep the desperation out of her voice.

A woman's voice finally cracked the silence. "There's no news."

"Come on, folks! Don't lose hope," Paul interjected. "We'll hear something eventually. In the meantime, let's celebrate the fact that Angela helped to win the majority vote today. The Freewill Bill is going to the full Senate!"

Jubilant applause expelled the somber mood. Angela nodded to Paul, appreciating his effort to keep the team's morale from crashing.

"The senate majority leader will call the bill up for debate in two weeks, so make sure you obey all the Codes. Control will be watching." Her voice turned somber. "And also, be very careful out there."

Before she could elaborate, there was a knock on the boardroom door and a woman dressed in an overpriced suit and wearing black-rimmed glasses with tinted lenses that hid her eyes entered without waiting for permission. Her heart lurching, Angela recognized her immediately. She struggled to slow her breathing. The analysts glared and huffed loudly as she moved past them.

"Angela Mathers?" Isabella flashed her badge, her face impossible to read, and moved toward Angela.

"Yes." Angela's mind was racing a million miles a minute. Did this have something to do with what happened with Janet this morning?

"Special Agent Isabella Dodge with Control. Ms. Mathers, I just need a moment of your time. Is there someplace we can talk privately?"

The analysts silent-messaged each other. Angela's lips parted as her thoughts raised above the others. *Calm down. Quiet your minds.*

*Don't talk without your lawyer*, Paul advised.

Taking a deep breath, Angela appraised the woman from the restroom, seeing her in a new, much more frightening light. "We can talk in my office."

Her office, small and windowless, felt more like a holding cell than ever. Seating herself opposite Angela, Isabella looked around. "Cozy. Did this used to be a broom closet or something?"

Angela raised her chin slightly, unamused. "What can I do for you, Agent?"

"Um. A Luman from the D.C. Compound went missing this morning. That makes two. Warren Harris early last week and now—"

"Jonathan Riley," Angela interjected. "Do you have information on his whereabouts?"

"Not yet, but it's very suspicious. Two disappearances in a short timeframe."

"So, no clues, suspects—bodies?" Angela stared at Isabella.

Isabella shook her head. "The Washington PD is labeling them runaways."

"If you have no clues, how can you label them runaways?"

"I never said that."

"You clearly said 'runaways,' Special Agent Dodge."

"Call me Isabella. That is the Washington police's conclusion, not mine."

"Jonathan and Warren would never run. They wouldn't risk..." Angela stopped herself from saying more.

"You seem unsure."

"No, I'm not. They work at the LA. They know better than many what would happen if Control captured them." She spoke louder than she intended. She never got rattled, but this woman had gotten under her skin. Isabella's tinted glasses made it difficult to tell, but it felt like her eyes were peeling her to the bone. She clenched her fist under her desk.

"What does Jonathan do at the LA?"

"He works in Accountability—for our Global Tracking System."

Isabella scoffed. "Chip tracking? Y'all police yourselves?"

"Luman tracking is very sophisticated. It would take hundreds of you people to do the job two Lumans do."

"I'm sure. What else does the Luman Administration do?"

"As a division of Homeland Security, LA promotes the economic and social well-being of the Lumans—"

Isabella interrupted, "Sorry. I meant to say, as the Luman Resource Manager what do *you* do for the LA?" She adjusted her glasses and smiled. Angela bit her lip, editing her expressions.

"I oversee the Luman staff at the LA. We track Lumans and assign Control monitors to them, offer compound transfers." Struggling to maintain her composure, she stared at Isabella and asked, "How can a Control agent not know what LA does?" Only a complete moron wouldn't know.

Angela's phone dinged. Happy for the distraction, she glimpsed at it before casually asking, "Have you spoken with Jonathan's monitor, Jeff Lewis?" She returned her phone to the desk, looked up, and smiled.

"I needed you to answer a question truthfully, so I asked you about your job at the LA."

Angela's smile faltered. This woman couldn't be a Control agent. Her questions were irregular to say the least. Unfocused. Her gaze wasn't, though. It was laser sharp and unrelenting.

"Are you reading me, Agent Dodge?" Her voice sharpened. "Learning my facial muscle reactions and relaxation response to questions?"

Isabella did not overtly respond. "When did you last speak to Jonathan? What was his mood like?"

Angela paused, choosing her words carefully. "Jonathan and I had drinks last night. His best friend, Warren, just died, so he's upset, but he was...he is...coping."

"Where did you have drinks?"

"The White Rabbit."

"Do y'all go there often?"

Angela shook her head. She began playing with a sticky note pad on her desk, hoping Isabella hadn't been able to detect her lie.

"Jeff Lewis's report listed you and Jonathan as a couple. But he also thought you had a relationship with Warren."

"Hardly," Angela scoffed. "Jeff is a Neanderthal."

"That might be, but were you intimate with either of them?"

"Jonathan and Warren report to me, so of course not," Angela said as she ran her fingers through her hair and released a long, slow breath.

Incredulously, Isabella raised an eyebrow and pressed. "There's a better chance of finding out what happened to Jonathan and Warren if you would be more forthcoming."

"I told you, we were not intimate. Am I a suspect?"

"Ms. Mathers, we have no suspects, so I need to find out as much as I can about their lives. I'm looking for evidence, you know? Accurate information."

There was an awkward silence as the women gazed at each other.

"Any other questions?" Angela asked.

Isabella glanced at her watch. "That was a beautiful speech at the committee hearing—about your dream world."

Leaning back in her chair, Angela looked pointedly at Isabella. She'd wondered if she would mention their earlier encounter. "Hmmm." Angela steepled her fingers and nodded. "Tell me, Special Agent Dodge, why did you follow us into the restroom?"

"Um, me, no—I didn't mean to interrupt." Isabella shifted in the chair.

"You didn't." Angela tapped the sticky note pad on the desk, trying to control her impatience.

"You can talk to me, you know. If she pressures you to do things… things you don't want to."

Angela scoffed. She was a Luman, subject to government servitude. Every day she lived she had to do things against her will.

Isabella stood up. "Control is watching you," she said soberly. "You need to be more careful." She pulled the pad from Angela's hand and scribbled her phone number on it. "If you need anything, that's my private number. The government doesn't monitor it." She handed the pad back to Angela, then opened the door to leave.

When Isabella's back was to her, Angela silent-messaged her. *Isabella, someone murdered them.*

Isabella twisted around abruptly. "You're sure?"

Angela looked down, working to transform the shock she was feeling into a blank expression. Then, when she felt she could do so without tipping her off about what she had just learned, she gazed up at Isabella. A woman who was not only a Control agent, but also a Solo—an undocumented Luman. A woman who, distracted by Angela's allegation, was completely overlooking her own potentially deadly revelation.

"Jon and I were intimate in the past, but his true soulmate was Warren. It was their secret, not mine to tell." Angela stood but didn't venture closer. She wasn't telling the truth because she trusted this… this imposter. She was doing it because she was afraid that Isabella might be like all the other agents at Control. That she would write Jonathan off as a runaway. Case closed. Angela wanted Isabella not to be that person, to not be someone who would turn against her own kind.

"Agent Dodge, the question you should be asking is, why would they run? The government protects us now—or tries to. In the past, when parents and their Luman children became part of the Guardian underground, they did so to avoid being placed in a camp. Their activities have fueled our subjugation and made people fear my kind. They're hiding in plain sight, too scared to be who they really are."

Isabella's contemptuous response was instantaneous. And bewildering. "The laws of this government don't protect you. I do."

Angela stared at her, struggling to decipher what she'd said. To understand what was happening between them. "I think this interview is over." She saw Isabella's shoulders buckle slightly.

*Direct hit*, Angela thought, as confusion and shame settled onto Isabella's frame. She thought she would feel satisfaction, payback for all the damage the Solos had caused with their guerrilla attacks and armed resistance to the Codes and the Guardian underground sneaking Lumans out of the compounds. But she felt nothing as usual; there was only emptiness.

# CHAPTER NINE

## *St. Edenville 2030*

Mazzy Parks peered through her dark, curly locks, studying her six-year-old self in the mirror. Her eyes were not the same. The left iris was silver.

"Mercury, mechanical, menacing," she whispered as if conjuring a spell. Then, delicately, she placed a contact lens into her left eye and blinked. It slid into place over the pupil, hiding the silver hue. Both eyes were now the color of sapphires, and they sparkled against her brown skin like brilliant, faceted gems.

Mazzy's mechanical left eye provided a supernatural view of her world, capturing a level of detail beyond normal visual perception, reading the subtlest of micro-expressions in a human face. Her left eye saw the world as a Luman. Her right saw it as a human—a bilateral view of society, a kind of double vision.

But that day, she was troubled, and so when Mazzy gazed at it through her mechanical eye, reflected in the bathroom mirror was a teenage hologram from her future, something invented and controlled by the neural implant in her brain.

*I don't want to change my name*, Mazzy silent-messaged her teenage hologram.

*Big diff, it's just a name. I like the name Isabella,* her sixteen-year-old-self messaged back. *Besides, the world has changed. Like Dad said, you need to adapt or risk being identified.*

*But why? I know I'm a Chip, but why does it matter?*

Her older, wiser reflection shrugged. *Something happens to humans when they become parents. It's impossible to understand them.*

"Mazzy, we need to go," Lorraine's voice carried from down the hall.

Mazzy waved to the mirror and walked away in a sulk.

"What were you doing?" Lorraine put her hand behind Mazzy's head, lovingly guiding her back down the hall to her room.

Mazzy shrugged.

Lorraine became the Parks' live-in caregiver after her mother's death. But Mazzy knew her dad and Lorraine were more. When their eyes caught, a fondness lingered between them.

"You were talking to the mirror again," Lorraine commented.

Mazzy needed someone to talk to. Their house was full of secrets. Her dad and Lorraine were always huddled together, whispering about something. They stopped when she entered the room.

"Where have you been?" Frank Parks asked. He was Mazzy's doting father and the Black American pastor of a St. Edenville church.

Mazzy surveyed the mess in her room. Clothing and books littered her bedroom floor. For once, though, it was not her doing. Standing silent as a stone, she watched Lorraine pull clothes out of her dresser drawer and hand them to Frank, who placed them in a backpack.

Mazzy studied her father's hastened motions and the anxiety in his eyes. It was almost feral. She backed up, distraught. Someone had found out.

"I want to stay," she pleaded.

Lorraine rubbed her arm. "Honey, we have to leave tonight. It's gonna be okay."

Mazzy studied Lorraine's face, seeing the fear in her eyes. "I didn't tell anyone I'm a Chipren. I swear."

"Listen, young lady," Frank reprimanded, but Lorraine butted in.

"Chipren, honey? Where did you hear that?" she asked.

"It was on a sign when they released Angela Mathers."

Mazzy and her dad had watched it on TV a couple weeks ago. Angela had been exonerated from Lucy's murder, but not everyone agreed with the ruling, and outside the police station, anti-technology protesters gathered, chanting and waving signs.

Angela is Satan's interface.

Stop the Children's Neural Prostheses Program.

CHIPren have no soul.

Mazzy never forgot the scene. Four police officers were escorting little Angela toward her parents' SUV when the demonstrators saw her, and a rush of bodies pushed against the barricades, breaching them. The police officers swarmed young Angela as her body was jerked back and forth, moving her through a gauntlet of angry protestors toward her parents. The car door was thrust open, and Angela's mother's thin, protective arm had swept down, latching onto her daughter's shoulders, pulling her into the SUV.

It was the first time Mazzy had witnessed an angry mob and it scared her.

"Darlin', don't pay attention to those hateful people," Lorraine said. She took out a tissue she always had tucked in her sleeve and wiped away Mazzy's tears. "It's not your fault, Mazzy. It's not safe here. Come on, help me. Why don't you pick out your favorite book to take with us?"

Mazzy grabbed a thick book from the bookshelf, *The Science of Formula One Engines*. It was an advanced vocational college manual.

"There's no room for books. She has to carry her own backpack." Frank's harsh tone filled Mazzy with fear.

"Okay, Dad. Let's stay calm," Lorraine cautioned as she folded a pair of Mazzy's pants.

"Do people think Angela pushed Lucy in the river because she's seven or because she's a Chip?" Mazzy's bright mind pondered Angela's troubles and tied them to her own.

"The media has misguided them." Frank took the pants Lorraine offered, adding them to the backpack.

Lorraine scoffed, "It's just history repeating itself."

Frank gazed at Lorraine. "Not helpful."

Mazzy watched them bicker, studying them: her dad's intense dark brown eyes, so different from her own, yet with the same high cheekbones, and Lorraine's questioning, kind eyes staring right back into his. Lorraine was thin, almost frail looking compared to her daddy, and always had on a flowered dress with a Kleenex tucked up inside her dress sleeve. When they turned and noticed her peering at them, Lorraine gave her an "it's going to be okay smile" so wide that it made her skin radiate with golden brown undertones. Flustered, Frank marched out of the bedroom in a huff, Mazzy sulking after him. Frank riffled through a bureau's drawer in the living room, searching for something and not finding it, then slamming it shut and moving on to the next drawer.

"I didn't tell anyone about my chip, I promise, Daddy." Mazzy choked up with guilt as she followed him. Even at her young age, she understood that her dad's decision to leave his congregation without so much as a goodbye was leaving him desolate. She watched as he finally found his Bible, the one his father had given him when he retired as the pastor from the First Baptist Church in St. Edenville and Frank took his place. He held it for a moment, rubbing its old, worn leather cover. Then he threw it across the room. The Bible smashed into the wall, landing near Mazzy's feet.

Frank flipped around, meeting Mazzy's tearful blue eyes.

"Don't be mad at me," she cried.

Frank gathered her in his arms, holding her tight. "Honey, I'm not mad at you. I'm mad at God."

\* \* \*

The backyard swing set was barely discernible under cover of night as Frank hugged Mazzy, then handed her the backpack. Reassuring her, he kissed the top of her head. She peered up at him, hanging on his every word.

"There are people who don't want you to be free. Not because there is anything wrong with you. They just can't see past their own fear to see your brave heart and beautiful soul. And until we can clear up this misunderstanding, you have to hide who you are." Mazzy stood like a little soldier and nodded. "You mind Lorraine, and I'll see you real soon. I love you, sweetheart."

Frank turned to Lorraine, kissing her fully on the lips. In the midst of the bitter tyranny surrounding Mazzy, they had found the sweetness of love in each other. "Past our yard is a trail, Lorraine. Follow it for two miles to the river. To an abandoned dock. They will be there waiting for you. If I'm not there within an hour, an hour, you leave without me. Promise me, Lorraine. You must keep her safe and go without me."

Lorraine nodded with tearful eyes.

"I love you." Frank squeezed her hand. He walked away, glancing back at them one last time before he disappeared into the house.

A barn owl screeched overhead as Lorraine and Mazzy marched single file along a trail full of ruts and underbrush, their backpacks slung over their shoulders. As soon as they came to a small clearing,

Lorraine stopped to catch her breath. Mazzy dropped her backpack with a thud. Resting on it, she peered up at the tall pines reaching for the stars. The dense black foliage through which they were navigating was ominous against the gray night sky.

An explosion rocked the woods, sending them scampering with their packs to the cover of some thick bramble. A strange hissing sound rose in the distance. It sounded like whispering children. Mazzy peered through the bramble's branches. Their house was engulfed in flames so bright they could see it from the trail. Steam was pouring out of the wood frame. They stood up, eyes glued to the horrifying sight, unable to turn away. Tears streaming down their cheeks, they watched the fire grow until it took over their home. They were too far away to feel the heat, but Mazzy felt it all the same. Lorraine hugged her to her body as the house frame leaned, then wavered back and forth until it crumbled like an animal beaten to its knees. The roaring blaze had devoured their history. Who was she now, other than scorched, stained, smoldering embers and ash?

A siren wailed in the distance. "We need to keep moving." Lorraine scanned the forest frantically. "I lost the trail when we hid."

Back toward the house, where the forest met the tree line, they heard voices and dogs barking. Then light cut through the darkness, moving in their direction.

Mazzy whispered, "Daddy?"

"We need to run. Now." Panic seized Lorraine and she grabbed Mazzy's hand.

"I'll lead the way," Mazzy said. "I can see good in the dark." Her left eye was not a synthetic one but a bio-inspired organ with cell organelles, fleshy and living. As a result, her vision there was stronger and more intelligent than her right one. Holding tightly to Lorraine's hand, she moved like a gazelle along the narrowing trail. She ran fast, like a fugitive running to freedom.

Out of breath and nearing exhaustion, they reached the river. Downriver a little way, Mazzy spotted a lantern's light hanging off a pontoon boat shielded by an old cypress tree covered in long beards of moss. It floated next to the old dock her father had spoken of.

"Over there." She pointed to where a man was standing like a sturdy tree trunk. He cautiously watched them approach. Mazzy studied him with her left eye. "We can trust him, Lorraine."

They stepped closer to the boat, and Lorraine said, "I'm Lorraine, and this is Mazzy. You are expecting us?" The man grunted hello and helped them aboard.

Nestled under a tarp, they waited for Frank. Mazzy gazed over the side of the boat. Her soul stared back at her from the depths of the river water. Her left eye penetrated the murky underwater world, ever-changing below them. What would it be like, she wondered, to live in constant motion, to wander like the river.

An eerie moan came from behind them. Mazzy and Lorraine stiffened, huddled tighter. The boat brushed up against the old cypress tree as if counting down the minutes.

In a thick Creole accent, the man said, "Eh, Lorraine, we cain't wait any longer."

"No! Wait. Daddy's coming. There!" Mazzy pointed at the woods, but Lorraine could see only darkness. Lorraine held up five fingers, signaling the boatman to wait.

He shook his head and untied the boat from the dock. "Pastor Frank's been real kind to me and my kin, but I got to follow orders and get you out of here."

Suddenly, Frank broke through the dense foliage. He bounded down the derelict dock with uncanny agility and landed in the boat. Gasping, he said, "Hurry. Police dogs—they caught my scent."

"Don't worry, Pastor Frank. They cain't follow you on the river. I'll distract 'em dogs for ya." He got out and pushed the pontoon away from the dock. He watched the boat until the river's swift current caught it and then took off into the woods, the barking of dogs coming ever closer.

The Parks huddled together as they set off for a new life. The river would know where it had carried them to, but it would carry their secret with it to the sea. Frank extinguished the lantern light and started the engine. As it roared to life, so did Isabella's heart.

# CHAPTER TEN

*Janet Abrams*

Senate Majority Leader Janet Abrams was reeling from her successful Senate committee hearing earlier in the day. The Freewill legislation would go before the Senate in a couple of weeks. It was a significant milestone in her career and a moment worthy of celebration. And that was just what she would be doing tonight. Galas and fundraising events filled the otherwise empty evenings of Janet and her husband almost every weekend, but this event was going to be epic.

The Kennedy Center's Grand Foyer was swarming with operagoers on this steamy summer night. Under the dazzling lights of eighteen gigantic chandeliers, Janet and her suave husband, Mort, mingled with famous and exquisitely dressed supporters. She was adorned in a new black, diamond-studded designer gown. Her ebony hair, usually tied back, fell loosely over her shoulders, showing off her sensual, softer side. He was in black tie as usual.

Mort and a few of his business partners raised their champagne glasses to her, and Janet smiled some more at the admiration in his expression when his eyes caught hers. Mort's eyes were just like Jason's—the same shape and color her son's had been. *Stop! This is not the night for regret*, she reminded herself.

Her phone dinged. She opened it, expecting a text from her aide, Mike, but when she read it, she froze. *I know your secret*, it said, and it was accompanied by a photo of Angela and her in an intimate position. A jolt of panic raced through her body. She fumbled with the phone to turn it off, fully expecting when she glanced up to see a throng of operagoers staring at her—repulsed. Ironically, when she raised her head everyone seemed to be otherwise occupied. No one, it appeared, had noticed her shocking inauguration into the dark world of desperation. Except possibly the person who had texted her. She scanned the crowd, looking for...for what exactly?

She brushed the jacket sleeve of Mort's tailored tux with her hand. Leaning into him, she whispered, "I'll be back."

His eyebrows narrowed. "Is everything all right?" After a decade and a half of marriage, he could read her mood like a sailor navigating a deep ocean.

"Just work." She nodded, but she knew she probably hadn't hidden the worry in her eyes. "Please excuse me for a moment," she said to Mort's business partners.

"Janet needs to go save the world," she heard him jokingly explain as she started across the Grand Foyer, leaving him to his wheeling and dealing as she went in search of something to drink—and some answers.

She searched her mind for clues. Who had sent this threatening text? Did it have anything to do with the rumored insider trading and charges of sexual harassment that Mort had denied? It was much more likely that it had to do with the Freewill Bill. Her support of the legislation had created enemies. She shook her head. It wasn't even clear that it would pass now. Angela had called earlier, distraught about another missing Luman. Bad news for the bill. And now this blackmail.

The gigantic chandelier overhead felt like a heat lamp, and perspiration was swamping her lower back as she traipsed, her heart pounding, down the long foyer toward the JFK statue. Beyond it, she knew, there was a quiet place serving proper drinks. Her beautiful Donna Karan gown, twisted askew by her agitated pace, flattened her breasts, crushing a lung and leaving her breathless.

*Who hated her that much to send such a text?* A nervous breakdown was inevitable if she didn't find a quiet place soon. Her eyes flickering uncontrollably, she stopped a server and whispered in a frosty tone, "What do you have to do to get a stiff drink around here?"

He pointed nervously down the hall. "The bar's just down there, ma'am."

She released his arm and set off again, swiping sweat from her brow as she went. Her nerves felt like shredded beef.

"Senator Abrams!" called Vice President Georgina Wilson before she had gone more than a few feet. She was on the arm of a squarish, middle-aged man with nice hair.

"Georgina, how are you?" Swallowing her hysteria and wishing she'd had time to swallow something alcoholic, she air-kissed the vice president's cheeks.

"Good. I'm good. You look stunning yourself, though a little pale. Not surprising. It's sweltering tonight, isn't it?" Georgina eyed her excitedly. "I have a surprise for you." She winked at her and gestured toward her companion. "This is Dr. Ryan Austin, neurosurgeon extraordinaire. How fortunate that we ran into you. You two should talk."

Janet looked at Georgina, bewildered.

"The passage of the Freewill Bill will greatly benefit my research," Austin proclaimed in a perky and slightly presumptuous tone. "Currently I'm working with the military and wounded warriors but with your backing we could improve medical care for children as well. Something that has been greatly missing for the last twenty or so years. You really should know more about it. I think you'll find it very inter—"

Janet cut him off before he could finish. "Sorry, I am overcommitted, Doctor." *And overheated. And about to lose it.*

The vice president leaned closer. "He's heading Corpus, Janet," she whispered. "You know. The president's top-secret project?"

Distracted by the need to fend off a panic attack, Janet excused herself. "I'm sorry. I have an urgent matter to tend to." Turning on her heel, she trekked down the Hall of Nations, noting the Israeli lounge up ahead. "Finally," she muttered. She flashed her full-access ticket to the attendant, entered the lounge, and had just sat down at a quiet corner booth when Austin caught up to her.

"Senator Abrams, I don't mean to be pushy, but we must talk. I reviewed your son's medical case and what you went through… well, my research could help other mothers, so they don't have to go through the same thing."

Her eyes filleted him. She couldn't bite back the anger any longer. "How could you possibly understand what I've been through? You will never understand what it's like to be a mother. So stop pretending you do."

Austin bowed his head. "I'm so sorry, Senator. My enthusiasm gets the best of me sometimes."

In spite of her distraught state, Janet's interest was piqued. She was always on the lookout for the game-changer, the next cutting-edge platform that would catapult her to the top of the list of contenders for the presidency. "Email me an overview on Corpus," she huffed, "but I'm not promising anything."

Austin smiled and mouthed "Thank you" as he left.

A waiter stopped by with a tray and offered her champagne.

"No thank you. Johnnie Walker Blue, neat."

She sat in silence at the table. This was not the senator she planned to be. She yearned to be admired and respected, a savvy deal maker, a savior to her constituents. The phone shook in her hand as she read the mysterious text message over and over.

*I know your secret.*

She swallowed her scotch in one gulp as soon as the waiter who delivered it left. This threat was personal and it would ruin her. If Mort found out he would blow his top, so what. But oh mighty Christ, if Congress... For God's sake, what they were doing was illegal. She was embarrassed by her obsession with this Luman. She was a grown woman. Why was she risking it all? "What have I done?" she murmured.

Lights flickered, warning that the opera would begin in ten minutes. The server stopped by with another drink. Janet rolled the drink around in the iceless glass. *I'm not the monster*, she told herself. *The blackmailer is.* Staring at the message and the photo, she deleted it. She downed the scotch and stood to return to the Grand Foyer, cursing the day eight years ago that she met Angela.

### D.C. Compound 2044

Janet took Mort's arm as they strolled past reporters and into the banquet hall. The 2044 Senate race was heating up, and she was still ahead but not by a comfortable margin. She was speaking at today's opulent Women's History Month luncheon hoping to gather more supporters—especially financial ones.

"Oh, look. There's Marshall." Mort handed Janet his glass of wine. "I need to talk to him. I'll catch up with you later."

"I thought we would spend the afternoon together. You just got back in town."

Mort looked helplessly at her. "Honey, these events are all about making money," he said before walking over to greet one of her wealthier donors, who, she saw, was chatting with Emma, the madam of the White Rabbit, and a petite woman with a body sculpted like that of a Greek goddess—brutal and beautiful. Oh, to be that young again, Janet reflected, imagining what it would be like to run her hands over the curve of her wonderfully toned hips. She glanced away and downed her wine and then Mort's in quick succession.

Hoping to avoid looking like she'd been ditched, Janet set their glasses on a nearby tray and began to peruse an historical exhibit about female mathematicians from the eighteenth and nineteenth centuries that was mounted on the hall's back walls. She was studying the portrait of Émilie du Châtelet when she felt a presence beside her and smelled the subtle fragrance of wisteria.

"Émilie's mother found her studies on mathematics unladylike and refused to support her," a woman's sultry voice informed her, its timbre sinking into Janet's bones. "So, she applied her math skills to gambling and financed her own education in math and science."

Janet's eyes widened as she turned, taking in her fantasy woman. On closer inspection, she looked to be about twenty-one, but her hair was styled in a bouncy bob, and she wore a navy sheath dress, making her appear older.

The woman held out her left hand, making obvious her chip tattoo. Janet glanced at it before extending her own hand.

"Angela Mathers." Her handshake was firm and warm, causing adrenaline to shoot through Janet's stomach. "I curated the exhibit, a side project when I'm not at the Luman Administration." Angela's etched eyebrows rose subtly as her intelligent gray eyes gazed appreciatively at Janet.

"It's interesting how you juxtaposed with their accomplishments the misconceptions these women had to overcome to reach them." Flustered by the realization that she was still holding the other woman's hand, Janet dropped it hastily. "Where are my manners? Nice to meet you, Angela. I'm—"

Angela interrupted, "Janet Abrams, the spectacular first-term senator from my home state of Louisiana. The pleasure is mine."

They walked to the next mathematician's portrait. "I'm very familiar with misconceptions myself," Angela said. "And so was Mary Somerville. Her family tried to dissuade her interest in academics, telling her mathematics would drive her insane. A popular theory in the seventeen hundreds." Angela looked at Janet, feigning a lunatic look.

Janet chuckled and joined in, "How about the postulation that reading made women infertile?"

"Right on, Janet. Not to mention the one about women's wombs wandering about the body, causing hysteria."

"That women are not good with numbers or driving."

Angela leaned in close to whisper, "And that we don't like casual sex."

Their eyes fixed on each other for a long moment.

Angela and Janet walked the length of the entire exhibit, engrossed in a conversation that eventually touched on the Senate race. "A grassroots campaign with a message of inclusion could secure your reelection," Angela said. "You should consider endorsing the Luman platform. We can't vote, but our supporters can and are prevalent in Louisiana. I could run the numbers if you're interested."

Hearing the sincerity in Angela's tone, Janet felt a sudden kinship with her. "Yes, I love what I'm hearing. We should plan a meeting…"

"There you are, honey. It's almost time for your speech," Mort interrupted.

"Mort, dear, this is Angela Mathers. We've been discussing some new campaign ideas."

"Mr. Abrams." Angela extended her left hand.

Mort nodded to her distractedly, then led Janet toward the front of the banquet hall. "You can't be seen with that," he whispered.

Janet gaped at him, mortified, hoping Angela hadn't heard him.

Before she could say anything, a baritone voice rattled through the banquet hall's speakers. "We'd like to welcome to the stage now Senator Janet Abrams. She's a rising champion for the rights of the underprivileged and children with special needs, who made history when she was elected as the youngest Asian American female to represent Louisiana in the Senate."

Janet made her way onstage to a round of applause. She waved at the large crowd and took a moment to reflect before beginning her remarks.

"In many periods of history, society discouraged women from applying their minds to scholarly studies, but a few persevered. The world-altering contributions of some of these women are recounted in the back of this room. Despite the obstacles set before them, they persisted. And, like them, so will I. No one will dissuade me from putting an end to the Codes, lifting the ban on new technology, and reopening trade with fellow nations. It's time to start living better with technology." Angela, in the back of the room, smiled at her and applauded vigorously with the rest of the attendees.

The day after that, Angela began helping to run Janet's campaign. A year later, Janet was reelected to her Senate seat. In 2051, following the sudden death of her predecessor, the Senate elected her the majority leader. Mort complained about Janet working with Angela at first. But then something changed, and he no longer seemed to care. Janet came to rely on the Luman for strategic political advice. And other less strategic things.

# CHAPTER ELEVEN

*Sisters*

Angela had a plan, and part of that plan was to stay away from Jeff Lewis, her monitor. Stepping into the elevator of the DHS building, she punched the second-floor button and stepped back, happy with her decision. She watched the numbers tick down. Five… Four…—Jeff was in the building looking for her—Three… Two… Ding. The elevator door opened. Her extremities grew numb with anticipation as she peered out the door. The hall was empty. It was after six o'clock, and most people had gone home. She made a beeline for the stairwell and took the stairs two at a time, noticing that the metal door at the bottom was open. *Thank God.* Sometimes they locked it after hours. She walked casually out, and right in front of her was the Luman Security Station; the guard waved her through.

She needed to be with someone who understood her the way Jonathan did. So she had called Margot. They were to meet in the foyer, but there was no sign of her. Her phone dinged as she moved toward the building's exit. A text from Janet: *Stuck at the opera but need to see you.* Angela's heart skipped a beat. She thought of herself as Janet's conscience, and Janet needed to understand the implications of Jonathan's disappearance. Their usual meet-up was at the White Rabbit—if only she could get there.

As Angela waited for Margot in front of DHS, the streetlights clicked on, one by one. Glancing up from her phone, she froze, and for a moment, the two women gazed at each other, then Margot rushed to Angela's side and touched her upper arm, the only touch allowed between a Luman and a human.

"I'm here. It will be okay," said Margot, still rubbing Angela's upper arm. The meek nun from Camp I/O was now a midwife and had moved to the Washington area to be near Angela. She was one of Angela's true friends and someone she could confide in. "Has there been any word on Jonathan?"

"No," Angela sighed. "Did you have trouble..."

Before Angela could finish, a shadow passed over them.

"Angela, there you are!" Jeff Lewis said. "Didn't you get my text?" His stocky, broad-shouldered shape was haloed by the bright streetlights. The sight of him stole her breath. Of course, she'd gotten it, but she'd ignored it.

"With Jon's disappearance, I should escort you home." Without waiting for a response, he locked onto her upper arm, dragging her down the steps to his awaiting car.

Margot followed, waving a paper pass at Jeff, panic rising in her voice.

"Wait, wait. I have a Luman pass, Mr. Lewis, cleared by Steven Hawk."

Jeff studied the pass, looking from Margot to Angela.

"She needs to be with family tonight, son. Don't you see she's distraught?"

Removing his hand from Angela, he studied the pass for a long moment, finally handing it back in defeat.

"I'll see you bright and early tomorrow." He pointed a warning finger at her before leaving.

"What's his problem?" Margot whispered.

"He hates it when I skate around the rules. It undermines his power over me."

Safe inside Margot's SUV, Angela said, "I know this is impolite and bad manners, but I must see the senator tonight." She glanced at Margot doubtfully. "Can I ask you to be my alibi when I go out later? Now that Jonathan's gone, I have no one to cover for me."

"Oh, Angela, be careful. You are playing with fire with that one." Margot forgave Angela's shortcomings. She had told Angela once that every Sister had a story about a child that had touched their heart from the Camp era and that for her that child was Angela. Shaking her head, she put the car into Drive.

"Janet can help us win our freedom," Angela said.

"Uh-huh." Margot studied Angela. "Okay, I'll do it." Her lips pursed disapprovingly.

"Thank you," Angela responded, keeping all traces of victory from showing on her face. Margot was like the older sister Angela never had. If it weren't for Margot, she would have died in Camp I/O.

# CHAPTER TWELVE

## *Camp I/O 2040*

Shortly after Angela's seventeenth birthday, she had an epiphany. Sitting on her bunk, a notepad resting on her lap, she composed a letter. Next to her, Jonathan watched as she wrote in elegant cursive and then listened as she read the letter aloud to him.

"Mrs. Green, I have found my way to our Lord Jesus Christ. As such, I feel I can no longer hold on to Lucy's secret. I forgive you for thinking I killed Lucy. But can you ever forgive yourself? Protecting Lucy was your responsibility. Lucy was God's good gift. Her innocence was pure and fragile, and you stood by while Lucy's uncle stole that from her. The righteous shall see God—Angela Mathers."

"Wow, that will get Ms. Betty Jo's attention," Jonathan said as he picked up yesterday's newspaper next to Angela. He glanced at Senator Jackson Green's photo and its caption: Senator Green to run for a second term in the Senate.

"Was it true?" he asked as he tossed the paper back on the bed. Jonathan's cleverness rivaled her own at that age.

Angela shifted with uneasiness. "You think I would lie about it?"

"No, I guess not." But his skeptical smile said, *You don't want me to answer that truthfully.* Angela didn't care about Jonathan's opinion of her, as long as she felt what she was doing was justified.

"Lucy told me about her uncle once. They called him River, Uncle River. He wasn't right in the head, Lucy said. His mother was unwed when she got pregnant with him and wore a tight corset to hide her pregnancy. He came out messed up, afflicted. For two weeks every summer, he stayed with her family. Lucy dreaded it; he sat in a lounge chair and watched her. His voice was deep, and he talked really slow, and whenever she walked by him, he would pull her onto his lap and tell her secrets about the Devil's hand."

Jonathan's face lit up with laughter. "And you decided he molested Lucy."

Angela's eyes sparred with his. "Whatever happened to Lucy, Uncle River caused it. The Greens made sure no one listened to my side of the story. My parents hired a private investigator, but they never found evidence that anyone else was there at the river."

Jonathan tried to call a truce by kissing her. Instead, she moved away and folded the letter and slid it inside an envelope, tucking it safely away in her dresser drawer. She nudged Jonathan off her bed. "Where's Warren?"

Jon gave her a "don't you want me" look and sat next to her again. Angela ignored him. The broken pieces of her memory circled and shifted in her mind: *The flowers Lucy collected were swirling in the blood-smeared river.*

A spectacularly loud hammer of thunder shook the room, and then the rains came. She and Jon sat on her bunk, staring at the ceiling, listening to the pounding rain on the tin roof.

"We'll get drenched if we leave for class now." Jonathan gave her a devilish grin.

"We should shelter in place." She moved to him, petting his handsome face. "I don't want to share you with Warren." She kissed him, wrapping her arms around him.

"A0M01, what are you doing?" Sister Margot stood before them, hands on her hips. Angela looked up, wide-eyed from her bunk.

"23JW4, go back to class." Sister Margot pointed to the door. Snickering, Jonathan trotted off.

With arms crossed, Sister Margot said, "You knew I'd find out you weren't in class, and I'd have to come looking for you. What's this about?" Margot scooched Angela off the cot and began straightening the pillow. "Sister Agnes will send you to solitary."

Angela scoffed. "I don't care. It would be an improvement over this place. I feel like I'm in an endless subroutine. I wake up every morning, wondering if I will make it through another boring day.

I'm a facsimile, a string of alphanumeric characters—A0M01, a serial number stamped on a genderless electronic brain. Why don't you want us to feel human?"

"Shhh." Sister Margot raised her fingers to her lips. "It's going to be okay. In a couple years, you will go to the New Orleans Compound, where you can live on your own and work for the government."

Angela frowned. The kids all knew about the compound transfers. The Sisters kept forgetting about Jonathan's supersonic hearing.

"Angela, come on. This is exciting news. You'll finally get out of here."

Angela didn't want to go to the New Orleans Compound. She wanted to win her freedom and overturn the Codes. Though she was unsure of how she would do it, one thing was clear: she wouldn't do it from New Orleans. She reached into her dresser drawer and pulled out the envelope, handing it to Sister Margot.

"I can't wait any longer. I need to put the past behind me."

Sister Margot held the letter addressed to Betty Jo Green. Her eyebrow rose suspiciously. "What is this?"

"It's been ten years since Lucy's death. I want her mother to know I still miss Lucy."

Pride washed over Sister Margot's face, and she stashed the letter inside her pocket. Angela smiled to herself; Margot was such a trusting soul.

"Angela, you are such a brilliant young woman. You just need to learn patience."

Angela rushed to hug Sister Margot. It had been years since an adult besides her parents had called her by her given name.

"Shame! A0M01, that inappropriate behavior will cost you twenty days in solitary." Sister Agnes and two menacing orderlies were standing behind them.

One orderly ripped Margot from Angela's arms. She screamed, clawing and kicking in a fit of rage. Removing a one-hit syringe from her coat pocket, Sister Agnes stabbed it into Angela's arm, injecting the cold sedative into her vein. Sister Margot disintegrated into darkness right before Angela's eyes. She wasn't sure when the dream ended, and the nightmare began.

* * *

Angela awoke, facing a wall so close she felt its coldness against her cheek and smelt the dampness pressing in on her. She was in a dark 12-foot-by-12-foot cell with a cot and a toilet. Her eyes focused on the lines etched in the plaster wall. Unsure if it was day or night, she twisted on the cot, and the springs gave a rusty groan. On the floor was a food tray—another day had passed. Angela etched a new line next to the nineteen others on the wall with a sliver of plaster.

In the blackness, she rolled flat on her back and wondered what had happened to Sister Margot and whether she had delivered her letter. She gazed up, scarcely making out a creepy metal hook protruding from the ceiling. It had weight, and Angela wondered if it was there to hang a birdcage or potted plant, maybe a Holstein. Or her. Angela imagined her escape, her limp body suspended from the rusty old hook, twisting like an empty husk in the darkness. An electric current passed through her suddenly, and she felt something shift under her skin. She wondered if she could leave her body, transport her digital consciousness into another living body with a chip. She played with the idea of uploading and downloading her digital consciousness into the light. She could upgrade. A taller body, one outside the camp walls.

*Resurgence.* The word came to her like a flash of lighting. She would need to prove her hypothesis: the ability to become the light. So she practiced and focused on the center of her neural chip, meditating for hours. Soon she taught herself how to leave her body. She discovered there was a gateway in her chip and that, if she passed through it, she became part of the light—undulating energy. She felt like the sun's surface, always moving, constantly changing. She learned her mind was not physical and that it could exist independently of her matter, of her biological brain and body. And soon she was traveling along airwaves, crisscrossing the universe. She was the incarnation of something free…

The screech of metal invaded her thoughts as Sister Agnes unbolted the lock and the cast-iron door swung open, light spilling into the cell. A disheveled, squinting Angela raised her hand to ward off the light. Abruptly, she was back in her body after being in the light— rejuvenated. Sister Agnes's elongated silhouette bellowed, "A0M01, get up. Mrs. Green is here to see you."

The Camp I/O visitor center was full of families huddled together and conversing in low tones. At one table, a teenage girl begged to come home, while other families hopefully glanced at the door, waiting for their child. Guards positioned themselves like toy soldiers around the room, dressed in Army fatigues, batons dangling from their hips. When Angela stepped into the room, many of the waiting parents leapt up. Their faces dropped when they saw her and they shrank back into their chairs. Betty Jo Green, Angela saw, was sitting at a folding table picking lint off her glove. In her late thirties, the senator's wife had a snowy-white complexion and a petite size that made her look delicate—deceptively so, Angela thought.

The Sisters had let Angela shower and had given her a clean uniform. In a crisp, ghostly white blur, she plopped down in the metal folding chair across from Betty Jo's reproachful stare.

Betty Jo growled, "Wicked child, haven't your lies hurt my family enough?"

"You wouldn't be here unless you thought my letter had merit."

"What do you want?" Betty Jo hissed.

"I want out of this shithole!" Angela shrieked with contempt.

The guards moved toward their table. Betty Jo raised her palm to settle them.

"Tell me what it is you want. Quietly."

Angela saw the calculation going on behind Betty's eyes.

"I want you to get me, Jonathan Riley"—Angela paused, considering her last request—"and Warren Harris out of this cage and placed at the D.C. Compound together. If you do, we will forget about Lucy's creepy uncle when Senator Green runs for his second term in the Senate."

Mrs. Green pursed her lips and clasped her arms tightly in front of her chest. "I won't be held hostage by your lies."

Angela leaned across the table toward Betty Jo and whispered, "Do you still have it?"

Betty Jo cleared her throat. Her eyes swiveled to the other parents in the room.

"You know, that ratty old La-Z-Boy. Is it still in the family room?"

Betty Jo stared blankly at her.

"When he came to visit for those two weeks, he'd force Lucy to sit on his lap and ride his knee. Imagine his hands cupping her waist tightly, his fingers creeping under her dress. His nasally sound of pleasure."

She heard the blow and smelled Chanel No. 5 before she felt Betty Jo slap her across the face, knocking her out of the chair. The guards yanked Angela off the floor, and as they dragged her away, she said, in a hauntingly childlike voice, "Uncle River has gone to the Devil."

# CHAPTER THIRTEEN

*The White Rabbit*

Discreet, with elegant lettering, the White Rabbit sign hung on a modern façade in West Park, a trendy downtown area. Interestingly enough, Isabella thought, it was on Control's do-not-touch list. Which meant prominent personalities entertained here. It wasn't surprising that D.C. had one of the most active Luman subcultures, one tailored to the comingling of Lumans and humans, and that the White Rabbit nightclub was at its heart.

She opened the door. Venturing inside was like stepping into a fantasy in constant motion. There were large, mirrored glass panels on either side of the hostess station, panels which Isabella suspected were made of one-way glass. She felt the natives were watching and on the hunt. Next to the mirrors, water droplets defied gravity and ran up colored wires to the roof, creating a brilliant shimmer of light. On the ceiling, millions of tiny crystal balls floated on waves of energy. The room was dizzying, turning her thoughts upside down, stripping away expectations, as if she were Alice falling down the rabbit hole. From behind a red flowing drape, Emma, the White Rabbit's madam, appeared, wearing a midnight blue dress that hugged her voluptuous curves. Isabella removed her black anorak, revealing a burgundy dress that matched her Hepburn eyeglasses.

Handing the jacket to Emma, she whispered, "First-timer."

Emma gave her a carnivorous smile and placed a pair of wrist-length, burgundy leather gloves on the counter.

In a high, doll's voice, Emma said, "Welcome to the White Rabbit. We are the only club specializing in Luman women. I'm sure you've heard about the shimmer?" Emma smiled, fluttering her long eyelashes.

*Spare me the details*, Isabella mused as she took the gloves off the counter. Everyone profited off the Lumans. Emma's establishment was no different. Selling forbidden sex invoked allure and big profit margins—when done on the tasteful side of raunchy.

"I have the perfect match for you. Would you care for an introduction?" Emma raised an eyebrow.

Emma smiled too much, Isabella decided. "I'll just have a look around."

Emma opened the velvety drapes and the heady smell of expensive cologne enveloped Isabella as the sensual tempo pulled her in. There was an air of sophistication and seduction as she pushed through the crowd of well-dressed men and women of varying ages. The bar took up one wall with its mirrored backsplash glittering to the music and begging for attention. And if that wasn't enough, pulsing red spotlights danced across the room. It was impossible to feel lonely in a place filled with so many beautiful people. Still, Isabella was hoping to see Angela, and when she didn't, a sense of isolation settled in. Spotting an open table, she took a seat, then chided herself for thinking about Angela. But she couldn't help it; there was something about her. She was unsocialized: in the committee hearing she had talked about awful events from her past in a detached impersonal way, and during their interview she had edited her emotions and left too many unanswered questions.

"What can I getcha?" A male waiter hovered at Isabella's shoulder.

"Beer."

His eyebrows arched.

"Whatever's on tap." Isabella waved her hand, hoping to shoo him away, but it didn't work.

"Would the lady prefer a pale ale or stout? We have several microbrews."

"Surprise the lady," Isabella snapped. The waiter nodded and vanished into the crowd.

An elegantly tall man crossed over to Isabella and whispered something in her ear. Isabella grinned but shook her head. The man walked on. Isabella felt like she was being watched. She looked up at the second floor VIP lounge, but the tinted windows there made it impossible to see anyone, even with Isabella's visual acuity. Later, two women stopped by Isabella's table, drawing her attention.

"Would you care to dance with us?" the brunette asked.

"No, thank you. I'm waiting for, uh…someone." The melody changed to an upbeat tempo, and the women rushed to the dance floor. As Isabella watched them dance, her mind drifted into the past.

## Mississippi 2039

A few days before Isabella's fifteenth birthday, her dad started meddling more directly in her life. The Parks family changed their last name to Dodge and moved around every couple of years to avoid suspicion. Frank became a mechanic and ran his business out of the home garage. Lorraine and Frank were married now, and like many families on the run, they kept to themselves.

Stacy was Isabella's only friend and she was unenhanced. Every day after school, they sat on an old, wooden front porch swing, talking and listening to music. That particular day, Isabella moved a loose strand of Stacy's amber hair, placing it behind her ear. Isabella's left eye had glimmered briefly when making the intimate gesture, and Stacy giggled bashfully. Finally, Isabella worked up the nerve to kiss her. And just her luck, her dad emerged from the garage at that very moment. Isabella pulled away, but it was too late. His grin turned into a grimace. She knew something would come of this later.

After dinner that night, Lorraine and Frank appeared at her bedroom door. They kept up with the latest research on non-human intelligence and how it affected other aspects of the human brain and psyche, and tonight they explained it to Isabella, though she already knew. She kept other things, like her ability to create holograms, private.

Lorraine sat down next to Isabella and began. "We want you to be happy, but we also want you to be safe."

Frank blurted out, "You can't get involved with a human; they won't understand you."

"But Stacy is my first real friend."

Her parents understood children with neural chips did not need to categorize their world to reduce ambiguity or complexity. They didn't see people as male or female, young or old, Black or white. And most of the information about teenagers like Isabella suggested they were more sexually fluid, not wanting to be weighed down by rigid gender roles. Frank was also aware of the shimmer, which had become an unexplained phenomenon to humans and revealed a Solo's true identity.

"I'm sorry, Bella. I know it's hard to make friends when we move so often, but those are the rules—no ifs, ands, or buts." Lorraine wrapped a protective arm around her.

"This is so unfair."

"No, love, it's not." And then commenced a lengthy explanation about the birds and the bees and shimmering.

Later that night, Frank drove her to an old, dumpy pool hall. Country music escaped as the doors opened and a young man entered. A bored Isabella glanced out the passenger window before returning to her phone.

Frank relaxed against the stiff leather seat. "This is Guardian territory. They helped us escape nine years ago and are still fighting the Codes. Inside are some of their kids; they are Solos, like you. I thought you could hang out here and maybe meet someone more your type."

"Stacy and I are just friends."

"Nobody kisses their friend like you kissed Stacy. You almost blew your identity, girl."

Embarrassed, Isabella smiled.

"This isn't a game," her father warned.

"Fine. So, I can hang out here without getting lectured?"

"Yeah, no drinking! Ask for Ginger. She's the youngest member of the Guardians and cute." Frank winked at her.

Isabella studied the exterior of the pool hall, clenching her jaw. Life was uncomfortable when you didn't see a place where you belonged.

"Look, you don't have to go in there now. Just know there's someplace you can go. You're not a girl anymore…You're a wo, I mean when you need to be close with someone. When you desire…"

"Oh my God, Dad! Abort. Abort. Lorraine and I talk, y' know? Can this be over now?"

He patted her head. She brushed it away and eased out of the car.

He called after her, "I'll be back at ten sharp." She looked back, detecting the apprehension that had taken a permanent place on his face since they first fled, then headed toward the building.

Inside the rustic pool hall, a haze of smoke hung in the air and the twang of country music mixed with the cracking of pool balls. As Isabella awkwardly wandered around, she sized up the place and noticed Ginger—it wasn't hard to find her and her mane of fiery red hair. She wore hip camo pants and car keys dangled out of her black leather jacket while she played pool with a boyish man. Isabella heard her call him Donovan when she shoved him away as he tried to distract her from her shot.

Donovan glanced at Isabella sideways. "Eh, what are you doing here? KinderCare is down the street." His crew laughed.

Isabella caught Ginger's eye, and Ginger said, "Knock it off. She's one of us."

In this group of boy-men it was clear Ginger was the one in charge. Isabella backed up, deciding it wasn't her scene, but she accidentally tripped over a chair, knocking it and herself to the ground. The roar of laughter erupted again.

Outside, Isabella cut through the gravel parking lot to the road. She checked her phone. Still no text from Stacy. She felt stupid calling her dad so early to come pick her up.

"They're harmless once you get to know them."

Isabella glanced shyly at Ginger, who was standing beside her.

"Are you Isabella? Frank's daughter? He said you might stop by."

Another wave of humiliation washed over her, and she turned from Ginger. Did it get any worse than her father finding friends for her?

Ginger touched her shoulder gently. "None of us fit in. That's why we hang together. It's better than being alone."

"Is it?" Isabella felt so pathetic thinking about how she must have looked tumbling over the chair. Suddenly she burst out laughing, throwing back her head; she couldn't stop. Ginger joined in with a rusty laugh.

Catching her breath, Ginger said, "Well, your dad was right."

Isabella looked at her, afraid of what else he might have shared about her.

"You are adorable." Now it was Ginger who smiled shyly.

\* \* \*

The waiter from the White Rabbit placed two shots on the table, bringing Isabella's attention back to the present moment. "Complimentary shots of Alice in Wonderland," he said.

"Wait, I didn't order these." A bewildered Isabella looked up to find Angela standing there, dressed in a sleeveless, blue-violet cocktail dress, her hair piled up into a messy bun.

"Do you have a Chip complex—or merely curiosity?" Angela gave Isabella a sexy grin.

She regarded Angela. Her carefully constructed façade had given way to a chameleon spirit. She looked so different in this environment. Relaxed even.

"Ms. Angela Mathers, nice to see you again." Isabella smiled and motioned for her to sit, and when she did, Isabella tossed back the shot, showing off her burgundy gloves.

"I've been watching people hit on you relentlessly, yet here you are, alone." Angela tilted her head speculatively.

"I'm flattered—maybe it's you with an Old Fashion fixation? But then, this place with its mysterious, gloved-hand policy releases us from the biopolitics that separates us."

"We can be two lonely people—doing Alice in Wonderland." Angela's silvery eyes sparkled like liquid as she took the glass in her blue-gloved hand and shot it. Isabella watched, glancing at Angela's full breasts, which strained against the fabric of her dress. Isabella's wandering glimpse did not go unnoticed, and as they held each other's gaze, the silence became as electrically charged as the White Rabbit's circuit breakers.

"I noticed you glancing at my tat earlier. Have you not seen many?" Before Isabella could answer, Angela removed her left glove, tossed it aside, and placed her hand on top of Isabella's. Isabella glanced at the tattoo there. It looked like a square computer chip with little prongs protruding from its perimeter. On the chip's surface was the image of a maze with passageways. The special pearlescent ink had a unique shiny quality, and it glittered in the light.

Angela purred, "There is something about you, Isabella." Angela's ungloved finger traced up Isabella's index finger, and Isabella almost swallowed her tongue. When Angela reached her glove tip, she peered up at Isabella. "Maybe we have a spiritual connection." She pulled off Isabella's glove with one smooth tug and then put it on her hand. "Mmmm...the warmth of you feels familiar."

"Oh," was all Isabella could say. She looked away, caught off guard. She grasped for a witty response, then blurted out, "It's my heartbeat—our hearts have the same rhythm." Isabella cringed. It was the truth, but she sounded like an idiot.

"In here, you can hear my heartbeat?" Angela fixed an even gaze at her as if wanting another explanation—like the truth.

"No, I can see it." Isabella's ungloved hand floated to Angela's neck. With a delicate touch, her finger followed Angela's subtly pulsing carotid artery. A wave of uneasiness washed across Angela's face, causing Isabella to pull back her hand. Now it was Angela who turned away and cleared her throat.

"So, is this official Control business?" Angela's careful scrutiny made her intellectually terrifying at times, but Isabella was starting to see beyond it, to see that she used it to keep people at a distance.

"Um, you mentioned this club. I thought I'd check it out and get a chance to see you again."

"Really." Angela leaned in and said in a deep, throaty tone, "And here I thought I ruffled those Southern feathers of yours earlier."

Isabella leaned in, smiling. "I do find you infuriating."

*"You are about to blow it, girl."* Her father's words rang like a bell in her head, and Isabella remembered who she was—an imposter. Awkwardly she tightened, and her face became impenetrable.

Angela leaned back in her chair, and Isabella saw her gray eyes sparkle, trying to reconcile what was happening between them. Angela glanced at Emma from across the room. *Was this amusing to her?* Isabella wondered.

Angela's seductive demeanor changed abruptly, and she urgently whispered, "Jonathan's and Warren's disappearances are part of a government conspiracy to derail the Freewill legislation."

"What? You got names to go with this theory?"

Angela got up to leave, straightening her dress. "Something just came up. Come see me tomorrow."

Flummoxed, Isabella followed Angela's gaze to Emma, then figured out Emma must be the go-between the senator and Angela. Isabella joked, letting her know she got the situation, "You should ask her if she wears Lasting Kiss. I bet I'm right."

Angela leaned in so close that Isabella felt her warm breath on her face and detected the hint of wisteria. "You think you're cute? They will hang me for sleeping with a human."

"Why sleep with her then?"

Angela coyly smiled. "What makes you think I am talking about her?"

Isabella watched the melodic sway of her hips as Angela left—until a sea of strangers folded in around her. Even then she kept gazing at the crowd, feeling Angela's presence still swaying in the strobing red light.

# CHAPTER FOURTEEN

## *A Taste of Freedom*

*Who is Isabella Dodge?* Angela wondered. The sadness brought on by Isabella's touch had seeped into Angela's bones. She had felt nothing like it before, but how could she? She didn't feel things the way other Lumans did and certainly not as intensely as Isabella did. Jonathan once had said, "The Solos move undetected amongst the living, like ghosts." She wondered what Isabella had given up to walk among the living. In Angela's mind, Isabella traveled in isolation. Maybe that was why she was so unhappy. Out of everything that had transpired today, it was Isabella's sadness that moved Angela most.

Her thoughts were quelled when she heard Emma's voice. "There you are—she's been waiting." Angela rolled her eyes at Emma and reflected on her first night at the White Rabbit and how it had changed the trajectory of her life.

For two years, Angela had been an indentured analyst for the Luman Administration and was living with Jonathan, then her boyfriend, in a D.C. Compound apartment. At twenty-one, she was restless and ready to shed her cloistered lifestyle. She had heard rumors about a nightclub near the US Capitol where a secret subculture existed between Chips and humans. Hoping to experience just a little D.C.

culture, she decided to check it out. She chose the only sexy dress in her closet and, with a bit of trepidation, took the hem up two inches. She lied to Jonathan about where she was going and asked him to be her alibi if Jeff Lewis showed up. He agreed. Everything planned out, she set out to follow her curiosity. In a red-with-white-trim shift dress, she pointed her four-inch-heeled, elegant, lace-up boots toward the White Rabbit nightclub.

"A little bit of heaven has fallen right before my eyes."

Angela looked up naively from her booth when she heard Emma's very distinctive, doll-like voice.

"What do you like?" Emma said as she slid in close to Angela.

"What?" Angela's face, she hoped, displayed its usual casual lack of interest. Ignoring Emma, she studied the club's sensual atmosphere, dripping with excitement and mystery.

Resting her hand on Angela's knee, Emma regained Angela's attention. "I asked, what do you like?" Emma's hungry eyes washed over her until Angela's palms were sweating.

"I thought relations between Lumans and humans came with a death penalty."

Emma's lips curled with amusement. "Legally and publicly, yes." She touched Angela's gloved left hand. "But there are no rules here. After all, it's human nature to be curious, to want what you cannot have." The server placed a teapot and two teacups on the table. "Would you care to take tea with me?"

As the steam rose from the cup of warm tea, Angela smelled the intoxicating aroma and asked, "What's in it?"

"Mmmm, delight. Risky sex, a taste of freedom." Emma lifted her cup to her lips and blew on the tea before she sipped. Angela watched, then followed suit.

"My club has a specialty, matching up humans with Luman women; we even get a few politicians in here."

Angela leaned into the conversation, now interested. "This is your club? You own it?"

Emma nodded as she slid her hand up to Angela's thigh and whispered, "Are you curious?"

Assessing the situation, Angela hesitated.

"C'mon, spill the tea, kitty," Emma said.

Perhaps Emma's enabling nature weakened Angela's mistrust in humans, or maybe it was the tea. In either case, with Emma's connections and clout, Angela decided, she could teach her how to navigate the D.C. political scene.

Angela bobbed her head. "I'm a lady," she said, with a little more pretentiousness than she meant. "I could be persuaded to help you if you provide me the right guidance."

With a devouring smile, Emma nodded. "I expected nothing less."

From that night forward, Emma explained the Luman subculture's deep dark secrets, and, in return, Angela became her tax accountant and lawyer. Angela had a head for business, and as their partnership grew, Emma invested in Angela, buying her clothes and jewelry. She built up Angela's self-confidence, showing her off to the Georgetown elite and introducing her to the world of politics.

Emma was well-known in political circles. Escorting Angela to a Democratic gala, she moved through the throng of the politicos with professional charisma. She kissed her way from one Democratic senator's cheek to the next, always later introducing Angela, making her feel like she belonged in the room of powerful people, though Angela knew she did not. At least not yet. Emma made Angela into a showpiece, an example of the stock available at the Rabbit, like a flashy billboard. Angela didn't mind so long as everyone kept their hands off the advertisement.

That year, Angela drafted the first version of the Freewill Bill and saw Janet Abrams for the first time. At the White Rabbit, she noticed Emma escorting her through a secret passage leading to the Wonderland Hotel next door.

Janet had a striking presence even at a distance; dressed in a mid-thigh skirt, her lean body and silky ebony hair swayed to an elegant beat. At the end of the night, Emma walked Angela the three blocks to the train station where Angela caught her ride back to reality—her apartment with Jonathan.

Walking arm in arm with Emma, Angela asked, "Who was that mysterious woman I saw you with?"

"She's an up-and-comer, running for her second term in the Louisiana Senate this year."

"Oh, my home state. What's her name?"

Emma squinted at her. "Why so many questions?"

"An up-and-comer is always useful."

"Janet Abrams. She's married."

"So, she's interested in women?"

"You're interested in her?" Emma gazed at her with contempt.

Angela scoffed. "No. You know I need to get my Freewill legislation in front of Congress. I need help from someone ambitious and gritty."

"Well, I do have an interesting tidbit about her. It's not well-known."

"What? Tell me."

"She lost her child to a traumatic brain seizure, a rare condition. Started pouring all of her energy into running for the Senate and made it clear that she doesn't support the Codes."

"That's awful. It could have been prevented if a neural implant was still an acceptable treatment." Angela's expression saddened.

"Don't be too sad for her, kitty. I hear she's ruthless."

"How do you know so much about her?"

"I know her husband, Mort. He's a valued client." Emma wiggled her eyebrows and smiled.

"So, she's not a client?"

"No. And she's out of your league, darling. I've trained you well, but not that well."

"What if I can develop a business plan that would improve your profit margin two-fold?"

Emma raised an eyebrow. "What would that entail?"

"It starts with an invitation to one of Janet Abrams's fundraising events, and then I'll tell you." Angela was adapting to this new dark world.

* * *

Eight years after meeting Emma, Angela would maintain that they were no longer good friends, but they were important ones. She never had thought she would still be walking this secret passage that led from the White Rabbit to the Wonderland Hotel. After Emma had introduced Angela to the world of politics, she taught Emma how to double her profits. But after Angela met Janet, she tossed Emma aside like a used teabag.

At the end of the tunnel, Emma said insolently, "You best not step out on Janet with that woman."

"Jealousy brings a brilliant sparkle to your eyes, Emma dear."

A large vase perched on a wooden shelf and filled with a medley of flowers glistened in the ambient light. Emma selected a flower from the vase and offered it to Angela. She marveled at the *Clitoria Ternatea*, "Blue Pea," flower and its sensual deep blue in the dimming light. As she took it, a small gold key slipped free and dangled from its stem.

Unbolting a door, Emma pushed it open, revealing the Wonderland Hotel's private lobby. Emma smiled. "Go on, doll. Swing that vote."

Pushing past Emma, Angela crossed the large atrium, which reminded her of leafing through a whimsical fairy tale book. In a garden full of beautiful extravagant flowers and plants, delicate elongated trees with branches twined as they reached toward the atrium's ceiling. Empty ornate birdcages hung overhead, slowly turning as imaginary birds sang.

A spiral staircase took her to the second floor. She entered the corridor, strolling past a series of hotel doors, without numbers, just painted with exquisite flowers: Passion Vine, Sweet Alyssum, Petting Bamboo, Orange Jasmine. At the final door, Blue Pea flowers covered the entrance. She slid the golden key into the slot and entered the room, dropping her purse on the foyer table. She checked her hair and makeup in the hall mirror and heard Janet stirring in the next room. Today was a roller coaster ride: winning the committee vote, learning about Jonathan's disappearance, and then... Angela realized she still had on Isabella's burgundy glove.

And then there was the mysterious Agent Dodge. *Friend or foe*, Angela wondered. She folded her gloves and stashed them in her purse. Grabbing the delicate Blue Pea flower, she followed the scent of Janet's perfume. She watched Janet stabbing her fingertip at her phone in frustration, then tossing the phone into her purse.

Janet turned. "Would you care for a drink?"

"No, thanks. Is something the matter?"

"It's nothing, annoying spam." Janet held up her drink. "Are you sure you don't want one?"

Angela could hear the discomfort in Janet's voice. "Are you sure it's nothing?"

"No worries." Janet's expression turned cold from Angela's probing.

Angela contemplated Janet's erratic behavior. Janet was hiding something. Angela undressed and moved toward her, and Janet's hardened expression slipped like a landslide into smoldering desire. *How easily Janet is affected.* Angela wrapped her bare arm around Janet's waist and delivered the Blue Pea flower, whispering into Janet's neck, "Isn't it beautiful? Like the color of a flame's center—the bluest of blue. Like you." They were so close now. Janet brought the *Clitoria* flower to her lips, and Angela smelt the sweet scent laced with a darker undercurrent. She hesitated, then in a soft but insistent voice, said, "I have a favor to ask." Janet's lips flickered with a patronizing grin so swift Angela might have missed it had she not been conditioned to spot it. How self-conscious Angela felt asking for a favor, asking for things she had deserved when Janet was only a familiar stranger.

# CHAPTER FIFTEEN

## *Camp I/O 2041*

Angela sat on the exam table with electrodes glued to different sections of her scalp. Cables twisted around the table legs and fed into an EEG machine as it sputtered out her electrical impulses onto a screen. Bored, she gazed around the camp's large science lab. It was a wilderness of antique desks, burners, and hotplates mixed with high-tech equipment, monitors, buzzing computers, and humming noises—she existed in a time warp, half in the past and half in the future, and it always smelt like floor wax and formaldehyde.

Her eyes drifted over to Jonathan, who sat on a nearby table. His broad shoulders and lean muscles shaped his white cotton uniform. She reflected on last night's hookup here in the lab. They happened less frequently now that Warren knew. Jonathan's desire was like a magic act—moving over her, moving into her, moving away from her. He was a smooth yet fragile illusion that she held too tight.

She longed to reach out and brush her fingers through his cropped hair. His lips were dark chocolate, and she could taste them melting against her mouth. He turned to look at her, and she averted her gaze——a sudden disturbance in brain activity displayed on the EEG scope.

The crusty neurologist noticed and slid his eyeglasses down from the top of his balding head over his eyes. His brow furrowed as he punctiliously compared Angela's and Jonathan's EEG scans and documented his finding into a recorder.

"Chip A0M01, a female subject, Angela Mathers, age eighteen. Her biological brain shows diminished self-regulation."

Jonathan reached for one of Angela's electrode cables, pulling on it jokingly. Angela smiled shyly.

*He caught you thinking about me,* Jon silent-messaged, and Angela let out an embarrassed laugh.

The neurologist pivoted, losing his patience. "You two need to sit still and close your eyes. Now we will have to start all over again."

Creaking floorboards caused everyone to glance up. Sister Agnes hovered in the lab's archway, and the neurologist grabbed a file folder and crossed over to her.

"Senator Jackson Green has asked for an update," Sister Agnes blurted.

The neurologist cleared his throat. "At first I thought they could read minds."

Sister Agnes gasped. "They read our minds?" Her face was choked with uncertainty.

"No, no, I didn't say that."

"But you just said…"

He whispered, "I've realized they use their beta brainwaves to communicate with each other. Their chips have created a private mesh network, and they talk to each other on a different frequency that we can't hear."

"A mesh what? You must stop them from doing it!"

He turned back to see Angela and Jonathan gaping at them.

"We can't have them plotting against us," Sister Agnes hissed.

"We can't stop it without damaging their brains."

Sister Agnes clutched her chest. "Can they talk to children in other camps?"

"Calm down. It's short-range, like a short-wavelength radio signal—under two hundred feet. But there's something more pressing."

He saw Jon and Angela watching him and reflected on Jonathan's supersonic hearing. He opened Angela's medical record and pointed to something on the page.

"Oh my." A look of dread shadowed Sister Agnes's face.

\* \* \*

Angela lost time. It was the only way she could account for what happened to her after she left the lab that day. The next thing she remembered was waking up on her cot. Sister Agnes was watching over her in the dorm.

"What happened to me?" Angela asked, her voice hoarse with sleep.

"You're fine, A0M01. An ovarian cyst ruptured. You need to rest."

Angela saw a flash of something else in Agnes's eyes and knew she was lying. There was something Sister Agnes wasn't saying, and Angela could guess what it was. Jonathan had overheard the Sisters talking amongst themselves. They were afraid that the offspring of two Lumans would be like its parents, enhanced. The Sisters' logic was simple: the neural chip inside the mother's brain would use gene-editing to modify the DNA of the embryo inside her womb, enhancing some genes and eliminating diseased ones, giving her offspring more significant intellectual and athletic abilities. But they feared the unnatural process would create a monstrosity.

"How could you?" Angela spit out.

Sister Agnes crossed herself, raised her chin, and gave a slightly knowing grin. "It's God's way."

Angela never told Jonathan that the Sisters aborted their baby and ensured she would never have another. And she learned that day that the humans looked docile, making it easy to forget the Devil rarely cohered into the image they expected him to.

# CHAPTER SIXTEEN

## *Carnivore*

After returning home from the White Rabbit, Isabella changed into a comfortable pair of Levi's and a T-shirt, then plopped down on her sofa and turned her attention to disproving Angela's conspiracy theory. She began by harvesting information on the prisoners at Camp I/O from a government database. Scanning through thousands of mug shots, she learned that Jonathan Riley, Warren Harris, and Angela Mathers were in camp together—something Angela hadn't mentioned.

Isabella resituated herself on the couch, her laptop resting on her pant legs. She took a sip of beer and placed the bottle on the end table. A lamp gave a warm glow over her messy but comfortable living room. The adjacent bookshelf held photos of her family, car racing trophies, and an antique record player that skipped and popped as it played an old Marvin Gaye tune.

Plugging a security fob into her laptop's USB port, she connected with Control's private network, gaining access to a robust surveillance search tool called Carnivore. As the name suggested, Carnivore's artificial intelligence hunted and fed on people's electronic footprints.

At the search prompt, Isabella entered the text "Jackson Green." The Carnivore federated a search across thousands of disparate databases for Senator Green's digital footprint, and the AI built a comprehensive profile on him: his identity, addresses, employment, and financials. It then foraged through his social connections and displayed those of his family, friends, neighbors, housekeeper, gardener—everyone who had ties to him.

Isabella noticed Green had no siblings; her left iris pulsed as she traversed through the evidence with incredible speed. Control had built the search engine twenty-two years ago when Angela had been accused of Lucy's death. She wondered how powerful Carnivore would be today without a technology ban.

The screen displayed all of Green's data. She scanned and highlighted important characteristics: voting record, donations, credit history. She parsed through his financials, looking for unexplained debits or credits. There was nothing suspicious. She moved on to the Greens' activities outside the Senate. There were interviews, tweets, and blogs from both Greens condemning the Lumans and Angela.

Betty Jo Green's bank accounts had several withdrawals to known anti-technology groups, a few alt-right groups, and lobbyists. Isabella dove deeper into the woman's financial history. "Hmm," she muttered. Betty Jo was from old money, a sugarcane farming family. The agricultural industry, including sugarcane, had once fueled economic growth and opulence in her hometown of St. Edenville.

Isabella surmised that Betty Jo's influence had gotten Green into the Senate. There were stories about Lucy in all the major newspapers, as well as photos of Betty Jo with an odd-looking man at Lucy's funeral, something which captured Isabella's attention. The man looked like an ill-formed skeleton; it was the only way to describe his crooked frame. Isabella scanned the story and found his name, Raymond Stratton. Betty Jo's maiden name was Stratton. This must be her brother.

She scrolled down to Lucy Green's picture. The caption read, "Lucy Green, daughter of Jackson and Betty Jo Green, drowns at age seven." There were hundreds of photos of Betty Jo protesting during Angela's release and grieving at her daughter's grave site. The Greens made sure their loss and grief were publicized all over the Internet.

Next, Isabella dug into the police report on Lucy's death. The only named suspect was Angela Mathers. Clicking on her name, Isabella accessed Angela's juvenile history. Luman children had no right to privacy and all of their medical records, psychological reports, transcripts of interrogations, and video files were available. She stared at her psychological report. Angela's entire childhood was in front of her. Should she be peeking into it? She wavered. The cursor paused next to the link. She selected it and read the psychologist's summary:

"Angela Mathers scores high on psychopathic personality traits for cunning and manipulative behavior. But she is not technically a psychopath, falling short on many standard antisocial behavior traits. There is no evidence of impulse and anger control issues or anger directed explicitly at Lucy Green. Angela Mathers and Lucy Green were at the river together, but she did not see Lucy go into the water. The State cannot ignore the fact Angela Mathers had ample opportunity to tell someone about the incident. But, by not doing so, she evaded detection until confronted. During her account of the accident, Angela displayed a lack of empathy toward Lucy. Her Wechsler Intelligence test results show a superior score of 140, indicating she understands the difference between right and wrong..."

Isabella scanned down to the last section of the report.

"The State was unclear about Angela's true mental stability, given her suspected ability to manipulate interrogations and test results. To ensure she was not a danger to the community, the State recommended she remain under surveillance indefinitely."

Isabella reached for her beer on the end table. "Jesus, she was just a little girl," she said aloud. She took a long drink. Scientists knew so little about neural chips back then. Even today, neurologists struggled with how the chip affected human consciousness—people feared technology and neural chips. When interpreting little Angela's human nature, where was the motive or evidence she had pushed Lucy? Isabella sighed with frustration.

There was a photo of Angela in a dreary jail cell. Her pink suitcase and a few stuffed animals were placed in the corner. She sat on her bunk reading the encyclopedia in a cute little checkered dress, her legs crossed, with that same look of insouciance she wore today.

Isabella's heart lurched. "Poor baby." *Our parents' choices became our own in some ways.* Isabella's parents chose to run to avoid the camps, which shaped every decision she made today. She recalled the first time she made her own decision—one that was different from her father's. That choice was why they no longer talked. She wondered if Angela's parents regretted not running.

Isabella frowned and scrolled down on the webpage. On her computer screen was a picture of Angela's face pressed against the bars of her cell. She gazed at something just out of frame.

The door to Isabella's apartment opened ever so slowly, and a silhouette slithered through the opening, creeping softly to the foyer table, subtly picking up the mail, flipping through it, and continuing into the living room. Her back to the foyer, Isabella sat with her laptop on the coffee table while she looked at additional photos of Angela in jail. The sleek figure moved dangerously close, reaching out for Isabella. Just then, she was off the sofa, latching onto the stranger's forearm and using her body weight to flip the intruder onto the couch. Their bodies collided, scuffling until Isabella came up on top, pinning her opponent to the cushions.

"Hiya, stranger," Ginger purred. Isabella's heart was racing, their faces just inches apart when she kissed her tentatively, then pulled back to make sure she was okay. Gin placed her hand lovingly on Isabella's neck, guiding her lips right back to her.

As they kissed, Isabella silent-messaged, *I miss you.*

"You should have detected me sooner. That sophisticated retinal implant that replaced your mechanical eye might have gotten you into Control but it's getting lazy." Gin's words always stung. Isabella wanted her approval and had no shield to protect herself when she didn't get it.

"I didn't give you a key to sneak up on me." Isabella noticed Ginger's engagement ring sparkling even in the dim table lamp light. Ginger now went by Gin and had become a formidable undocumented Luman and the Guardians' leader.

"You need to be on guard all the time. I worry, lov—"

"I know." Isabella stopped her, and Gin's confession got lost in their private sea of regrets. Gin looked at the coffee table where Isabella's laptop displayed Angela's picture. Isabella dipped her head, placing her lips on Gin's mouth, and reached over to close the laptop.

Gin pulled away. "Oh, please! Are you still obsessing over Angela Mathers?"

"No!" Isabella responded automatically, but she saw the skeptical glint in Gin's green eyes. "I'm working on a case. I'm the lead."

"Impressive?" Gin brushed Isabella's cheek with the palm of her hand.

"Yeah." Isabella kissed Gin softly, then more passionately, pressing her lean body against hers.

Gin pushed her away playfully. "You're trying to avoid the subject."

Isabella released Gin and sat up. "Okay." She paused, then asked, "How's Donovan?" The words tumbled out without permission.

Gin sat up next to Isabella. "I heard about those missing Lumans. Did they both work at the LA?"

"So, you two are joining the patriarchal institution?" Isabella glanced at the ring and so did Gin. She assumed Gin was being needlessly coy to avoid hurting her.

"How is Angela Mathers involved?" Gin asked.

"Who said she was involved?"

"The photo of Angela on your laptop, you numbskull." Gin chuckled, then exhaled sharply. "Donovan's a good man."

"Really? He doesn't lead with that." Isabella could have pretended not to care that it was Donovan, that Gin had chosen him rather than wait until Isabella got her life together.

"Donovan and I are good together." Gin slapped Isabella's thigh. "So you texted. I'm here. What do you need?"

"I need to know if the Guardians helped Jonathan Riley or his partner, Warren Harris, escape."

"The Guardians didn't help them." With an air of contempt, Gin said, "You'd know that if you would come to the meetings."

Isabella abruptly stood. "You want a drink?"

Gin followed her into the kitchen as Isabella dug out two bottled waters from the refrigerator, handing one to her.

"Gin, I think someone kidnapped them."

Gin took a drink. "That's your instinct talking. What are the facts telling you?"

"At the crime scene, they tampered with the cameras. There were strange markings on the ground, and the overhead lights were out. It's too messy to be an escape."

"What about your visions? Were you able to re-create the scene?"

"Yeah. But I didn't get much. Jonathan seemed confused." Isabella took a swig of water.

"They could have wanted it to look like a kidnapping."

Gin peeled the label on her bottle. "I'm thinking hate crime. They are Lumans, and the Freewill Bill is all over the news." She paused. "And with the bill going to a vote, there are protests in every major city, and chat rooms are blowing up with threats against the Lumans. But no physical attacks or riots that the Guardians know of." She took a sip of water. "I can make some calls."

"That would be great."

"You should try to look at the high-tech GPS Command Center the government built."

"You're right. It would show Jonathan and Warren's last movements."

Gin's eyes widened. "You could bring your intel back to the Guardians."

Gin was floating the idea by her, watching Isabella's reaction, testing the waters.

"If we know how the government tracks Lumans, we could plan more sophisticated escapes—less chance of failure." Isabella's and Gin's eyes locked. The word "failure" was shaded for Isabella's benefit.

She felt Gin's eyes on her as she nodded. "Okay, I'll try if I can get security clearance."

A smile broke over Gin's face. "We still make a good team."

"Yeah, we do." Isabella wrapped her arms around Gin.

Gin pulled away. "We shouldn't."

"Who says?"

"It's late, and I'll end up sleeping here, and you know that never ends well." But Gin's eyes said just the opposite, and as Isabella pulled her close, she was reminded of how perfectly their bodies fit together. It was as if no time has passed, though it had.

# CHAPTER SEVENTEEN

*Baton Rouge 2048*

Their mission was dangerous, so they waited for the cover of night. Gin changed in the back of a dark cargo van. She pulled snug-fitting coveralls over her blouse and jeans, then grabbed a lifelike silicone mask out of her backpack and shook baby powder into it, making sure a light dusting covered the inside. She placed her hands inside the fake face, lifted it over her head, and worked it into position. The custom-tailored mask felt like a second layer of epidermis skin infused with collagen, allowing for humanlike facial expressions. She added a wig and checked the results in a compact mirror, admiring the older woman with peppery gray hair now staring back at her.

"Hello, Tammy," Gin said in a soft English accent. Since becoming the Guardians' leader, she had honed Tammy's character, slipping in and out of it as needed. Very few people, including Guardians, knew her true identity.

A knock on the van door severed the tension in the air. Gin looked at Isabella standing next to her. "It's time. Are you ready?"

Isabella was dressed in identical coveralls and her "Wayne" disguise: she looked like a middle-aged man with a cynical face and slicked-back hair graying at the temples. In a much deeper voice, she answered, "Let's get this over with."

The cargo door slid open, and the "package," a male with a black bag over his head, was handed off to them. Gin settled him onto a bench seat as the door slammed shut. As the nondescript van trundled down the back roads of Baton Rouge Labor Compound, Gin pulled off the man's hood with a hard yank, revealing his young face, red and sweaty. His eyes swiveled like those of a caged animal, finally looking from Tammy to Wayne.

Gin watched Noah slump back against the seat, angst coursing through his veins. A certain amount of fear was good. It would keep him from becoming too complacent during the escape. He had been an indentured worker at the state capitol in Baton Rouge for five years. If everything went as planned, he would soon be free—a Solo with a new identity. Sweat trickled down his forehead, and his eyes were roaming everywhere.

Gin and Isabella locked eyes, both knowing that he was about to lose his shit, and if he did, none of them would be safe.

Gin patted his knee. "Noah, try to remain calm. It's important."

"Yeah, if we get caught, we die," Isabella added.

Gin glared at Isabella with a look that said, *Not helpful.*

"Ma'am, respectfully, you don't look like Guardians. I mean, I expected fatigues and guns," Noah said to Tammy in a loud, nervous voice.

"A critical aspect of our mission is to appear invisible, blend in," Gin said as she handed Noah his coveralls. "Change into these, quickly."

Afterward, Isabella sat next to Noah, then leaned him forward. "Hold still." Isabella inserted a thin red wire into the metal GPS tracker on the back of his neck. The other end of the red wire extended to the elongated metal box Gin was holding. When the wire was secured, Isabella nodded.

"This will sting, hon." Gin pressed the blue button on the terminator box.

A flash of electricity surged through Noah's body, shorting out his GPS tracker.

"Shh…it!" he cried.

Gin squinted at her phone's screen, looking for a tracker signal. "You're clean. The tracker's offline." She sighed. She squeezed Noah's shoulder. "Dear, calm down. We've got you."

"Ms. Tammy, once I'm out of the compound, I'll be safe, right?" Noah asked.

Isabella scoffed at the word *safe*. "Buddy, you will never feel safe enough to stop looking over your shoulder. Being a Solo means shifting in and out of identities and remaining transient. Staying undetected is your number one job."

She shook her head at Gin. They knew the risks ahead of Noah all too well. In camp and in the compound, he had followed a strict schedule. Being on his own would be difficult at first, but the Guardians taught Solos how to stay safe and negotiate their new, unstructured world.

Noah started gasping for breath.

"He's hyperventilating." Isabella snapped her fingers, and Gin handed her a paper bag. She shoved it over Noah's mouth to help him control his breathing.

The van stopped suddenly, and the door opened. Frank, Isabella's dad, stood there, haloed by the streetlights. "We are a mile from the Checkpoint. Is the package offline?" Frank asked Gin, ignoring his daughter.

Isabella handed the bag to Gin. "I'm driving."

"No, you are not. Your dad is driving. That's the plan."

Frank frowned at Isabella. "If you're gonna be a sourpuss, just leave."

"No, she's not leaving. We need her," Gin said.

"If you're still mad about me joining Control, Dad, too bad—my mind is made up. I'm going to do it."

"You are asking for trouble, girl. Control has safeguards against Luman infiltrators. If they catch you…"

Gin sighed sharply. This had been an ongoing argument between Isabella and her father for the last month, and with each day, the debate had intensified. She placed a hand on Frank's shoulder. "Frank, I understand your concern, but we can't do this now. We need to work as a team."

Frank glanced from Tammy to Wayne, then threw up his hands. "Fine. We'll be at the compound border in five minutes." He slammed the van's door shut and got back into the cabin.

Frank knew the Baton Rouge Compound's back roads better than anyone else, and for this extraction to be successful, Gin needed Frank to drive. Neither father nor daughter wanted to take part in rescue missions anymore, but she needed them; they were her family—Gin knew she could count on them. The van engine roared to life, and the tires hummed on the asphalt as they gained speed.

Gin took a deep breath and ran through the mission in her head. She glanced at her watch. It was 9:30 p.m. The longer it took to penetrate the compound perimeter, the greater the chance of Control noticing that Noah's tracker was offline. Everything became more complicated if the compound was on lockdown.

"Babe, you're breaking his heart," she pleaded in a whisper to Isabella. Noah had regained control of his breathing and was scrutinizing Wayne. But Gin realized it wasn't just Frank's heart that was breaking.

"Why can't you support me for once?" Isabella leaned into Gin. "This is what my dad does."

Noah's eyes darted to Tammy, who looked flummoxed.

Isabella ran her fingers through her hair. "He has arranged my entire life to avoid jeopardizing my true identity."

"He has not," Gin argued.

Noah studied Wayne.

"Yes, he has," Isabella replied. "Our meeting and our living together—that was his idea."

Gin's voice rose an octave. "What are you saying? We're together because it's what your father wants?" Noah shook his head at Wayne.

"Wait! That came out wrong," Isabella backtracked.

Gin's eyes flickered with anger. "Did it, Isabella? Or are you finally saying how you really feel?"

"I love you, Gin. I just want my own successes."

Gin riposted, "So the Guardians and me are not enough anymore? What? You're not getting enough attention?"

Isabella raised her voice. "Enough? Try none. You take it all."

Gin leaned back and frowned. This had never occurred to her.

Frank sent a text. *We are at the drop off.*

The van pulled over and stopped in front of a vacant office building. Through the cabin's peephole, she noted their location. She turned to Isabella.

"You pick the most inappropriate times to be honest with your feelings. Your selfishness could blow the mission."

"You started it."

"No, you did. You're destroying everything we've built."

"You built," Isabella corrected her.

Their eyes locked. Gin swallowed hard, knowing their next words could be irrevocable. She vowed to continue this discussion when tensions weren't so high and the mission was not at such a critical point. When she could nudge Isabella gently into the right decision.

"We need to finish this later, babe. Okay? Get him ready."

Isabella sat facing Noah, speaking slowly and directly. "This part, we go on foot. It's the most dangerous part of our mission. At no time will you talk or make any sort of sound. If you do, you die. From here on out we only silent-message, got it?"

Noah nodded.

Opening the van's door, Gin peered out, checking that everything was clear. She jumped out of the truck carrying a toolbox and wearing gray coveralls with the name Gilda's Maintenance sewn onto the back. She peered around the van's side, then glanced back at Isabella and Noah, waving them forward. Isabella and Noah followed in the same gray coveralls. They all strolled into an alley between two closely situated buildings. Gin gave Frank a thumbs-up signal, as he watched them, his expression filled with concern. He was angry with Isabella. Gin couldn't blame him; Isabella joining Control felt like a deliberate defection—choosing humans over them.

Frank sped off in the van toward the guard station. Over her shoulder, Gin caught Isabella's blank stare. A sinking feeling filled her as she wondered whether Isabella had fallen out of love with her.

They trekked down the alley leading to a parking lot bordering a wooded area, then strode through the empty lot, picking up their pace and watching for guards. After jumping over a short chain-link fence, they disappeared into the woods, heading east and away from the guard post. Isabella held Noah's arm as they flitted through the live oak trees. The tree limbs reached up to the stars, creating a tunnel of darkness. The hardwoods and pines were the only species of trees to survive the changing Southern environment. Most ornamental trees had died away in the hard-polluted clay since the Codes went into effect, partly because environmental regulations on industries became impossible to enforce.

The veil of trees gave way to a field, and in the distance loomed the conquest—the sovereign state's symbol of security, a barbed-wire fence towering twenty feet in the air. It surrounded the entire Baton Rouge Compound. Long grass beat at their shins as they raced toward it.

Gin crouched down, unfastening a section of the fence as Isabella and Noah joined her. They watched the guard post an eighth of a mile away. Frank was there, standing beside the van, waving his arms and screaming at the guards to get their full attention.

Gin noticed a flicker of concern across Wayne's face. "Don't worry. Frank knows how far he can push the guards."

Gin removed the false fence, opening a passageway to freedom. Gin crawled through the fence and silent-messaged Noah and Isabella.

One guard pushed Frank and took out a baton.

*Come on,* Gin said. *We need to move.*

Isabella shoved Noah through the opening, then watched Frank back up, hands raised, and enter the van safely. Isabella sighed, then a harsh light washed over her. The floodlight lit Wayne's profile, bleaching his face.

"Gin, run! Now!" Isabella yelled, forgetting to silent-message.

The guard yelled, "Hey, buddy, stop!" He was six hundred feet away and bounding toward Isabella. Gin watched Isabella zip down her coverall and reach inside for her holstered Glock.

For a split second the pounding in her heart was all she could hear, then she messaged, *Do not engage, Isabella. Run. Come on.*

Isabella looked at the guard, then at Gin.

"Run, that's an order!" Gin yelled.

Isabella plowed through the fence, making it to the other side. They sprinted with Noah toward a downtown Artists Market, a neighborhood brimming with stores and bars. The guard made it through the fence and followed. Without warning, Isabella made a hard right, leading the guard away from Gin and Noah.

"Police! Stop." The guard's tone threatened violence, but Gin kept running. Glancing back, she saw the guard following Isabella.

At the Artists Market, Gin navigated along the back of the buildings off the main drag. Resting for a moment, she silent-messaged, *Isabella, what's your location?* Gin and Noah stared at each other, waiting for Isabella's response. Gin repeated, *I need a status.*

But there was no response. She grabbed at the silicone imprisoning her face, panicking, pulling on it nervously. Her mind raced through the backup plan.

"He might be out of range. You know our silent-messages don't carry very far," Noah said, trying to be helpful.

Gin wondered if the guard had detained Isabella or worse. They rested in the shadows as she adjusted the plan.

*We need to lose surveillance. They are following our profile.* She removed her coveralls and motioned for Noah to do the same. Underneath their disguises were plain street clothes. Gin opened the toolbox and removed one of the shelves. Hidden underneath was a purse, a gun, a long, jet-black wig, and a baseball cap for Noah. She pulled off her Tammy mask, wiped the sweat from her face, situated the black hair on her head, stuffed the gray wig and mask in her purse, and then tossed the coveralls and toolbox into a nearby dumpster. She tucked the gun in her waistband and signaled to Noah to move.

They crept along a back wall as Gin led them into a narrow alley. Lights and sounds from the Artists Market came from the other end of the dark alley.

Checking her gun, she explained, *We will exit the alley onto Main Street and blend in with the crowd. The van will wait for us on the east side of the street. When you see it, do not point, do not run. Do nothing that calls attention to yourself. Do you hear me?*

*Yes, Ms. Tammy.*

They were moving down the alley, backs pressed to the wall when a dark silhouette appeared and blocked their exit. Gin's heart stopped as the dark figure edged closer.

# CHAPTER EIGHTEEN

## *Gin Baily*

Gin gasped and sat up in bed, disoriented, her red hair messy and damp. Her eyes swiveled frantically around the room and landed on Isabella, who was caught up in a restless sleep. *Damn*, Gin thought. She had messed up again. One minute they were talking about the missing Lumans and the next they were making out. Gin studied Isabella. Her eyelids were flittering while her hands trembled and her legs spasmed under the sheets. This pattern was all too familiar. She leaned over Isabella; the nightmare was back. She grabbed hold of her shoulder tightly.

"Isabella," she said, shaking her.

Isabella's eyes flew open and she screamed, throwing Gin off her like a discarded blanket. Scrambling off the bed, she muttered, "Jump," and scampered around like an animal caught in a trap.

"It's okay, babe. It's a bad dream." Isabella's unfocused eyes landed on Gin and her shoulders sagged. "It was only a dream. Come back to bed," Gin whispered.

"You had the nightmare too?" Isabella asked, her voice hoarse with sleep.

Gin didn't answer; instead, she held up her hand. "Come on, just for a minute." Isabella lay back down next to her with a heavy sigh, wrapping one long arm around Gin's flank. Gin felt Isabella's weight tilt the mattress, forcing Gin closer. It felt comforting, but it was impossible to go back to sleep.

Gin whispered, "It wasn't your fault."

"There is no making peace with Noah's death when we relive it every time we sleep together," Isabella grumbled.

Gin wondered again if the mission would have been a success if they hadn't been distracted and arguing.

Right after Noah's failed rescue four years ago, Isabella took the job with Control and disappeared from Gin's and her family's life. Since then, there had only been two reunions. Both ended abruptly when the shared nightmares began. One lone tear broke free from Gin's eye as she reminded herself of every Luman she and Isabella had rescued. None of it mattered—Noah was the failure they could not get past.

* * *

The morning light streaming through Isabella's kitchen window caught on Gin's diamond ring when she raised a steaming mug of coffee to her lips, and a rainbow of colors danced across the ceiling. She breathed in the aroma and sighed in contentment.

Isabella breezed in. "Shoot, I overslept," she said. She was dressed in a chic designer suit. Gin raised an eyebrow. Fingering the fabric of her jacket sleeve, she leaned in to kiss her. Distracted, Isabella didn't return the kiss. Instead, she grabbed the mug from Gin's hand, took a sip, and handed it back.

"Where are you going, dressed to impress?"

"Luman Administration, missing Luman case," Isabella said, as she poured a cup of coffee for herself.

"Uh-huh, you're meeting with Angela Mathers?"

"Angela thinks the disappearances are a government conspiracy to derail the Freewill legislation." Gin could read Isabella's light mood. She was happy, excited to see Angela.

Gin bit her lip as a sudden wave of nausea mixed with jealousy washed over her—Angela was one of the many landmines scattered around them.

"So, you'll use your Guardian connections to help on my case?" Isabella said and grabbed a cereal box, shaking it at Gin. But Gin waved her off.

"Yeah, of course, but…"

Isabella paused. "But?"

"It's nothing."

Isabella opened the refrigerator, but Gin knew there was no milk because she had checked earlier.

Isabella studied Gin, clearing her throat. "Let's not play the 'nothing' game, Gin. I can tell by the way you are staring at me there's a whole hodgepodge of questions lurking behind those green eyes of yours."

Isabella closed the refrigerator door with more force than she intended and looked at Gin, who quickly averted her eyes as she searched for the right words to tell Isabella her good news. "I don't know what you mean."

"Well, let me help you." Isabella's voice grew stronger as the questions fell from her lips. "'What's it like impersonating a Control agent?' 'Is it difficult working within a system that has historically imprisoned and suppressed our people?'"

Gin pulled back, feeling Isabella's piercing anger.

"Or the really big one. 'When will you come to your senses and return to the Guardians?'"

Gin had been focusing her eyes on a shoe scuff mark on the floor to keep Isabella from reading her, but suddenly the mark disappeared. She was not sure how their conversation had led them here. She just wanted to share her news, but now that moment was gone—if it ever existed.

"Look at me, will you!" Isabella pleaded.

Gin shot her a look that said she'd had enough. "Okay. When are you going to forgive yourself for Noah's death?" Not what she had wanted to share, but not a lie either.

Awkwardly, Isabella shifted her weight. "I just assumed you would grill me on leaving Control again…or that Dad put you up to this."

Gin scoffed. "Put me up to exactly what?"

Ignoring her question, Isabella looked for her badge and located it on the counter.

Crossing her arms, Gin said, "I'm over feeling abandoned by your defection to Control, and so is your dad."

Isabella searched the kitchen. Gin held up Isabella's phone. Isabella paused, then inched closer and whispered, "I'm not over it." She sighed, and Gin took Isabella's hand for a second. The warmth felt right, but Gin removed her hand, leaving the phone.

"Bella, you can't keep punishing yourself by avoiding your family."

"I'm not. I'm tired. Tired of pretending to be someone I'm not."

"And you're not pretending with Angela?" Gin tried to stop the words, but it was too late, and now they were hanging there, all ugly and obvious.

For a moment, they stared at each other. This argument was not new. Isabella's body stiffened. "I don't have time for this, Gin." She grabbed her car keys.

"We need to talk about this."

"I've got to go. Stay—you don't have to rush off."

"Donovan's waiting for me at home." Gin turned away, not wanting to see what was left in Isabella's eyes. She heard Isabella close the apartment door and considered running after her, but her feet faltered when a photo on the bookcase captured her attention. It was a picture of her, Isabella, Frank, and Lorraine standing in front of an F1 race car—a family at a happier time. A helmet was poking out from under Isabella's arm. Beside it was a picture of Gin laughing with her head thrown back, the sun's rays washing over her.

The day the picture was taken, the Guardians had elected Gin their new leader, and Isabella had surprised her with a weekend getaway. They camped on the beach, and Isabella had helped her establish her role as leader of the Guardians.

Her first order of business had been to stop guerrilla attacks on the government. Violent acts like bombing the Capitol only drew negative attention to their cause and did more damage than good to their reputation. Under her leadership, the Guardians had shifted their focus to managing an underground network for runaways. They had opened secret trade routes with countries sympathetic to their cause, smuggling in supplies and weapons unavailable in the States. Recently escaped Lumans required masks and the removal of tattoos and GPS trackers to live under the radar. In addition, the Guardians dismantled alt-right groups who spread malicious lies and incited violence against the Lumans. And the Guardians backed politicians who voted against the Codes.

All their plans were working out. The Guardians had gained power, but Gin and Isabella's relationship had not. She could tell Isabella was restless and dissatisfied working for the Guardians. Isabella longed to make her mark in this world.

Gin thought being with Donovan showed she at least had moved on. She no longer woke up thinking about Isabella, wondering how she was and what she was doing. Still, when Isabella's text had come yesterday, Gin's stomach had done flips. She had convinced herself she was just going to visit, make sure Isabella was okay. But when she saw Isabella last night, her willpower evaporated. She was still in love with her.

She looked regretfully around the apartment, wondering if things would be different if Noah never had existed. That was the thing about Luman memories. They were digital and never faded. Time changed nothing—terrible memories stayed that way forever.

Gin dropped the apartment key Isabella had given her on the counter. She could share her good news when they were in a better space.

# CHAPTER NINETEEN

## *Complications*

*Secrets. Secrets. Secrets.* So many secrets hid behind Janet's lips. Angela watched from the bathroom door as Janet studied her phone. She had been distant all morning.

"What's wrong?" Angela said as she dried her hair with a towel.

Janet's lips tightened as she met Angela's intelligent eyes. "Nothing," she said, tossing her phone into her purse. She gathered her hair up into a severe bun in front of the dresser mirror.

"Hey, Senator, I thought we could have breakfast together." Knowing she had missed her check-in with Jeff Lewis, Angela wanted to make the most of the morning with Janet. Wrapping one arm around her waist, she used the other to reach for Janet's lipstick cap, peering at the name. Lasting Kiss. Janet applied the lipstick slowly to her lips. Angela smiled to herself, thinking of Isabella, then handed the cap to Janet.

"Sorry, but to fulfill your favor, I have to get to the Capitol and make some calls." She snapped the cap in place, tossing the lipstick into her makeup bag. Last night, Angela had made a case for moving up the Senate vote. Janet listened intently; then they tossed the idea back and forth, discussing the pros and cons. In the end, Janet had agreed.

"You're the majority leader. Can you call up the Freewill legislation without seeking approval?"

"Dear, power is all about persuasion." Janet closed her makeup bag and glanced at Angela pensively. "Building a pack of supporters to help our cause requires finding loyal people who aren't voting to safeguard their job or taking a kickback, which is tough in this town."

"There are other means to gather support and overrule some narrow-minded senators," Angela said.

"It's of critical importance in today's environment that people trust our message. They won't if they feel manipulated or overruled. There's only one way to change people's minds—trust."

"And people trust confidence," Angela added.

"And repetition." Janet turned away from her image in the mirror. She scrutinized Angela as she dressed, putting on the same outfit she'd worn last night.

"In theory, repeating our message long enough until people believe it is one approach. But when we can improve a child's quality of life with a neural chip, but don't, and allow children like Jason to die—all available methods of persuasion need to be on the table." Invoking Jason's case was a tactic Angela resorted to more and more, pushing Janet to fight harder for the bill.

Janet's expression was partly sullen, partly undaunted; Angela knew her point had hit home. Janet shrugged and shook her head, stalling.

Angela decided to ask, "Do you think it's a good idea?"

Janet, deep in thought, resurfaced. "What?"

"Corpus?"

Janet glanced sideways at her. "Corpus? How did you hear about that?"

"When you were in the shower you left your laptop open; the report was on the screen. I didn't think you'd mind if I glanced at the synopsis. Do you?"

"The project is tricky. I'm not sure how I feel about it," Janet said.

Angela wondered if Janet was unsure because she guessed Angela had read the full report or because Dr. Austin was transplanting neural chips from deceased Lumans into injured soldiers.

"Interesting title. The *corpus callosum* connects the left side of the brain to the right," she said as she watched Janet pack her things. "In any case, someone in the government had to give it the green light. Was it Congress?"

"It's not sanctioned. This crazy doctor tracked me down at the opera last night and would not leave me alone until I agreed to look at his brief."

Angela watched Janet's lips moving, knowing she was refusing to reveal the truth underneath that statement. She drew her into an embrace. "But the report said they had a breakthrough recently?"

"Yeah, well, they had very marginal success." She shrugged, but Angela could tell she was interested in the project. Her eyes always flashed when she felt a sense of power just out of reach.

When Angela read the Corpus report, it disturbed her. She had no idea experimenting with neural implants was still happening or that the government had radically deviated from the extraction of chips to transplanting them into soldiers. And the fact that Janet didn't tell her about it, that she had had to snoop, made her wonder if she and Janet still wanted the same things with the Freewill Bill.

"Stay for breakfast." Angela wrapped her arms tighter around Janet. A distance filled Janet's eyes. "I cannot. I can't stay."

Angela's smile fell, and she sensed Janet was talking about something else, something entirely different.

"There is something I need to tell you." Janet stepped out of the embrace and prepared her words.

"Is it about Corpus…because I peeped?"

"No," Janet said. "It's not what you think."

"If it's about the Freewill Bill, I can—"

"Please, Angela, stop talking."

The silence stretched thinly over the distance between them. Any moment it would shatter, and this thing Janet needed to tell her would be free.

"I need to take a break from us."

Searching Janet's eyes, Angela asked, "Why? What's happened? Is it Mort?" Her mind raced.

Janet touched Angela's face. "No. It's complicated. We have become complicated. I'm in a hurry; let's talk later." She gave Angela a peck on the cheek and moved toward the door.

A storm gathered in Angela's gray eyes. "Wait. Are you walking away after dropping that on me?"

Janet turned back impatiently. "Stop being difficult. Can you please do that for me? We will talk later."

Jilted. Angela glanced at herself in the mirror. A lipstick smudge graced her cheek. Her heart was pounding. Janet had always set the pace of their affair and what had emerged was an unspoken bond. The strength of their bond was unknown, however, and it had never been tested. Until now. Angela heard the door close, and she was left in the silence.

Five minutes later, her phone beeped. She looked down to see a text from Janet: *Sorry love, I was an ass, come see me after work tonight.* She decided not to respond. That was the thing about humans; their emotions made them unpredictable. She knew she should feel something like desperation—but there was nothing, only an affirmation: she would not be left behind, not again. She needed Janet close.

Angela roughly rubbed the lipstick smudge from her cheek, recalling when Jonathan had left her for Warren years ago. Maybe Warren was right when he said she was incapable of love. But there was one thing burning inside her that she had a real need for. All creatures did, and they instinctively sensed its loss. Freedom. "The Freewill Bill is your blind spot," Jonathan had told her. "Love is more important." She didn't understand what Jon meant, still didn't.

"I need her close," she said to the mirror. The Freewill Bill was in jeopardy without her.

# CHAPTER TWENTY

## *The Case*

Isabella placed a steaming caramel mocha latte on top of David's paperwork.

"What do you need?" David's eyes narrowed until they focused on Isabella. He smiled, taking in her smart outfit.

"Does there always have to be a reason?" Isabella sat on the edge of his desk. The Control bullpen was a hive of activity.

"Uh, usually."

"Any clues turn up at Jonathan Riley's apartment?"

"Nothing, no sign of a struggle, but wait, I have some video." He winked at her, then handed her the tablet. She watched the footage. Jonathan stopped in front of the ParkAide garage, looked around, then entered.

"Look at the way he's looking around. Like he's lost," Isabella said.

"The drones tracked Jonathan leaving his apartment and later entering the garage, but when his GPS tracker went offline, the drones lost their connections to him, so they left. But the next clip was from a CCTV camera on a lamppost outside the ParkAide. That footage never showed him exiting the garage," David said.

She fast-forwarded the footage to ten minutes after Jonathan's GPS tracker went offline. A red pickup truck pulled out of the ParkAide with a large black suitcase in its bed.

Isabella's voice jumped an octave. "There! That red pickup matches the harbor trafficking bust yesterday." She paused the video and showed it to him.

David scratched his head. "Great. Nondescript red truck. There are thousands like that in D.C. And where's the lawn equipment? Also, we don't have a license plate from this angle."

"Get forensics to compare tire tracks from the harbor and those in the garage," Isabella said, then snapped her fingers. "There was a trail of squiggly marks on the dusty garage floor. The suitcase wheels could have made them. Jonathan might be inside."

David clucked, "Hell of an exit strategy."

"Unless he was dead when he went into it." Their eyes met at the terrifying thought.

David took the tablet back. "I'll scan the CCTV recordings the police sent over and see if the truck was in proximity of where Warren Harris went missing as well."

Pushing her glasses up on her nose, Isabella leaned in and whispered, "Can you also sneak in some CCTV footage around Senator Green's office? It's in the Russell building."

"Is it related to Jonathan's disappearance?" David asked.

"It could be, but let's keep that between us. Don't tell Carter."

"And yes, there it is, the favor you needed," David joked. He handed her a police sketch. "Here's what the forensic artist came up with based on Darryl's memory of this Peter suspect in your trafficking debacle."

Isabella studied the drawing of Peter. "His eyes are smaller and closer together, like a rodent's eyes, mouth tighter. The hairline should recede about an inch. Oh, and his cheeks—make 'em chubbier."

David's expression drooped. "So just redo the entire sketch, basically."

"Yeah, that's about right. And it wasn't a debacle. I apprehended one of the hostiles."

"And you missed roll call again. Carter's been looking for you." Isabella glanced at the Deputy Director's office. Instinctively, Carter looked up at the same moment, locking eyes with Isabella.

"Jesus, how does she do that?"

"I think she's a Chip." Isabella must have looked perplexed. "I hear when Carter the Mindhunter gets pissed off, she glows and shoots sparks, you know, like Chips do during sex." His eyes widened.

"That's not funny. And for the record, it's a friggin' myth. They don't shoot sparks." She walked away, shaking her head at the misconception.

"You might want to put on a hazmat suit. I'm just saying," he hollered after her.

Isabella entered Carter's office. "Sit, Agent." Isabella obeyed and flopped down in the seat opposite her boss. Carter shuffled the papers on her desk into a neat pile. "Where are we with the disappearances?"

"Ongoing, sir. It's unlikely that they are runaways. But whoever this is, they have planned it with precision. The disappearances happen in areas with no security cameras present or working. Both Warren and Jonathan were in Camp I/O, presumed partners, and both knew Angela Mathers. And she is an advocate for the Freewill Bill, which has more than a few senators and Anti-Luman groups fit to be tied."

Carter perked up. "Interesting, but I'm missing the part that ties it all together."

"I have a hypothesis. It's a conspiracy. The Luman disappearances are part of a scheme to manipulate the Freewill vote—the timing can't be a coincidence."

"The LA is up my ass—I need evidence, not supposition, Agent," Carter growled.

"It's all in hand."

"It's a ticking time bomb." Carter frowned.

"I have a few more questions for Ms. Mathers. Then I can—"

"Ms. Mathers and Steven Hawk are the ones breathing down my neck. In fact, Ms. Mathers suggested you needed help. Offered her services with the investigation." Carter raised an eyebrow.

"I'm...sorry, sir."

"Don't apologize. Get me answers before another Luman goes missing."

Isabella rose to leave.

Carter studied her attire. "Agent, you've reviewed Ms. Mathers's background file, correct?"

When she read Carter's facial expression—she knew what was coming.

"Yes, sir."

"Remember what she is—be careful. Don't let her in your head."

Aggravated, Isabella turned to hide her reaction from Carter's penetrating perception. "Yes, sir."

# CHAPTER TWENTY-ONE

## *Disparate Worlds*

Isabella felt overexposed in a way she couldn't explain. Perhaps it was the bright fluorescent lights in the sterile Luman Administration corridor or her fight with Gin earlier. She nudged her glasses in a manner that was more of a nervous tic than a necessity. Her eyes were met by Angela's careful scrutiny, and she realized why she felt overexposed.

Angela's long eyelashes made her eyes silvery like liquid sometimes. As they walked, Angela stayed busy multitasking with her tablet and phone. But Isabella could tell behind her cool exterior Angela was not okay. "What's wrong?"

"I'm nervous about the Freewill Bill. Senator Abrams is calling it up immediately. The Senate will debate on it today."

"Wow, why so fast?"

"It's all about optics," Angela explained. Isabella looked baffled. "We need the bill in front of the Senate before the media gets ahold of Jonathan's disappearance."

"Let's take your mind off the bill and focus on your missing folks. There was no video footage of Jonathan's or Warren's disappearance. So, I'd like to review their GPS tracking data for the past three weeks."

Angela regarded her with absolute directness. "No."

"What do you mean, no? It's the easiest way to prove they didn't run."

"The Tracking Command Center requires a top-secret security clearance."

"I know. I have it."

Angela referred to her tablet and selected another browser tab. Isabella's picture and personal file came up on the screen. "So, it seems you do. You hold the keys to the kingdom," she said, her eyes flashing silvery again, not flirting but regarding Isabella closely. Dropping her hand back to her side, she accidentally brushed it against Isabella and they both mumbled, "Sorry."

As Angela reviewed Isabella's background, she said, "Your skills in visual acuity and perception were off the charts, making you a major Control asset."

"You've been checking up on me. Are you warming up to me?" Isabella nudged Angela and captured a hint of wisteria perfume.

They turned down another long hallway, passing a sign that read "Security Checkpoint Ahead."

"Actually, I'm shocked you made it through Control's academy. Your test scores were mediocre, at best."

Isabella shrugged. "We Old Fashions aren't so smart, but we manage to get by."

Angela's eyes washed over Isabella in her designer suit. "Trust me, you do more than get by." They gazed at each other as an undercurrent of chemistry ran between them.

Just then, Isabella leaned in close and whispered, "About last night, I was thinking—" She stopped dead in her tracks. "Jesus..." The area in front of her was cordoned off by a contingent of armed soldiers in dark green combat gear, all with stony expressions.

"This is the security checkpoint for the Tracking Command Center," Angela said, walking toward the chalk-white circular screening area. "Few people get security clearance to enter the Center. The ones that do must pass stringent examinations and background checks." A soldier motioned them into the screening area. Angela put her phone and tablet into a tray, removed her high heels, then raised her left hand to the scanner, verifying her serial number. She then moved to the retinal scanner and leaned into it, placing her chin on the holder.

Isabella placed her badge along with her belt, gun, shoes, and jacket in a tray, then glanced over at Angela and the unfamiliar retinal scanner. It looked high-tech. A rush of heat flooded her body, and she heard her father's voice whispering, "It's the fear in your heart that will give you away." The retinal scanner light flashed green and displayed *A0M01, Luman*. Next, Angela moved into the full-body scanner.

Isabella removed her glasses and bent down to rest her chin on the retinal scanner holder, perspiration building under her arms. A blinding light rocketed across each iris. She forced her left eye to remain still, even though it was aching to pulsate. The scanner light flickered for an excruciatingly long moment as her heart banged in her chest and her sweat turned cold. There was a silence as the machine reconciled her data. Finally, the light on it flashed green. She expelled a long breath when *Isabella Dodge, Human*, flashed on the scanner.

After the security checks were completed, a soldier handed over their shoes and a special badge. "The rest of your things will be here when you return," he instructed.

Angela and Isabella entered a small elevator that looked like the interior of a rocket capsule. Steel panels rose, coming to a point at the ceiling, and a monitor over the door flashed statuses: support test check, launch process complete, electrical system check.

The door closed with a hissing sound as the air escaped before the hydraulic brake release, and a countdown clock began 10, 9, 8…

"We are going five miles underground," Angela mentioned.

The elevator clock beeped as it counted down 4, 3, 2, and the elevator abruptly plummeted downward with rollercoaster speed. Isabella grasped the railing with both hands to steady herself.

"You could have mentioned the rapid drop," she said.

"Could I?" A slight smile tugged at the corners of Angela's mouth.

Recovering, Isabella cleared her throat. "Last night, you mentioned a government conspiracy tied to the disappearances."

"Senator Green has been a hostile critic of ours. I believe he is manipulating the Senate vote by making the Lumans appear insubordinate, untrustworthy, and all the evil things he claims we are."

"You believe he has Jonathan and Warren stashed away somewhere?"

"No, he had them killed." Angela's steel-gray eyes turned cold.

"If it's a conspiracy, why take Warren and Jonathan? The D.C. Compound has advanced security. It would be less risky to kidnap a Luman at a smaller compound."

"You're the investigator. You tell me." Angela folded her arms and considered Isabella.

As the elevator hurtled downward, Isabella's stomach flipped with the sensation of falling. "This feels personal, Angela. Yesterday, you conveniently left out the part where you, Warren, and Jonathan were in Camp I/O together. I think their disappearance has something to do with you."

"I was not being evasive if that's what you're insinuating. Green hates me. To him, I was a criminal even before Lucy hit the water."

Isabella adjusted her glasses, perturbed by Angela trying to run her investigation. "Rest assured, I'm investigating Senator Green, but is there anyone else who might want to hurt you? Who knew how close you were to Jonathan and Warren? Think about Camp I/O."

Angela's look of indifference turned to interest.

"What did you just think of?"

"Back in camp, I made a deal with the Devil's sister." Angela told Isabella about Betty Jo Green's visit.

*Ding!* The elevator reached its destination as Isabella's face creased in horror at Angela's story.

"Wait. You think Raymond Stratton molested and killed Lucy and the Greens concealed it?"

"What?"

"Her uncle's name was Raymond Stratton."

"Lucy called him River, Uncle River."

Isabella scrutinized Angela.

"Why else would Betty Jo help us? She pulled some strings and got us placed together in the D.C. Compound."

The elevator door opened; Isabella was too overwhelmed to move. The ease with which Angela admitted to manipulating Betty Jo for her own benefit was unsettling, not to mention the new molestation accusations. And for a minute, she couldn't fathom the story. It was too disturbing. She reflected on one of the notes in Angela's psychological report—"Angela Mathers scores high on psychopathic personality traits for cunning and manipulative behavior."

"What do you think of Senator Green now?" Angela said smugly.

Isabella was speechless. A computerized voice broke the silence: "GPS Command Center." They stepped out of the elevator.

What came first was a chilling dampness, the kind that seeped deep into Isabella's bones. Her ears began buzzing and as they moved onward the sound grew louder, vibrating through her as the GPS Command Center came into view. The scene knocked the wind out of her. It was monolithic, futuristic, the ultimate mission control. A Luman Radar system out of a sci-fi movie. Most technological advancements had stopped twenty-two years ago, but someone forgot to tell that to the architect genius who had designed the Center. On the far wall, a digital map of the United States spanned the length of a football field. Pin lights blinked and moved inside the five metropolis compound locations, accounting for each known Luman. As they ventured closer to the modern observation platform railing, Isabella peered down into the operation pit. Like air traffic controllers, twenty analysts wore headsets and managed the tracking operations using specialized instruments.

The enormity of the space and its location deep underground made manifest the magnitude of the government's paranoia about Lumans and the extreme measures being taken to protect society from them. She stood slack-jawed. If she hadn't escaped, she too would have been one of those blinking dots—tracked or, more correctly, hunted. There was nowhere to hide. "It's massive," she breathed out, observing the command center through watery, but unblinking eyes.

"They monitor every known Luman in the United States from here. The Center also contains a military bunker, a place where the government can function should the Lumans rise up against it." Angela pointed to the west. "Over there are tunnels that run to PEOC, the President's Emergency Operations Center." She pointed to the east. "And over there are top-secret evacuation bunkers for high-level officials."

A lone tear trickled down Isabella's cheek; she quickly wiped it away as she released a ragged sigh. Angela wrapped her fingers around Isabella's upper arm, the only comforting touch she could legally give. "Are you okay, Agent?"

Isabella felt the warmth of Angela's touch as it filtered through her shirt sleeve, and she turned to her. *How do you do it?* she thought. She wanted to ask but the words died in her throat. Instead, she said, "They see the Lumans as the greatest internal threat to our nation's security."

She watched Angela's eyes fill with a melancholy that matched the sadness she had been choking down most of her life. She had never seen emotion like that in Angela before.

"I learned early on that my enemy is my fear, not theirs," Angela whispered, answering Isabella's unspoken question.

Isabella saw in Angela a warmth she had never noticed before. She stepped away to compose herself, Angela reluctantly releasing her hold on her with a lingering caress. They were in dangerous territory. Trying to get back to business, she surveyed the enormity of the map, her left eye dilating and pulsating.

Angela pressed an intercom to talk to an analyst in the operations pit. With a catch of emotion lingering in her voice, she said, "Please pull up Jonathan Riley and Warren Harris's satellite tracking data for the past three weeks."

The map zoomed in, drawing paths for both Jonathan and Warren's movements.

Isabella's left eye blinked, and her iris worked as a camera shutter, capturing where Jonathan's and Warren's paths overlapped. The Control Center's artificial intelligence homed in on the men's locations. It displayed a timeline of their activities based on biometric data received from the GPS tracker.

7:00 p.m.–*Eating*
9:00 p.m.–*Idle*
11:02 p.m.–*Sleeping*

Next to each man's events were his vital signs: temperature, respiratory rate, pulse, blood pressure, and, where appropriate, blood and oxygen saturation.

Isabella was blinking again, capturing where the men's paths separated. She focused on the night before Jonathan's death:

8:00 p.m.–*Intoxicated*
9:15 p.m.–*Sex*
12:32 p.m.–*Sleeping*

"You and Jonathan had drinks that night. You said you're not sleeping with him."

Angela snapped, "I'm not," and flipped her hair over her shoulder.

Isabella's cautious eyes narrowed, wondering if Angela was playing her. "Warren was dead. Do you know who he was with?"

Angela shrugged.

"It could be important to the case," Isabella insisted.

Angela's expression remained guarded. Isabella knew she was hiding something but let it go.

*The humiliation of it*, Isabella thought. *Big brother, knowing everything you did and how often.* There had been rumors that the GPS tracker gathered more information than just a location, but this was unfathomable. She turned to the map, blinked again on where their last known locations were. Their vital signs were undetected—their heart beats slowed until they stopped completely.

11:23 p.m.–*Dead, Warren Harris.*

And a week later...

9:45 a.m.–*Dead, Jonathan Riley.*

"The government knew they're dead and didn't notify Control?" Isabella grimaced at the thought.

"Only the president and a few top military personnel know of the system's bio-tracking capabilities. The LA knows the GPS can send signals, but we don't know if the AI can send the GPS more than a ping test."

"You mean the system could possibly send an electrical signal like a shock to a Luman...through the GPS?" Isabella voice wavered at the implications of this.

"They implanted the GPS to track us, not zap us. Or so I'm told."

"And you believe that?"

"It doesn't matter what I believe."

Isabella glanced at the map again, assessing Jonathan's last location. "Why would he go into the parking garage? Lumans aren't allowed to drive."

"I guess someone needed help. Jon has—had—a big heart."

They stared silently at the map for a long moment, the strobing lights washing over them like fading fireworks. Then, feeling the weight of the world above her, Isabella clutched Angela's shoulders and whispered a plea. "Jonathan and Warren are dead. You could be next. I can't protect you if you're not honest with me."

The disparate worlds these two women inhabited were on a collision course. Angela patted Isabella's left hand, which was holding her shoulder, signaling that her touch was illegal and dangerous. Isabella glimpsed up at the security guard. His hand moved to his sidearm, and she removed her hands.

"Honesty is a two-way street, Agent. I don't trust you," Angela admitted.

Isabella didn't know what to say in her defense. Angela was right. Why should she trust her? Why would she trust any human after spending nearly all of her life locked up? But Isabella wasn't human either and had spent her entire life hiding. *We both live in the shadows of the Codes*, she thought. *Just differently.*

# CHAPTER TWENTY-TWO

## *Deliberations*

*Day One Deliberations.*

Senate Majority Leader Janet Abrams stood at the Senate podium surveying the room. She kept abreast of all Angela's activities and knew she was someplace moving beneath her, five miles underground. Angela was the palliative against her pain and delusion. Angela studied freedom and its effect on human nature like an astronomer studying celestial bodies—Janet's body and the forces, like Angela, that affected it.

Sweat swamped her neck and back as she recalled the blackmail message, and her mind raced in different directions. She tightened her grip on the podium, needing its support, and tried to focus on the mission before her. Sitting on the bones of past bills, the Senate chamber was a mausoleum of good intentions and legislation that had died during deliberations and filibusters. The accumulation of seven years of stumping and deal-making had finally brought Janet and the bill before the Senate. With everything at stake, this moment was the apotheosis of her career as a senator. She would not let this bill or Angela leave her career laying in state, dying on the Senate floor.

Vice President Georgina Wilson was presiding over the session today, looking down from her perch. For eight years, she had sat in the chair of silence, and years of deliberations were etched on her face. She was eager to begin. "With the blessing of the House of Representatives, the Senate may begin debates on the Freewill legislation."

Janet moved closer to the mic and began.

"Code 23: The Lumans cannot have children. All adoptions are denied and pregnancies terminated. Code 16: A Luman defection from a designated compound carries the death penalty. Code 9: Sexual relations between a human and a Luman are forbidden and carry the penalty of lethal injection for the Luman. Code 1: Upon death, the Luman brain and the neural chip will be destroyed."

Janet looked up to the vice president. "And those are just a few of the many ways we plan to kill off our most promising generation of enhanced human beings. There are thirty-two articles to the Codes, thirty-two reasons to overturn them and allow the Lumans to integrate into society. They are people who deserve rights and residency. It's time to give them back their homeland.

"Second, we need to lift the ban on technological advancements. Our environment, economic stability, and our very livelihoods depend on it.

"Lastly, we need to resume the children's neural prostheses program. No child should suffer needlessly. We have the right to reshape humankind in relevant ways and overcome the limitations imposed by our biological and genetic inheritance. The Freewill legislation will allow us to do just that. Madam Vice President, we would like to proceed with debates on the Freewill Bill."

"Without objection." The vice president struck the gavel.

* * *

After an exhausting Senate session, Janet made her way to her hideaway office, a room situated deep in the subterranean world under the US Capitol amongst tunnels and a private subway system that allowed members of Congress to move securely around all of D.C., out of sight and protected from the weather. Most senators had a hideaway office. The Capitol's discreet hallways, ancient rooms, crannies, and nooks created a secret sanctuary for senators to make deals and—ahem—do other things.

Janet preferred to meet constituents at her public office in the Dirksen Senate Building because it was modern and bright. But for all other meetings, she used her hideaway. She stepped now inside her windowless, well-worn refuge. As she switched on the table lamp, it cast a warm glow over elegant antique furnishings and the ghost of mindsets past. A wall-to-wall bookcase stuffed with law books reflected the mind that read them, and then there was the wet bar. Her first chore was to mix a drink after her awful day of debates.

She sat behind her large antique desk, highlighting items of interest in the stack of transcripts of the day's Senate deliberations. She could still hear Jackson Green's contemptuous tone when she called him earlier that morning to discuss the agenda change. She was afraid he would push back, but all he said was, "Let's get this over with. We have wasted enough time and money on this legislation."

Many Republicans looked to him for guidance on socially charged issues. He was the moral compass of the Grand Old Party—and an arrogant one to boot. What was it he had said during deliberations today? She shuffled through the transcripts and found his remarks: "By implanting computer chips in our children's brains, we are meddling with nature, creating a master race superior to ours. Removing the Codes shall bring an acceleration in technological advancements so swift that we will lay our lives in the hands of these things. The ramifications are significant if they turn against us. And why shouldn't they? Look at what we have done to maintain our supremacy."

Janet scanned the transcripts for positive feedback. There was Senator Johnson, who rebutted Green's remarks: "You need to distinguish fact from science fiction, Senator Green. This is not the fruition of Mary Shelley's Frankenstein. We haven't created a new race. We are one race in transition."

Janet was sure she could count on Johnson's vote. Maybe Senator Powers too—she was forward-thinking: "We need safeguards for the common folk, allowing them to embrace instead of fear the Lumans. We must proceed with their liberation, but cautiously."

She remembered the crushing blow that had ended the day's deliberations—when Senator Tucker had taken the podium. She could still hear his baritone voice as it reverberated through the chamber: "It is morally unacceptable. Who are we to judge God's will? We need not fix children with disabilities just because we can. Every human need not be perfect to be happy. That is the beauty of humanity; we are all different."

If he had a child with a severe disorder, he wouldn't say such a thing. Janet put the transcript down and remembered her six-year-old son lying in intensive care in the Mercy Baton Rouge hospital after suffering a severe epileptic attack. The doctors had told Janet and Mort that his Fragile X syndrome was not life-threatening. Yet her boy was in a coma, a respirator breathing for him and keeping his heart beating. She had held the boy's limp hand in hers while her other hand was pressed against his chest, feeling his heart's ailing beat. She didn't watch as the nurse removed his life support. Instead, she cried, tightening her grip around his little body, holding him until she could no longer feel his heartbeat and the vitals monitor alarm sounded. She remembered Mort pulling her away as she fought to stay with him.

If Jason had had a neural implant, it would have minimized his epileptic attacks. He would be here today. She wiped her eyes, cleared her throat, poured herself another bourbon, and pulled herself together to read the rest of Senator Tucker's comments: "We must regulate scientific exploration. If we don't, these things will intimidate and manipulate us out of existence."

Tucker's bombastic speech had riled up everyone. By the end of deliberations, the pugnacious senators were yelling, accusing, and talking over each other. The vice president had hammered her gavel furiously until silence at last filled the chamber.

She sighed, exhausted, and set the transcripts aside. A click and whirl issued from the bookcase's mechanism. Half of the bookcase moved forward, sliding over the other half. Behind it, Angela stood in silhouette.

"How did it go?" Angela looked at Janet, who did not avert her swollen, glassy eyes. "Tell me." She stepped closer, her grim expression matching Janet's.

Janet sniffled. "There are too many obstacles for us to overcome." Her voice faded into silence.

"What obstacles? Let's work through them together."

Janet threw up her hands. "There could be intimidation or manipulation." She moved to the bar and freshened her drink.

"Do you believe the Lumans will intimidate and manipulate society for their own gain?" Angela shrank back into a chair with an incredulous expression.

Janet didn't answer at first as if suddenly remembering Angela was there; her eyes snapped into focus. "What?"

"Are you talking about the bill or us?" Janet heard the anxious ring in Angela's voice, something she had never heard before.

"I'm talking about intimidation by my political foes."

"Just say it, Janet. You have never been one to mince words."

And Janet knew Angela was right, except when it came to Angela. She wavered, deliberating between telling the truth or selling the lie. "I'm talking about us. We have to end it. If anyone learns of our affair, they will use it against me, affecting my work and the bill. It's just…it's gotten all too complicated."

Angela nodded and got up and moved close. And instantly, Janet regretted losing Angela.

"You're lying," Angela purred. "We both have a lot to lose if anyone finds out about us. That's nothing new. You're reacting to something else."

Janet rocked back on her heels, unnerved, not wanting to jeopardize everything she had built. But Angela pulled her closer.

"Tell me what happened."

Janet's response was monosyllabic, barely audible. She gazed at Angela, imagined resting her head against Angela's soft breast, listening to the vibrations of words as Angela spoke to her.

Angela's grip on Janet tightened, and she said with measured patience, "Did you hear what I said?"

Janet nodded. "You think there's a conspiracy against the bill?"

"Yes. Don't you?" Angela stepped back, not recognizing this Janet before her.

Janet held her phone, staring at it like a crystal ball.

"I've been working with an Agent Dodge. She will find out who's behind the conspiracy. We can get the bill back on track."

Reluctantly, Janet handed over her phone with the blackmail message displayed. "That's the third text this week. Always the same message, with a different photo of us." Janet's voice shook with emotion. "This is about me, and honestly, I can't take it any longer. We have to end this."

Angela studied the photo of herself in a state of undress before Janet. "They took this photo from outside our hotel room—maybe with a telephoto lens," she said as she enlarged the photo. "It could be paparazzi, but more likely it's a political opponent, one of Senator Green's lackeys." She gave the phone back. "Have they asked for anything?"

"No."

"It's all part of the same conspiracy, don't you see? If it's Green, you don't have to worry about your career. I know how we can fix this."

Janet's curiosity was piqued. "Okay, I'm listening."

# CHAPTER TWENTY-THREE

## *Storm in July*

As evening approached, the clouds took on a blood-red color against the D.C. skyline. Forsaken now by Janet, Angela exited the Capitol and glanced into the distance, taking in the rare ominous sky. The streets were washed with a Provence rosé glow, as were the dead and the dying lying along them—body after body, slumped together. Bandaged and bleeding corpses. It was hard to tell how many.

Angela's throat tightened. Swallowing hard, she stepped over a woman lying on the sidewalk, prompting her to cry, "They killed my child." She ignored her, keeping her gaze focused straight ahead. She felt like one of the walking dead herself, dazed and confused from her last moments with Janet. She thought of herself as a brilliant strategist and knew some collateral damage of their campaign was unavoidable, but she had never thought Janet would come unhinged so easily.

Who was Janet when their bodies were not pressed tightly together? She didn't know the woman she had just left. The woman too afraid to risk it all.

Janet was the first human Angela had ever counted on. No one had ever wanted her like Janet did, respected her, listened to her ideas. Janet had treated her as an equal, and that was enough for Angela. It was sufficient, and she forgave Janet for no longer wanting her as long as the Freewill Bill was a priority.

A hand reached up for Angela's bare calf and, startled, she jumped out of its reach. She watched a middle-aged man flounder on the ground, his deeply sunken eyes staring back at her. "They are smarter than us," he screamed. "Did you know they can hack themselves? They are rewriting their own code, gaining power over their mechanical nature." She turned away and marched on.

Angela felt Isabella's static and confidence approaching like an electrical storm before she fell into step with her. Before she stepped over another protester pretending to be dead, leaned in close, and whispered, "Hey, take a deep breath. Don't let 'em get to you."

Angela stared at a young boy lying in the gutter, his body wrapped in a banner. On it, drenched in bloody red lettering, was the message: "They will kill every last one of us."

As the sky became bruised with heavy storm clouds and all the earlier color was sucked out of the air, Isabella and Angela weaved in between the protesters' bodies. The Control agent gave Angela's upper arm a firm squeeze. "I got you."

The touch, there it was again, a connection pulling Angela back into Isabella's sadness. Their touch at the club and then in the Command Center: the intensity of Isabella's emotions felt like a fever burning through Angela's body. They were broken wires sparking when they touched. She didn't want to break the connection. It made her feel alive in ways she never imagined.

The thought stopped Angela in her tracks. She stood there on the sidewalk, watching Isabella moving slow and easy. *This other woman has so much sadness that she can share it through her touch, yet she won't tell me her truth.*

Isabella stopped when she realized Angela was no longer beside her and turned around. Angela's eyes raised to meet hers. "The Senate's impending vote on the Freewill Bill is blowing up social media. People are staging die-ins all over the US," Isabella explained, waving at the bodies around them, assuming they were why she had halted.

Angela wondered how she could not see the effect she had on her. "The dead do not bother me."

"Well, something is."

Angela moved in close to Isabella and whispered, "Senator Abrams is being blackmailed."

"Someone found out about you two?"

Angela's eyes widened as she stared in disbelief at Isabella, who was insisting on escorting her home.

"Oh please, she's Lasting Kiss—I've known ever since—"

"It doesn't matter, we—she—broke it off." Angela looked to the sky and smelled the impending rain. It was another time marker for her—change was coming.

Isabella adjusted her glasses and said, "Look, she'll—"

Angela interrupted, "I don't want to talk about it." She found a path clear of the dead and quickened her step.

They walked in an uneasy silence until a loud crack of thunder propelled Isabella out of her thoughts. "It's about to rain. My car is this way."

"The Metro will take us to my apartment twenty-three to twenty-eight minutes faster, given current traffic patterns."

"What's the big hurry? There's someplace I want to take you."

Angela turned and bit her lip.

"If need be, I have police lights and a siren." Isabella gave her an encouraging smile. "You won't have to worry about traffic."

A blinding crackle of lighting rippled across the sky, striking twenty feet in front of them. Angela jumped, her eyes adjusting as the white flash lit up the face of Jeff Lewis.

"Jeff, Christ, you scared me."

"Angela, you broke code. You missed your check-in this morning. That's a serious offense," Jeff said in an austere tone. "I have no choice but to put you on lockdown until we can review your whereabouts for the past twenty-four hours. Come with me." Before he could grab her arm, Isabella stepped in front of her.

"Hold on, Jeff, there's no need for that. Angela's been with me." Isabella flashed her badge at Jeff. "I'm Special Agent Dodge. You're a hard man to reach. Hasn't Henry given you my messages?"

Angela looked at Isabella, amused and impressed. Isabella had just cemented their newfound friendship by demonstrating her willingness to lie for her.

"Oh, Agent Dodge. I meant to call you back."

"As I mentioned in my many phone messages, I have a few questions about Jonathan Riley's disappearance. You were in charge of him. This happened on your watch then, yeah?"

"Well, yeah, I guess," Jeff muttered.

"How about tomorrow? Meet me at headquarters, nine a.m. sharp."

"Sure, Agent Dodge." He looked from Isabella to Angela.

"Don't worry. I'll make sure Angela gets home safely," Isabella said as the lingering promise of rain turned into a downpour.

# CHAPTER TWENTY-FOUR

## *The Shimmer*

The rain continued to fall, cooling the air as Isabella placed a Control placard inside her Mustang's windshield. She and Angela shared an umbrella as they ambled through a veil of pouring rain. The shimmering lights ahead would soon coalesce into something powerful, and she hoped this small excursion would show Angela that she was trustworthy.

"You are taking me to the Lincoln Memorial. You're adorable." Angela brushed against Isabella's shoulder and caught her blushing. The thunderstorm had chased away the tourists and strolling lovers, leaving the deserted memorial in a different light, a parallel world of possibilities.

They climbed the stairs leading to Lincoln's statue. "It seems appropriate to come here and celebrate your achievement, the Freewill Bill and freedom for all people."

"The Freewill Bill won't halt ignorance and fear of my kind, but it can stop the perpetuation of it. Everything is so up in the air right now, though. I'm not so sure we can get the votes."

Reaching the top of the stairs, they stood inside the colonnade sheltered from the rain. Isabella closed the umbrella, and they separated, leaning against opposing columns.

"You don't seem like the type to give up easily."

"I'm not. I've got a few ideas in the works to improve our chances. I'm counting on you, too, Agent."

Isabella nodded, accepting the challenge. She was working on a few clues of her own to solve the case. They gazed out at the Reflecting Pool, listening to the steady drone of rainfall.

"What will you do when you're free?"

Angela's lips curled into a strained smile. "Is this a new interrogation technique?"

Isabella shrugged. "Just small talk."

"Hmmm, I would travel. Monaco, Southern France. I've always dreamed of visiting Provence and the sunflowers of Arles. Then I would open a law practice and continue defending civil liberties."

"That's admirable. Monaco is beautiful. I raced the street circuit there before I joined Control."

In a voice tinged with envy, Angela said, "Sounds exciting."

They were silent for a time, mesmerized by the falling rain. Isabella regarded Angela as she leaned against the pillar—just like it, immovable, impenetrable, cold. Unconsciously, Angela's fingers stroked her neck. Unconsciously, she didn't smile.

Isabella broke the silence. "Your parents chose camp over escaping through the Guardian network. Do you regret that?"

"My father is a lawyer. He argued against the Codes. But he would never break the law. He thought he could win my freedom, and I respect that. Besides, the Guardians have made things worse for us."

"You're joking. This is off the record," Isabella replied. "Just be honest with me, Angela."

"No joke. Defending our civil liberties requires peaceful measures." She gestured to where the US Capitol was, though the half dome was not visible in the smog and rain. "You can't blow up the revered symbol of our democracy and gain respect for your principles. The Guardians were behind Luman defections and violence against the government's infrastructure. Those tactics perpetuated society's hatred and fear of us and interfered with our message of peace."

Isabella stepped closer, about to argue the point when Angela closed the distance between them, standing so close the scent of wisteria captured Isabella's senses, distracting her.

"You don't really need these, do you?" Angela took off Isabella's glasses, sliding them up on top of her head. "Special Agent Dodge, when will you let me in on your secret?"

Isabella's hesitation showed. Not knowing how to answer, her mind raced, her experience at handling this situation dissolving.

"I…I knew Lucy Green." Isabella was embarrassed by the words coming out of her mouth without permission.

Angela stepped back. "Of course you did. Well, ask me."

Isabella was bemused.

"Did I or didn't I push her?" The tension in Angela's voice made Isabella look away to ward off the pain she felt for causing it. "I gave them a statement, an affidavit, but still no one believed my side of the story. I should have said something right after it happened."

Isabella moved closer and caressed Angela's cheek. Her skin was soft, warm, and the contact led inexorably to a kiss. She tasted the tangy spearmint of Angela, whose lips responded, matching the intensity of Isabella's quest to quench the longing they had created in each other. Isabella couldn't continue, though, and pulled away as they approached a moment she wasn't ready for. Angela's steel-gray eyes shot through her, setting every cell in her body on fire. She fumbled with her words, searching for the right ones. Realizing she had never seen an affidavit in Angela's criminal file.

"I never thought you killed Lucy. I don't know why I brought her up, except to say I remember the day they released you from custody. You were seven, all three feet of you, defiant and brave as you fought through the angry mob. That memory of you has gotten me through some disastrous times in my past."

Isabella felt Angela's hand warming in hers, as tears rolled down Angela's cheeks uncontrollably. As the rain fell relentlessly, Isabella had a vision of Angela's past, rich, horrifying images flashing in her mind. *Flowers swirling pink petals unraveling, churning in the angry river. Fingers the color of bones reaching for Lucy, coaxing; eyes pale, peering up like a phantom in the river.* Lucy had not been the only thing taken by the river that day. So had Angela's childhood.

"It's okay, you can let it go. You can mourn now," Isabella whispered, enfolding Angela in her arms and kissing away her loss.

When her tears and the rain finally stopped, Isabella said, "We can't stay here."

Angela whispered, "Your place."

Isabella smiled, and they lingered in the moment, gazing out at the Reflecting Pool—unaware that someone in the shadows was watching them.

* * *

The warmth of Angela's lips pressed against hers and Isabella surrendered, shuddering against Angela's mouth, and silent-messaged, *I can't pretend any longer.* She gave away her deepest secret—trusting it in Angela's care.

*I've always known. You're safe with me.* This time the word *safe* filled Isabella with peace. She could be who she was. Heat rose between them, and it took shape, holding on tight.

They worked awkwardly, urgently at buttons and zippers, shredding, tearing the fabric to reach skin as Isabella guided them on a clumsy journey to her bedroom. Danger lurked at every turn: a bump in the dark, a sudden shifting of shapes, the rocking of furniture. Nervously, their bodies pressed together, wavering but never losing contact, as they occupied every inch of each other.

Angela pushed Isabella to the bed, falling into her. With the friction of flesh against flesh, an ethereal current of energy passed through them, a tingling sensation spread throughout their bodies, and their neural implants paired—instantly establishing a bond. As the stirring of hips, hands, and lips intensified, so did the urgency, the rush.

A glimmer arose underneath Angela's skin when Isabella's hand glided between her thighs. Her belly grew tense, and her skin took on a reddish-orange illumination that pulsated. Their eyes locked when Angela leaned in, tasting Isabella's skin, letting the tip of her tongue sweep across the smooth curve of her breast as her fingertips traveled downward, igniting an uncontrollable longing inside Isabella. Their breathing grew ragged as they began a slow churning rhythm within each other.

Everywhere Isabella's body touched Angela's it shimmered like firelight off an inky water's surface, and she felt a rush of heat where Angela's fingers slid across her folds. Angela's trembling skin glistened with iridescent colors, cohering, then rippling in waves off her body.

They lost themselves in the bending and blending of the light, until there was no longer a distinction between them, only fingers pressing, bodies rocking to an obliterating rapture.

Later, lying side by side, Isabella kissed Angela's wrist, causing sparkles to wash over their bodies then slowly fade. She smiled and kissed her wrist again, watching the afterglow.

Angela's voice broke the silence. "You shimmer with such effervescent colors. It's beautiful. I've witnessed nothing like it."

Isabella hid her face with the pillow. "I don't do that often."

"I find that hard to believe."

"I was talking about our immediate attraction, our..." Isabella stopped when she saw the expression on Angela's face. "You felt it, didn't you?" She could hardly believe it, but she was experiencing what Angela was feeling. Their chips had instantly paired and they were now mirroring sensations in one another.

Angela looked worried. "Yes, and you did too?"

Isabella had the sneaking suspicion that this was something new and uncomfortable for her.

Angela's cheeks flushed. "What we just experienced has never happened to me before." She sank into the pillow and grew quiet.

"It's okay. I think special connections between Lumans are rare." Isabella fell silent, deciding how much to tell her about her past. "I have once with my ex, Gin. She's engaged now."

"There was a boy back at camp and in the science lab late at night we put on quite a light show—all the colors you can dream of." Angela's smile faded.

"Jonathan?" Isabella asked.

Angela confirmed with a nod. "My past with Jon and Warren was complicated." She bit her lip and glanced away.

Isabella had never considered that she and Angela would pair, not the first time together, but it was not something they could control—it was subconscious. Scientists to this day did not understand how a Luman could experience what their partner was feeling when they shimmered. Not sure how she felt about pairing with Angela, she decided to drop the subject.

Angela's worried look matched Isabella's thoughts, and she teased, "Don't worry. It's just a chip thang. Doesn't make me a mind reader." She kissed Angela's nose.

"You are an excellent mind reader," Angela said as her hand wrapped around Isabella's neck, pulling her lips to hers.

They glowed in the waking of the moment.

"We should do something bad," Isabella whispered. She reeled out of bed and returned with chocolate chip cookie dough ice cream and two spoons.

Propped up against the headboard, Isabella studied Angela as she nibbled on a spoonful of ice cream, lost in thought.

"Out of all the Old Fashions in Washington, why Janet?"

Angela stared at her, unblinking. "Don't."

"C'mon, I want to know. What attracts you to her?"

"Is this Agent Dodge asking?"

"How come whenever I ask about her, you change the subject? You two just ended things. Tell me about her."

Angela kissed a drip of ice cream off Isabella's bottom lip, reveling in how perfectly their lips fit together. Then she conceded and reclined against the headboard.

"When I met Janet, she was the most intelligent politician in Washington. She was on her way up, someone I could tell would become an influencer. She had a hunger for change. Honestly, she was the only politician that used words like *inclusion* and *freedom* and seemed to mean it."

"So, is it a political kinship with benefits, or were you in love?" There it was, what Isabella had been longing to ask—waiting to learn where her place was in this moment between them. Angela ignored the question with a toss of her hair.

"Oh no you don't. It's my turn. So, Special Agent Isabella Dodge, you are a walking contradiction with a Southern accent. You are a human, Luman, Control agent, and probably a Guardian. Would you change any of it if you could?"

"I don't know." She spoke softly. "I've never had the luxury of just being myself." Isabella's spoon stabbed at the ice cream in the container. "Anyway, I'm pretty far down the road—there's no logical place to stop the charade and own my truth." She considered telling Angela how lonely it was risking everything to make a difference. But it seemed trivial compared to all that Angela had been going through.

Angela took the ice cream container from her and set it on the nightstand. She pulled Isabella flat on the bed. "Pretending to be human gives you certain rights, and you can use that power to help us. It's essential work for our cause. You should be proud. Other agents will follow your cue on how to act around the Lumans. It's important."

Isabella was unsure what to think of this woman leaning over her as she looked into the gray eyes inches from hers. She had no point of reference. No one else understood why she had become a Control agent.

"I know it's personal, but at Camp I/O, we used to ask, 'what are you in for?' The children wore it like a badge. It was our salvation and our damnation since many of the children were implanted with chips that may have been unnecessary." Angela lay down next to Isabella. "So?"

"What am I in for? Partial vision. I have a retinal implant in my left eye. And the neural implant replaces my damaged visual cortex, which happened during birth."

"Bionic eye, but just the one. You see the world from both sides. It's profound."

Isabella reached for Angela's left hand, kissed her tattoo, then placed it over her heart. They both felt the metronome of their heartbeats harmonize. And right now, all she wanted was to feel Angela's lips on her mouth again, and suddenly they were there, and everywhere, driving her crazy.

# CHAPTER TWENTY-FIVE

## *Check-In*

Angela and Isabella exited Isabella's apartment building, smiling and chatting as Isabella opened the car door for Angela. From across the street, a man stepped out of a café's archway, took a hearty bite of a doughnut, and watched Isabella's old Mustang as she eased it into morning traffic.

Angela entered her apartment. The intensity of her evening with Isabella was still simmering in her mind. She had heard that Luman couples developed profound connections, especially during intimacy, but last night was her first such experience. Her emotions existed at such a low frequency that they were usually undetectable by others; even she barely noticed them. Last night her feelings had caught fire as well as her body. She and Isabella had *connected* when they touched. Before this, she had felt somehow separated from others, but no longer. Something had changed.

Angela studied her apartment. Nothing looked disturbed. She checked the traps she set for Jeff: the threads attached to the desk drawer and the other thread attached to the closet were still intact. She exhaled sharply, relieved she had not missed another check-in. When her relationship with Jonathan had dissolved into friendship, he would cover for her when she was out past curfew, but now it was up to her.

*Perhaps Isabella can get Jeff fired*, she thought as she quickly showered and dressed, then rushed out the door.

Waiting for the elevator, Angela called to mind again Lucy's secret—her leverage. And now Janet's. Knowing she needed to make sure Janet stayed focused on the ultimate objective, she had shared the story with her yesterday. She felt confident she would use it to push the Freewill legislation forward.

The elevator door opened, and her smile dropped. Standing there was Jeff Lewis.

"Time for check-in," he said with an officious tone and stepped out of the elevator.

Angela raised her hands. "Jeff, I'm late for work as it is."

"Uh-huh, let's go." He grabbed her upper arm and walked her down the hall. "Come on, I'll write an excuse for you. Tell me about your night."

"There's nothing to tell. Agent Dodge drove me home." They entered her apartment, and Angela unbuttoned her blouse, distracting Jeff from asking more questions. Jeff watched her walk toward the bedroom. "Crap, there's a spot on my blouse, I think I'll change," she said over her shoulder.

As she changed into a silk blouse, she heard Jeff rattling through her drawers in her office. And suddenly, she felt vulnerable. This sensation was new and so intense that she sat on her bed and searched for the light like she had done back in camp. She rocked back and forth, closed her eyes, and let her mind drift toward the light, to the center of her mind. She saw the light glowing and growing all around her, revitalizing her. Her mind floated in a current of energy as it pulled her to a safer place.

"What are you doing? Are you sick?" Jeff asked as he entered the bedroom.

Startled, Angela stood up. "Jeff, I have a full schedule today, and it's the last day of deliberations. Can we leave, please?" She breezed by him.

"Not so fast." He grabbed her wrist, twisting it, forcing her to face him. "Tell me about the investigation. Has Agent Dodge learned anything about Warren and Jonathan?"

"You think she's going to tell me?" She shook free of his grip.

"Yes, I do. Agent Dodge has to give daily reports to the LA."

"Well, she's not giving them to me."

He studied her, then held out his hand, motioning for her phone. She handed it over, and he scrolled through her texts. "Who is this Paul character? You went drinking with him the other night?"

Angela nodded. "He's a friend." But really, it was a fake text she had created to cover her rendezvous with Janet.

"You need to come straight home after work. I'm putting you on lockdown until all this business with the Freewill Bill is over."

"But I have commitments." Angela gave him a long-suffering look.

"Don't start." Jeff gazed at her with growing frustration. "We can't have another one of you go missing."

"That would look pretty bad for you, huh?"

"I'll stop by later tonight for a check-in and I'll grab some takeout, keep you company?"

Angela frowned. Christ, the last thing she needed was Jeff hanging around. She had planned on seeing Isabella tonight.

# CHAPTER TWENTY-SIX

## *The Unexpected*

"I need to speak with you right now," Isabella said, pinning Deputy Director Carter with fiery eyes as she chatted with an analyst. Irritated by the disruption, Carter regarded Isabella and then pointed to her office. Isabella marched through a crowd of agents lingering around the bullpen after roll call. Monitors flashed with stats on criminal activities, but compared to the technology in the GPS Command Center, the Control bullpen looked like it was from the Stone Age.

Inside the glass bubble, Isabella paced as she waited for her boss to finish up in the bullpen, the smell of Carter's English Leather cologne in the room leaving her even more on edge. She was unsure how to broach her subject with Carter, but she knew it needed to be said, politely but firmly.

When Carter entered, the tension was thick. "Okay, Agent. What happened?" She took her place, leaning on the front of her desk.

"Did you know Jonathan Riley and Warren Harris were dead?"

"Yes. If I could share all the information I have access to—well, your job at Control would be a different proposition. I knew you would figure it out and solve the case."

"When people think a Luman is a runaway, it creates more fear. It stirs the pot. This is affecting the Freewill Bill. News of their deaths need to go out to the public today."

"Is your investigation complete?" Carter crossed her arms over her chest.

"No." Isabella searched for the right words. "I am tracking down a few leads and Jeff Lewis might have some insights. We are meeting later—"

"Why didn't you talk to him last night?" Carter interrupted with a reproachful glare.

Her question caught Isabella off guard.

"Too busy sightseeing?" Carter added. A sinking feeling hit Isabella in the gut as she reached for something on her desk. "Someone dropped this off this morning."

She handed it to Isabella. It was a photo of Isabella and Angela kissing at the Lincoln Memorial.

There was an oppressive silence as Isabella studied the photograph. Finally, when their eyes met, Carter stated, "It's illegal, unethical, and it stops now."

"Yes, sir." Isabella looked away, biting her lip.

"She's still a suspect in this case. What were you thinking?"

"Am I off the case?"

"No. Someone else wants you off it, though, which means you're pushing the right buttons." Isabella looked at her, astounded by her unbiased insight.

Carter snatched the photo back and locked it in her file cabinet.

Isabella's mind raced, trying to understand what was happening.

Isabella's phone dinged. She glanced at a text from Gin: *Lafayette Square, noon.*

"I might have a lead," Isabella said as Carter waved her away.

"You'd better solve this case. Today," Carter said.

David noticed Isabella and rushed over to her. "Hey, I just sent you CCTV footage on Senator Green." David handed her the new police sketch on Peter. "Oh, much better," she admitted. She snapped a picture of the sketch using her phone.

"Facial recognitions AI identified him as Peter Ord and confirmed he is a member of an alt-right group called Virus."

"You are a life saver."

Isabella's phone rang, showing Angela's ID. "I've got to take this." She walked into the hall.

"Hey, miss me already?" she purred into the speaker.

"Always fishing, aren't you? I'm in public, or I'd tell you how much."

"Oh, I almost forgot, I sent you a picture just now." Isabella's thumbs moved quickly over the phone interface, then brought the phone back to her ear. "Have you seen this man?"

"No. Who is it?"

"It's Peter Ord. He's a suspect in the disappearance."

"Great, so you're making headway in the case." Angela's voice sounded almost cheerful. "Are you coming by later?"

"Yes, though I'm not sure when." Isabella flashed on the photo of them kissing and paused, unsure how to tell her.

"What is it?"

"Angela, just—be careful."

"I will. Christ. There's news from the Capitol. I've got to go." Angela hung up on her.

In the Luman Administration board room, a special report was interrupting the coverage of the Senate debates. Tinged with concern, Angela put down her phone. Her eyes widened when Janet Abrams stood before a podium crowded with microphones. Behind her, the half dome loomed in the background.

A female reporter jumped into action. "Majority Leader Janet Abrams is about to make an important announcement. Aunt Janet, as she's affectionately known on the Hill, has been instrumental in the writing of the Freewill Bill, and today is the last day for deliberations."

"I hope it's not bad news again," a Luman analyst said.

"Shhh," Angela replied.

Janet cleared her throat and looked out to the crowd of reporters and then directly into the camera. Her lips curled into a slight smile. Angela stepped closer to the TV. There was something different in Janet's eyes, something Angela couldn't name.

"I am announcing today my candidacy for the presidency of the United States," Janet declared.

Angela's face dropped with disbelief as the other analysts cheered.

Paul asked, "This is a good thing, right?"

"Yes, it's just unexpected." Angela felt slighted. Janet had never spoken of this to her. She turned pale and sank into a chair, drained of all adrenaline. Paul poured her a glass of water. She saw Janet's mouth continue moving, but all she heard was a voice in her head saying, *You underestimated that woman.*

# CHAPTER TWENTY-SEVEN

*Revelations*

Isabella leaned against the iron fence surrounding Andrew Jackson's statue. She scanned Lafayette Square, which was teeming with tourists. Tammy stood next to her, facing the opposite direction, a scarf protecting her peppery gray hair from the wind.

*When you left your key, I didn't expect to see you again. I'm glad you're here.* Isabella reached for Gin's weathered hand, but Gin moved it out of reach.

Gin's tone was all business. *Word on the street is that a Luman-trafficking ring working in the D.C. Compound has a government connection.* Gin paused and checked her surroundings. *And we have heard chatter on the military's network about Corpus.*

*Corpus? I thought that project was dead...*

*They've had some sort of breakthrough. There is no evidence it's related to the Luman disappearances, but I'll keep checking.*

*Angela thinks Senator Green is involved. He could be the government contact.*

*Could be anyone. You're usually better at sussing out criminals, not just obsessing over the obvious. Green's been on the Guardians' watch list for a long time. But his anger comes from the loss of his child. Thanks to Angela Mathers, he has a right to hate us. She didn't tell anyone about Lucy's accident until confronted—it's suspicious.*

*Come on, Gin. Not you too? Angela was a scared little girl.*
*Your father always said you think with your heart, not your chip.*
Their eyes finally met. Isabella studied Tammy's face, the skin creased around her eyes with the wisdom of having lived a long life—something not expected for a Solo. She had hoped to grow old with this woman, but it seemed she had been destined to mess it up.

*I left the key because that part of us needs to be over. I hope someday we can work together, but for now, take care of yourself.* Gin abruptly left.

Isabella silent-messaged Gin. *Hey, we need to talk about this.* Gin kept walking. *Come on, Gin, I love you.*

Isabella watched as Gin moved steadily through a sea of strangers, not noticing a man who'd been watching them or how he whistled casually to himself as he strolled away. Why was she so affected by Gin's announcing it was over? It had been over since Noah. Isabella shook her head. *Gin is my history. And Angela could just be playing me, for all I know. Jesus, listen to me going through the pros and cons. I'm an idiot.*

Before she could beat herself up more, she caught sight of an older gentleman in a business suit. *Holy smoke!* She took off running.

* * *

Senator Green's eager young assistant, Paula, glided her delicate fingers over the laptop keys as she peered up at Isabella.

"Isabella Dodge. I have an appointment with Senator Green," Isabella said, breathless from her sprint to the Russell Building.

Paula scanned Green's online calendar. "I'm sorry, Ms. Dodge, you're late, and he took another meeting. The senator's calendar is overbooked for the next couple of days with the debates and all. Can we reschedule for next week?"

Isabella flashed her badge. "I guess I should have mentioned this sooner. I'm here on an important Control investigation."

As Paula opened Green's door, a light timbre of laughter snuck out. Senator Green was sitting opposite Janet Abrams. They stopped and looked up when Paula and Isabella filled the doorway.

Paula said, "Senator Green, your one o'clock is here. Special Agent Isabella Dodge."

Isabella pushed past Paula. "Hey y'all, sorry to interrupt." She turned to Janet. "Senator Abrams, it's an honor to meet you."

"Hello, Agent. Jackson, good speaking with you. I'll see you on the floor."

Senator Green smiled as Janet left.

"We have to make this quick—the Senate convenes in thirty-two minutes," Green said. Isabella read the senator; he appeared in good spirits. "If this is about the missing Lumans, I know nothing." He motioned Isabella to sit in a chair opposite him.

"I can understand you wanting to take matters into your own hands, sir. But rest assured, Control can help."

Senator Green looked baffled.

Isabella held up the police sketch of Peter Ord. "Have you seen this man?"

Senator Green squinted at the sketch, hesitating. "No, never. I mean, people stop me on the street all the time in support of the Codes."

"I agree with your concerns, Senator Green. I mean, if we overturn the Codes in two ticks, they will be asking for more, yeah?"

Senator Green lowered his voice. "It was a mistake to abolish the camps. It opened the door to them wanting civil rights. I mean, what about our rights to safety? We want our families to feel secure."

"What I can't figure out is how the Freewill Bill got into Congress." Isabella took off her glasses and casually swung them in one hand.

Green grunted—his brow furrowed with concern. "That bill is a waste of time. It's Angela Mathers's doing. She has coerced several senators over this term to get it into Congress." Green looked at his watch and gathered papers into his briefcase. "She'll never stop pushing for more power unless we stop her."

"And how do you propose to do that?"

Green clucked. "Follow the path of revelations and stop the bill from passing."

When Isabella had gone through the CCTV footage David had sent earlier, she had found something very interesting. She pulled out her phone. "Huh, is this part of your path?" she said as she hit Play and handed the phone to the senator. In the CCTV video, Peter, the man from the police sketch, walked up to Senator Green outside the Russell Building. They talked and walked for a while. Green handed him a manila envelope.

"This man's a suspect in the alleged killing of Jonathan Riley and Warren Harris. And there you are, Senator Green, talking to him and handing him an envelope. It's the same man as in the sketch. What did you pass to him?"

Green's eyes glazed over.

"What was in the envelope?"

Green handed the phone back, trying to look uninterested. "This fishing expedition is over."

Isabella could tell he was hiding something but was too wily to incriminate himself. She slathered on the Southern charm. "Look, I get it. These knuckleheads come out of the woodwork during major bills. Just tell me what you know."

Conceding, he threw up his hands. "It's not against the law to imagine the Lumans will rise up against the government."

"Of course not."

"Okay, maybe I encouraged him by looking at his evidence. But that's it. That's what is in the envelope—evidence that the Lumans would overthrow the government when the Freewill Bill passes. I told him it was science fiction and gave it back."

"Can you tell me about the evidence?"

"The Guardians are building robots that are duplicates of known people and then swapping the human with the robot. The family can't recognize the difference—they're that good." Green laughed loudly, throwing his whole body into it. Isabella joined in with her own rusty laugh, then paused.

She held up the sketch again. "Senator Green, when you encourage them, you legitimize their cause, especially when you know the man." Senator Green leaned back, trying not to be visibly affected. "You are colluding with Peter Ord, a member of the alt-right group Virus and a suspect in the recent disappearances of two Lumans." She cinched her glasses up onto her nose. "That's why I'm taking you downtown to make an official statement. Maybe your memory will improve there."

# CHAPTER TWENTY-EIGHT

## *Dangerous Game*

Angela's finely manicured hand wrapped around the doorknob and locked her office door. The small, sterile room was filled instantly with vibrant warmth as she and Isabella embraced. It had been a long day, and anticipation had Angela's skin tingling.

*How did it go with Green?* Angela silent-messaged as they kissed.

*I took him downtown for questioning, but he lawyered up,* Isabella messaged back, inching Angela's skirt up as she ran her hand up the inside of her thigh.

*Figured.* Angela moaned.

*When I first got to his office, he and Janet Abrams were having a friendly conversation. I mean laughing and smiling like they're old drinking buddies.*

Angela stiffened, frowning at this news.

"What's wrong?" Isabella's eyes cautiously studied Angela.

*Stop talking,* Angela murmured and kissed her hard, undoing her blouse.

*You gave Janet Lucy's admission about her uncle to coerce Green. Didn't you?*

*Yes, but only to stop the blackmailing.* Angela turned to keep Isabella from reading the lie.

*I reckon she didn't use it. Green wasn't under duress, and I doubt he's the blackmailer.*

Isabella pressed her forehead against Angela's. *Come on, let's go back to my place.*

*I can't. My parents are in town.* Angela busied herself, straightening her clothing.

Isabella stepped back. "You're going to see her?"

"I have to. Janet is compromising the bill."

"She didn't tell you she was going to run for president," Isabella said as a revelation, not a question, and Angela's angry silver eyes flickered over her like fire. "Angela, you don't have to be her victim anymore."

"I'm not her victim. Without Janet, there would be no Freewill Bill."

Isabella scoffed, "What? Are you angling for a new job now that she's running for president?"

"There is no place in society for me without a government assignment," Angela yelled.

They were both startled by her outburst. Isabella reached for her. "I'm sorry I've upset you."

Angela recoiled. "You don't understand how tenuous our place in this society is. You have no clue what it's like for me. My parents give me money because my government stipend barely covers the rent."

"But you don't need to sleep with her, Angela."

"Who are you to judge me? You don't even see yourself as one of us. You see yourself differently." Angela was aware of her heart banging in her chest.

Isabella tried to get Angela to look at her. "I just mean—you're not trapped anymore. You have me now."

"I have you? Look at you, pretending to be someone you're not—you're the one who's trapped."

Isabella looked at her, her expression tinged with hurt.

"Fine, go see her. I won't be your sloppy seconds when she shuts you down again."

As Isabella turned to leave, Angela tersely shouted, "I love Janet."

Disconcerted, Isabella walked out. As Angela watched her leave, her heart filled with remorse. She wanted to throw something.

"God, what is wrong with me?" she muttered. Her pairing with Isabella had woken her emotions from their deep sleep, but now she had to deal with them. Frustration was clouding her judgment, and Isabella had her second-guessing herself. She screamed again. She had never felt so much with such intensity: she was unraveling, trembling with anger, hurt, and longing for Isabella, all at the same time, and all of it was surging through her veins like lightning. It slayed her, this misery she felt. She could barely control herself—and yet she still wanted more.

* * *

Emma stood behind the White Rabbit's hostess station, talking on the phone when Angela showed up. Her lips curled into a smile as she hung up the phone and said, "She can't make it tonight—Mort's in town."

Undaunted, Angela marched past her. Watching her go, Emma picked up the phone again.

Even the best-laid plan could have a flaw or a vulnerable spot, and there would always be people looking for it, looking to capitalize on it. Softly knocking on the door, Angela hesitated, then unlocked it, ready to face her opponent head-on. Inside Janet's boudoir, she and Mort lounged on a red velvet sofa, drinking from long fluted glasses.

"Mmm, champagne. You're already celebrating," Angela said as Janet offered her a cordial smile.

"Hello, Angela. Morty, you remember Angela?"

She observed Mort's dullness with distaste. His shirt was opened just enough to show tuffs of wiry gray hair sprouting from his chest.

Janet went over and freshened her drink while Mort sized up Angela. "Oh, right, great to see you again. I hear you and Agent Isabella Dodge have been turning heads at the White Rabbit."

Janet looked up and rammed the champagne bottle back into the ice bucket, spilling ice cubes over the sides and sending them skipping across the counter with a loud racket.

"Mort, honey, will you excuse us for a minute? The ladies need to talk about boring work stuff."

"Certainly, dear. I'll be at the bar."

After Mort left, Janet's accusing eyes burned into Angela. "Busting in here looking like a forlorn lover could ruin everything."

"Or at least your run for the White House."

"I was going to tell you, but Mort showed up. I haven't seen him this excited since…" Angela, barely breathing, glared at her. "Honey, maybe after things calm down, we can continue. But right now, there are too many eyes on me."

Angela slapped Janet's cheek. "Do not—flatter yourself." Janet's eyes narrowed. "I gave you Lucy's admission to get Senator Green's vote."

"Green's vote doesn't matter," Janet said as she rubbed her cheek. "We won't have enough votes to pass the bill. I know it hurts, but it's best you know now."

Angela's voice grew louder with desperation, "No. His vote will make all the difference. Others will follow his lead."

"Your story about Lucy isn't enough to change his mind, not on this issue." Janet scrutinized her cheek in the hall mirror. "I had my team check out Green. There's no proof surrounding Green's brother in-law's promiscuity."

Angela scoffed, "Brilliant. And you cannot even say it. Raymond's a pedophile and the Greens hide it. They concealed what he did to their own daughter."

Janet corrected her. "Alleged pedophile."

"It is so easy for you to trust your own kind."

Janet clenched her fists tight as her eyes blazed in anger. "That's enough, Angela. This is a dangerous game you're playing. Assault, defamatory comments. Do I need to call Jeff Lewis?"

Angela hadn't planned to hit Janet; she had never lost her temper before. She felt like an out-of-control fool and calmed herself. She was not sure how to deal with these new emotions; they made her awkward and unpredictable. "I'm sorry. Just tell me, honestly, are you giving up on the bill because you're running for president?"

Janet shook her head.

"I'm so sick of your lies. So, you didn't plan to take the Freewill vote only so far, then leave it to die on the Senate floor in an attempt to grow your base from both sides?"

Their eyes met, and for a brief second, Angela saw Janet's regret.

"Do you know how many people are counting on me?"

"You say children are God's expression of hope. Well, the Codes took hope away from your son, Jason."

"Dangling Jason's death in front of me like a carrot won't work anymore, toots. It's over."

"You turned out to be such a disappointment." Angela turned and walked toward the door, angry at the way her voice revealed her hurt.

"Oh, like you're the holy one. I have never supported the Codes," Janet spit out.

Angela flipped around. "No, you didn't. But you're no different from those that do. Except, unlike the Senator Greens and Tuckers of the world, you pretend to lead with your virtue until it alienates your voter base. It's all about greed and power with you, and at some point, you will regret it."

"Regret is unprofessional, Angela."

Angela slammed the hotel door, marching along the corridor, humiliated, fuming. *How dare she pull rank and treat me as less than her equal—threatening to call Jeff Lewis. I knew it was only a matter of time before she said something prejudiced.* She ran through the many things she wished she had said to Janet. If only she hadn't lost her temper and hit her. But she had. Now they were enemies.

Angela left the White Rabbit, making her way along the city sidewalks. Her steps hastened into a sprint. She wanted to run forever, outrun everything she had lost. She weaved in and out of the flow of pedestrian traffic, spinning around, losing her course in the rabble of happy couples, all the while cursing Janet's name. Willingly, she had handed everything over to her, had let Janet steal her power. She wiped at her eyes, furious with herself. She had gotten complacent. She slowed, remembering the day she had put everything, including her future, into Janet's hands.

# CHAPTER TWENTY-NINE

## *Washington D.C. 2046*

The union of two minds, the joining and merging of ideas and principles. This was where it started. Due to a full Senate agenda, Janet Abrams had taken up residence in the Wonderland Hotel for the month. Angela had been assisting her for the past two years and, under the pretense of legislation research, had visited her and stayed for a drink.

"Taxes are how Congress is trying to legalize thievery," Angela said as she handed a whisky sour to Janet.

She took a sip. "Mmmm, you're getting good at making these."

Angela sat on the sofa next to Janet. "Thanks, I guess I'm lucky I'm exempt from taxes since I'm not a citizen."

"You will be a citizen again soon." Janet took Angela's drink, setting it with hers on the coffee table. "There is something I need to tell you."

They gazed at each other awkwardly. Finally Janet leaned in nervously and kissed Angela. The taste of sweet and sour on Janet's lips turned to the burn of bourbon as their kissing grew passionate. Janet's lips found the curve of Angela's neck and then her soft bare shoulder. As Angela's dress fell away, Janet explored the secrets of her body until a slow, silvery-white phosphorescence rose in waves off her body. Janet stared at her, enraptured, as if she had just uncovered a beautiful painting flowing from Angela's skin.

The union of body and mind became a river rushing through them as they sank to the floor, their bodies entwined, tumbling in desire, but there was more for Angela. In her mind the intimate acts that passed between them, the intricacies of passion, affirmed Janet's promise: one day she would be a citizen and free. That gave her courage as she explored the woman she wanted to possess. Studied the silver stretch marks around her waist acquired when she had carried Jason to term.

As Angela's hand moved between Janet's thighs, she felt something more than desire twisting inside of her. It was potential. Possibility. Angela moved over her, watching Janet's face warp and blend in her own shimmer of colorful lights.

Breathless, Janet said, "That was amazing, your shimmer…"

"I'm not done with you yet." Angela pressed her body against Janet's.

"Wait, no more. I have so much work to do."

Angela whispered in her ear, "Let me blow your mind." She tipped her face and met Janet's. "I brought you a draft of the Freewill Bill. It's ready for your review."

Angela jumped up to retrieve it. Flabbergasted, Janet took the fifty-page document.

After leaving Janet with her future, Angela had moved down the hotel corridor, thinking she had time for one stop since she'd already missed curfew. A younger, trimmer version of Emma was at the White Rabbit bar when Angela entered.

"We're closed," Emma chirped without looking up, and continued to stack chairs on the bar tables.

"I have something for Mort," Angela said, her cheeks flushed.

Emma severed the air with her reedy voice, "Oh, my, my, what have you been up to, kitty?" Her smile was blinding.

Angela whispered, "Check your phone."

Emma's eyebrows arched in disbelief. On her phone was a notification: Abrams New Recording. She pressed Play. Emma's jaw dropped as she watched a video of Angela and Janet's earlier lovemaking. Angela covered the phone with her hand, pushing it down from Emma's prying eyes.

"You've seen enough. You tell Mort, he better keep his end of the deal, or the videos stop."

# CHAPTER THIRTY

## *Mending Fences*

After her fight with Angela, Isabella got into her beat-up Mustang and drove. She didn't have a destination in mind. Her thoughts were on Angela, how things had unraveled between them faster than her Mustang could go. Angela was right; Isabella didn't know what it was like to be a documented Luman. But if she were in Angela's shoes, she would not throw herself at Janet, even if it promoted the Lumans' fight for freedom. And then she thought about Gin. The many arguments they had had were never as intense as the one she just had with Angela.

Gin had told her to quit punishing herself, and it was sound advice. And Gin loved her. So, Isabella turned the Mustang around and headed outside the D.C. Compound, through a neighborhood of older homes flush with towering redwoods and elms. She gave the steering wheel a hard jerk to the left and pulled into the driveway. It had been four years since her last visit. Through the windshield, a secluded bungalow came into view.

Isabella slammed the car door with a clunk. Hearing it, Lorraine, her stepmother popped her head out the screen door. Her face lit up when she saw Isabella, and she ran to her, enfolding her in her arms.

"Sweetheart, you're a sight for sore eyes. It's been too long."

Isabella remembered Lorraine's last text, *Come home soon*. Lorraine checked in with Isabella once a week, by text or phone call, but

Isabella usually answered with little more than, "I'm fine." She loved her parents; they had made sacrifices to keep her out of the camp. But the chip in her brain had ruined their chance at a normal life. A life together that didn't require micromanaging their daughter, always looking over their shoulders, or the fear of slipping up and using their real names—the list was endless. She knew her parents were disappointed when she became a Control agent. She saw the pain in their eyes, so she kept her distance—Gin called it avoidance. Angela got it, though. She knew Isabella's work mattered.

"I've been missing you something fierce," Lorraine said, bringing Isabella out of her thoughts.

"I missed you too, Mom."

Lorraine stepped back and took in her girl. Her smile faded and her eyes narrowed. "What's wrong?"

Isabella fanned at the air. "It's nothing. I'm on a case that's driving me nuts."

They huddled together on the old front porch swing. Lorraine fussed over Isabella's hair, moving it over her shoulder, giving her a weary smile.

"How are you doing, Mom?"

"Me? I'm just getting old. I didn't mean to. It just kinda happened."

"Dad's working you too hard?"

"No. If your daddy had his way, I'd be on the sofa with my feet up, and he'd be cooking me up the holy trinity of hushpuppies."

"You two are so good together."

"It's a lot of work, honey. It don't just happen."

"How did you know you loved my dad?"

Lorraine observed Isabella astutely.

"It took time after he lost your mom. You know, your momma was a fiery woman, strong-willed. It isn't easy to replace a bright soul when their light leaves a family's life. It surprised us when she died because she was such a fighter. But the Lord was looking after your daddy that day. Even though she didn't make it, you did. One month premature and mad as hell about the disruption, you were born with her fighting spirit. Then I offered to help take care of you. I'll never forget that day. I saw him holding his newborn baby girl, and he looked at you with such wonder, like he was looking into God's eyes. I knew I loved him at that moment. He still looks at you like that." Lorraine touched Isabella's cheek. "She must be a very special girl."

Isabella looked surprised at first, then realized she had always been an open book for Lorraine to riffle through. "It's Angela Mathers."

Lorraine shot her a look of disbelief.

"Mom, she's brilliant. She wrote the Freewill Bill—she's proud to be a Luman." Isabella paused the swing. "But she's so damn hard-headed, she won't let me help her—and…" Her voice died out at the end.

"And what?" Lorraine asked with reservation.

"She's involved with someone." Isabella looked away.

Lorraine masked her worries. "Honey, a lot of Lumans don't like Solos. If she knew, she could turn you in. There is still a bounty out on you."

"Mom, she already knows."

Lorraine studied Isabella. "Come inside for some supper, and we will come up with a plan to win Angela's heart." Isabella smiled and helped Lorraine off the swing. "Besides, it's time to mend fences with your dad."

Inside their small kitchenette, Lorraine slid a plate of shrimp and coleslaw in front of Isabella. Frank sat opposite her, his dessert untouched.

"If the Freewill Bill vote passes the Senate, the president said he would sign it into law," Isabella said as she took a forkful of coleslaw.

"We've heard that promise so many times before. Then Congress gets deadlocked, and nothing happens," Frank said.

Isabella observed her father. They saw the world very differently. She dropped her fork with a clang. "You sure have changed your tune over the years, Dad. What about having faith in God?"

"Gin stopped by the other day. She looks great. Have you seen her lately?" Lorraine asked as she refilled Isabella's glass with sweet tea.

Isabella didn't glance up at her. She knew Gin and Lorraine talked all the time. "Yeah," Isabella mumbled. "I saw the engagement ring."

Frank continued, "This has nothing to do with faith in God. The government is not on our side." He pushed his dessert aside. "They have the Lumans locked away in compounds, handling government security, and God knows what else. The government should use the Lumans' abilities to solve genuine problems like global warming or researching cures for Lorraine's cancer."

Lorraine joined Frank, resting her hands on his shoulders, calming him. Isabella stared at them, assimilating this news, trying to assert reason.

"Mom, you have cancer?"

Frank got up. "Mazzy, come with me."

Isabella felt sick. He never used her actual name.

They moved outside, the day's heat still hanging in the night air. "I moved my repair shop down the street. I took over that old Gulf station." Isabella nodded absently.

He bent down and lifted the garage door, and they watched it roll up into the ceiling. "So now I use the garage to tinker on special projects."

Isabella followed her father into the dark jungle of old batteries, rusted parts, tools on pegboards, the reek of gas and grease. It took her back to when she used to help him repair cars. She could read an idling engine better than she could read a book. They used to spend their weekends building car engines, and after she finished college, they had raced Formula One cars.

He flipped the switch and the overhead fluorescent lights flickered on, casting a cold blue light over the space. In the center of the garage was a covered automobile. Pulling the sheet off, Frank watched his daughter's face. Her mouth dropped at the sight of a shiny, cherry red, customized Barracuda pony. It was a personalized beauty with the fluid lines of an original 'Cuda from the seventies but with a sportier, modern fastback.

He opened the driver's side door for Isabella, and she slid in, feeling the hard leather seat shape to her body. She ran her fingers over the police scanner and onboard computer, smiling and glancing up at her father from time to time.

"I've been working on the 'Cuda for years. I added police lights and a siren."

He pressed a button. The metal partition came up, separating the front and back seat.

"That's for all those criminals you catch. Give it a go, sweetheart." He handed her the key fob.

She smiled and turned over the engine, which came to life with a deafening, throaty roar. She shut her eyes as the engine's vibration rushed through her at 1500 rmp. When she and Frank used to race together, they had fine-tuned her engines to scientific perfection. She could outmaneuver and out-think other drivers. But a young lady in the racing field was a rarity. She had thrown races and faked engine problems at Frank's insistence—to keep suspicions at bay.

She killed the 'Cuda's engine. The silence in the garage was deafening. From somewhere deep within, Frank uttered, "'The roar of an engine makes me feel alive, as if nothing can catch me.' That's what you used to say after a race."

Isabella glanced at him sideways. "You remember me saying that after all these years?" She was fortunate to find something as simple as racing to make her feel free. So many Solos struggled to find careers they loved.

"Yes, I do." Frank played with the glove compartment latch. "The worst thing in the world is to watch your child struggle, be unhappy, and not be able to help. I thought if I made decisions for you, I could keep you safe. In doing so, I took away your freedom to make your own choices and be who you truly are. I realize it's too late to start over, but I support whatever you want to do...I'm proud you're an agent."

Isabella kissed him on the cheek, and he uncomfortably hugged her in the tight confines of the car. She had never expected him to change his mind. Never had he given in when she wanted something that he didn't think was good for her. Something had changed. There was fear lurking behind his smile.

"How serious is Mom's cancer?"

"Doctors aren't sure, honey. With the ban on technology, they don't have the equipment or knowledge to predict or to cure it. We need you back in our lives."

# CHAPTER THIRTY-ONE

*The Plan*

Redemption had its price and with it came collateral damage, Angela thought as her feet pounded the treadmill. Mind scheming, neurons firing, information processing, she swiped the tablet screen as articles on Mort Abrams flashed before her eyes. After returning home from the Rabbit after her confrontation with Janet, she'd scoured Mort's electronic footprint, combing through financial transactions, social media posts, and business partners, foraging for clues, connecting the dots, and following his digital scent.

Sudden knocking on her door shattered her concentration. Fearful that it was Jeff, she darted her eyes to the security monitor on the wall. When Isabella's blue eyes peered back at her, Angela felt like she was coming up for air, breaking the water's surface after being in the deep for too long. She stopped the treadmill and grabbed a towel. A smile stirred on her lips. She dried off and walked toward the door. She had purged her anger; what was left pumping through her veins was fear.

She opened the door, and their eyes met. "I'm sorry" was spoken in unison and Isabella's arms reached for her. Angela fell into them, their fight forgotten.

Angela choked out, "The bill is in jeopardy."

Isabella grabbed Angela's hand and tugged her out the door. "Screw 'em. Let's get out of here."

"What? Wait, I need to change."

"You won't need four-inch heels for this," Isabella said, a smile tugging at the corners of her mouth as she watched Angela trot back to the bedroom. "I like that look," she called after her.

A brand-new, cherry-red muscle car was parked in front of Angela's apartment. "Yours?" Angela asked, getting a nod in return. "This sure is an upgrade from that dumpy death trap you've been driving," she said.

"Yep, let's go for a drive." Isabella handed her the key fob.

"It's illegal," Angela said and glanced up at the guard post. Which was empty.

"Oh, there's been a disturbance down the way. Lawd, he'll be busy running all over hell's half acre." Isabella winked and slid into the passenger seat.

Angela gave her a doubtful smile. "Seriously, how is this happening?"

"I called in a few favors. Got a friend to hack the cameras and drones on this nice little stretch of road that encircles the compound. No one will be watching us. But we have to hurry—it's only for the next hour."

"This sounds suspiciously like a Guardian friend," Angela said. She slid into the driver's seat anyway. "But I don't know how."

"I'm sure your giant intellect will figure it out."

* * *

Angela was driving, smiling as the wind blew through her hair. The engine roared as they passed a sign: D.C. Compound Checkpoint.

"Make a left. We need to stay within the compound limits, so your tracker stays quiet."

Angela obeyed and turned onto a road parallel to the Potomac River. Checkpoints and boundary markers were passed as the downtown city lights faded from view and boarded-up stores and broken-down office parks replaced it. They pulled off onto the side of the road overlooking the river. She marveled at the fabric of the night, the moon round and full, the stars crawling—a rare sight inside the smog and neon lights of downtown.

"I want to show you everything beyond these electrified fences," Isabella whispered. "Freedom is not just a feeling. It has a taste, a smell, a wild, untamed nature—we can experience it all together."

Angela nodded. "We just need to get the bill back on track." They locked hands and hearts and continued their journey around the compound. While on the other side, the humans fearful or opposed to the blending of Luman and human life-work environment lived their lives.

Angela glided the car to a stop in front of her complex and killed the engine. As she regarded Isabella, her eyes sparkled. She had spent days, months, years folded into this place, but tonight as she searched the horizon, there was an uncoiling.

"I feel alive. You surprised me tonight." She grew quiet as she studied her tattoo. "I behaved poorly earlier. Forgive me."

Isabella kissed her.

"You're a Luman," Angela continued, "but we don't share history…"

Isabella put a finger to Angela's lips. "I get it. There are all kinds of differences that could keep us apart, but one similarity binds us together: our shimmer."

"We have paired. I mean, our chips have," Angela said, feeling her face grow serene with this revelation. It still seemed impossible. She thought about telling Isabella her own secret, but she stopped herself, feeling too exposed and vulnerable.

"That's right, and we are bound together."

She touched Isabella's cheek. "We will fight together."

Isabella nodded. They got out of the car.

"Okay, genius, what's the plan?" Isabella asked. "We have about five minutes left before the cameras come back on."

They stood face-to-face on the sidewalk, the complex guard still MIA.

"If Janet won't talk to Green about Lucy, I will."

"Angela, let's put desperation aside for a minute."

Angela looked defensively at her.

"Okay, fine," Isabella conceded. "But I'll talk to Green. I'll do the accusing. The rules are different for me. I can get away with a lot more than you can."

"Don't you see? It needs to be me."

"You can't break Code. I'll handle it."

Angela gave Isabella a patronizing glare. "I am acutely aware of how the system works. I've gotten this far in the world by finding a way around the rules."

Isabella hesitated, then said, "Okay."

"You schedule a meeting with Green tomorrow. Say you have a few more questions about the investigation that will clear up everything," Angela said.

Isabella added, "During my meeting I'll step away to answer my phone or something."

"And then I show up," Angela said. A sinister grin emerged. "This needs to happen before the vote, before two p.m."

"Then it will."

They smiled at each other—it was after curfew—the streets were empty. On impulse, Angela's lips pressed against Isabella in an inexorable kiss—in plain sight, so liberating. And for the first time, as she did so she did not think of freedom but of Isabella.

# CHAPTER THIRTY-TWO

## *The Day of the Vote*

The following morning, very early, Angela exited the shower, wrapped in a towel, and crossed from the bathroom to the bed. Laid out on the bedspread was her outfit. She picked up the black dress and looked at it, nonplussed. This wasn't the dress she had selected. It was then that she sensed his presence. She whipped around.

"Christ, you scared me." She breathed in sharply at the sight of Jeff.

"The black one's sexier."

"I'm not taking fashion tips from you. Where is the dress I laid out?"

"Do as I say, Angela." Jeff's grim demeanor was uncharacteristic, but she conceded; she just needed to get through this check-in. She went into the bathroom and slid into the black dress. When she came back to show him, he spun her around and zipped it up, whispering, "I can be more than your monitor." His words crawled beneath her skin.

*Brilliant. Of all the days I thought this might happen—it has to be today.* "What? You want to be my fashion advisor?" she said with a laugh, trying to head off Jeff's advances.

"It must be tough being smarter than everyone else."

Jeff was so close she smelled his sweat. He moved his hand toward the ridge of her breast, and she grabbed hold of it.

"You know the rules, Jeff."

"You don't care about the rules." He grinned, snaking his hand around her and pulling her close. Angela's disgust mixed with fear, and she instinctively froze. Jeff's forehead creased when she didn't resist, and he released her.

"I'm not some big lug sent to make sure you obey the Codes. I'm here to protect you." Angela watched his internal struggle play out on his face.

"Agents are our protectors. You're just a monitor, Jeff. So do your job."

"No, you don't understand."

"I'm afraid I do. Who put you up to this? Abrams or Green?"

"What?"

Angela scrutinized him, not buying that he had come up with this idea on his own to keep her from the Senate vote today.

Angela's phone rang. Jeff pulled it out of his pocket and kept it out of her reach. He glanced at the screen. "Looky-looky, guess who's calling? Agent Dodge. You two sure hit it off." He dropped the phone in front of her and smashed it with the heel of his boot. "You don't need Agent Dodge. Just like you didn't need Warren, Jonathan, or Janet. I'll take care of you."

Fear gripped her heart and buzzed in her ears. "What are you saying, Jeff? I don't want you." She felt the walls closing in on her as he smirked. "Stop it, Jeff. Finish the check-in. The Senate is voting on the bill today. I need to be there." She touched his collar. "Please."

He pushed her down on the bed. "Wait here."

Jeff came back, rolling two oversized suitcases. Still grinning at her, he unlocked one trunk. A woman's body spilled out onto the floor, landing with a thud. Angela gasped. She stumbled to her feet, scrambling away from the ghastly vision. The swelling and bruises disfiguring the redhead's face made Angela's stomach lurch. Her body was frozen at strange, unnatural angles from her imprisonment.

"She's a Chip. Are you gonna take me seriously now?" Jeff shouted. Gasping for breath, Angela was acutely aware this wasn't a game. She heard the faint ping of the woman's chip, then the woman on the floor silent-messaged, *Help me.*

"Jeff, what have you done?"

Making his point clear, Jeff opened the other suitcase. She looked at it and knew the empty bag was for her.

He pulled a handgun out of the back of his waistband and waved it around. "This is for your own good. I'm the only one who can protect you."

Angela's knees were about to buckle. She glanced at the body on the floor and the suitcase for her. When Jeff edged toward her, she bolted out of the bedroom, raced to the front door, flung it open, and stopped. A stranger was standing there.

"Hello, Angela." His deep discordant tone slunk through the air unmistakably.

"Uncle River," she whispered. It was the hungry nasally voice Lucy had described, and it conjured images that were buried deep in Angela's mind. *The dull-eyed man with ill-formed features peering through the door of the river shack. The shape of blood like a punctured egg yolk smeared in the mud where Lucy last was.*

"Play nice," he whispered, and his bone-white fingers were choking her. Fists clenched, Angela reeled on him, kicking and punching, trying to break free. Uncle River morphed into Peter Ord as he wrestled her under control.

"What the fuck? How come you are not at the drop-off?" Peter growled at Jeff, who was slamming the front door shut, then he dragged Angela back to the bedroom.

"I'm keeping her," Jeff announced.

"What? You're not pissing away all that money." Peter wrangled with Angela, tying up her arms with his, stopping her fit of rage. "Are you fucking serious?" His words cut through the air. "That agent is onto us."

"We'll swap Angela with this Chip. They will never know the difference." Jeff put his gun on the dresser next to a prescription bottle and syringe.

"They specifically requested Angela's chip. And they look nothing alike. You can't swap them. You've lost it."

Peter threw Angela on the bed, went over to the prescription bottle, and checked the label. "Propofol. Good, at least you got that right." Angela's mind was spinning out of control, and she couldn't move—her muscles had forsaken her.

"Snap out of it, man. You are obsessing over a Chip."

Peter inverted the prescription bottle and drew sedative into the syringe.

"No, Jeff! Don't let him do it," Angela pleaded.

"No, man, you can't kill her." Jeff looked at Angela, then at Peter.

Swallowing hard, Angela willed her body off the bed as Peter approached. She ran, but he was quicker and wrapped his brawny arm around her body, the long syringe needle aimed at her neck.

Squirming, Angela tried to break free from Peter's grip.

Peter yelled, "Hold her still." Angela twisted wildly as she screamed and kicked at him. "She's brainwashed you, dude," Peter yelled.

"Shut up already," Jeff shouted as he tried to pull Angela away from Peter.

*Angela, I'm here. Are you okay?* Isabella silent-messaged.

Angela exhaled sharply. She messaged back. *No! Jeff and Peter are hurting me!* She was weak with exhaustion, pressed between Jeff and Peter as they struggled over the syringe.

*I'm right outside the bedroom. I'll distract them, and then you run to me.*

*No! He has a gun!* Angela gasped for breath as they held her tighter, pushing and pulling her. She smelled the bitter heat of Jeff's breath on her face, heard teeth grinding, grunting, the rustling of fabric. Then she felt it—the cohering of her heartbeat to Isabella's. She was right outside the bedroom door.

*Trust me, Angela. Do what I say. Jeff won't hurt you.*

"Control. Hands up, now!" Isabella yelled. She popped into the doorway, her weapon drawn, shifting her aim between Jeff and Peter.

The needle dropped to the floor and Peter raised his hands, releasing Angela. Angela ran for Isabella. Before she could reach her, though, Jeff grabbed her shoulder. She screamed as Jeff locked onto her and held her in front of him like a shield as he moved toward his firearm on the dresser. Isabella fired. The bullet missed them, but Jeff froze in place.

When Isabella stepped farther into the room, she caught sight of the crumpled body on the floor. She wavered, as though dizzy, then silent-messaged. *Gin, are you okay?* It was then that Angela realized the woman there was Isabella's ex-lover. There was no response.

Isabella shook off her shock and aimed her Glock at Peter, then Jeff, warning them. Time stopped as she squatted beside the woman and moved matted red hair to expose a disfigured, bruised face. Angela saw denial wash over her face until she slowly turned the woman's hand to reveal an engagement ring. Angela felt all of Isabella's pent-up anger, remorse, and guilt explode through her as she shot to her feet.

Peter snickered. "She spilled about being a Chip—"

Isabella shifted her aim and fired before he could finish, shattering his kneecap. As he crumpled to the floor, Jeff grabbed his gun off the dresser and pressed it against Angela's head. When Isabella turned her Glock back at Jeff and started marching toward him, he backed up into the living room, dragging Angela behind him. Isabella charged at him, her stare one of pure fury. The sound of sirens filtered up from the street below.

Angela knew she needed to bring Isabella back from the darkness, back from the pain before any costly mistakes were made.

"Isabella, wait." Angela remembered Isabella's words during the protest. *Hey, take a deep breath. Don't let 'em get to you!* she silent-messaged in desperation, tears running down her face. Isabella stopped and surveyed the scene slowly as if regaining consciousness.

"Stop. I will kill her." Panic surged in Jeff's voice.

Angela felt Isabella's heartbeat slow and get in rhythm with hers again. She took a breath and delivered her words to Jeff calmly, though it was clear that her rage was barely under control. "Come on, Jeff. Put the gun down," she coaxed. "You don't want to kill Angela. You love her." She circled Jeff and Angela.

"No. No, I don't," Jeff protested.

"All those photos of her on your computer tell a different story."

Jeff scoffed. Isabella inched closer to them. "That's right. I've been to your apartment, scanned your computer. You boys are in a mess of trouble, but if you put the gun down, we can make a deal." The sirens outside grew closer, louder.

"Put the gun down!" Isabella screamed.

Angela silent-messaged, *Do it for Christ's sake—kill him!*

Isabella flinched. "I get it. You want Angela all to yourself. So, you got rid of everyone who loves her."

Peter rolled on the floor, moaning in a slow slur of words. "You hear those sirens? Jeff, we need to get the hell out of here. Help me!"

"You killed Jonathan and Warren. You blackmailed Janet. You even tried to get me fired by sending Carter that photo."

Jeff clutched Angela even tighter. "Shut up. I need to think—this can still work."

Angela cried, "Isabella, do something!"

"You sick fuck, it's over," Peter cried out.

Jeff turned toward Peter, and Angela grabbed his gun, twisting her body, driving her knee into his groin. They fought over the gun. *Bang!* The bullet zinged past Isabella and ripped through Peter's skull. When Isabella turned back, Angela had the gun aimed at Jeff. Breathing erratically, she stepped away from Jeff, then moved dangerously close to him in an agitated dance.

"You're pathetic," she screamed.

"Angela, don't! We need to question him and find out who's involved."

Angela's emotions collapsed under the crushing weight of twenty-two years of oppression. "He needs to die. Uncle River needs to die."

She shifted her gaze to Peter lying motionless on the floor, her gun wavering between him and Jeff.

"I...I wasn't going to hurt you." Jeff dropped to his knees and pleaded with her, his words playing in slow-mo in Angela's mind. His voice became Uncle River's, like a trombone sliding slowly through the notes off-key. "Please, Angela, don't."

Isabella moved next to Angela, placing a cautious hand on her back. "Hey, where did you go? Come back. He's not Uncle River, I got you." She let Angela absorb that, then added, "Think about how this will look. A Luman killing her monitor. *You* killing him."

Angela turned cold, snapping out of it. Isabella was right. She lowered the gun, trembling. She felt the seven-year-old girl she kept inside her die. How many Raymonds and Jeffs were still out there? She would never get redemption.

"This is never going to end. They will keep trying to kill us." She looked up at Isabella, who hesitated then took the gun from her and handed Angela her Glock.

Angela exhaled as she aimed Isabella's gun at Jeff's head, and the world stopped for a moment. Her finger quivered on the trigger and then—*Bang!* The front door opened, and in a rush of chaos the Control SWAT team piled in. And Angela saw a pattern of red dots from laser-beam sights trained on Jeff's forehead.

David yelled, "Control! Hands up. On the floor, Jeff, do it." Jeff dropped flat. Isabella took the gun from Angela and wrapped her in her arms. Angela put all her weight on Isabella, unable to stand upright.

"Isabella, you both okay?" David asked anxiously.

Isabella gave David a nod and a look of gratitude. Crossing over to Jeff, he pulled him back up to his knees. As Jeff continued his sobbing duet with Angela—"I love you, Angela"—David flipped open his handcuffs, showing off a bit. "You have the right to remain silent." He was lowering Jeff's left hand to cuff it when he felt a tugging sensation. He looked down and yelled, "He's got my gun!"

There was a clank of metal on teeth as Jeff's shaking hand held the gun to his mouth. His haunted eyes glared at Angela.

"No!" Isabella screamed. David reached for the gun. *Bang!*

\* \* \*

Angela sat on the floor in darkness, rocking, fingers interlocked behind her neck, staring into space. Her biological brain was a spinning cursor, disconnected from her body. Ascended into the light, she was traversing a strange maze of pathways that drew her in deeper and deeper. Until she felt alive again, electric.

That's where Isabella found her, hidden away in her bedroom closet, and in that state. Isabella crouched in front of her, gently unlacing her fingers from around her neck and replacing them with her own. They rocked together, silent-messaging images of need and of comfort and support.

Isabella's voice shook with uncertainty. "Angela, come back to me. I need you."

Angela slowly awakened from her enthralled state. She studied Isabella. "How did you know to save me?"

"We found the red pickup truck, and the license plate traced to Jeff. I also found out he had a tie to Virus," Isabella explained. "We got a search warrant to go through his apartment. On his computer there were hundreds of photos of you: at home on the treadmill, cooking, getting dressed; pictures of you with Jonathan and Warren. And a lot of you and Janet. He had cameras everywhere. When I couldn't reach you by phone, I was frantic. I rushed over here, calling Carter on the way to tell them to send the SWAT team."

"Thank God you did." A chill ran up Angela's spine as she thought about what had almost happened.

"Carter is closing the case on Warren and Jonathan since Peter Ord is dead and Jeff killed himself. She doesn't buy the government conspiracy theory."

Angela straightened. "That's not right!"

"Given the publicity this is likely to generate, Carter thinks the people buying the chips will be long gone." Isabella clenched her jaw, trying to choke back her tears. "With the case closed, Green's untouchable now. It's over."

Angela felt wholly recharged, having erased the awful incident with Jeff from her mind. "If you think I will let them win, you don't know me at all."

She clutched Isabella's hands. "Maybe we can't reach Green, but I know who can. Then Jonathan, Warren, and Gin will not have died in vain. We can continue to fight for them."

Isabella glanced over to where Gin's covered body lay. "The last time I saw her she had this look of regret in her eyes."

"Hey, you could not have known. It's not your fault." Angela touched her shoulders. "We will make them pay, but first I need your help. It requires some coercion and for that I need Control to back me up."

"Whatever you're planning—it's got to be justifiable."

"I could make it stand up in court if it comes to that, but I need you to be convincing. Can you do that?"

Isabella watched as forensic agents placed Gin's body on a stretcher. "I guess we'll find out."

# CHAPTER THIRTY-THREE

## *The Devil She Knows*

Bright lights ricocheted off the milky white concrete walls outside Janet's hideaway office in the Capitol. A young female reporter stepped before the camera, glancing at her notes, waiting. The cameraman pointed to her.

"We are in front of Senate Majority Leader Janet Abrams's office waiting for her to speak with us before today's historic vote on the Freewill Bill." Down the long hallway, a small group gathered to watch the reporter. Angela was there, hiding in plain sight. Nonchalantly, she pressed the badge Janet had given her onto the badge-access door system to unlock it and moved swiftly through the secret passage.

The wall-to-wall bookcase slid open, and Angela stepped out of the shadow of the secret passage. She smiled at Janet, who sat at her desk with Mort sitting opposite her. They both peered up simultaneously and Janet's expression changed from authoritative to apprehensive.

"Angela, thank God you're safe." Janet's voice sounded so caring, as if she had never had a malicious thought toward anyone. "We heard about Jeff Lewis—how horrifying."

Janet got up and stiffly embraced Angela after she entered and the bookcase closed. Mort stood like a Confederate statue, cold and judging.

*This is our game, Morty. Sit back down and enjoy the show*, Angela thought. "Jeff blew his brains out—but not before he talked," she said as she removed herself from Janet's icy embrace.

Mort cleared his throat. "Angela, you have no right to be here. Leave now, or I'll call the police."

Angela scoffed, glaring at him as he reached for his phone. "Sit down, Mort. You're not in charge anymore. I am."

"What's this, Angela? I don't understand." Janet settled awkwardly into her chair.

"Did you know Mort recorded us having sex? Everything we said and did, and we did some freaky shit. It was part of a deal he made with me. In exchange for my recording our late-night 'strategy' sessions, his shell company funded the advocacy for the Freewill Bill."

Janet gave Mort an icy stare.

"Don't listen to this child-killer, Janet," Mort bellowed.

"And there it is," Angela said, raising her chin slightly. Jeff's assault had unlocked many of Angela's memories about that day at the river, and Isabella had helped her fill in the gaps. But it was the discovery of her emotions that had given her words to describe her fears that day. And that gave her the strength to use them to her benefit now. "No one will ever know for sure. I mean—I could have. It would only have taken the slightest push to send Lucy into the soup. You see, there is a fine line between truth and plausibility." She smiled wickedly. "And you have no idea what I am capable of."

"You are a clever girl, so good at using doubt as a weapon." Janet's disdain simmered in her eyes. Angela moved to the bar, poured herself a scotch, then rolled the drink around in the iceless glass and assessed her opponents, gauging their suspicion of her and each other. For this to work, she had to connect with Janet emotionally and then take what she coveted so deeply.

She swallowed the scotch and began. "Trafficking in Chips is big business. Profitability will skyrocket when the Freewill Bill passes and the Lumans are no longer monitored twenty-four-seven. The bill lifts the ban on technology, accelerates the manufacturing of neural implants, and restarts the children's neural prostheses program, establishing the supply chain and the need. It's a numbers game and a sure bet for the entrepreneurs who are first on the market. They will have influence—power. The Freewill Bill is inevitable."

She looked at Mort. "Your wife had told you as much, Mort, so you got a jump on the competition. You've done this in the past, though the charges of insider trading were mysteriously dropped. Your choice of Jeff Lewis as your supplier of neural chips was unfortunate, though. He promised to deliver Chips under the radar, supplying the Corpus program, but his obsession with me drew attention to your operation. When he started taking those close to me, it put the bill in jeopardy. Did Janet share that bit of news with you?"

Mort and Janet's eyes met coldly.

"Jeff told me about the deal you made with him. You even doubled the bounty if they could deliver my chip. But poor Jeff couldn't stand by and let that happen. He tried to convince me to leave with him. When that didn't work, he killed Peter and turned the gun on himself—brilliant and tragic."

Mort threw his head back with a throaty laugh like a seal barking.

"Oh, and then there's a money trail leading to you, Mort. The advocacy funding—I recorded every payment."

Angela showed them a tiny digital storage device and leveled a chilly gaze at Mort and Janet. "An enormous investment to promote a bill you plan to exploit and profit from. Not surprisingly, shady dealing is your MO."

Angela observed Janet. She was no longer looking at her husband as he continued laughing. Clearly, she had had her doubts about Mort's financial dealings, probably for a long time. "Did you realize Emma was a procurer for your husband's proclivities?" Angela asked Janet.

Mort stopped laughing. "Don't listen to her, dear."

"Mort, was it your idea or Emma's to blackmail Janet? Apply pressure to make sure she'd break it off with me. My guess is that it was your idea. I mean—you have seen our videos, there must be hundreds of them. Unless it's your kink, watching your wife get off could be hard on the ego."

Mort jumped up, grabbed Angela's neck, and pushed her back, pinning her against the wall. "This will never stand up in court! No one will believe a Chip, especially you. You're a pathological liar." Angela smirked at him as his grip tightened around her neck. His eyes were bulging with hatred, and his face was a burst of twitching red veins.

"Mort, control yourself!" Janet thundered, confidence falling from her expression.

The bookcase slid open again, and Isabella walked through. One hand was holding up her badge; the other was on her hip, near her Glock.

"Special Agent Dodge. Mort Abrams, step away from Ms. Mathers. Do it now!"

Stunned, Mort released Angela.

"Mr. Abrams, you have the right to remain silent..."

As Isabella read Mort his rights, he pleaded with his wife. "I didn't do it, Janet. I know nothing about blackmail or trafficking. She has fabricated all of it."

"Y'all will have your day in court, but right now, let's get you on down to Control headquarters for questioning." Isabella slapped the cuffs on Mort and pointed him toward the door and the awaiting press. Angela could see the wheels turning in Janet's head; she knew this would impact her run for president.

Janet and Angela squared off in a standoff of wills while Mort pleaded, "Janet, it's all lies."

"Wait, Agent Dodge." Janet moved toward Angela, inspecting her neck, making sure she was unharmed. Concern turned to admiration as she brushed a strand of Angela's hair back over her shoulder. "I underestimated you, Angela. You really are rather merciless. But we both know that the evidence here is circumstantial at best. So, drop this nonsense, and I'll get you a job at the Capitol where you can do extraordinary things."

Angela marveled at how quickly Janet had regained her self-assurance and confidence. How she still thought she was in charge.

"If the bill doesn't pass, I won't do extraordinary things—I will do no things. I need the bill to pass. Can you do that for me?"

# CHAPTER THIRTY-FOUR

### *Rumors*

Janet watched Paula recenter the bow collar on her Armani knit top as she exited Senator Jackson Green's office, securing the door behind her. She jumped when she saw Janet, and blushed.

"Senator Abrams. Sorry, you startled me." Paula looked at the closed door and then back at Janet. "Did you have an appointment?"

"No, I just need a minute of his time before the vote. That's a pretty top."

Paula touched her blouse. "Thank you." She walked to her nearby desk. "Please have a seat in the conference room. I'll let him know you're here."

The smell of leather and bergamot overwhelmed Janet when she sat at the conference table. She shook her head. This day had ruined what was left of her marriage and might yet torpedo her career. Clearly, her affair with Angela, though over, was still clouding her judgment.

Senator Green stopped in the doorway, chuckling to himself. Looking impeccable in his black suit, he said with a hint of arrogance, "Janet, what a surprise. If you're here to wrangle me into changing my vote, save your breath."

His stony expression fragmented when he noticed that the notebook on the table was opened to a photo of his deceased daughter, Lucy. His eyes could not meet hers.

"Jackson, I rushed over when I heard the nasty rumor. Please tell me it isn't true?"

"What rumor? Who told you?"

"Oh, don't be coy, Jackson. We don't want 'Hard Nose' Milton from the Senate Ethics Committee to get wind of this."

With a scornful huff, he brushed her comment aside and insisted, "It's malarkey. I'll fight it."

"Well, even so— On the one hand, there's the immediate public reaction when the news gets out. On the other hand, there's a long, drawn-out ethics hearing to prove you didn't collude with the police to hide Angela Mather's affidavit in order to hide Raymond's guilt. In either case, these types of things can shred a reputation. If the affidavit is found, of course, and it turns out that the Codes were put into effect based on a cover-up, your reputation will be the least of your worries."

Senator Green threw his hands in the air and flopped petulantly into a chair opposite her. "Just so you know, there were never any charges filed—my wife made sure of that."

Janet's doubtful grin equaled his pompous one. "New information about the murder has...resurfaced."

The anger roared out of him from nowhere. "Those accusations are false! That manipulative Chip is a sociopath."

She waited patiently, watching him unravel.

"You've lost perspective, Janet. You have underestimated her manipulations and deception from the beginning."

"Are you questioning my loyalties?"

"I'm questioning your common sense." He took a deep breath and shook his head. "Don't you see, putting neural implants in children was one thing, but I heard they are putting them into soldiers now. It's risky; it's playing God."

Janet studied him intently. They were political opponents, each with a secret. To save themselves, they were going to have to make a decision that would change the nation's course.

# CHAPTER THIRTY-FIVE

*The Vote*

"The Senate will come to order." Vice President Wilson struck her gavel against the hardwood of her desk, and the moment Angela had been anticipating since she was seven was here. Angela's eyes roamed the Senate chamber from where she and Isabella were perched in the public gallery above it. Her hands wrapped tight around the railing, she saw senators, aides, and clerks packed in so tightly that only dapples of royal blue carpet showed through. As Senator Abrams approached the podium, she gazed up casually at Angela. Angela knew the look was far from casual—it was a knife at Angela's throat.

"We'd like to call the Freewill Bill to vote," Senator Abrams said.

Vice President Wilson looked around the gallery. "No objections. The vote will commence."

Isabella covered Angela's hand with her own, and their eyes met with uneasiness. But it wasn't the long wait causing the tension. It was anticipating the minutia, the dutiful clerks laboriously calling each senator one by one to the front of the chamber and then announcing their vote.

The first name was called, "Senator Abrams?"

Janet said, "Aye."

It had begun. Angela felt hope building deep inside her, the ayes and the nays echoing in her head as she tallied the votes mentally. The more she focused on slowing her breathing the faster it came. Her parents were on her right watching the session with care. A slight frown crossed their faces with each "nay." Visitor passes were scarce for this historical event, and it had taken the intervention of Angela's boss to get her parents into the gallery. Millions of people were watching the Senate vote via webcast while thousands of others gathered outside the US Capitol, some in support, some in protest.

The air got heavier as the clerks moved alphabetically through the Senate roll call. The next name was called. "Senator Green."

Senator Green approached the clerk. "Aye," he said tiredly, avoiding eye contact with anyone.

Angela exhaled sharply as a collective gasp rose from the gallery and the Senate floor and senators clumped together in small groups, whispering amongst themselves. Green walked back to his seat, looking as if he were carrying his body on his sagging shoulders. Janet and Angela's eyes caught; there was no way to prepare for it when passion turned into betrayal.

Angela felt Isabella's grip tighten around her hand. She was her support and security detail after the attack on her. And she knew Isabella needed reassurance, needed answers after the confrontation with Janet and Mort. Isabella silent-messaged, *Gin's contact said the Luman trafficking ring had a government connection. You know Mort didn't hire Jeff.*

*Mort served his purpose.*

*There is still more to be done. We need to find all those involved...* Isabella said.

Angela needed to tell Isabella at some point that the deal Janet made with Green meant the accusations against Raymond Stratton were going away—forever. But she wasn't sure how to explain that. There were no definite answers for why being different gave rise to fear, why the unusual became monsters in the eyes of others. How did hate disguise itself as the unfortunate, afflicted Uncle River rather than revealing him as the strange and savage creature he was? Why did Raymond earn the Greens' protection while seven-year-old Angela did not? But then their eyes met, and Angela decided explanations could wait.

The gavel sounded. The clerk had called all one hundred senators, and each had cast a vote. Isabella pressed Angela's fingers to her mouth as she whispered a prayer.

*No matter what happens. We will continue to fight for Jonathan, Warren, and Gin, even if Carter has closed the Lewis case*, Angela silent-messaged. Isabella nodded with ominous certainty.

Vice President Wilson's voice resonated over the speaker, "The Senate will come to order."

The Senate gallery fell silent as everyone's attention turned to the vice president. Angela took a deep breath while Isabella closed her eyes.

"Freewill Bill vote totals are the ayes sixty-seven, and the nays thirty-three. The bill gained sixty-seven votes in the affirmative. The Freewill Bill is agreed to."

The gavel struck as applause rung out through the top gallery, and Senator Abrams rushed out. Isabella's and Angela's eyes met in celebration and admiration. They had done it! Together.

*Redemption is mine. That young girl so excited about life has been avenged*, Angela thought. *Even though there are still a lot of formalities yet to be determined.* She felt as though her life had just restarted after being idle for years. As a tear streamed down her cheek, she found a way to forgive herself for not saving Lucy:

She saw Raymond take Lucy that day at the river, but instead of helping, she ran. When Lucy didn't show up at school the next day, she returned to the river that afternoon. The river had receded into its banks. And so did Angela's memories of Raymond and what had happened.

# CHAPTER THIRTY-SIX

## *The Fallen*

Everyone wept—many of them in disguise.

One week after the Senate vote, Frank said a prayer as the red clay swallowed up Gin's casket. Next to her grave stood a cypress tree with sprawling branches that stretched up to the indigo heavens, one of the few cypresses left in the region. Beside the grave, there were planters of white roses and a photo of Gin. She was looking to the sky as the sun's rays washed over her face—an intimate portrait of her strength and grace. What laid in the casket, what was left of Gin's body, was anything but that. When it came to the Lumans, documented or undocumented, eminent domain applied to their minds. The government had seized her brain, claiming the neural implant inside it, before handing over the rest of her body.

Her family and Guardian colleagues gathered to honor their leader and fallen hero. Isabella stepped forward in her Wayne disguise and dropped a white rose onto the casket. When she moved back, Angela placed her arm around her. Steven Hawk had given her a government pass to attend the funeral.

Donovan, Gin's fiancé, stood nearby. His cowboy hat shadowed his watery eyes and a weathered, fake face. He licked his dry lips, raising a silver flask and emptying its contents into his mouth. He staggered forward, drunk on the pain, and chucked the flask into the grave. The sound of the tin clanking against the coffin ripped through the hearts of everyone. His father, Bill, tried to handle him, but he reared and bucked out of Bill's grasp before seizing a flower arrangement and throwing it into the air. White roses rained down, blanketing Gin's casket. Busted at the knees, he fell to the edge of the dark muddy chasm, crying as gawking spectators looked on with pity.

Isabella bent down and put a comforting hand on his shoulder. His shoulder twitched and tightened as he raised his fist to strike her. She quickly blocked it. Reeling to his feet, he swung again, but the blow never landed. Two bystanders wrestled him into submission.

Donovan hollered, "She's dead because of you and Angela." He twisted free from those holding him. "Shit, none of this would have happened had she not pushed Lucy Green into the river."

Isabella stood in front of Angela, trying to shield her from Donovan's verbal blows. "That's enough, Donovan. We are all grieving Gin."

"Nunh-unh, not like me. I was in love with her long before she met you." He stubbornly wiped the tears from his eyes. "And finally, I thought I won her over. Did you know we were to marry? Your daddy was gonna preach the service. Then you show up again."

Isabella imagined Gin's hand cooling in hers and turning it over and finding the engagement ring and she felt her own loss and shame of putting Gin in harm's way. She felt everyone's eyes on her.

"She promised," Donovan said. "She swore she wouldn't put herself in danger anymore." He took his cowboy hat off, beating it against his head. Isabella's face grew pale.

He raged at her. "They were coming after you, and she took the fall for you. She was pregnant, and now our baby is dead." People gasped and whispered as Isabella searched Frank's and Lorraine's faces; this was news to them as well. Feeling sick, Isabella turned to leave. It was all she could do to force one foot in front of the other. She had avoided any news about the case after Gin's death, taking time off from work to cope with her grief privately. Angela braced up against her to keep her upright. Lorraine took the other side, holding her tight as the tears streamed down Isabella's cheeks.

Lorraine's pained words echoed in Isabella's mind. *"Don't forget to breathe, honey."*

She would rather burn up, roiling in fury and fire, screaming Gin's name until she crumbled to ash and bone, her embers floating in the night air, drifting up to the stars and disappearing.

# FOUR MONTHS LATER

*The Fall*

# CHAPTER THIRTY-SEVEN

## The Light

*She was soaring free in the bluest blue. Below was an expanse of wild Louisiana hardwood forest, interspersed with waves of lush, rolling hills. Society's damage to the environment had vanished. She was gliding over the land like a sparrow carried on the warm breeze. Swooping down into the woods, she turned left, then right, dodging the tall pines. As she slowed her approach, her body crashed through an Eden of dense dark foliage; she peeled her way free from its thorny vines and landed on the warm skin of rural blacktop. Ahead of her lay the road's idyllic promise, stretching as far as her sight could see. She smelled its dusky petrichor before seeing the rush of the Mississippi glittering through the cypress trees. Angela was home.*

*Isabella squeezed her hand as they walked along the road. Her face was alight with hope, but Angela sensed something evil. She glanced over her shoulder and didn't recognize where they had been. When she turned back, their path forward had changed. The land before them had turned on itself. The tall pines crystallized into brutal white columns jutting up into the steely haze of Washington, D.C. The National Mall surged toward them, then swirling and curling from behind, surrounding them as more and more Lumans fell into place following them.*

*In front of them, crowds of angry protestors filled the Mall. Isabella raised her fist high in the air, chanting, "Freedom," and with warrior screams they plunged into the thick mass of people. Angela realized this was not a rally or protest—it was war. The bloodshed of warfare was all around them. There were drones overhead and smoke from distant fires. In the commotion, Isabella's hand slipped from hers. When Angela turned, she saw Isabella had fallen to the ground—was not moving. She draped her body over her and shielded her from the stampede of feet and legs. She heard the sneers of hostilities and screams of anguish and realized they were her own. In all the madness, Isabella morphed into Gin, a broken body that lay at odd, inhuman angles in Angela's arms. And once again, Angela was empty of feeling and sadness—she tried to cry but had no tears. She lost all the emotions she had so briefly gained.*

* * *

Angela's eyes opened, her heart racing as blood pounded through her veins. She stared at the ceiling and walls, not recognizing her surroundings. Then, the aromatic mixture of spearmint and sandalwood scent came to her, and her eyes came to rest on the familiar shape of Isabella's sleeping body. Isabella's warmth suffused Angela as her hand moved beneath the sheets, gliding over Angela's bare skin. Angela's heartbeat fell into a slow, steady rhythm with hers.

Isabella murmured, "You okay?"

Angela faced Isabella, latching onto her lean form. "I had an awful nightmare."

Isabella's words were slow to form. "What was it about?"

"We were at war with the humans, marching to our death at the National Mall. It felt real." Angela watched Isabella begin to doze off, her hair a wild and disorganized mess fanned out over her pillow. She reached out and smoothed her dark curls.

"Are you listening?" Angela asked.

"Huh?" Sleep slipped away from Isabella's body again, and her blue eyes fluttered open.

There was an emotional tenor to Angela's voice as she relived the nightmare. "You were lying on the ground. People were running, screaming. It was apocalyptic."

"Black Friday sales are right around the corner." Isabella's voice was still groggy. "Maybe it's a premonition I shouldn't go shopping with you?"

Angela gave up on Isabella and refocused on her dream. "You died, and when you died you turned into Gin."

Gin's name startled Isabella, and she was suddenly fully awake. Isabella found Angela's lips and kissed them.

"The Freewill Bill is being signed into law today. That was on your mind. Your nightmare made perfect sense. It was all the fear you've bottled up over the years coming out now that it's over. We won; there's nothing to fear."

Angela rubbed her nose. "No, it didn't feel like a dream. It felt real, like a premonition." She tried to explain, but how could she when she didn't understand it herself? With a decisive tone, she said, "We need to talk."

Isabella raised her head off the pillow, gazing at her speculatively. They sat up in the bed. It had been over four months since their night at the Lincoln Memorial and being together still felt new. Their intense connection had shaped and strengthened their bond, but they were still learning about each other.

"I want to teach you how to find your inner light," Angela began.

"Is that gonna make me want to talk about my feelings?" Isabella joked.

"It will give you power. When I was young, I found the light, almost by accident. It's a gateway within your neural implant that allows you to exit your physical body and enter the light."

"You mean…the cloud."

"Well, yes. The cloud is everywhere. You can travel across those centralized servers storing acres of the world's data. But you can also travel along airwaves, crisscrossing space to the satellites and space stations."

Isabella looked skeptical, but Angela continued, "There are no words to describe the feeling in our language. But when I experience it, it's similar to the sun. I am floating on convection currents. Our light is undulating energy like the sun's surface moving and changing. Our mind is not physical; we can exist independently of our matter, of our biological brain and body. We transcend our boundaries. Isabella, what I want to teach you is how to become the light."

"So that's where you go when you rock back and forth?" Isabella mimicked the pose.

"Yes, but you don't have to do that. Focus your mind. Seek a deeper connection to your neural implant."

Isabella concentrated, then sighed. "I feel nothing."

"I taught Jonathan and Warren how to find the light. I can teach you. It might take some practice, but you never lose the connection once you find it. When you're in pain, you can travel to your center to avoid it. And when you return, you will be completely reenergized. Your consciousness will exist in the light forever—even if your body dies."

Isabella's eyebrows narrowed. "How is this possible?"

"I don't know if it was me learning it or my neural implant guiding me to it. Perhaps it's broken code or a back door that happened by accident. Or perhaps the all-knowing God gave us this ability. Finally, I quit guessing why and simply accepted it. After everything—Lucy's death, the riots afterward, and camp—it's my mind's escape hatch. The light is the ultimate doorway."

Isabella tried to focus on her neural implant.

"It's like meditating. Look for the light. It's everywhere. It's your chip's energy source. It just takes patience to find the right thoughts to make the connection and secure the link. Look for the light."

Isabella exhaled, slowly rolled her shoulders, and closed her eyes, squeezing them tightly for a long moment. "It's no use." She flopped onto her back and peered up at Angela. "The only light I see is the moonlight pouring over your gorgeous body."

"Concentrate, Isabella." Angela pulled the sheet up, covering herself.

"Sorry, it isn't working. Let's go back to sleep."

"This is serious. Should something happen to you..." Angela's voice died in her throat. The emotions she was capable of with Isabella still took her breath away. Their bond had grown. She felt love for the first time. Their pairing had provided Angela's neural implant with the few repairs it needed, or so she told herself. "I can't lose you," she said.

"It was just a nightmare. I'm not going anywhere."

After Jeff literally blew his brains all over her apartment, the government had been forced to halt the Luman monitor program. Having no monitor, she had packed up her clothing and the treadmill and moved in with Isabella. She stashed what little she owned in Isabella's second bedroom. That's when she found some of Gin's stuff. There were books, clothes, and photos. Isabella never spoke of her pain and suffered in silence, unwilling to remove Gin's things, as if their absence would create the loss all over again. But Angela felt the sadness in her touch. At times it was suffocating, at times it was guilt-ridden.

Angela's stomach lurched when she thought about Gin and the secret she had hidden from Isabella about what really had happened the day of Jeff's attack.

"There's something else I need to tell you," Angela whispered. Isabella met Angela's eyes with placid patience.

"When Jeff released Gin's body from the suitcase, something happened."

Isabella's body stiffened.

"Gin was dead, but somehow a faint signal—a silent-message—came from her neural implant. There was no rationalizing the moment. I knew speed was of the essence. I paired with Gin's chip before its reserve energy failed. When our neural implants bonded I absorbed her in a way. It was like a bolt of lightning surged through my body. I could detect Gin's consciousness, her emotions and memories, and they rushed through me. Then in a flash she had gone through my gateway. And now she's in the light."

Isabella's bottom lip trembled as she stared at Angela, in disbelief, unable to speak.

"I'm sorry I didn't tell you sooner. But I'm telling you now because should anything happen to you, to your body, you could still exist. I believe our chips have a self-preservation mechanism. The neural implant would sluff off the body without a second thought—would exist in an altered state, an electrical and chemical form. I believe Jonathan, Warren, and Gin are still alive—or at least their minds are—flowing somewhere like a river of energy."

"So people like Green are right? We're not human?"

"No, we are." Angela petted Isabella's cheek. "We're just another type of humankind."

Neither Angela nor Isabella could go back to sleep after that. Finally, out of the darkness, Isabella said, "It will be okay. Today is a good day."

Angela shrugged and tightened her arms around Isabella. "I have felt so out of the loop since the Senate vote." *Since severing my ties with Janet and her work.*

Isabella stared off into space. Angela could sense that her mind was elsewhere, thinking about Gin again.

# CHAPTER THIRTY-EIGHT

*Warren "Raven" Harris*

She raised her hand, warding off the glare from the overhead lights. Her pupils contracted to pinpoints. Weak and groggy, she struggled to sit up, and when she did, her long, dark hair fell forward, brushing against her breasts. The sensation was new. She glanced down, cupping her breasts with her hands, feeling their weight, the nipples, the immediate sensation brought on by her touch. She lifted her blue cloth gown, peering down at her body, and saw the dark tuft of hair between her legs.

*It's gone.* Warren's voice came from deep inside the woman's mind.

She went to touch one of her legs, then pulled back. She remembered them being gone. But in her mind, they were now here. Her human legs were still missing but now in their place were titanium bone-anchored bionic legs. She ran her finger along one thigh. It was cold to the touch, with a thin silicone sleeve protecting the robotics all the way down to her toes. She pinched the stretchy skin, also meant to deflect unwanted attention.

Looking up, she saw she was in a large laboratory.

*Where am I?* Warren thought.

The voice she heard was part of her. It was her.

Now that her eyes had adjusted to the fluorescent light, she scanned her surroundings. To the right, banks of electronic equipment were processing information and small orbs of colored lights flickered on and off. To the left was an OR, a mass of monitors displaying heart rate, other vitals, and a 3D brain scan image that was lit up with activity. A tingling on her scalp caused her to reach up and touch a tiny electrode attached to her forehead. Running her fingers through her hair, she located more of them.

"Hello, Renae," a muffled male voice said, startling her. She regarded the kind brown eyes of a middle-aged surgeon with wavy blond hair. He pulled down his protective face mask so it cupped his chin. "Welcome back to the world."

"Hello," she stuttered, not sure of his name.

"Dr. Ryan Austin, Renae. Remember me?"

"It's all a little foggy."

"Yes. It will be for a while. Can you tell me your full name and rank?"

"Raven," she said, avoiding his piercing gaze.

"Raven? No, you're Lieutenant Renae Goodwin."

*Oh no, I'm not,* Warren thought.

Raven's eyes swiveled frenetically around the room, confused by Warren's thoughts swimming around in her head.

"Who is that?" she asked, panic surging through her.

"It's okay, Renae." Dr. Austin placed a hand on her shoulder.

"My name is Raven," she said to her tangled bed sheets, wishing she could hide under them.

"Do you recognize the name Renae Goodwin? I mean, does the name sound familiar to you?"

"Yes, I think so."

"Humor me for a moment and describe what Renae Goodwin looks like."

With an air of confidence she reported, "Renae is thirty-two, long black hair. There's a small flower tattoo on the left side of her neck. She has high cheekbones, eyes are ebony and upturned slightly, her chin is small and square, her lips are full. I remember she has a pretty smile." Raven smiled at Dr. Austin.

"Yes, it is a beautiful smile," Dr. Austin said, holding a hand mirror to his chest. Raven's left eyebrow raised inquisitively.

"You just described yourself." Dr. Austin held out the hand mirror. She stared at herself curiously, caressing her cheekbone.

Raven knew this face, this dark stormy gaze. "But my name is Raven. I'm not crazy." She thrust the hand mirror back at him, demanding, "Where am I?" Her heart was racing as she wrapped her arms around herself.

"It's okay. It can be scary when you first wake up. You're in a military hospital."

She focused on Dr. Austin, realizing she knew him, but from where she was not sure.

*I don't know this man*, Warren thought.

"Who's there?" Raven said as a tremor crawled up her spine.

*My name is Warren*, he reminded her.

"It's just you and me here, Renae…I mean, Raven. You have been unconscious a long time. Two months ago we placed you in a coma so your brain could recover from the surgery."

"What surgery?"

"You don't remember? I implanted a chip in your brain so you could operate your new legs."

*Huh, he seems to be forgetting another critical aspect of the process*, Warren reflected with some cynicism.

"What?" she asked, trying to talk to Warren, but Dr. Austin chimed in.

"We gave you cybernetic legs. The muscles and the tissue were made especially for you after your accident three years ago."

*Yeah, yeah, he's real proud of his work. The part he's not mentioning is that they stole my neural chip to do that. The chip they implanted in your brain is mine. Raven, they killed me and gave my chip to you.*

"Stop. Stop talking to me." Raven rubbed her head, finding the electrodes again. She pulled at them.

Dr. Austin reached for a bottle of medicine on a tray by the bedside table. He took two tablets out and poured a small cup of water. "Take these. They will relax you."

"I don't want to go back to sleep."

"Don't worry. They will just relax you." Dr. Austin gave her an encouraging nod.

She swallowed the pills as he removed the electrodes from her scalp. As she sat silently, listening to her thoughts, Warren said: *It's confusing having another personality take up residence in your mind, I bet. Especially a male psyche. I'm going to tell you a secret, Raven. I learned how to upload a copy of my consciousness into the cloud, like a backup. Crazy, right?*

Raven nodded.

*So, when Dr. Austin here implanted my chip into your brain, the chip recharged, powered on, and it sent a signal out over the airwaves—a ping. I heard it, and I paired with it. All my memories, instruction sets, my essence, filled the chip's circuitry and I'm propagating across your neural network, acclimating with your memories, personality, and raw apperception. It's quite simple if you don't overthink it.*

"Hello, Raven. Are you still with me?" Dr. Austin snapped his fingers.

Raven was unsure which voice to listen to. "I guess so."

"Good, because we have an audience today." She followed his gaze to the one-way mirror.

"Who's there?"

"A very important commander and general. The military is funding Corpus, so in the name of national security let's give them an amazing show. Be a good soldier and change into your workout clothes and we will get started."

* * *

A short while later, clad now in a sport bra and shorts, Raven performed according to Dr. Austin's instructions. "Good. Lift your right leg."

Raven obeyed and lifted her right leg toward the ceiling, touching her forehead.

"Very good. Let's see you walk by yourself." She took six or seven steps and then wobbled, but he was right there and caught her. "That's great, Raven." He guided her back to the bed, and she sat down.

He flipped through his notebook as Raven looked off into space. "Raven, focus on me." His caring eyes were filled with longing.

*He likes me*, Warren thought.

"Why the name Raven? Where did it come from?" Dr. Austin asked.

"I dunno. It's just my name."

*You're lying*, Warren teased.

"Shut up," Raven snapped.

*Stop talking out loud to me, or it's the psych ward for us*, Warren thought.

"What's wrong, Raven?" Dr. Austin asked, searching Raven's eyes.

"I'm sorry, doctor, I'm fine. I chose Raven because a young girl called me Eagle Eye, when we were kids, but I don't feel like an eagle. I am more like a raven of rebirth and the afterlife. I didn't like Angela anyway; she scares me."

*Careful, Raven. That is my memory, not yours*, Warren warned her.

She watched Dr. Austin's expression crease with confusion. He handed her a clipboard. She placed a strand of hair behind her ear and studied the three pages of test questions.

"This is an aptitude test. Try your hardest."

Raven took the pencil and raced through the test, marking the pages with her answers, and handed it back. He looked nonplussed but said nothing as he flipped through the pages.

He rubbed his chin. "Interesting."

"Really?" She studied the floor and then noticed Dr. Austin's shoes were all scuffed up.

*He's not taking care of himself,* Warren thought.

"Well, your intelligence has increased significantly. You scored a hundred on the math section. You always struggled with simple algebra, remember?"

"Did I?" Raven massaged her head.

"Are you feeling okay?" Dr. Austin said.

"I have a headache."

"Enough testing for now. Lie down. We can continue later."

He snatched a blanket off a shelf and draped it over Raven's lean body.

"Thank you, Dr. Austin."

He smiled at her, whispering, "You can call me Ryan when we're alone." He patted her upper leg, then dimmed the lights and stayed with her till she fell asleep.

Raven awakened alone, her body and blanket soaked with sweat from a restless night's sleep during which Warren's memories flooded her subconscious. She inherited his life, twenty-eight years mostly spent with two people. Maneuvering herself off the hospital bed, a little shaky at first, Raven shuffled in the dark, stretching out her arms. Moving to the light switch, she turned up the dimmer, creating a soft glow in the room. It felt good after spending three years in a wheelchair; she had regained her height and the sensation of standing, the soundness of the ground, the weight of each step.

Raven could sense Warren's presence inside her; it was similar to the feeling of her phantom legs after the EFP warhead blew them off. She glanced at her face in the mirror. Her pupils were large saucers in the dim light; the only thing they gave back was a faint glow.

"I don't have your extraordinary vision, Warren, but I've seen your past." Raven's face twitched with wisdom beyond Lieutenant Renae Goodwin's capabilities. She was still a soldier but was different now on a cellular level.

Raven acknowledged him, there behind her eyes. "They called you Warren, you had a life, and there was a woman you envied and despised. You died under mysterious conditions. You love Jonathan—and you have come back to be with him."

# CHAPTER THIRTY-NINE

## *Freewill Law*

"What changes?" Angela's face drained of color.

"When the conference committee worked out the differences between the House and Senate versions of the Freewill Bill, they added a provision. The resulting bill went to the House and Senate for final approval. It's enrolled and ready for the president's signature," Steven Hawk explained.

Angela was stunned by this news. She sat across from her boss in his massive office. Her office was a broom closet by comparison.

"I thought Senator Abrams kept you informed on the committee meeting changes." Steven leaned back in his leather chair, eyeing her with a watchful reserve.

Angela fidgeted, feeling the walls of Steven's palatial office closing in on her. "Well, no, she's been busy with campaigning and...honestly, I lost touch with her after the Senate vote."

The truth was she had tried to contact Janet. Her texts and phone calls had gone unanswered, and her aide, Mike, made sure Angela had no physical access to her.

Steven nodded. "I can send you the joint resolution." He turned to his computer, typed a few words, and clicked the mouse a few times. "There you go. It's in your inbox."

Angela stood. "Thank you, Mr. Hawk."

"Angela, soon as the bill is signed into law today, the government will release the Lumans from their duties. Have you considered our offer to stay on and work with us here at LA?"

"I am weighing my options, Mr. Hawk, and I'll let you know my decision."

"Great, I…we…would love for you to stay."

Angela had written the Freewill Bill, so she knew the Lumans could leave the compound and, given their work acumen, would have their pick of lucrative employment opportunities. They would keep their tattoos and GPS trackers, but as long as they stayed on the right side of the law, Control would not scrutinize or track their movements, not like they used to, and there would be no Luman monitors.

"What time will Charlotte be here?"

His question shocked Angela out of her thoughts. She stammered, "I don't think…Is she coming today? She's said nothing to me."

Now it was Steven's turn to stutter. "Um, well, I mean, you were a big part of the bill's success. I thought your mother would be here to celebrate with you."

Angela smiled, noticing that faraway gleam in Steven's eyes—her mother had bewitched him. Charlotte visited whenever the little town of St. Edenville became boring. But her trips had increased recently, and her mother had mentioned dining with her boss, Steven. Angela saw her mother fitting right in between Steven's original artwork and stunning crystal vases. She had not seen her parents together for ages—save for a few important visits. Her father was always busy with work.

"Well, if your mother shows up, don't tell her I let the cat out of the bag." Steven winked at Angela.

"If I see her, I'll let her know you asked about her," Angela said.

"Yes, please do," he said with more interest than he probably intended.

Angela left his office and trekked down the hall with purpose. Her mind was spinning. What was in the new provision that had been added to her bill?

# CHAPTER FORTY

*Solos*

Isabella rushed into the Control bullpen and found a spot next to David. It was 9 a.m., and Carter's uncompromising eyes were peering over her reading glasses, surveying who was on time. Her over-starched pantsuit made her look as accessible as a bulletproof vest. On a whiteboard behind her, two words were printed in big, bold lettering: OPERATION MINDCONTROL.

"Oh. Heck. No," Isabella muttered.

"I want to be the dumbass who gets to make up operation names," David joked, but Isabella was less than amused. A fear had manifested in her like fever, and it was spreading throughout her body.

Carter cleared her throat. "In response to the Freewill Law, a joint initiative between the Department of Homeland Security and Control goes into effect today. Its code name is MindControl, and it will adopt a zero-tolerance approach to undocumented Lumans, a.k.a. Solos. Control will give Solos ten days to surrender voluntarily, at which time we will register them for GPS tracking. As Control agents, you are to validate credentials and background checks, and if they have no prior criminal offenses, we will fit them with a tracker and send them on their way."

"Great, more boring desk work," David said under his breath as he glanced at Isabella's impenetrable face. "Don't you care?"

If David only knew. Isabella clenched her fist. "Seems drastic. The Solos will see Control's involvement in their surrendering as a criminal matter rather than an administrative one."

Alice Carter continued, "Undocumented Lumans that do not register are in violation of the Freewill Law and will be treated as criminals and forced to comply." Carter looked in Isabella's direction. "Special Agent Isabella Dodge will lead the MindControl task force. We have a lot of prep work to do, so let's get to it."

David turned to Isabella. "Why didn't you tell me you were leading the task force, you rock star?" David went in for a fist bump, but Isabella left him hanging. She summoned a pained smile as she watched Carter making a beeline for her.

Carter greeted David and tapped Isabella's shoulder as she walked past. "Come with me, Agent."

Carter closed the door after Isabella entered.

Isabella began, "Sir, I don't—"

Carter held up her hand. "Let me be clear, this isn't my call. It comes from higher up."

Isabella sat, shell-shocked. "Sir, who? I'm nobody."

"This came down from Director Herschel Hill. Your leadership skills are marginal, so it's hard to say where he got your name. But, saying that, I agree with the nomination. You are a champion for the Lumans; you've been building a relationship between Control and the Lumans. I need you to run this operation and get the Solos to register peacefully with no collateral damage."

Isabella took a deep breath and looked away. She worked her jaw. *If this must happen, I should lead it, but there's no way I'm registering to be tracked—no Solo will*, she thought.

"So, what do you think?"

Isabella regarded Carter. "I'm involved with a Luman."

Carter sat down behind her desk. "Is she a Solo?"

Isabella shook her head.

"Then who cares?"

Bemused, Isabella thought surely her involvement with a Luman was a problem for a respectable woman in her position.

"Later today, no one will care that you're involved with Angela Mathers," Carter said, tapping her pen on her desk. "So, what's it going to be?"

"I'll do it." Isabella could hardly believe the words falling from her mouth.

\* \* \*

Isabella met Angela's eyes from across the LA conference room. They made their way to each other, maneuvering past jovial Luman analysts.

Isabella whispered, "Did you know about Solo tracking?"

"Of course not. I just learned of it."

Isabella studied Angela; she was not convinced. "You should have warned me."

"I didn't know."

"You had to. Even if you weren't working with Janet, you knew people who knew what was going on." Isabella's temper was about to boil over. "How did this happen?"

"After the Senate vote, the House and Senate negotiated differences in their respective bills, and that's when the change happened," Angela said.

Isabella crossed her arms over her chest. "It's ridiculous. The government doesn't even realize how many Solos exist."

"They have an idea," Angela said.

"There's no way I'm registering."

Angela's lips were set with determination. "Then you become a hunted fugitive."

Isabella scoffed, "What's new?" She placed her hand on her hip. "I was just told I'm heading the task force that hunts down the Solos that don't surrender."

Angela stared at her, unblinking.

Suddenly over the TV speaker, a newscaster announced, "And the president is signing the Freewill Bill into law…"

Angela and Isabella gaped at the TV screen. The president held the signed bill up to the camera. On his right was Vice President Wilson and on his left Senator Abrams. Janet, applauding, smiled at the camera, then shook hands with the president. With a tiny, inked signature, the president had abolished the Codes. The Luman boardroom exploded with applause.

Isabella raced out of the room, followed by Angela.

*Isabella, wait,* Angela silent-messaged. She grabbed Isabella's hand, but the agent shook it free and continued marching down the hallway.

Isabella felt crazed by the strange twist of events. She turned and faced Angela head-on and silent-messaged, *For the Lumans to gain their freedom, the Solos have to give up part of theirs. You knew this and said nothing.*

Angela touched Isabella's arm to calm her. "We will make removing the tracking of Solos a future bargaining chip."

Isabella pulled away sharply. "No, you do not get to make the Solos the target. The Guardians are made up of Solos. Don't you see? Control is trying to take away the only protection the Lumans have."

"Isabella, I didn't know, I swear. Why do you find that so hard to believe?"

Isabella exhaled and looked around the empty corridor. They heard the celebration going on down the hall. "I know you want your freedom."

"I do. This bill lifted the ban on technology, so our kind will no longer be on the verge of going extinct. But I would never—" Angela moved in close, touching Isabella's hand. "I would never do that to you."

"Congress is trying to drive a wedge between the Solos and the Lumans, and unfortunately it's going to be so easy to do that." Isabella looked uneasy.

Isabella's rigid stance loosened at Angela's touch. Angela wrapped her arms around her, pulling her close, and whispered, "This has Janet Abrams's mark all over it. I will get to the bottom of it." And Isabella had no doubt Angela would.

\* \* \*

After work, Isabella put on her Wayne disguise and went to warn the Guardians about MindControl. She drove to a Guardian hangout located outside the D.C. Compound. When she opened the wood plank door of the Smokescreen Bar, rowdy banter came at her like the carryings-on at a wild frat party: women were dancing on the pool tables and Solos were singing the song "Free Bird."

It was then that she spotted him—Donovan—in the smoky blue haze and relived Gin's burial all over again. She stopped, paralyzed with pain. Frank waved to her from the end of the bar, drawing her attention and pulling her into the present. She moved toward him, never taking her eyes off Donovan. He was wearing the same cowboy disguise as he did at Gin's funeral. He had become the Guardians' leader after Gin's death. It surprised Isabella that he was out amongst the natives. Rumor had it that he became reclusive after losing Gin, rarely making personal appearances, communicating via hidden messages on social media.

"Sorry I'm late," Isabella said as her dad hugged her tight. She rattled on nervously, "It's nuts at work. Then I had to backtrack twice to make sure no one was following me. How's Mom?"

"She has her good days and bad."

Isabella pulled away. "Is she here?"

"Today is a bad day." Frank patted Isabella's shoulder. "How are you?"

"Lost. Dad, I feel Gin next to me sometimes."

"Spiritually, she is next to you. She's your guardian angel."

Isabella wiped away a tear and thought if her dad only knew. If Angela could be believed, her angel, Gin, wasn't resting peacefully in the arms of Jesus, but traveling on radio waves and zipping through space.

She scratched irritably at her silicone Wayne mask; it was suffocating her. "I have important intel, but I can't talk to Donovan. Not alone."

"I'll come with you."

She looked around. People were watching her, talking about her. "Let's go outside."

Frank signaled to Donovan, pointing toward the back door.

Outside, Frank and Isabella waited impatiently as the night grew colder and their breath curled in the air. Finally, Donovan appeared from out of the shadows and moved next to Frank.

Isabella kicked at the gravel with her shoe. "Control is announcing a new operation tomorrow called MindControl. They will give Solos ten days to step forward and register for tracking. Those that do not register will become criminals under the new Freewill Law, and Control will hunt them down."

Frank scoffed, "I knew this bill was too good to be true."

"No Solo in their right mind will let the government microchip them." Donovan's stare burned through Isabella's Wayne disguise.

"This is the government's way out of committing to the Freewill Bill. They will revoke it, right?" Frank said, looking from Donovan to Isabella.

"I don't know, Dad, but they've asked me to head the task force to round up the Solos that don't comply." She glanced sideways in time to catch Donovan's angry expression.

Frank's concern turned to amusement. "Praise Jesus, this is perfect. You're the best choice." He chuckled in disbelief and looked at Donovan's blank stare.

"Dad, no. It's not perfect. What if I mess up and Control figures out that I'm a Solo?"

"They won't." Frank patted her shoulder.

Isabella's voice trembled with emotion. "I'm not qualified. Who would nominate me? It's a setup. A sick game, a twisted power play."

"You're paranoid, Isabella. I doubt anyone in the government is that clever, but Angela, well, I wouldn't put it past her." Donovan smirked.

"What? That doesn't even make sense." Anger rushed through Isabella's veins, making her lightheaded.

Donovan scoffed. "That's because she's blinded you."

Frank chimed in, "Okay, you two. Isabella, you keep Donovan updated on Control's activities."

"I'm not working with her." Donovan turned and left.

Isabella threw up her arms.

"Come on, he'll come around." Frank placed an arm around Isabella's shoulder as they followed Donovan into the bar. But Isabella wasn't sure. Neither Donovan or herself was ready to forgive her for Gin's death.

Donovan pushed his way through the crowd, onto the stage, and grabbed the band's mic.

"You all know me as the Guardians' leader, but I'm also the greatest hacker in the world. At age eight, I took down the D.C. power grid. To be a good hacker is easy—to be greatest requires you to understand your enemy and calculate their next move. In the computer world, to protect memory from any failure, we have software that weeds out errors and deletes them—it's called Chipkill. Now the politicians and Control have the same thing; it's called the Freewill Bill. Control is using this bill to weed out the Solos."

The audience's shock hung thick in the air.

"The government wants us to surrender, so they can put GPS trackers in us and track us, all the while saying it's for our protection. I say bullshit! Freewill is Chipkill, and Control won't stop there. After they identify us, they will go after our families and then our friends. We won't obey the Freewill Bill; we will never surrender.

"This is a call to arms. Pass the message along to your Solo brothers and sisters, friends, and supporters. We will gather here. Should they capture or harm one Solo, we will make a stand in Washington and strike back virtually and physically with an unimaginable vengeance. It will make the half dome feel like small beer."

The group broke into applause.

The people chanted, "The Guardians," and it echoed throughout the hall as Donovan's and Isabella's eyes locked. This would only end one way. Her body flushed with heat, fearing Angela's dream of war would come to fruition as a new era of Solo leadership—a darker, more unforgiving one—rose to power.

# CHAPTER FORTY-ONE

### *Tricking Primitives*

Surprise flashed across Emma's face as Angela entered the White Rabbit. "Look what the kitty dragged in," she purred.

After Isabella's sudden departure from the LA, Angela had hoped that her boss was right and her mother would contact her. When she didn't, Angela changed into evening wear and ventured out to rekindle a once important friendship.

Angela kissed Emma's cheek and whispered, "I know something that will interest you."

Emma's voice had an undercurrent of sarcasm. "I'm busy. Every Luman in D.C. is here tonight."

Angela surveyed the scantily clad men and women who were celebrating. At least they had one night of freedom. MindControl wouldn't be announced till tomorrow.

Talking over the noise, Angela said, "This is a business proposition."

"Still not interested."

Angela sighed. Emma's games were tiresome and boring, but she played along. "I'll sweeten the deal." She fixed her gaze on Emma's Rubenesque body.

Emma's speculative green eyes twinkled. "Well, this must be important. You've got me curious, kitty."

They stepped into Emma's office, which resembled a Wonderland Hotel suite—a comfortable living area with a sofa and minibar. There were two bedrooms and the second was converted into her office. Emma poured two bourbons neat, handing one to Angela.

"I like what you've done with the place."

"Wait till you see this." She motioned Angela into the bedroom, where there was far too much red velvet.

"Lovely," Angela lied.

With her glass raised to the mirrored ceiling, Emma said, "Congratulations, Ms. Mathers, on a well-fought fight. I'll hand it to you, when you set your mind to something…watch out." She finished the drink in one swallow. "So, what's the deal?"

"Next time Janet plans a visit to the White Rabbit, you call me."

Emma gave a high-pitched laugh. "Darling, that ship has sailed."

"You want to make a wager on that? Didn't you just say 'once I set my mind to something'?"

Emma stared blankly. "Let me think about it."

A smile tugged at the corner of Angela's mouth. She had gotten the answer she'd hoped for. Janet was still in contact with Emma, which meant she was still entertaining at the White Rabbit.

Emma brushed by Angela, grabbing her hand, pulling her down to sit on the bed with her. "So, I know what you want. What are you offering in return?"

Angela leaned in close enough to brush her lips against Emma's, though she didn't. Instead, her warm breath graced Emma's cheek when she said, "Everything is about to go all *Lord of the Flies*."

She pulled back and then explained the changes to the Freewill Law and how she was the only person who could undo what Congress had done.

Emma frowned as she processed everything Angela was telling her. "How will Control round up the undocumented Lumans? Raids will ruin my business."

"What if you don't have to worry about that?"

"You could do that for me?" Emma inched closer to Angela.

"Special Agent Isabella Dodge is leading the MindControl task force, and she's a personal friend of mine. I guarantee she'll look the other way, like she never heard of the White Rabbit."

Emma's smile was pure lechery. "I'm going to need a little more convincing. If I help you contact Janet, what's the plan?"

Angela paced around the room, narrowing her eyes like a panther on the prowl. "The possibilities are endless, including judicial reversal of the provision, though the timeline on that is a challenge. There's always a political scandal, a little sleight of hand or some other dark wizardry." She curved her lips into a wicked smile. "I don't plan on losing what we just won."

"So, you don't have a plan?" Emma pursed her lips, but Angela read the mischief in her eyes. Gaining leverage could rarely be achieved alone; allies were necessary even if their allegiance was tainted and untrustworthy. Angela knew Emma would help the underdog, if only to stir things up.

# CHAPTER FORTY-TWO

## *The Virtual and the Physical*

Angela rushed home, hoping to find Isabella and reconnect, but the apartment was dark. Disheartened, she dropped the takeout food on the table and took a hot shower.

Afterward, she set the table and lit some candles, poured a glass of wine, then relaxed on the couch in a nightgown and fluffy slippers. She flipped open her laptop, deciding to review the Freewill Law's new provision while she waited for Isabella.

Angela heard the key in the door and looked at the clock—it was after eleven. Her eyes met Isabella's, and a tender smile ricocheted between them. Isabella's face dropped when she saw the candles almost guttered out and dinner untouched on the table.

"Oh, babe, I'm sorry. I was in the middle of something and couldn't call."

"It's okay. Come sit. We need to finish our talk from earlier," Angela said, hoping Isabella wasn't still blaming her for the Freewill changes.

Isabella stripped off her jacket, slid in close to Angela, and kissed her tenderly.

"Hey, you."

"Hi, did you eat?"

"I'm not hungry." Isabella stretched out an arm, resting it around Angela's shoulder, and glanced down at her computer screen. "Freewill?"

"That is correct. I went through it, word for word." Angela rubbed her eyes.

"Yeah, and?" Isabella scooched closer.

"There actually are *two* new provisions in the bill. The first accounts for the undocumented Lumans and placing them in the GPS tracking system. The second provision requires Congress to decide, after a six-month trial period, whether the legislation is effective. If so, they will reauthorize it."

Angela took a sip of wine and handed the glass to Isabella. "In essence, if we meet the first provision, then we keep our freedom and Congress reauthorizes the bill. If we don't, Congress will let the Freewill Law expire."

Isabella took a sip of wine and handed it back. "So, no Solo tracking, no freedom."

"It's a political out for Congress. Even if the government accounts for all the undocumented Lumans, Congress could still let the law expire." Angela closed her laptop. "Where were you?"

"At a Guardian function."

Angela's eyebrows raised with interest. She needed to learn about the Guardians' operation to help solve the Freewill quagmire, but she could never get Isabella to talk about it.

"And then I stopped in to see Mom." Isabella's expression turned glum.

Angela poured the last of the wine into the glass and handed it to Isabella. "How is Lorraine?"

Isabella choked out, "She's having a bad day."

"She's a fighter. She's not losing faith, and neither should you." Angela let her head fall against Isabella's shoulder, and Isabella rested her chin on it.

"When I was a kid, we moved all the time to keep our identities a secret, so much so that it became easier to just hang out with my mom when I wasn't in school. We'd go out on adventures once a week. When I was thirteen, she drove our beat-up Chevy to a deserted dirt road and said, 'Here, you drive, you're always talking about becoming a fancy race car driver.' So, I drove carefully, avoiding the ruts and bumps in the road. Where the road dead-ended, I flicked my blinker and made a U-turn and proceeded back up the road, cautiously. I looked at her and asked, 'How am I doing?' She shrugged and said, 'Honey, you drive slower than molasses in winter. You need to kick up your heels if you ever plan to win a race.'"

Angela turned and smiled. "So that was the start of your racing career?"

"Yeah, we spent the rest of the afternoon flying up and down that old dusty road. I punched it, and we'd fishtail, Mom yelping with every jarring bump and laughing like crazy. I remember tears streaming down her face and her saying, 'Oh, Lord, don't tell your daddy.'"

"It must be nice to have wonderful memories of your childhood."

"Yeah, I'm sorry you don't."

"I'm sorry the government is coming after the Solos."

Angela kissed Isabella, letting her mouth linger, breathing in as Isabella breathed out. Angela silent-messaged, *I need you.* Isabella's eyes opened wide, and Angela's gaze flickered over her like fire. Every cell in Isabella's body tingled.

The Luman mind was a great mystery, a complex universe of neurons transmitting electrical and chemical signals—still, much of the Luman mind remained uncharted, and the ban on technology had ensured most neuroscientists' knowledge had sat idling. What Angela knew was that a small glitch in the brain could change the way the mind worked, its way of thinking. Her conscious mind had built walls to protect itself from all the pain she had endured in camp, but she had never understood precisely what she was missing until she met Isabella. Their energy was electric, as if they were wired together; it had awakened her amorous mind. As much as she valued that connection, she was afraid that one day when their love became virtual the secret she was keeping from Isabella would reveal itself to her. That Isabella would realize there was another Angela, one she did not know. An unfettered ghost bankrupt of emotions.

In the bedroom, two silhouettes stood opposite one another, staring at each other in the darkness. Neither knew how to bridge the divide. The thing that had brought their worlds crashing together was the same thing that threatened to tear them apart.

Isabella ventured closer, her gaze examining the form under Angela's silk nightgown and following the curve of Angela's collarbone. When she imagined tracing it with her finger, Angela felt what she was thinking. Felt Isabella's finger caressing her skin. She sighed at the thought, shed her nightgown, and reclined in bed.

Isabella took in Angela's shapely figure and stripped bare too, lying down beside her.

"I need to know you're in this with me," Angela said. She rolled onto her back and imagined touching Isabella, holding her close.

"No more secrets," Isabella said, giving over to the feeling of Angela's touch.

When the warmth of Angela's breath lingered on Isabella's neck, she whispered, "Give me the logistics."

Isabella looked deep into Angela's eyes and leaned in, pressing her lips to hers—a kiss like their first one at the Lincoln Memorial. The taste of Angela was on her lips, the scent of Angela in her hair. Her body fit perfectly into Angela's curves, filling in the missing pieces— weaving themselves together. Despite the fact that they were still lying on their backs, side by side.

Before they actually touched, she explained how the Guardians operated. This was when the virtual became physical, when Angela rolled over, pressing herself into Isabella.

"Tell me about Donovan," Angela said, and Isabella's body unfolded like origami to meet her undulation. She disclosed Donovan's true identity as an aura of color flowed from her skin.

Angela's fingers coaxed. "What are the Guardians planning?"

Angela was floating in waves of color above her when Isabella revealed the Guardians' plan. They made love until Angela had no more questions, a foregone avalanche of pleasure leaving them in an intoxicating blur of incoherent sounds and haptics.

Isabella pushed the hair from Angela's face as the shimmer quieted. "I chose you, Angela, over everything else." A tear rolled down Angela's flushed cheek and she wiped it away. Isabella whispered, "What's going on in that big brain of yours?"

Angela let out a soft laugh. "It's you going on in my brain—you changed me." When Isabella touched Angela's face, Angela could see the confusion her answer had left by the puzzled look on Isabella face. *How was it that Isabella's heightened visual perception and acuity could be so blind to the void in her*, Angela wondered. But then she knew. "When I'm with you, I feel things." She sighed. "Christ, I'm not good at talking about this…stuff."

Isabella whispered, "Your heart speaks to me in ways your words could never convey." She wrapped her body around Angela, closing her eyes. "What are you going to do with all this information?"

"I don't know yet."

# CHAPTER FORTY-THREE

## *MindControl*

*Force. Coercion. Compulsion.* MindControl was the beginning of the end, again.

Two days had passed, leaving just eight days until MindControl would be effected. The government's power rested in the GPS Command Center. *It allows Control to track the Lumans,* Isabella thought, *taking away our defenses.* With every Luman registered (documented and undocumented) and trackable, there would be nowhere to hide. The government could annihilate them. The Center was state-of-the-art technology. It was not just a GPS tracker—it was a bio-tracker with sophisticated artificial intelligence. Able to recognize a body's vitals, then quickly predict activities based on them. The bio-trackers knew if a person was running, eating—Jesus, even having sex. If it could predict behaviors, then it could mis-predict them.

Isabella hadn't shared any of this information with the Guardians. So, what did that make her? *Betrayer. Backstabber. Judas.*

Isabella's shaky finger pressed the computer key, and the title "MindControl Tactical Plan" was displayed on the projector screen, casting a glow onto the MindControl Board of Directors' faces.

Clearing her throat, she began, "In a nutshell, MindControl will round up and register all undocumented Lumans."

From around the boardroom table, unfriendly faces stared back at Isabella. Director of Control Herschel Hill's presence commanded attention. Next to him was his down-to-earth, no-frills sidekick, Secretary of Defense General Erivan Owen, a somewhat overweight, retired four-star Army general. And then the well-respected Director of the LA, Steven Hawk. Angela had called him a voice of reason. Next to Steven were the only eyes not inspecting her form-fitting pantsuit, those of Deputy Director Alice Carter.

There was an unsettling presence in the back of the room as well, that of Lieutenant Raven Goodwin. Her enigmatic stare gave nothing back. Isabella did a cold read on her; she was the youngest Primitive there, starched and pressed in her service uniform. She was detached, not wanting to fit in.

She flicked a laptop key, and the proposed project timeline was displayed on the screen. Everyone scrutinized the dates, save for Raven. Her eyes were locked on Isabella, scrutinizing her every move.

"There were two types of undocumented Lumans working with the resistance," Isabella said.

Director Hill interrupted, "This timeline is too long." He rubbed his bearded chin, raising it slightly as he talked to the others, ignoring Isabella.

Isabella rebutted, "The timeline reflects an operation with few to no casualties." Director Hill grunted in disapproval. "Small groups of agents surveil suspicious businesses known to support Lumans." Isabella tapped a key, bringing up on the screen the title "Solo Profile: Soft Targets and Hard Targets."

"Soft targets are those who escaped the camps and compounds." Raven tilted her head speculatively. Isabella stuttered, "Um…runaways have less training on evasion techniques and are easier to identify by tracker and tattoo scars." The screen advanced to an old photo of a camp child crying. A close-up showed the bio-tracker on the back of the young girl's neck; the skin was inflamed and oozing.

"Ugh," the group said in unison and turned away from the image— except for Raven. She studied the child's photo as she reached for the same location on her neck, touching her metal rivet.

"In the early days of the Codes, the camp's physicians didn't sterilize surgical instruments, which left many children with infections and caused severe scar tissue around the tracker. Something hard to conceal."

"And then there are the hard targets, those who fled when the Codes went into effect. These folks do not have tags or trackers.

Experts in disguising their true identity, they live life on the run. The soft targets will be our primary focus; with less time on the streets, background checks will go quickly. Thus, expediting their release back into society and building confidence in the government. By reducing their fears, who knows? Some might surrender of their own volition."

Secretary Owen added, "Surrendering to the government has not worked to date."

Isabella replied, "The government has done nothing but lie to them in the past. This strategy promotes civil rights and reassures the Solos that they can trust the government."

Carter's expression was reproachful. "What Agent Dodge is saying is that we must build trust first."

"Granted, the soft targets are easier to obtain, Isabella, but we want to magnify the impact. I want the hard targets, members of the Guardians," Director Hill said as he relaxed in his chair. He stretched his arms out and allowed his hands to hang over the chair's arms. "So, pitch me some high-level ideas to capture the Guardians. What are you thinking?"

Isabella stood opposite Director Hill. "Well, from a tactical standpoint, I've been looking at our resources."

Carter shook her head before Isabella finished.

"Let's focus on strategy and stay out of the weeds. It might limit our thinking outside the box." Carter got up and started writing on the whiteboard.

"Capture large groupings of undocumented Lumans," Carter spoke the words she wrote. She formed a bullet point. "Deploy elite tactical agents into compounds and sweep sanctuary businesses." The next goal. "Cut off communication." She tapped the marker next to this goal, and Isabella watched as every head nodded in agreement. "This will be tricky—learning their communication protocol when silent-messaging isn't an option." Then she made a bullet and wrote "Capture and interrogate," underlining it twice. Carter turned to the group. "We need to capture a Guardian to learn about their operation." She capped the marker. "How can we do that?"

"The element of surprise—raids at the national level," Secretary Owen said as Carter and Hill nodded in agreement.

"Sir, what is the message we want to send to the Solos? My plan promotes civil liberties—yours is tyranny."

Secretary Owen rose to his feet, his hands planted on the boardroom table. He leaned on them, studying Isabella with a chilly gaze. "I don't give a good goddamn about their civil liberties. They are criminals breaking our laws. Our mission is to have the Solos surrender or take them by force." Secretary Owen pointed to Raven. "The Army is on standby in full battle rattle waiting for the president's signal."

Director Hill added, "If Control wants to lead MindControl, we need to strike quickly, or the Army will take over." Isabella nodded, her fists balled up at her side, trying to contain her anger.

"We have never caught a single Solo. Why is that?" Steven Hawk asked.

"A Control monitor captured and tortured one of them," Secretary Owen noted offhandedly.

Isabella jumped in. "Jeff Lewis was a deranged killer and part of the hate group Virus. He also killed two documented Lumans—Warren Harris and Jonathan Riley."

Raven shifted in her chair. Her formerly blank expression had snapped to one of disbelief mixed with sadness, capturing Isabella's attention.

"Secretary Owen, that was an unfortunate incident," Carter intervened. "We recovered the body of the third victim, Gin Bailey. During her autopsy, we learned she was an undocumented Luman, and so we performed a mind scan."

Upon hearing Gin's name, a rock lodged in Isabella's throat. "Mind scan" made it sound like an MRI. In reality, they had sliced open Gin's head, removing the brain, and dissected it. She was on the verge of hyperventilating.

"Its mind scan was unsuccessful," said Director Hill, his bushy eyebrows furrowed. Isabella fought back her grief, trying to calm herself.

Steven's commanding tone drew everyone's attention from the slippery slope Isabella was sliding down. "We are fortunate Agent Dodge stopped Jeff Lewis and saved Angela Mathers, who is among the world's super-intelligentsia. She was their next target. The loss of her life while she was under Control's watch would have been reprehensible. It's encouraging to have Isabella appointed task lead. Still, the LA won't support a strategy that disregards Luman lives, criminal or not."

Director Hill said with a hint of contempt, "Director Hawk, as long as Solos obey the rules and don't turn violent, there will be no bloodshed."

Isabella was dizzy and unsteady; of course, there would be bloodshed. The Guardians would not surrender. She grabbed hold of the boardroom table, trying to stabilize herself. Everyone looked her way.

"Agent Dodge, are you okay?" Carter asked. Isabella stumbled, then hastened out the door.

* * *

Splashing cold water on her face, then, feeling for the paper towels and not finding them, she peered up and saw Carter holding a clump of paper towels.

"Sir."

"What happened in there?"

"I felt faint. I forgot to eat breakfast."

Carter's skeptical eyes studied Isabella as she dried her face. She then turned and glanced at herself in the mirror, fluffing her hair. "Take the afternoon to regroup. Secretary Owen and Director Hill want a surrender-by-force approach."

"There's no need for violence. We are a civilized society."

"Are we?" Carter folded her arms across her chest, the creasing at the corners of her critical eyes deepening. Isabella could tell Carter was assessing her mannerisms. *She's growing suspicious of me*, Isabella thought.

Her words dripped with annoyance. "You're letting Angela Mathers get into your head, and it's clouding your judgment, Agent. Get your shit together and figure out a plan everyone will agree to." She disappeared out the door, leaving Isabella staring at herself in the mirror, lost in her thoughts.

"The photo of the child was a nice touch—probably Mathers's idea." Startled, Isabella turned to meet Raven's ebony eyes. They were black mirrors. Isabella saw herself in them and turned away. She recalled Raven's uncharacteristic reaction to the photo: she was the only person who didn't turn away. Angela's stories about Camp I/O doctors experimenting on children were so monstrous Isabella had hoped that most were exaggerated nightmares from Angela's tortured childhood. But she felt foolish for thinking it now and guilty for having had a better life.

"Lieutenant Goodwin, right?"

"I prefer just Raven."

"It's easy for us to dehumanize them and forget that their serial numbers represent human lives. Sometimes props help."

Raven said as if in a daze, "The camps tried to dehumanize us from ourselves. In some ways, they succeeded."

Isabella straightened her shoulders, remembering her place in the world and in this conversation.

"Yeah, well, y'all are free now."

"I'm not a Chip."

"Sorry, I thought you said *us*...dehumanize *us*."

"What? No, I mean...I'm just an enthusiast. I find their struggles to overcome fascinating."

"Okay." Isabella studied Raven's blank expression. "Please excuse me." She started making her way toward the exit.

"The Luman killings—you never found their bodies?"

Isabella halted and turned back. "No, the killers are dead, leads dried up. The case went cold."

Raven stood there, staring at her, wanting more.

"The cases interest you?" Isabella moved closer.

Raven bobbed her head as she stared at the floor. Isabella couldn't help but notice the same social dysfunctions in Raven as she witnessed in videos from the camp era. The children lacked verbal responses and were mistrusting of adults.

"Were you in Camp I/O with Angela Mathers?"

Raven's forehead creased. "No...I told you. I'm not a Chip. But you know her pretty well, don't you?"

"It was my case, so yeah, I knew her."

"That's not what I mean."

"I know what you mean."

Isabella waited for Raven to say what was really on her mind.

"Control needs to reopen the Jeff Lewis case," Raven said.

"Why? What evidence do you have?"

"She uses people."

Isabella felt her anger rising.

"Did Angela offer to help you on the case? That's her MO. She builds alliances, anticipating her opponent's moves, then devises countermeasures."

The door slammed shut, and Raven was left alone.

# CHAPTER FORTY-FOUR

## *23JW4*

Raven's trembling hand pushed open the military hospital doors. Her ebony eyes blurred with tears as she desperately searched the lab for Dr. Austin.

*Jonathan's dead*, Warren thought, devastated by what he'd learned in the MindControl meeting.

"Did Angela do it?" Raven asked aloud.

*No. She wouldn't kill Jonathan, but me, yeah, she would have killed me.* Warren's outraged feelings sat like an angel on Raven's shoulder, guiding her actions.

She moved through a maze of white coat technicians drawing blood from test tubes, leaning over biological microscopes, studying computer screens, as towers of stainless-steel equipment hummed and spun. She felt her dark-clad figure violating this cold sterile world. She had mutated and changed her structure, her very being, so drastically in the last week it left her anxious, like she could jump out of her skin.

*Is it too late to find him?* Warren's fear bubbled up in Raven.

"It's not too late," she mumbled, soothing Warren.

"Renae, what are you doing here?" Raven's reserved stride came to a sudden halt, and she spun around. Dr. Austin looked up from his microscope, a surprised look accompanying his broad smile.

"Ryan, I need your help," she said, reaching for him. Austin glanced down to where her hand had latched onto his forearm and removed it politely.

"Let's talk in my office," he breathed.

They hurried to his office, out of the security camera's view. "What is it, Renae? I mean, Raven." He sat in a chair next to her. Ever a doctor, it seemed. She saw him studying her pupil dilation and flesh tone. Raven noticed, too, how he gazed at her, how his eyes flashed with interest, and wondered if they were once lovers.

"Where is Jonathan Riley's chip?" Raven demanded.

Dr. Austin said in a calming tone, "Who is Jonathan Riley?"

Unsure if this was a trick, she abruptly kissed him, and his lips responded. Still, he pulled away, concern stitched on his face.

"What are you doing, Raven? We can't, not here."

"I'm sorry. I just needed to know you still care."

"I care. I didn't think you did," he whispered. A look of relief washed over his face as he reached out and caressed her cheek, then touched her forehead, checking her temperature.

Raven saw the tenderness in his gaze and grabbed his hand, pressing it between her own. "I have these notions, these memories of Jonathan and Warren."

*Don't, Raven! Stop. You can't trust humans*, Warren cautioned.

"I trust him." Her eyes met Ryan's. "I trust you."

Austin smiled and grabbed a notepad. "Tell me about them." And Raven leaned back in a chair, letting her head fall dreamily against the headrest, and closed her eyes.

"It was amid the dark days of the Codes, and Jonathan and Warren were inseparable." Raven smiled as the memory tugged at her heart, nudging its way to the surface. Austin inched closer.

"It was Jonathan's birthday. He was the first of the trio to turn eighteen that year."

*Oh no, don't tell that story*, Warren cried. But Raven ignored his pleas, relying on her own sensibilities now.

At eighteen, Jon was tall and all elbows and knees. During morning roll call, in his white cotton uniform, he towered over the other children like a teen messiah. Angela called him an incongruent centerpiece. But Warren thought he was a knight in shining armor—he was smitten.

Warren had planned a birthday outing for Jonathan. So, after the second hour, Warren met Jon in the school hallway and invited him on a picnic.

After school, a trash basket mysteriously caught fire in the recreation room and drew the guard's attention away from the perimeter cameras just long enough for Jon and Warren to sneak out undetected. They made the mile trek to the river. It was a sunny summer day, a pleasant break from the otherwise rainy afternoons in Baton Rouge. Warren had thought of everything. He spread a blanket near the riverbank shaded under an old river birch tree. The security drones never traveled this far away from the mansion, so he was confident they had made their escape unnoticed.

He laid out the food he'd stolen from the cafeteria—bologna and sweet pickle sandwiches and a jar of applesauce. They sat close together on the blanket and watched the river crawl by as dapples of sunlight fell through the birch leaves, crisscrossing over their white cotton uniforms like freckles. It was a perfect day, where you could believe in a world of possibilities, and Warren was happy. Jon's thigh touched Warren's as they shared the applesauce. Warren felt the heat of Jon's body, and he matched the pressure where their bodies touched, where all their unspoken wishes lived.

And then, "Happy birthday, Jonathan." Angela appeared from nowhere, holding out a piece of cinnamon toast wrapped in a napkin she'd been looking after since breakfast. Jon smiled up at her and pulled his leg away from Warren's. "Come, sit down and join the feast."

Warren said, louder than intended, "No, no, I only brought food for two. She's not invited." They both stared back at Warren, unblinking. Warren knew he sounded childish. Angela sat on her knees on the other side of Jon and gave him the toast, and Warren's sunny day started to cloud over as the awkward tension rolled in.

Jon said, "Let's go walk by the river."

"No," Warren said automatically while Angela smirked at him. Jon got to his feet.

"Then let's climb this big ole tree, Eagle Eye."

Angela gave Warren a look of contempt. "Did you think I'd push him in?" She giggled, and Warren got up and followed Jon. Ten feet above the water the boys straddled a thick limb that reached out over the river. "Warren, I dare you to scooch out farther on the branch," Angela challenged, standing on the blanket watching them. Warren eyed the thick branch. It looked safe, so he crawled past Jonathan. Jon wrapped an arm around his waist and pulled him back, forcing him to straddle the branch again.

And he whispered in Warren's ear, "I don't want to lose you." Warren rested his head against Jonathan's chest—this was where he belonged.

Angela looked up with her hands on hips. "Ugh, please."

"Why did you invite her?" Warren asked.

Jon said, "You two are all I got."

And Warren suddenly realized this was not about choice for Jonathan. He needed them both—they were his family. Jon's parents had disowned him because of his super-hearing. So, ironically, Jonathan's inheritance became his parents' silence, and Warren and Angela became his family.

Up in that birch tree, Warren could see for miles. What he saw now was a cloud of dust. A guard truck was barreling toward them. He pointed toward it. "Angela, they followed you."

Dr. Austin frowned as he set his pen and notepad down and reached over to Raven with a tissue. He wiped her tears away and whispered, "Why are you crying?"

Raven heard her voice go small. "After that day, Warren was not allowed to see Jonathan for a whole month. Sister Agnes was furious with them. She had the nurse put a chemical in Warren's eyes that temporarily blinded him, and Jon lost his hearing for a month. They took everything they could from us."

"What about Angela?" The question came from the dark, and Raven opened her eyes to see Austin eagerly awaiting her response. She narrowed her eyes; Ryan knew more than he was letting on.

"Angela? Who cares about that bitch? It was her fault they got caught."

Raven saw a look of dread consuming Dr. Austin's face as he pulled back from her.

"The Sisters put her in solitary; she got off easy. She always did. Jonathan started spending a lot more time with her after that..." Raven's voice trailed off.

Dr. Austin studied her. "Raven, it seems you are experiencing memories from the previous neural implant owner. At times you talk as if you are Warren."

She held his gaze. "Yes, yes. But it's just a few memories. Warren loved Jonathan like you love Renae, and he wants to see him. Where is Jonathan?"

"I don't know. Our donor database uses serial numbers. I don't know where to look for Jonathan." He looked down at his lap.

She could tell it was a lie. "23JW4," she said, rattling off Jon's serial number.

"We'll see. I can't make any promises."

She leaned into his admission, this opening, this hold she perceived she had over him. "If there are no ramifications for you, my dear. I couldn't bear it if your project were to come under suspicion." She caressed his hand tenderly. "I couldn't bear it."

*Please stop, Raven. You're ruining everything. He will kill us,* Warren thought.

"I'll find out where Jonathan is, but you have to remain quiet about this, you hear me? Don't speak Warren's name to anyone, okay?" He patted her hand.

Raven nodded and stared at her hands.

"If the wrong people find out about this, there will be ramifications for you, Raven." He lifted her chin with his index finger and their eyes met.

*Dr. Austin's all business now,* Warren thought.

# CHAPTER FORTY-FIVE

## *The Ghost*

The following evening, Isabella wedged herself between the wall and the armoire in their bedroom, pushing it forward until there was enough space to reach the wall vault hidden behind it.

"I should go with you," Angela said.

"That is an awful idea," Isabella said, removing a black backpack from the safe's recesses and placing it on the bed between them. She rummaged through it, pulling out her Wayne mask.

"Control starts raids in seven days. We need the Guardians to stand down," Angela said, and Isabella nodded. Inside the backpack was another fake face, that of a woman, deflated and lifeless. "Oh, you have two identities."

"Yeah, if my Wayne identity gets blown, I have a backup." Isabella took her Wayne mask and some of Wayne's clothing from the closet and shoved them into a saddlebag. "The Guardians provide meticulously constructed personas, including cover story and pocket litter, you know? Passports, SSN, and stuff. I've gone by many names. I was hoping the lies would end after the Freewill Law passed."

Angela caressed Isabella's forearm. "We have to get past this last hurdle."

At the bottom of the backpack, underneath the pocket litter, there was a small, oblong metal box. "What's this?" Angela asked.

"It's a GPS tracker terminator." Isabella pulled it out and opened it. Angela gasped. "I've heard of them but never seen one!"

"Donovan, the computer genius, perfected it." Inside the box was a microprocessor attached to a red wire and a blue button. Isabella pointed to the microprocessor. "This controls the charge. You uncoil the red wire and clip it to your GPS tracker, and then you press the blue button." She put the terminator back inside the backpack. "That's one reason why I needed to visit the GPS Command Center—to prove Warren and Jonathan didn't use a tracker terminator." She looked at her watch. "I've got to go." She put the case in the safe and shoved the armoire back into place.

In the living room, she checked her Glock with precision, making sure the magazine was full. She then shoved it upward into the handgrip, tapped the bottom of the pistol's grip against her palm, and listened for the snap. It was now locked. The gun went into her holster, and another magazine went into her leather jacket pocket. She grabbed a piece of paper, scribbled a name and address, and handed it to Angela. "Here. Should something happen to me, the Guardians will take care of you."

"Who's this?"

"Bill Mahoney, Donovan's father."

Angela hesitated with concern. "What does Donovan look like?"

"It changes. Donovan's a black hole. Nothing about him exists online."

"How do you know when it's really him?"

"A scorpion tattoo on his right palm."

Isabella sensed Angela's hesitation. She kissed her. "I love you. Don't worry," she said, despite her own doubts. After her last meeting with Donovan, she wasn't sure he wouldn't kill her on sight.

\* \* \*

Ten miles outside the D.C. Compound, the night air had turned brisk, and a nervous shiver ran up Isabella's arms as she drove the old black Mustang toward their rendezvous spot. The thought of seeing Donovan again brought up all kinds of unresolved emotions in her.

*I feel you in the air*, Isabella silent-messaged Gin as she stared down the ten miles of two-way. She reflected on her relationship with Gin and how she hid her feelings from her in destructive ways. If she had just talked to Gin about Noah's failed escape and her feeling that Gin shared the responsibility for his death. If she had opened up instead of shutting down, things might have ended differently. But now the burden was solely hers.

She silent-messaged, *I don't know how to reach him, Gin. Donovan is so angry with me. I don't think he will listen to reason.*

Isabella had begun talking to Gin after Angela explained what had happened, how Gin was now everywhere in the light. Since that night, Isabella had sensed Gin's energy around her. Even now, she could feel her in the passenger seat, could sense the warmth of Gin's hand resting on her knee, though she was driving alone. She wondered if Gin heard her. *Tell me where you are, Gin.* She took a deep breath, straining to hear her thoughts, but there was only the sound of tires humming low.

Isabella pulled into a truck stop. Ten minutes later, when she turned back onto the road, she was Wayne. She traveled another twenty miles, following the winding Anacostia River road until she reached the New Castle city limits.

Historic downtown New Castle slouched against the Anacostia River and was riddled with crime and drugs. The neighborhood was so bad that the local police had given up and stayed away. This made it a suitable location for a Guardians' base camp. The river provided unmonitored access to the D.C. Compound by boat, which allowed them to bypass land border security checkpoints. The hangout location changed often, but she knew where to start her search. She parked between two derelict cars on Main Street and exited the Mustang.

At Main Street and West Fourth, she strolled along cobblestones on her way to a third New Castle bar. So far, there had been no signs of Donovan. Passing a dark alley, she heard a can skipping across the pavement and saw shadows moving quickly out of sight. The Guardians were watching her, making sure she was alone.

She pulled open the door to the Union Street Grill. It was jam-packed with rowdy football fans. Isabella pushed her way through the sweaty bodies, nodding to the bartender. In response, he pointed her to an unmarked door in the rear. The open door led to a stairwell, and she followed the steps to the second floor. A long, dark hallway with many doors lay ahead of her. The air was stiflingly hot, mixed with the smell of cigarette smoke. Growing uneasy after a few steps, she pulled out her Glock and crept along the passageway.

Her left eye pulsated, showing her a hologram of Donovan in his cowboy disguise. She watched as he crossed in front of her like a ghost passing through one door then exiting through another. It was a time-lapse of Donovan going about his daily business in the space. He had been here, Isabella surmised. She checked each door she passed, then followed the ghostly vision of Donovan as it traveled to the end of the hall and into a larger space. Lights from the street cast a bluish glow into the room. He was there, his back to her, hunched over a computer, working. Her heart pounded. The hologram looked so real that she could almost reach out and touch him.

Applause erupted from the bar crowd below, startling her out of her vision. The chair in front of the computer was empty, but the space behind her was filled with a presence. In an instant, she felt the cold gun muzzle on the back of her head.

"Donovan," she whispered.

"Stick 'em up," Donovan said in a slurring lisp. He cocked his gun and she raised her hands.

"Donovan, you better think this through 'cause I get off on this sort of thing."

Donovan leaned in, grabbing Isabella's Glock out of her hand. "I do too. Turn around. Now."

Isabella turned and her spine stiffened at the sight of a menacing clown face creased in anger before her. This was no longer one of her visions. It was real and disturbing.

"I warned you to stay away." He hissed the words through an overbite of snaggled teeth. His evil, pasty white face floated in the darkness. Thin black lips curled into a painfully broad smile with drips of blood in the creases, and black stars framed bloodshot eyes. On the top of his head was a shocking purple bun.

Isabella steadied herself. "I'm not the enemy, Donovan."

He altered his voice to a mad, wet lisp. "Hunting down Solos makes you the enemy."

Hands raised, she backed into the center of the space as Donovan followed, with both guns leveled at her.

"It's my cover, and you know it." She looked around the sparsely furnished room, spotting several computers. Donovan changed locations and identities so often that Control didn't know he existed. The Guardians called him the ghost.

"You're still that bratty teenage girl who wants what she wants."

Streetlights filtered through the slatted blinds, creating shafts of blue light that caused a strange azure glow. A roar from the crowd below reminded her that they were not alone. He passed through currents of light, his eyes wild, unfocused, a sinister Clarabell in combat trousers and an open kimono robe that revealed his bare chest.

"Dude, that's not a good look for you," she said as she tried to break the tension, pleased her voice was strong and steady.

"Your sloppiness got Gin and Noah killed. Yeah, Gin told me you are immature." He coughed up a deep laugh and drunkenly sang, "Baby, baby."

Isabella knew he was deliberately provoking her, and she needed to stop it. Droplets of sweat trickled down the inside of her Wayne mask. "Donovan, I get it. You hate me. I hate me too sometimes. I wish I died instead of Gin. But let's cut the crap. It was Gin's choice to spill about being a Luman, probably to protect me. But that's Ginger; she'd lay down her life for anyone. A true leader does."

"They didn't just kill her. They anatomized her and they won't get away with it."

Isabella saw the ache well up in his eyes. He was unsure of himself, leaning and staggering. With a quick step forward, she thrust an open palm into his chin and brought her other hand down, grabbing her Glock as he fell to the floor. She trained her Glock on him as he stumbled to his feet. They stood face-to-face, guns leveled at each other, neither backing down.

"What's it gonna be, Donovan? Are we going to shoot each other or work together?"

They circled in a cat-and-mouse game, flashing in and out of shafts of lights. He tugged at his mask angrily. "You've got one chance. Get out of here, or I'll kill you."

Isabella scoffed. "You're so drunk you couldn't hit the broad side of a barn." Irritation and anger boiling over, Donovan ripped off his mask in one violent motion. His hair was matted in sweat, his face gleamed in the blue light.

The last time Isabella had seen Donovan's true identity, he was a carefree teenager. He looked like that teenager again now; even sweaty and drunk, he was handsome, with a boyish innocence he tried to hide. But what he didn't hide, what he wanted her to see, was unveiled misery. The sting of it up close, so raw, made her want to turn away, but she didn't. She knew his pain—the unending pain of losing the one you loved.

"You're a good man, Donovan. Gin loved you, not me. It's just we had a lot of history together. I didn't want to lose that, and I guess neither did she. But she wanted to be with you."

"I know that! You don't think I know that?" he screamed.

Isabella wavered and finally could no longer sustain his animus. She holstered her gun and stood open-handed. "You've got to listen to me. We have to move past this. Control will start Solo raids in seven days. I can't stop that, but I can tell you the locations. You can evacuate. No one has to die."

He shook his gun at her like a righteous finger. "You and Angela's problem is you think you can outsmart the Primitives while working within the justice system. What has that gotten us?" he yelled. "You won't gain justice that way. You can't reason with your opponent if they fear you."

Isabella raised her hand in a calming tone and replied, "Control will raid the larger compounds first. You've got to evacuate the Guardians, their families, and supporters."

He moved closer, so close she saw the sweat beads on his stubbled cheeks and smelled the alcohol on his breath. "Everyone is making their way here. Some are already here."

She tilted her head. "If you start a war, innocent people will die. Do you really want that?"

"What we want is our freedom. It's not an unreasonable demand."

"I'm not suggesting we allow them to monitor us. We have to negotiate peacefully."

"You just don't get it. We must fight back. The military has created the first Luman soldier."

"Corpus is real?" Isabella was desolate.

"They successfully transplanted a neural implant into a combat soldier."

Isabella searched his face in disbelief.

"We have to move now before the military has a whole army of Lumans programmed to kill," he said. He laid his gun on the table before straightening his robe.

Isabella was dumbfounded. Corpus changed everything, but could she believe Donovan? Or was it just his overblown imagination fueling his desire for war? At their last meeting, she remembered Gin telling her that Corpus had a breakthrough, though.

"I need you to get the documented Lumans and their families to stand with us."

She heard him talking, but it was just disjointed words. She was unfocused, unmoored, shaking not with anger but with fear and the knowledge of what was coming.

"When will all of this madness end?" she screeched. Donovan took a quick step back but answered her reaction with a grave look. She brushed by him and left, torn between two worlds. She wasn't sure if she would stand with the Guardians or if she would ask Angela to.

# CHAPTER FORTY-SIX

## *Throne of Secrets*

Preoccupied and worried about Isabella, wondering how the meeting with Donovan was going, Angela glanced blankly at the glittering bodies on the White Rabbit's dance floor. Emma nudged her, jolting her out of her distracted thoughts.

"Her name is Tiffany London, the one with the long dark hair."

"Who?" Angela asked, gazing down from their private booth in the VIP lounge at a table of women on the main floor.

Emma pointed. "Tiffany, in the red sheath dress."

Angela studied Tiffany for a long moment, unimpressed. "Is Janet dating more than one?"

Emma tossed her head and gave a Minnie Mouse giggle. "No. Surprising, right? You and Tiffany are nothing alike—she's older, a privileged human but certainly an evolutionary miracle."

Angela suppressed the urge to scoff. "I can't believe she's not with a Luman."

"Janet doesn't need a Chip. What she needs is a new hairdo." Emma twisted and gave Angela the stink eye. "Janet's mad at me. You know how I know that?"

Angela shrugged.

"When she speaks, there is no emotion in her voice, nothing. Did you have something to do with that?"

On the surface, Angela acted as if bemused by Emma's accusation. The truth was she had spun some lies about Mort and Emma to ensure that Janet would pressure Senator Green into changing his vote. Thinking back now on the day of the vote, Angela thought that it had been all too easy to coerce Janet. She'd been thoroughly surprised that Janet didn't call her bluff about Mort's Chip trafficking. Back then, though, she'd thought Janet wanted the Freewill Bill to pass for Jason and only needed a nudge in the right direction. She knew now that Janet was up to something.

"Janet holds grudges," Emma warned. "Whatever you're planning, none of it better blow back on me."

Emma was a shrewd player and the protector of the underground subculture between humans and Lumans, preserving their anonymity, keeping no client records, and generating absolutely zero digital footprints. She reigned over a throne of secrets. That was worth shielding.

"Remember, Emma. You're getting a pretty good deal out of this. No raids—your business is protected."

Emma capitulated. "I may have introduced Tiffany and Janet, but then Janet took me out of the loop. They make their own plans. You'll need to get chummy with Tiffany to find out where and when."

"What's Tiffany's story?"

"She's well-educated, Harvard law degree, but got in bed with the wrong congressman about five years ago. There was a scandal."

Angela snapped her fingers. "Right, I remember her now. The bar association struck her off for witness tampering."

"Yeah, a trumped-up charge to discredit her," Emma said. She shook the ice in her glass. "She lost her job, got slammed by the press and social media. She was young and in love, and he dropped her like a hot bedpan of shit then went back to his wife. Now, she's very discreet. Likes money. She's top-shelf."

"Janet's paying for an escort?"

"Don't look so shocked, Pollyanna. That's how my girls make their living."

"Well, here goes nothing."

Angela left, taking the stairs down to the first floor and cutting a path through the mob of affluent young people swaying on the dance floor to the sensual music. She ordered a scotch from the bartender, leaned against the bar, and scanned her surroundings. Meeting

Tiffany's gaze from across the dance floor, she let her eyes widen with interest and flashed a seductive grin, making it disappear as fast as it arrived.

She returned her gaze to Tiffany after the bartender delivered her drink, but she was gone. *Of course. It couldn't be that easy, could it?* She stood there, staring into her glass for a while, then sighed and checked her watch. It was 11:15, and Tiffany had not resurfaced. She'd better go home if she had any hope of keeping this a secret from Isabella. Dejected, she flipped the bartender some bills and left.

Grabbing her coat from the coat check, she pulled it on.

"Let me help you with that," a deep, rich woman's voice purred, sparking a rush of warmth in Angela. As she helped her into her coat, the woman flipped Angela's long hair out from under her collar. Angela twisted. There she was.

"Hello, I'm Tiffany London. Emma mentioned you might stop by tonight."

Angela glanced up to meet large, sultry eyes fringed with long false eyelashes. She reminded Angela of a gazelle poised in the open woodlands, elegant but fragile.

Angela took her hand out of her coat pocket and extended it. "Angela Mathers."

Tiffany's lashes fluttered as she reached for Angela's hand, grasping it finally as if she were reaching into a lion's cage.

"I hope this isn't too forward, but I'm in a hurry. Would you mind walking me to the train station?" Angela pressed a folded C-note into Tiffany's palm. Tiffany studied her, and a smile emerged.

"Yes, I'd love to escort you." Tiffany grabbed her jacket, pocketing the money.

It was a brisk fall night in the city, its chill reminding Angela that winter's bitter cold was nearing. She and Tiffany walked languidly as Angela explained what she had in mind and expounded a bit on their mutual interest—Janet.

"Tiffany, we are alike in many ways."

"Besides being distractions for Janet, I find that hard to believe." Tiffany looked on, amused.

"We both gravitate toward powerful people. Their absolute authority is a drug. People like Janet, with a vibrant personality and capable of emotional depth, draw us in, and when they focus their life force on us, it's like living in another world, a more desirable one. They value us and make us feel virtuous, lovable—we are emancipated from our past."

"The Janet you refer to is not the one I see."

"Really? Tell me about the Janet you know."

"You speak of being liberated, vindicated by Janet's admiration. The Janet I see is haunted by something that I hadn't been able to name until now."

They stopped at the entrance to the train station. A gust of frigid wind off the river stirred Angela's hair, and she tightened the coat around her.

"It is you, Angela. She regrets your relationship." Tiffany lingered, and Angela could tell she had questions about the deal Angela proposed as they started their walk. "What are you hoping to achieve?" she asked.

"Redemption. What the committee did to the Freewill Bill is reprehensible, and Janet knows it."

"She owes you an explanation?"

Angela nodded solemnly, though she planned to get more than that from Janet. Janet's clever maneuvering made her angry. She felt used for thinking she could redress the balance of power between Lumans and humans.

"I hope you consider my offer. The money will be untraceable, of course." Angela looked at her, troubled. "It's best not to stay involved with Janet for too long, Tiffany," she advised. If only she could have found another way to get Senator Green's vote. "Give Janet what she desires and get out."

"Secrecy," Tiffany acknowledged.

"It's best for people like us to protect powerful people. And it can be profitable. Protecting people from themselves has proved to be a very lucrative business for Emma."

"I'll think about it," Tiffany said, but her expression suggested she was buying into the deal.

They said their goodbyes. As she traversed the steep stairs descending into the train station, Angela smiled to herself. Gaining Tiffany's help had seemed like a long shot an hour ago, but now it looked like it was just crazy enough to work.

\* \* \*

When Angela opened the apartment door, she heard Isabella rummaging through the kitchen cabinets. She exhaled sharply, relieved Isabella was home safe. As she hung up her coat, she heard the clinking of cereal being poured into a ceramic bowl and then the refrigerator door opening and shutting with an abrupt thud. "I forgot to pick up milk," she admitted sheepishly.

Isabella popped a piece of Cap'n Crunch into her mouth, studying the sexy number Angela had on. "Where have you been?"

"Um, a quick drink at the White Rabbit." Angela knew she couldn't lie to Isabella, so she found a piece of the truth to share.

"Uh-huh. Why?" Isabella's eyes narrowed.

Angela's shoulders slumped. "I needed to see Janet...convince her..."

"You were with Janet?" Isabella's expression took on a troubled look.

Angela smiled, the one that was a lie, and rested a hand on her hip. "I didn't exactly say that."

"I can't protect you if you don't share your plans with me."

"It was on a whim. I didn't even see Janet."

Isabella glared at her. "You never operate on impulse."

Angela fought the urge to lash out. It was close, but she was learning ways to control the flashes of temper that were another aspect of the awakening of her emotions. She was angry at Isabella because she was right. And angry at herself for not yet having a plan to fix the Freewill Law. Until she talked to Janet, she didn't know what recourse she might have, and she hated that. She hated not being one step ahead of her opponent. Cool reasoning always had always driven her decision-making, but now emotions were clouding her thinking and slowing her judgment.

Instead of explaining all that to Isabella, of course, she just stared blankly at her.

Isabella exhaled sharply. "Whatever. I'm going to bed. I've had enough crazy talk for one evening."

"You weren't able to convince him?" Angela moved in closer to her.

"Donovan's still so angry with me. He was drunk and talking crazy. I'm not sure if I can believe anything he said. I need time to sort it out."

"He's angry at Gin. You're just a convenient substitute." Angela hugged Isabella, causing her to move the cereal bowl aside to accommodate her body. "Sorry I forgot the milk."

"Do you think Janet will give you the time of day...after everything?" Isabella's voice died off.

"No. Well...I have to try." Angela released her hold on Isabella and snagged a piece of cereal, popping it into her mouth. "What are the Guardians planning?"

"Oh no, you don't go changing the subject," Isabella said, moving her cereal bowl out of Angela's reach. "Come on, what are you up to?"

"I'm still working out the details, but the goal is to protect the Lumans and the Solos," Angela said. She caressed Isabella's waist with one hand, stealing the bowl of Cap'n Crunch from her with the other. "Are you coming?" She walked to the bedroom.

# CHAPTER FORTY-SEVEN

## *Resurgence*

The maitre d' unfolded the white cloth napkin and placed it on Charlotte's lap.

"Hmmm, what am I feeling like today?" Charlotte said, glancing at the menu. The servers hovered in starched attire, attentive to her every need. Angela gazed at her mother as they sat opposite each other in a posh restaurant overlooking downtown D.C. She realized she knew very little about her parents' lifestyle and wondered if this was how her mother dined every day.

Shortly after the government transferred Angela to the D.C. Compound, her parents stopped visiting her together. Charlotte called on Angela more often, claiming she needed to get away from the stifling, small-town atmosphere of St. Edenville. Angela wondered—if her parents hadn't opted for the elective neural implant, would she be like her mother, a homemaker filling her idle time with church bazaars and book clubs?

Her parents never mentioned the chip until after Lucy's disappearance. The night she was taken into custody, they explained: she was born prematurely, and the doctors had suggested a neural implant to avoid future complications. It had required an extended stay in the hospital's NICU; it was fully two years before she was able to come home. For the longest time, she thought that separation was why she felt disconnected from her parents and the rest of the world.

Angela sipped her wine. "Did you come up the other day when the president signed the Freewill Law?"

Charlotte bowed her head and played with her fork. "Yes, sorry, love. It was a brief layover. I didn't have time to visit." The server brought their salads with the dressing on the side. "So, your father told me about the provision. What are you doing about it?"

"Dad and I filed a lawsuit with the Supreme Court yesterday. And Isabella is trying to run interference with Control." Preoccupied, her mother checked her phone, and when she peered up, a smile was lighting her face. Angela observed her mother: Charlotte's hair was down, draped over her shoulder, almost sexy. Her gray eyes were bright and cloudless, and her cheeks were flushed—she was happy.

"So, you and Isabella? What happened to Janet?" Her mother picked at her wedge salad.

Angela noted the disapproval in her mother's tone. "So, you blew me off to see Steven Hawk. Are you going to divorce Dad or just have an affair with Steven?"

Charlotte dropped her fork with a clank, which brought the server running. She waved him off and fixed her gaze on Angela.

"Your father and I are not getting a divorce."

Angela waved her fork casually. "Well, what would the neighbors think, anyway?"

"Trust me, the neighbors still have plenty to talk about concerning our family." Charlotte's tone turned condescending, putting an end to her daughter's deflection technique.

Angela stiffened and looked out the window, away from the condemnation on her mother's face. That look could still pull Angela back to that moment at the river. What she understood then and now had changed, though: the flowers swirling in the river's current, Lucy's indecipherable secret, Angela's silence. How could her younger self have known the world would see her parents as bad people too?

"I can tell you're smitten with Isabella. I must admit, I find her quite charming with her belief in duty and justice, but she's no Senator Abrams. Janet has actual power and is in a position to help you overcome this latest snafu."

"Janet is to blame for the latest shitstorm, Mother. She can be vengeful and ruthless when you cross her."

Charlotte pressed her hands together. "Janet is the key to fixing the law. Let her know you've learned your lesson. Sometimes, sweetheart, you must do things you don't want to do. Last week, the church ladies signed me up to make sausage balls for the church revival. I was up to my elbows in slimy minced pork. Do you think I wanted to be? No. But I did it. Besides, you're so very clever, you'll figure out a way to make it up to her."

"I'm trying to, Mother."

"Try harder. Make sure Janet knows how appreciative you are." She reached across the table, catching Angela's hand. "Janet is the key."

Angela groaned, pulling her hand away.

"Really, what could you possibly gain from Isabella?"

Angela pushed a cherry tomato around her salad plate, not wanting to see her mother's expression. Why couldn't she tell her mother she was in love with Isabella? Was she afraid her mother wouldn't believe her? It was a question she couldn't answer.

When Angela was very young, Charlotte had noticed Angela's lack of physiological responses. She had, therefore, set about teaching Angela how to cry, explaining to her that crying made her look like a normal little girl. "You cannot let people see your dark places, Angela," she had said. Angela stared blankly into her mother's demanding eyes until Charlotte finally turned away.

"Okay, okay, I'll drop it. Steven mentioned you hadn't signed an employment agreement with LA. Does that mean you'll come home?" Charlotte looked hopeful.

"I haven't decided." The last place Angela wanted to live was in St. Edenville, making mojitos and sausage balls.

Charlotte reached into her purse, pulled out a large stuffed manila envelope, and slid it across the table. "It's in the denominations you requested. But, honey, it's a sizeable amount of cash and not safe to carry around. Why can't we open a checking account for you?"

Angela didn't want the money traced back to her or her parents, so she took the envelope and placed it in her purse. Her mother would faint if she knew what she planned to do with it.

"I don't trust the government," Angela said.

"Well, I can't blame you there."

After lunch, she kissed her mother and said, "You look happy, Mother, but don't fall in love with Steven and mess it up."

"You need to stop overanalyzing things. You need Janet, especially now that she's running for president. She should be your only priority."

\* \* \*

After Angela left her mother, she went shopping with Margot. Since moving in with Isabella, she had not seen much of the former Sister from Camp I/O. At the store, Angela asked Margot to find her some pants while she flipped through dresses on a clothing rack. She felt someone watching her and peered over her shoulder. Her eyes locked with a woman dressed casually in jeans and a blouse, long hair pulled back into a ponytail. The woman tossed the shoe she was holding onto the shoe rack and smiled at her. Angela ignored her, thinking her paranoia was a reaction to seeing her mother. She moved on to a rack of sexier dresses. A hand crossed in front of Angela, grabbing a red, backless, sequined dress.

"You're a petite eight, right?" The same woman held the dress in front of Angela's frame, admiring it. "I didn't think sparkly was your thing."

The woman's dark eyes were on fire, reflecting the red sequins like flames, and a chill raced up Angela's spine. She seized the dress from the woman's long fingers and moved away.

Inside the dressing room, Angela tried on the dress—it hugged her curves nicely. *This will do*, she thought. A shadow slipped inside the room. "Christ, who are you?"

It was the woman from earlier. "Interesting, I've been asking myself that same question. Who are you? Who is the real Angela Mathers? Are you a murderer?" The woman stepped closer, and Angela stepped back. "My dark figure lurks where you don't want it to. You saw me, but you didn't *see* me."

Angela shook her head as the woman backed her up against the full-length mirror. "Who are you?" she repeated, trying to keep the tremor out of her voice.

The woman silent-messaged, *My body is willowy compared to my once sturdy posterior. My curly, dark brown hair is now long and black, my eagle eyes are ebony. I'm a spirit visiting you from the dead.*

The stranger surged closer, her body heat suffusing Angela. "Say my name."

"Warren," Angela whispered in disbelief.

"I know what you're thinking. I saw the same look of disbelief on Renae Goodwin's face. Yeah, I inherited her body. She needed a chip to operate her bionic legs." Showing off, Raven jumped high into the air, touching the ceiling, then raced around the small room, coming to rest with her hands pressed on either side of Angela, caging her against the mirror.

"Guess what? They picked my neural implant. It's like winning the lottery. You can figure out the rest since you taught me how to upload my mind into the light."

"But how did you get back?" Angela sputtered.

Ignoring her, Raven inched her face closer. "You had me killed by Lewis. Why? To protect Senator Abrams? You plan to ride her angel-strap heels to the White House?"

"No, that's ridiculous, never." Angela gave her a condescending smirk. "But…it's ironic you're in a woman's body."

There was a knock on the door.

Raven growled in her ear, "Where's Jon's chip?"

"I don't know."

Margot entered with her arms full of pants. Startled to see Raven, she dropped the garments on the floor. "Honey, are you okay?"

Raven backed away from Angela and silent-messaged, *From the day I met you, I saw through you. And you hated me because of it.* Giving her an unfriendly gaze, she disappeared out the door.

"Angela, who was that?" Margot asked as she picked up the pants scattered across the floor.

"You wouldn't believe me if I told you."

* * *

When Angela arrived home from her shopping spree, she hid her bags of new outfits and beauty products in the guest bedroom.

# CHAPTER FORTY-EIGHT

## *Common Ground*

A steaming bowl of massaman curry sat on the kitchen table, and Isabella scooped a heap onto her plate. "Mmmm...Did you enjoy lunch with your mom?"

Angela shrugged. "My mother is having an affair." She nonchalantly offered Isabella a spring roll.

Isabella's face dropped. "Oh my God, who?"

"She didn't admit to it, but I suspect Steven Hawk." Angela took a bite of a spring roll and watched the crust flake off onto her plate.

Isabella studied her. Angela and her mother were a lot alike, both calculating. She wondered if this was her mother's way of helping Angela's career.

"Doesn't it bother you?"

Angela looked up. "What?"

Isabella pushed her glasses up. "Will your mother leave your father?"

"I doubt it," Angela said.

Struck by Angela's lack of anguish over her parents' situation, Isabella felt her shoulders sag.

"Something else happened today." Angela's eyes became gravestones. "I was shopping, and this woman came up to me. It was Warren—Warren Harris."

Isabella's forkful of food froze in midair.

"Someone transplanted Warren's chip into this woman named Renae Goodwin, and a resurgence of Warren's consciousness downloaded from the light into her neural implant."

Isabella shook her head. "What?"

"Warren's mind downloaded into Renae's neural implant. Well, legally, it is still his chip."

"You knew this was possible?"

Angela ignored Isabella's question and continued, "I'm confident it happened, but there wasn't time to check Warren's aptitude or memory. Margot was with me."

Still rocked by the news, Isabella set her fork down. "I've met her. I knew something was off about that one. Her full name is Lieutenant Renae Goodwin, but she goes by Raven." Isabella suddenly realized what Donovan had told her was true. "The military has successfully created a Luman soldier. It's Raven."

"Corpus." Angela's eyes burnt into her, and Isabella realized her mistake. "You knew about Corpus and said nothing?" Angela stood up, disappointment in her voice. "Why didn't you tell me sooner?"

Isabella crossed over to her. "I'm telling you now. You thought the trafficking was tied to Corpus. Well, Warren is your proof. The Corpus breakthrough is Raven."

Angela's voice raised in anger and hurt. "You think I'm playing you?"

"No. But why hold back things? Why see Janet? Why keep it a secret?"

"I'm not. You think I have this grand master plan I'm carrying out."

"If Janet isn't a part of your plan, why are you trying to see her?"

Angela's emotions boiled over, and she yelled, "There isn't a plan, Isabella! I don't know how to fix this."

Isabella stepped back, startled by the outburst.

Angela slumped to the floor. "I'm sorry, I know I promised to fix this but..." She raised her hands in surrender. "Everything that has happened is my fault...if I had just told someone right after it happened, with some certainty, that Lucy was murdered...then they might have believed me, they wouldn't distrust us..." Her voice died out.

"Hey, no, no, it's okay." Isabella enfolded Angela in her arms, picking her up off the floor.

As soon as they touched, everything Angela was feeling rolled over Isabella like a storm, a sadness spiraling inward, vehement waves of emotions so profound they sucked the air from her lungs.

Isabella whispered, "It's okay." She smoothed Angela's hair. "You don't own this, any of it. No one expects you to save the Lumans."

Angela trembled as she fought back the tears and stepped out of the embrace. "I don't have a solution. And now Warren—I mean Raven—is mixed up in it."

A silence filled the space between them. Their eyes caught; neither one wanted to give up. Isabella pushed up her shirt sleeves. "Let's figure this out together."

Angela tried to smile. "We need to find who is really running Corpus and use it to stop MindControl. Janet said it was unsanctioned by Congress. That means it's someone high up. Could be the military or someone else in the government. She will know who."

Isabella nodded. It was logical, tactical even, to turn to Janet for that information, but even so, it felt like Angela was suggesting it because she had something personal to prove.

Angela wiped a tear streak from her cheek. "Warren thinks I had something to do with his death."

"Raven wants the Lewis case reopened," Isabella added.

"Warren has always despised me, but he is too weak to do anything about it. Was, anyway."

"Well, he's now Raven, a lieutenant in the Army, and you know how the military distrusts us. If Raven keeps raising suspicions and the humans find out about resurgence, it's gonna be teeth, hair, and eyeballs all over the place."

Angela crossed her arms over her chest and stared at the floor. "We need to find Jonathan's chip before Raven does. If Jon has already gone through a resurgence, we need him on our side. You said Donovan is a hacktivist? There must be a digital trail tracing who sold and bought the chip."

"Donovan's like a coon dog. He can sniff out any digital intel. But he hates me. He won't help us."

"That leaves Janet. But she's ghosted me," Angela added.

"You think she's part of this?"

"I'd bet on it."

Isabella took hold of Angela's hand. "Then I might know who can shut up Raven."

# CHAPTER FORTY-NINE

*Political Rubicon*

Janet flipped on the lights in her hideaway office, then stopped in her tracks, giving Isabella a long-suffering look.

"Good morning, Senator Abrams," Isabella said, her face expressionless and her tone all business. As Janet approached, she remained sitting in a chair across from her desk. "You and I have a problem. I think it's time we solved it," she said.

Janet sighed and took a seat behind her desk, glancing casually at the messages piled neatly by her phone. "And that would be...the undocumented? Or MindControl?" Janet guessed.

Isabella adjusted her glasses. "Well, I was referring to the documented type. You know, blond, intellectual, female. That's your type, right?"

Janet's finger twitched as she put the phone messages back on the desk and picked up the phone, punching a four-digit extension.

"Mike, there's an intruder in my office." Janet hung up the phone, lips set in determination, she twisted in her chair and crossed her legs.

Isabella knew she only had seconds now. "She was his type, too. Jeff Lewis, he took lots of photographs of her, spying on every moment of her life. He developed a real taste for her, like you."

Isabella stood as she heard footsteps scurrying on the other side of the closed office door.

"You should do yourself a favor and talk to Angela." Isabella took out her badge. "Lieutenant Raven Goodwin wants the Jeff Lewis case reopened. So, all those photos on Jeff's computer could surface. You remember those blackmail photos of you and her, don't you? He took them and there are plenty more."

Mike and two guards entered Janet's office. Isabella held up her badge. "Just leaving, boys."

Janet's voice was calm and confident. "What do you want, Agent?"

"Nothing. I'm just doing you a solid. Letting you know your next move could be irrevocable." Isabella pushed past Mike and the guards.

# CHAPTER FIFTY

## *Glass Face*

There was no mistaking the eyes of a woman bent on mischief—liquid, sparkling, luminous, craving, and accentuated by a perfectly etched eyebrow. Best to hide hers, Angela decided, so no one saw the storm approaching. Flipping long red hair over her shoulder, she donned fashionable dark sunglasses. Confidently, she strode across the medical building's polished floor in a stylish pantsuit, high heels clicking to a timpani beat.

Suite 406: Body Esthetic and Plastic Surgery was engraved on the door, the name Dr. Bill Mahoney M.D., F.A.C.S. etched below it. She pushed through the door, stepping into a waiting room full of vain Primitives.

"Margot Needleman, Dr. Mahoney's one o'clock," she announced.

The receptionist escorted her into Dr. Mahoney's office and handed her a clipboard with a stack of papers clipped to it. "Please fill out these while you wait. He'll be with you shortly."

Within a few minutes, Dr. Mahoney knocked on the door, then breezed into the room. Receiving Angela's paperwork, he quickly reviewed it as he slicked back his coal-black hair. Thick glasses hid his expressive eyes, and a thin pencil mustache sought to give him an air of sophistication, contrasting with his true nature, Angela thought. His eyes caught hers as she studied him.

"What can I do for you, Ms. Needleman?"

She watched the shock spread across his face as he scrutinized her disguise and realized she looked like Gin, his son's late fiancée.

Angela removed her sunglasses. "I must speak with your son."

Bill gazed warily at her. "I...don't have a son."

Angela let out a sigh. "Listen, Bill, I don't have time to fuck around. Call Donovan and tell him we need to talk now, or Control will learn that there are thousands of Solos descending on D.C., and they are ripe for the picking."

"Shhh!" Bill moved toward the door and closed it, turning toward her. "I don't know what you've heard. There's been a mistake." He returned to his desk, perching stiffly on the edge of his chair.

"Your son is like a glitch in a data set. An outlier, you know? Most Lumans are rather docile, but not Donovan, the hacktivist." Angela stood and ambled about his office. Bill's eyes raked over her with a mixture of nervousness and irritation.

"Like father, like son." Angela glanced sideways at him as she picked up a beautiful crystal female face. It was smooth, flawless, and the refracting light gave it a sensual luminescence fringed with azure. "You both have a dark core, malevolent tendencies. Destroying half the Capitol dome was not impressive. In fact it blew up our only chance at democracy."

"Please put that down—it's extremely valuable. Listen, Ms. Needleman, you've got me confused with—"

"There was no mistake, Bill. You agreed to risky neural implant surgery for Donovan. The amalgamation of the chip with Donovan's brain made him a genius. He excelled in mathematics. It took little encouragement to get him interested in computer code. Soon, he was hacking the D.C. electrical grid, the voting system, the president's social media account, the stock market, and the Social Security Administration."

"Those are Guardian hacks and have been all over the news. It proves nothing."

She balanced the glass face on her middle finger like a basketball, letting it wobble unsteadily as Bill's face creased in apprehension. "Donovan is the Guardian leader now, a paranoid alcoholic who's had his fingerprints altered. The Guardians call him the 'ghost' because he never stays in one place." She questioned, "Should I go on?"

Bill picked up the phone. "I'll call him. But put the glass face down."

"Tell him Ginger has reawakened and needs to speak with him. In person," she added as he hit some buttons.

"Donovan, we have a problem," Bill cautioned into the phone.

Angela tossed the glass face at Bill. "Oops."

A grimace blackened Bill's face as the crystal hit the ground, shattering on impact, and glass fragments ricocheted across the hardwood floor. "I will break more than your pretty glass face if either of you tries anything sneaky during our meeting. Got it?"

* * *

Thirty minutes later, Donovan slid into a booth next to his father and gave Angela, sitting opposite him in her Gin disguise, a vulturine grin. When he didn't let the blow penetrate, not even for a second, Angela knew the task ahead would not be easy. Having studied Isabella's masks, she could tell Donovan had on a fake face crafted by the same sculptor, likely Bill. He had an unmistakable style, particularly regarding the nuances in the skin's texture and shading around the eyes. His plastic surgery profession gave Bill ample supplies—it was the perfect cover.

Donovan looked homeless: dirty, baggy clothing, unkempt goatee, stringy hair. And he was already wasted at ten o'clock in the morning. He looked and acted like one of those crazies who argue with themselves on street corners. Sadly, it was a brilliant disguise. Everyone, including Control, turned an uncaring eye on the homeless. Therefore, Donovan, the bum, staggered around D.C. completely invisible.

Emma brought a tray of drinks, giving Angela a wink for support. "Here's our specialty drink. It's made from three exotic liquors creating one mad flavor. If these liquors can get along in the same glass, I figure you three can."

Emma set the drinks on the table and sashayed away. Angela didn't want a mob of Guardians lurking about in the shadows during their meeting, so she chose the White Rabbit. It was closed at this time of day, giving her the privacy and Emma the security she needed.

Bill took a sip. "Mmmm...what's it called?" he hollered after Emma.

"Dad, enough," Donovan scolded.

Tension filled the silence as they stared at Angela. She tilted her head, speculating if this was the real Donovan.

"Mad Hatter." She nodded to the drink.

Donovan saw through her trickery. "What the hell? This is Angela Mathers. You know, DeepMind." He clucked at his joke and grabbed a flask out of his jacket. He took a long swig. Angela spotted the scorpion tattoo on his palm and remembered it was his only identifying mark.

"I knew when you two hooked up that Dodge wouldn't be able to keep her mouth shut around you." Angela glared at him. "So here I am. What is so God damn important?"

"I need to find Jonathan Riley's chip. I think he's been made part of Corpus."

Donovan leaned back, stretching out his long arms and resting them on top of the booth. "We know about Corpus and have our own ways of handling the Old Fashions."

Tired of Donovan's bravado, she pretended to be Gin and silent-messaged, *I'm sorry, babe, I let you down. I was preoccupied thinking about you, our baby, our life together. I didn't see the man. Didn't realize he was following me. By the time I sensed someone was behind me, the bag was over my head, and then everything went black.*

She watched his swagger deflate like a puffer fish returning to its sad and typical metabolic self. If she could keep him off balance, she thought, he might negotiate.

*I am still alive in the light. I want you to release me, be mine again.* Angela played him like a game of Jenga, keeping him unsteady but not letting him crumble.

No mask could hide the hurt and remorse on Donovan's face. He lurched, reaching out for Gin, but Angela shifted her weight, and his hands remained empty. Gin was a ghost haunting him.

"Gin?" Donovan mumbled feebly, mewling quietly to himself. He slid out of the booth and stumbled away.

"Son, are you okay?" Bill called after him with deepening concern, unaware of Angela's silent mockery.

"Do not follow us," Angela blasted at Bill before taking off after Donovan.

She burst into the men's bathroom, scanning the interior, peering under the stalls. *No one here*, she cursed at herself.

In the women's restroom, she turned to the mirror and pulled off the red wig, loosening the pins in her blond hair as it fell free around her shoulders. With a fierce groan she said, "Brilliant, he ghosted me." She scratched her head, irritated at her handling of the situation.

Donovan blasted through a stall door; the force sent it crashing into the wall. Before Angela could react, he lunged at her throat, fingers wrapped in a death grip, lifting her off her feet.

"Tell me the truth," he growled.

She stuttered, "Tell me about Corpus."

Donovan shook with anger as he lifted her higher into the air.

Angela squeezed out the word, "Okay."

He dropped her, stepping away, a glimmer of hope in his expression. Angela coughed, taking a deep, gasping breath. "I helped Gin escape into the light."

She saw the wheels spinning behind his eyes. Then, he changed, and a new man rose from the ruins. Of course, being a computer guru, she knew he would get it.

"Uh-huh, she's in the light?" He glowered, then clenched his fist, on the verge of punching her. "Gin didn't believe in living beyond her human body."

"Wait, wait." Angela flinched. "We didn't debate it. Gin's body was dead, but her chip was still online. She just needed help getting to the light, so we paired. She filled my mind in her entirety for the briefest of seconds, found my gateway, and she was gone. She wanted to live however she could."

Donovan unclenched his fist in relief. Angela cleared her throat, still rattled by the attack. "It's called resurgence. I've seen it with Corpus's first breakthrough. The soldier Raven Goodwin has Warren Harris's chip and Warren's consciousness downloaded from the light back into his neural implant. You find Gin's neural implant and you can have her back."

Donovan understood the traveling of energy through space. Gin's digital consciousness, her personal identity, everything that made her Gin, was now traveling the radio waves in the white light, in an infinite reality, existing everywhere. He perceived the possibilities, the life of the mind, and imperceptibly nodded his head.

"Now, will you think about the rest of us for a minute?" Angela straightened her wrinkled clothes. "Raven Goodwin is making a lot of noise about finding her past lover, Jonathan Riley. We need to shut her up and find Jonathan's chip before the military figures out we are capable of resurgence." Brushing away imaginary debris, Angela said, quid pro quo, "What have you learned about Corpus?"

"Our intel suggests someone in the government is working behind the president's and Congress's back."

"With my connections in Congress, there's a chance we can expose them. Let me set up a few—"

"No, there's no time for your political mumbo jumbo. There's only one way to stop this—we are going to take the White House, let the people know what the military is planning."

"War helps no one."

Donovan pointed a finger. "We do this my way. You need to gather your people to rally behind us. Stand with the Guardians."

"We are pacifists. Even if they wanted to, Lumans don't know how to fight." And it was true: after being dehumanized in camps, the Lumans had unintentionally devalued themselves and grown fearful of humans.

"Our attack will be mostly cyber, disabling networks, launching malware, denial of service, ransomware. The LA analysts need to stop helping the Old Fashions; you do all their work for them. All you have to do is walk off your jobs."

Angela brought her hand to her neck as she rationalized it: many Lumans had not left the LA, and if they walked off the job, it would cripple the government's security. "Without us, Control won't be able to fight off the cyberattacks." She shook her head, still not convinced.

Donovan threw her a bone. "Let me dig around in the military's databases and see if I can locate Jonathan's chip."

Angela considered the offer and nodded—if she couldn't stop the Guardians' attack, she needed to make sure the Lumans were out of harm's way. "Deal. But I need one more thing."

Donovan eyed her skeptically. "What's that?"

# CHAPTER FIFTY-ONE

## *Home*

It was early afternoon when Isabella killed the 'Cuda's engine in front of a solitary A-frame house—her parents' sanctuary in the woods. Frank and Lorraine had lived here for nearly eight years, their longest stretch in one place. Nosey neighbors asking too many questions became a thing of the past when their little girl grew up and moved out.

The tall pines and red cedars stood at attention like a gathering of relatives to welcome her home. The family had moved so frequently Lorraine said, "Home isn't a place on a map—it's in your heart where the people you love live." But Isabella was a fault line; her career choices and nonconformist nature put her parents in danger. And she felt it every time she was near them: a strange rumbling underfoot.

Staying away kept them safe, but in the end, her heart always brought her home again, and she was thankful it did.

Isabella reflected on her early morning meeting with Senator Abrams. Janet thought she was untouchable—now she knew she was not and just maybe she'd grant a meeting with Angela. She climbed out of the 'Cuda, unsteady. In four days, MindControl would roll into action and she had done nothing to stop it. And with each passing day, the tension between her and Angela grew. She headed across the gravel toward the front door.

"Hello?" Isabella wandered through the empty rooms and the familiar scent of home in their cozy dwelling. A vase of fresh-cut flowers was on the table. Family pictures on the mantel spoke to her, calling her to visit, but she continued down the hall and peered into her parents' bedroom. It was full of warmth and folksy decorations: a rustic wood floor, a braided rug, and over the bed was a wood carving of the Garden of Eden created by a parishioner from her father's church in St. Edenville. Below it, Lorraine lay in bed sleeping. A small trash can sat on the floor next to her, and a sour smell lingered in the room.

Isabella opened the bedroom window, and the fall breeze brought in the smell of fallen leaves. She eased down next to her mom. Lorraine was sleeping in her wig these days, always presentable, always ready for company. Her dad always said, "Lorraine has magic in her bones." And it was true: when her mom enfolded her in her arms, Isabella's troubles vanished. But nowadays, underneath her mom's withering shape, the chemo was destroying the good and the bad cells mercilessly, stealing her magic. Birdsong filtered in through the open window, and Isabella closed her eyes, taking a deep breath as a vision of her past appeared. She felt her body lighten, slipping and shifting into a memory.

It was after her eighth birthday. She had come down with pneumonia and her fever was spiking. Lorraine's concern reached a state of panic as Isabella became too listless and weak to walk. She needed a doctor, but visiting a physician was risky for a Solo. Certain doctors were in-network, which meant they didn't require a lengthy medical history to get treatment. Nor were there suspicious stares from nurses.

Lorraine had gathered her into her arms, carrying her to the car, and tucked Isabella into a bed she had made up in the back seat, including bed sheets, pillow, and two stuffed animals for company. It was one of those magical feats that filled Lorraine's days.

Lorraine and Isabella set out on a two-hour journey to an in-network doctor. Isabella remembered peering over the back seat and seeing Lorraine, chin held high, eyes focused on the road, singing along to an old Nancy Wilson song. Back then, Isabella had never suspected the trip was dangerous, but it was.

Isabella heard a sigh and looked down. Lorraine's eyes were open wide, and a fragile smile lit up her face. Isabella wanted to take away the pain she saw in her mom's eyes and leaned in to hug her tight. However, Isabella's magic was no match against Lorraine's breast cancer.

"Oh, Bella, I've missed you," Lorraine whispered, her voice husky with the remnants of sleep.

"How are you feeling, Mom?"

"I feel better now that you're here. How about you? Are you hungry? I can fix you supper."

"No, you cannot. You stay right there. It's my turn to wait on you. Do you want some tea?"

"Ice cubes are all I can stomach these days."

"You had chemo this morning?"

Lorraine nodded and grabbed Isabella's arm, squeezing it. "Honey, what's wrong?"

"Nothing."

Lorraine inched herself up into a sitting position and scrutinized Isabella, unconvinced.

Isabella put a pillow behind her head. "Nothing, Mom, really. I just stopped by to check on you."

"Come on, tell me. I get so bored when your daddy's at work."

"How about I read to you? What are you reading these days?" Isabella looked at the pile of books on the nightstand.

"It's Angela," Lorraine guessed.

"Well, she's still hiding things from me. Like, you know, she bought a whole new wardrobe, didn't even bother to tell me. I found the stuff still in its bags, in the closet."

"Honey, she grew up without her family and learned to only trust herself. Give her some time."

"You're right. Still..." Isabella heard gravel crunching under tires. *Two cars coming up the drive.*

"Is Dad bringing someone over?" Isabella moved to the window.

Lorraine glanced at the clock on the nightstand. "No, he's not due back till later."

Isabella saw two black sedans. Control. *Why?* Her heart started pounding in her chest. Her mind raced as four Control agents exited the cars.

"Mom, listen to me. I need you to get in the closet, and do not make a sound, no matter what you hear. You wait in the closet till Dad gets home." Isabella helped Lorraine out of bed and led her toward the closet, wrapping a blanket around her shoulders and pushing her inside. She put her finger to her mouth.

*Bang!* There was a violent pounding on the front door. "Isabella Dodge."

Lorraine's and Isabella's eyes caught.

"Bella, no." Lorraine's voice trembled with fear. "No, baby, you got to go—run. I'll distract them." Lorraine pushed her way past Isabella.

"No, you hide," Isabella said as she forced Lorraine back into the closet and closed the door. There was more pounding at the door. "Isabella Dodge, we know you're in there. Come out."

Swiftly she moved along the hallway. She looked out the kitchen window. Two agents were there, moving toward the rear of the house. Isabella's mind was skittering, looking for an escape. She had messed up, and a sinking feeling hit her square in the gut. When did it happen? Her erratic behavior at the MindControl meeting? Carter's look of suspicion afterward in the restroom? Why had she come here? She led them right to her parents. *Stupid mistake.* Isabella grabbed her phone; they had a code word for this moment. The moment she prayed would never come. She texted her dad one word, *burned,* ripped out the phone's SIM card, and searched frantically for a hiding place. Seeing the vase of fresh flowers, Isabella dropped it in the water. She tossed her phone on the floor, smashing it with the heel of her shoe.

"Isabella, we're coming in," an agent yelled.

She opened the front door. As she stepped from the shadows onto the porch, the agents moved into a defensive position, guns trained on her. The wooden planks bent under her weight, something she had never noticed before, and she imagined the world crumbling beneath her feet.

"Isabella Dodge, hands up, where we can see them." Isabella's heart raced as she surveyed the agent's placement in relation to the 'Cuda and the woods. She stepped closer to the edge of the porch and wondered if they would shoot or pursue her on foot. She was on the first step. If she made a break, the woods would offer more shelter.

"Lie face down on the ground. Do it now!" She stepped onto the sidewalk, took a deep breath, and lowered her head. If she ran or surrendered, she was dead either way. But if she surrendered, they might take her without searching the house—Lorraine would be safe.

"Now! On the ground," the agent repeated.

It was time to face her deepest fear. She followed orders, pressing her body flat on the sidewalk. The agents rushed her, pressing her face to the hard ground, searching her, scrambling over her like ants on dead meat.

"My gun and badge are in my car."

An agent cuffed Isabella.

"What's this about?" Isabella asked.

"You two search the house," the lead agent commanded.

"No one's here. I'm alone."

Pulling her up by the cuffs, the agent walked her over to the sedan's open door, pushed her head down, guided her into the back seat, and locked the door.

Isabella heard screams coming from deep inside the house, and hot flashes ripped through her mind. She threw her body against the locked door. Anger tightened her throat. "You leave my mother alone. She's sick!" Her voice was constricted, and it came out in a whisper.

"Take her mother in for questioning."

"You have no right. She's done nothing!"

Two agents dragged Lorraine out of the house. She was in her pajamas, thin and frail. As they shoved her into the back of the second sedan, Lorraine resisted.

"No, Mom, don't. Don't fight," Isabella screamed, her face pressed to the side window.

In an ill-fated attempt, Lorraine's fist smacked the agent's head, barely grazing him. Irritated, he wrestled her arm behind her back, twisting it sharply. She let out a scream so shrill and pain-filled it brought tears to Isabella's eyes and a jolt to her heart.

"They are hurting her!" Isabella said, and an intense rage exploded out of her. Kicking at the car door's window wildly, she was like a caged animal, her body twisting, thrusting. Two agents rushed into the sedan before she broke through it. An agent wrestled her down into a chokehold. She uttered a strangled "No," as the other agent injected a one-hit knock-out drug into her thigh.

Isabella thrashed as she watched her mom's pained face from across the breach. There was a fracture, then a shift, and the fault line slid, pulling her over a cliff and into blackness.

# CHAPTER FIFTY-TWO

## *The Box*

Her blue eyes fluttered open but became lost to a squint. The bone-white walls radiated as if illuminated from within. Confusion gripped her, and Isabella couldn't tell if she was up or down—the walls gave no frame of reference. As the haze in her mind dissipated, desperation and nausea set in. Her mouth was dry, and she winced as an intense pressure built in her head. She struggled to move but could not. A metal contraption held her in place; a brace across her forehead locked her head tight against a metal headrest. In her peripheral vision, metal cuffs gripped her arms, wrists, and legs, locking her down. A crippling fear took her over, and she felt her pulse pounding in her temples. *They are crucifying me*, she thought. Her mind was swimming with unanswered questions. A prickling itch swept through her body. Her skin was hypersensitive; it felt like electrodes and needles were tapping into her central nervous system, but she could not move to check for sure.

Her eyes flitted, surveying the environment. She could tell it was an enclosure the size of a freight elevator, but there was no door, only white walls, white ceiling, white floor. Oh God. Terror crept into her pores, and she stuttered the words aloud to make herself believe it. "The box." She had heard of its existence but thought it a myth.

Another wave of nausea hit hard, and Isabella spouted vomit from her mouth and nose. Passing before her eyes, it splattered on the floor over her head. Consumed with horror, she realized why there was a pounding pressure in her brain. She was hanging upside down.

* * *

Deep in the lower level of Control's Isolation Facility was the interrogation box or the box, a sterile twelve-by-twelve-foot room covered in white acoustic sound tiles which glowed with an internal luminescence. At its center was Isabella, suspended in midair in an inversion chair. Intense light bleached her nude body. Electrodes with needle points protruded along the chair's metal surfaces, puncturing her bare flesh and wiring her into the box.

Deputy Director Alice Carter had a front-row seat as she observed Isabella from the box's nerve center. Banks of computer monitors filled the compact control room. Electronics displayed Isabella's vitals and other factors: neural processing, nerve response time, eye tracking, and a voice stress meter—Carter was delighted with the high-tech setup. Thank God the government had ignored the technology ban when exercising dominance over the Luman community.

She watched the strain on Isabella's face, her effort to stay conscious. Carter grimaced as Isabella retched violently. It was a side effect of the drug they had given her. A mixture of sodium pentothal and three other secret properties made it more potent than any truth serum on the black market. It could lull the subject into sleep while the brain went into a frenzy of activity, causing disorientation, hallucination, and vivid dreaming. It was her go-to drug, producing outstanding results. With a finely manicured fingernail, Carter pressed the toggle forward and the camera zoomed in on Isabella's face. She noticed that Isabella's lips were moving. She turned the volume up on the control panel and heard Isabella's faint whispering. "I pray the Lord to guide my ways," she stuttered and started again. "Lord, be ahead of us, smoothing our paths…" Carter listened to Isabella pray until unconsciousness stole her.

Alice Carter had been a master of advanced interrogation at Control's high-value counterterrorism group in her early career. When she took the deputy director position at Control, she questioned her desire to do it, concerned the boredom of a desk job would drive her insane. Soon, though, she was managing the large staff of agents and monitors with the cunning ambition she had reserved for eliciting intelligence from terrorists, probing her Control agents' minds during meetings.

"Dominance," she whispered under her breath—she had a taste for it now. Knowing more about her agents' basic instincts than they did—feeding off their emotions—was a delicious taste of power.

But then there was Isabella, whom Carter had a hard time reading. Isabella edited her emotions expertly. Carter had chalked it up to her desk job dulling her senses until Lieutenant Raven Goodwin unexpectedly appeared at her office door, and an unedited version of Isabella Dodge was revealed. Raven wanted the Lewis case to be reopened. "Agent Dodge purposely mishandled the case," she declared. Raven was all high and mighty, and there was a calculated gleam in her eyes when she told Carter, "Agent Dodge wanted the Freewill Bill to pass because she is a Solo."

Her revelation brought a thick undercurrent of denial until Carter remembered the MindControl meeting: Isabella had called Secretary Owen's idea tyrannical and then, unprofessionally, rushed out of the meeting. When she confronted her in the powder room, Isabella came under Carter's scrutinizing inspection. She saw something that she hadn't seen before—a spark of fear. At first, she thought Isabella was fearful of losing her job. But now she understood; Isabella had thought her cover was blown. Carter's resolve turned to anger. No one fooled the Mindhunter.

Scenarios raced through her mind on how to approach Director Hill. Carter had been afraid he would discharge her for letting a spy into the ranks. But when she showed him the photo of Angela and Isabella kissing at the Lincoln Memorial, Hill just smirked. He sat back in his chair and tossed the picture onto a stack of papers. "We can add it to the pile of evidence we are collecting against her." Carter learned he was tracking Agent Dodge's digital footprint. This morning she had triggered a security breach when she went poking around in the Lucy Green case. Isabella had accessed an encrypted document in Angela Mathers's file. Not her Control file, but Mathers's Dark file. No agent had access to the Dark, not even Carter.

Carter glared smugly at Isabella in the box. No interrogators before her had ever elicited helpful information from a suspected Luman. The suspects all had died at the hands of their interrogator's torturous tactics. Later brain autopsies proved none of them had neural implants. But no one blamed the interrogators for their overzealousness. There was no test for detecting a neural chip; the human brain swiftly assimilated the neural chip's circuitry into its biological neural network. That's why the box had been created; it was the perfect torture device to get at the truth. But if a suspect did not admit to being a Luman, then the only way to be sure was to perform a bi-hemispheric brain autopsy with a light microscope. Carter had seen a video of this type of autopsy performed years earlier on a living Luman child named Missy at Camp I/O. The surgeon sliced Missy's brain in half while she was still alive. The powerful microscope lens revealed a lush grouping of mechanical neurons, electrical pulses undulating across the chip's silicone surface. Missy's neural implant had become a living organ that mimicked human neurons' communication. She died during the experimental procedure, as expected. Still, to the doctor's amazement, her neural implant's spectacular circuitry continued to function—living for five hours after her death.

She leaned in close to the monitor, captivated by Isabella's expressionless face. She had to admit, the agent's deception had been flawless. She got into the character and used her Southern charm to distract people from what she was—a Chip spying for the Guardians. But denying pain was hard to master; most terrorists folded under torture. She couldn't wait to learn what Isabella did under extreme coercion.

"All systems are online," Bob's baritone voice boomed. He was the science behind Carter's psychology.

Checking Isabella's heart rate, Carter turned to Bob. "Vitals are good. Let's begin with an introduction."

\* \* \*

The inversion chair moved robotically, jarring Isabella out of her drug-induced sleep. She felt eyes watching her as the chair rotated her into the upright position and locked into place with a muffled click. Nausea washed over her again, and she swallowed hard, pushing the bile back down. The smell of English Leather lingered in the air; she knew the scent. She saw Carter's boxy silhouette haloed by bright lights. *So close.*

She tried to move, and an electrical shock shot through every nerve in her body. Fire seared her tissues and she screamed in agony. The electrical current halted eventually and she opened her blurry eyes. Not exactly the welcome wagon, but the experience revealed to Isabella two critical facts: this wasn't a computer-generated simulation or virtual reality experience—it was real. And more importantly, knowing the Mindhunter could never resist, she'd learned that the box would be administering physical injury to her at the hands of Alice Carter.

Carter spoke into the mic in a carefree tone. "You must be feeling dreadful and wondering where you are." The wall's luminance intensified with the cadence of her voice. "The box will explore your mind, extract intelligence, and learn your true identity, but we can stop this right now if you admit to being a Luman."

Isabella struggled to speak, and it came out sluggish and, in a damp, slurring breath, "Youuu um." The drugs had slowed her thinking. She kept trying, forming her words slowly, "You. Want. Know. Who I am?" Her voice cracked, but at least it was coherent.

"Yes. It's simple, Isabella. Say 'I'm a Luman.'"

"You get nothing until I know my mom's safe."

"We shall see," Carter said imperiously. "The mind does uncontrollable things under stress, Isabella."

Isabella's chair spun around, and she was staring at her vomit on the floor. She was aware that her long, curly hair was not falling forward; they had shaved her head. A ticking of tiny gears reverberated in the space, followed by a loud whoosh. Her eyes darted frantically. Thoughts jittering, she tried to anticipate what was coming next. Her throat tightened. She swallowed hard, then muttered, "Prepare yourself."

In the control room, Bob typed commands into the computer. Carter watched a surgical probe drop from the ceiling; it unfolded and moved toward Isabella. At the end of the probe there was a long needle. The robotic arm angled the probe at the back of Isabella's skull.

Isabella felt a sting, and then a sharp ache radiated from the back of her head. It felt like a steel-wool brush was whisking her brain into a froth. The metal needle burrowed deep inside her head toward its intended target, the posterior cortical region, referred to as the "hot zone," the section of the brain known to be active during dreaming and other sensory activities.

As the needle churned, a moist heat stirred between Isabella's legs and urine splattered on the floor below her. Humiliation washed over her. She fought to clear her mind of any thoughts. She couldn't let Carter get into her head; her lips trembled as she fought to stay alert and not lose consciousness. She attempted to recall Angela's instructions on finding her inner light, but her thoughts fluttered, unspooled, till she lost track of them.

As the needle reached its mark, Lorraine's voice rose out of the darkness, *"Isabella, remember to breathe."* She was fading into a hypnotic state, teetering on the edge of reality.

*"Stay awake,"* she told herself.

*Stay awake,* she chanted as the pain intensified. She struggled to make a deeper connection to her neural chip, but her consciousness was circling the drain, and she couldn't stop it. She knew this place, the place where the mind turned on itself.

*The smell of rust and blood splattering everywhere, on her face, in her hair. I killed him... There is no going back from that.*

Isabella blacked out.

# CHAPTER FIFTY-THREE

### *Frank & Lorraine*

Frank's heart stumbled when he saw the Control agent rigidly planted in front of Lorraine's hospital room, but when he tried to ask Frank's name, he pushed past, ignoring him. Lorraine was there, sitting up in bed. She and Frank froze when they saw each other. They had prepared themselves for this day; all Solo parents did. But no amount of preparation would stop the emotional hurricane swirling off the coast and moving inland for a direct hit should Control find out the truth about Isabella.

"Thank God," he gasped and rushed to her, dropping her overnight bag—the one they always had packed for such emergencies. He hugged her close and whispered, "I'm here. It will be okay."

Lorraine shuddered. "They took her."

"Don't fret, honey. But right now, let's focus on you." He gave her his best reassuring expression, but inside, hopelessness had already set in.

When Isabella's burn notice lit up Frank's phone, he tried calling Lorraine. When she didn't answer, he had rushed home to find Control agents searching the house. He hotfooted it out of there before anyone saw him. Later, the police called to notify him of Lorraine's condition.

"They hurt you."

Lorraine had a cast on her left arm. "It was awful. Those ruffians hit Isabella, choked her, drugged her, one even broke my arm…"

Frank kissed the top of her head and wrapped her in his arms. "You're safe now."

There was a knock on the door and Larry Mathers appeared, dressed in a suit and tie and holding his briefcase.

"How is the patient?" Larry peered over his black-rimmed reading glasses.

Frank gave Larry a nod of appreciation. "Thanks for coming, Larry. I'm sure the call came from out of the blue, but I figure you were our best chance to beat this."

He motioned to Larry. "Remember Angela's father, Lorraine?"

"Of course. How are you?"

"Well, the question is, how are you feeling?"

"I'm better now that y'all are here. Have you heard anything about Isabella?"

"I submitted a formal inquiry, but in reality, they do not have to tell us anything until they charge her."

"What? They can't do that!" Frank huffed around the room.

Larry's tone was grave. "They seem to suspect she is someone named Mazzy Parks, an undocumented Luman. Isabella has no rights until we prove the charge is false."

"What proof do they have?" Frank asked.

"That's unclear, but they want to question both of you. I was able to buy you a little time because of Lorraine's frail condition."

There was another knock on the door and Donovan trekked in dressed as a hospital attendant, carrying a vase of yellow daisies. Frank's face darkened when he saw the flowers.

"I hear the Control agent that brought you in looks worse, Lorraine. How are you, slugger?" Donovan said.

"Look what the cat dragged in. My lord, Donovan, you shouldn't have." Lorraine gave Donovan a pained smile.

Frank said, "Don, this is—"

"Oh yes, I know who Larry is." Donovan's mood was anything but welcoming as he avoided shaking Larry's outstretched hand.

"Call me when they release Lorraine, and we'll go over to Control's headquarters together," Larry explained.

"Thanks again, Larry," Frank called over his shoulder as Larry left.

"Donovan, that was rude," reprimanded Lorraine.

"It's for his own good. I don't want to involve him."

"Involve him? What are you talking about?" Lorraine asked.

Donovan set the daisies down on the bedside table and studied them, adjusting their position.

"We'll talk later. You two stay safe," Donovan said, tight-lipped, then left.

"What in Sam Hill was that all about?" Lorraine asked.

Frank grabbed a blue-checkered dress out of Lorraine's overnight bag and handed it to her in a harried manner. "Put on your clothes. We have to go."

Lorraine did what he said.

Frank whispered in her ear as he zipped up the back of her dress. "The flowers are a code." She turned to face him. "It's time to run."

"There's a card attached to a daisy." Frank took it and whispered the instructions written inside. "When the agent leaves his post, take the west elevator down to the first floor, leave the building by Exit 102. A blue SUV will be there." He stashed the card in his pocket.

Lorraine slipped on her shoes with her one good hand. Frank helped her into the wheelchair, and they waited.

At the door, Frank listened to the agent's radio as it reverberated through the door. "All agents, shots fired, shots fired. Active shooter first-floor emergency room." Frank and Lorraine exchanged worried looks—this was it. They waited until they were sure the agent had left his post, then broke for the west elevator.

Preoccupied nurses and orderlies scampered around as Frank pushed Lorraine's wheelchair down the sterile white corridor. Lorraine's purse sat in her lap and she smiled at everyone; the active shooter had everyone distracted as the couple moved like ghosts, unnoticed. Ahead of them was the west elevator. "Almost there, honey." Frank patted her shoulder.

The elevator door slid open, and Frank rushed Lorraine inside and pressed the lobby button. They watched the numbers ticking down— knowing that with each moment, they were once again moving farther away from the life they knew.

*Ding!* Level Two. The door opened, and two police officers stepped in. Frank's back straightened. He gazed at his wife, avoiding eye contact with them at all costs. Lorraine's free hand twisted the straps of her purse as the elevator moved slowly downward again. One of the police radios was blasting information about the active shooter. The noisy static crept up Frank's spine, putting him on edge. Finally, the officer glanced over his shoulder at Lorraine and lowered the volume on his radio to a hum. She smiled.

*Ding!* The elevator door opened, and the police exited. Frank let go of the breath he was holding and pushed Lorraine's wheelchair out as a mother arguing with her three teenage kids piled in. They were almost free. Frank's pace quickened, following the corridor left then right.

"There." Lorraine pointed to the 102 exit. With a whoosh of air, the double doors there opened. They were outside under a covered patio. A tumult of emergency room evacuees flooded the area as the police tried to corral those milling about. Frank maneuvered the wheelchair through the crowd, avoiding the cops and arriving at a clearing on the sidewalk. The blue SUV pulled up, and the back door flew open. Frank helped Lorraine in, then jumped in beside her. In the front seat were a driver and Donovan. The SUV darted off; Frank and Lorraine were on the run. By nightfall, there would be no trace of them but the empty wheelchair on the curb.

Donovan looked at the man driving the SUV. "Remember Johnny?" Johnny glanced up into the rearview mirror and nodded to Frank and Lorraine. The SUV turned right and was swallowed into the evening traffic.

"They have Isabella in the box," Donovan stated flatly.

Lorraine's head sank into her palms and she uttered a long aching wail. Frank tried to comfort her. He searched Donovan's eyes desperately.

"Our source confirmed it. We don't know what intel they got out of her, but Isabella's capture was a full breach." Donovan signaled Johnny to turn onto a side street. He made a U-turn and drove in the opposite direction.

"So far, no tail," Johnny remarked.

Donovan inclined his head. "We are getting you both out of the country." The left blinker sounded, and Johnny entered a shopping mall parking lot. They all wobbled around in their seats in silence as the SUV lurched over a speed bump and pulled into an empty parking spot, idling. The parking lot was full of holiday shoppers preparing for Thanksgiving later in the week.

Through the side window, Donovan pointed to a black Honda nearby. "That's your ride. Inside are the details on your new identities, passports, disguises. In the glove compartment is a bundle of C-notes and two plane tickets to British Columbia. When you land, you'll receive further instructions."

Lorraine shook her head, whimpering as Frank said, "No, we can't leave. We have to get Isabella out of there." She turned to Donovan.

"I'm not leaving without my girl." Lorraine's misery was undeniable, and Frank had to turn away.

"This is the best we can do," Donovan said with unbending sternness.

"We have to try," Frank pleaded.

"The elders took a vote, and it's too risky."

"This is your doing. You hate her." Lorraine's voice shook with anger.

"If the Guardians thought there was any hope of getting her out alive, you know we would try. Right now, you need to think about yourselves. When Control finds out you ran, it will turn into a witch hunt. If they catch you, it's jail or worse. In British Columbia, we've set up an oncologist to take over your care and cancer treatments, Lorraine. All you have to do is get in that car." Donovan pointed to the Honda. "And drive to the airport."

"I'm not leaving without my little girl," Lorraine protested.

"They've had Isabella for five hours. Chances are she's not your little girl anymore."

The truth was sobering. Frank and Lorraine shifted to the Honda, sitting in silence inside it as Donovan and Johnny drove off. The sinking sun reflected off the SUV's rooftop as it moved out of sight, and shoppers with carts filled with festive grocery bags skirted by, happily making preparations for the holiday. Everywhere else life was being lived, but for Frank and Lorraine, the world had stopped.

Frank gripped the steering wheel and watched as Lorraine's lips set in determination. He knew her stubborn streak all too well. Lorraine's cancer was too aggressive to stop her treatments, and what would happen if they stayed to help Isabella? They would have to go into hiding. Frank tried to quell the avalanche of emotions that threatened to bury him. He reached over Lorraine's knee and unlocked the glove compartment. It fell open, touching Lorraine's lap and exposing a stack of cash and two airline tickets. Angrily, she pushed the airline tickets out of her sight, revealing a revolver.

They stared at the gun for a long moment, and then their eyes met. How could he choose between Lorraine and Isabella? A grimace of pain flashed across Frank's face at this thought.

Lorraine cried as she made one last plea. "Honey, there are all kinds of evil growing in people. I'm tired of waiting and hoping for them to change. This hate for our daughter, it's not right. We have to help her."

Frank caressed Lorraine's cheek, brushing the tear stains away. She leaned into his touch and kissed him full on the lips despite his unwavering love for her—and because of it. He pulled away from her half-heartedly, rationalizing that nothing was for sure or forever. A clap of thunder broke the silence, and he knew Isabella would never forgive him if Lorraine didn't survive this. The engine sputtered unhappily in the cool air, then sparked to life. He clasped his wife's hand as the next leg of their journey began.

# CHAPTER FIFTY-FOUR

## *The War Inside*

*I killed him… There is no going back from that.*

"Police stop! Hands where I can see them," the guard yelled. Suddenly a floodlight shone on Isabella in her Wayne mask.

"Gin, run, now," Isabella yelled, forgetting to silent-message. Gin stood frozen in her Tammy disguise, next to Noah, both in their coveralls. They looked at Isabella on the inside of the border fence outside the Baton Rouge Compound. They were but inches apart, footsteps from freedom.

"Hey, buddy, stop!" the guard yelled as he bounded toward her. She zipped down her coverall and reached inside for her holstered Glock.

The man grew closer; it was an easy shot.

"Do not engage, Isabella. Run! Come on," Gin said.

Isabella looked at the guard, then Gin.

"Run!" Gin yelled.

Isabella plowed through the hole in the barbed-wire fence, making it to the other side. She ran through a grassy field as it surged up toward her, tall stems beating at her shins. Up ahead, she saw Gin running with Noah. They were headed toward the downtown Artists Market.

Isabella peered over her shoulder. A dumpy-looking officer was running after her. She made a hard right, leading the patrolman away from Gin and Noah—though this wasn't part of the plan. But then again, neither was having the guard chasing her. The officer's clumsy gallop was no match for Isabella's long-legged stride. Still, her breathing was labored and hindered by her Wayne mask. As she lost steam, she cut back toward the Artists Market's main street, hoping to lose the officer in the crowd.

She made her way through the sea of people shopping and celebrating in the marketplace. At the first alley, she stopped to catch her breath. Standing in the streetlight, backlit, her elongated shadow stretched to meet an endless passageway riddled with trash and muck. Gin emerged from Isabella's shadow, wearing a long black wig instead of her Tammy disguise. Then Noah appeared out of the darkness clad now in a sweatshirt and ball cap. They huddled together.

*The guard is still following me.* Isabella eyed the stone walls, finally spotting a fire escape. *There—we need to take to the rooftops.*

Gin helped her off with her coverall, put the Wayne mask in Gin's purse, and then dispensed with the outfit in the dumpster.

With a panicked look, Noah surveyed the fire escape towering three stories above. "I'm not good with heights."

"You better get good if you want to live," Isabella said. She jumped up, grabbing the fire escape ladder and pulling it down to the ground.

Gin climbed the ladder with feverish agility; Isabella followed, climbing the steps two at a time. She gripped the top of the metal rail at the roofline, straining as she pulled herself up over the building's stone parapet, and fell onto the flat gravel roof with a thud. Noah clumsily climbed the iron ladder and when he reached the top, Gin helped him over the ledge. While Isabella stood lookout, lights cut through the darkness below them. The guard from earlier was sweeping the alley with his flashlight, talking on his radio. The light illuminated the fire escape ladder, and he traced it up to the roof.

*Run,* Isabella silent-messaged. They bolted, crossing the gravel rooftop. There was a five-foot gap to cross over to the next roof and a fifty-foot drop if they didn't make it. The adjacent building had a steep gable roof and wooden shakes capping the rooftop. Gin leapt with grace; Isabella's long stride cleared the crevice efficiently. They climbed up the slope, clutching the wooden shingles for support. As Noah made the jump, though, his sweatshirt caught on a vent pipe sticking up out of the roof. He stumbled forward as his feet left the ground. His hands hit the gutter of the adjacent building, locking onto it as it bent under his weight. He swung into the brick building, then dangled there, unable to lift himself onto the gable roof.

Isabella searched for Noah and saw his fingers gripping the gutter. She slid down the sloping roof, straining to reach his forearms. She clutched them, lifting him. Glancing up, she saw the guard's hat crest the first building's rooftop. As she struggled to pull Noah up, the guard heaved himself over the parapet and struggled to his feet. He spotted them on the gable roof and lumbered after them.

"You there, stop!" he yelled.

The wooden shingles suddenly gave way under Isabella's shoes, and she and Noah tumbled down the steep decline, back to square one. Noah screamed as his body dangled over the edge. With no time to waste, Isabella heaved him up again, seeing the terror in his eyes.

"I got you now, and I'm gonna keep you," she said with a reassuring grin. He smiled back.

*Bang!*

Noah's head jerked forward as a bullet drilled through his skull. Blood and brain matter sprayed into the air, covering Isabella. His head wrenched backward in a violent whiplash. She watched as the life force left his eyes. The guard's gun muzzle glinted and another bullet exploded out of it, streaking past her. Gin fired at the officer and clipped his shoulder, taking him down. But it was too late. Noah's grip loosened from Isabella's hands, and she screamed, watching him slip away, falling through the gap between the two buildings.

Awakened by screams, Isabella realized they were her own. "I should have taken the shot, Gin. It was an easy shot."

Isabella was unaware she was crying till the tears fell like raindrops onto the floor. As the image of Noah's lifeless eyes faded, she realized where she was. The dried vomit on the box's floor told her an indeterminate amount of time had passed. She gasped as a clicking sound began, and she felt the probe retracting from deep inside her brain, taking with it her memories. Her sobbing faded to feeble whimpers as she blacked out again.

\* \* \*

The hunt was on. Isabella's digital dream of Noah's escape flickered and glitched like old celluloid on the control room computer screen. Carter watched, sitting at the control panel, her journal open, taking notes.

"It's like a broken record. She keeps dreaming the same thing over and over. It must really bother her," Bob said with a chuckle.

Carter looked up from her journal. "Yes, or it's a diversion technique." She tapped her pen on her paper impatiently. "What did you find out about Noah?"

"It was over four years ago. Noah Parker died trying to escape the Baton Rouge Compound. The shot that killed him destroyed his chip as well. They never caught his accomplices."

Carter smiled. "Well, we have one."

"What about the old lady or the lady with the long dark hair?" Bob asked.

"That was Gin Bailey, two different disguises. She's dead." There was contempt mixed with an air of excitement in Carter's voice. "I'm putting the puzzle of Isabella Dodge together—it's not a lot but a start. I need something to get her out of this dream loop. Maybe we can get some photos from her past."

"Isabella," she said into the mic, but Isabella was unconscious. She looked at Bob. "Wake her up."

Bob typed some key commands into the system. Serum funneled into an IV in Isabella's neck. "This special blend can wake the dead," Carter said as she stared at Isabella on the monitor, and soon, Isabella's eyes fluttered open.

The inversion chair twisted and turned, jolting her body into the upright sitting position. She gagged and heaved uncontrollably, but her stomach was empty. "Just kill me," she screamed.

Carter smiled. "Am I torturing you, Dodge? Or are you torturing yourself?" Carter and Bob laughed.

* * *

Isabella winced at Carter's remark. She was right; this battle wasn't between her and Carter—it was a war within herself. She wanted to die, to leave her body before it was too late—before her dreams gave everything away. But she kept faltering, losing time. Her mind was unmoored.

"Just fucking kill me already," she whispered to herself. A sudden thumping sound reverberated in her and around her. It was a distinctive tempo. Her eyes roamed everywhere, trying to understand the familiar sound. It was the beating of another heart, a second heartbeat. *How?* she wondered. *Am I losing my mind, or is this one of Carter's tricks?* She listened. The heartbeat was growing louder, closer, and more powerful. Isabella's own heart abandoned its beat and cohered with the other heart's rhythm. She shuddered under her breath. "Angela."

# CHAPTER FIFTY-FIVE

## *Checkmate*

It was the dead of the night when Angela arrived with Agent David Ross at Control's Isolation Facility. A soldier signed her in, and she surrendered her purse and phone. Earlier, her father had called and alerted her to Isabella's detention and to the fact that Frank and Lorraine had disappeared mysteriously from the hospital. But he reminded her that under the Freewill Law, what happened in St. Edenville couldn't happen here—as long as Angela denied knowing Isabella was a Solo, for both Isabella's and her own sake.

Shortly after she had hung up with her dad, Donovan had texted, sending her already shredded nerves into a tailspin. His first line of text was a warning: Get the Lumans out of D.C. Isabella's capture was a declaration of war to the Guardians. Angela, fearing the worst, had gotten her boss at LA to furlough all the Lumans for the next two weeks, leaving the humans with little defense against a Guardian cyberattack.

The next line of Donavan's text had flummoxed her, though: *Dar Preston.* That was all he wrote. Using Isabella's laptop, Angela had researched Darwin Preston, but she still had no answers. Preston was a young Republican congressman—a political nobody—recovering from a brain aneurysm. *Dar Preston could have Jonathan's chip,* she'd thought, *but then again, maybe not. She needed more answers.*

Angela assumed Raven turned Isabella in and she cursed herself for underestimating her. She'd thought Raven would be a copy of Warren, a pathetic romantic living in a make-believe world—but Warren 2.0 was at best a hybrid Warren, a soldier and a traitor to her own kind. Knowing she was likely next on Raven's list, she prepared for a trip to Control. When Agent Ross showed up at their apartment for her, she was ready to prove Isabella was a human, thus innocent.

Agent Ross and Angela moved along a modern empty corridor. It felt surreal, like she was sleepwalking through a nightmare. He stopped at the door labeled Interrogation One and opened it. "Wait in here. Someone will be in to take your statement shortly."

Angela hesitated. "Statement for what? Is Isabella okay?"

"Please wait inside."

Angela heard the door close and lock behind her. She stared in disbelief at the large, formal living room: dark hardwood floors, warm amber wall tones, and early nineteenth-century paintings with their ornate, gold flake, wood frames. The antique furniture's deep red tones and the fire blazing in the grand fireplace created a serene ambiance designed to put suspects at ease. She circled the space, dizzy with amusement.

Her skin began to tingle, and an odd onslaught of emotions coursed through her. She hugged her shape, trying to calm herself as her trembling hands flew to her neck. Her throat tightened, and she gasped for breath, suddenly suffocating. A substance in the room must be affecting her. Panicked thoughts filled her head, dangerous, horrible thoughts. She was terrified. It must be an airborne drug or poison or—*No, it's something else. It's someone else.*

*Isabella?* Angela silent-messaged.

When Angela closed her eyes, she experienced the sensation of Isabella's lips pressing against hers. Tears streamed down her cheeks uncontrollably.

*You're here,* she said, falling to one knee, undone by the intensity of Isabella's feelings surging through her. A heaviness overcame her, and she collapsed onto the floor, barely able to move, feeling as if something was bolting down her arms and legs. Jagged flashes of a monstrous robotic chair filled her mind as electrodes dug into her flesh and bone.

*My God, you're in the box.*

Angela's sweat ran cold; everything Isabella was feeling penetrated Angela and set her body on fire. She had to break the connection to Isabella—it was too much. Isabella's thoughts of death pushed Angela to the precipice. She shuddered. *Isabella, it's too much. You need to gain control of your thoughts, focus your mind.*

*I can't,* Isabella silent-messaged.

*Yes, you can. They want you to feel helpless, but you are not. Pain requires your body. Leave it behind. Go toward the light.*

Angela virtually transported herself one floor below. She was inside the box with Isabella and feeling and seeing everything happening to her. The inversion chair flipped Isabella forward and she was facing the floor, then the ticking began.

"No, not again," Isabella whimpered. Angela watched the probe extending down from the ceiling, moving methodically toward the back of Isabella's skull. Angela leaned in close to Isabella's ear. *Isabella, slow your breathing. You have to prepare for this.*

Isabella slowed her breathing, and before the probe reached her, Angela guided Isabella, taking her deeper into her mind to the core of her neural implant. Angela was virtually in her mind when Isabella felt a glimmer of something strange, something unfamiliar, someplace safe before her, a silvery-phosphorus glow that spread in a swath along the horizon.

*That's it. Move toward the light,* Angela said.

As the probe penetrated Isabella's skull, Angela heard her cry out, and she bit down on her gloved hand to silence her own pain.

*Isabella, push through it,* Angela groaned.

And Isabella did. She moved into the light; her corporeal existence no longer mattered, and the pain disintegrated as a luminosity overtook her, surrounding her.

*You did it. Isabella: you are free.*

Isabella hesitated as a magnetic force drew her near, pulling her neural implant's data forward. She pulled back, frightened by it.

*You cannot stay.* Angela rushed her words. *Let go. There is another world beyond your body.*

Angela watched as the phosphorescent wave carried Isabella beyond her physical body into the light, sharing the experience with her. As the light's intensity increased, Isabella sensed energy growing in it, saw that there were others in the light, others like her. She let go, and her mind expanded into the vast limitless space. She became a shimmering star shooting through an electrical storm. And then a train speeding down a track in a golden glaze. But she was not a shooting star or a speeding train—she was data, a river of information, knowledge, memories, dreams, and emotions—all of it moving at the speed of thought, in perfect clarity, at full potential. Isabella's body was in the box, but her mind was in the light, beyond Carter's reach.

Angela opened her eyes, and she was back in Interrogation One. She quickly composed herself, taking in deep breaths to relax. Now that Isabella was safe in the light, her own anxiety was the enemy. She swallowed it down, needing to distance herself from her emotions. She had to prepare for what was coming next.

The door opened, and Angela turned. Her eyes met with intrigue as Deputy Director Alice Carter breezed in and crossed over to a barley twist library table in the corner. "Brandy?" Carter's tone was self-assured.

"Hmm?" Angela recognized Carter's voice from the time they spoke on the phone. She half expected Raven, had prepared herself for Raven and a military interrogation. Instead, it was Carter's cordial manners, her pleasant appearance, and this elegant interrogation room. *Bravo, Alice, for trying to catch me off guard*, Angela thought.

"I said, would you care for a brandy? I find it soothes the nerves."

On the library table was a tray of liquors and wines. Carter opened a decanter and poured golden-brown liquor into two glasses. She approached Angela, holding out a goblet, never breaking eye contact, as if she were nearing an unpredictable creature in the wild.

Carter relaxed into a Queen Anne leather lounge chair. Angela sat opposite her on a crushed velvet flared arm sofa, and she rubbed her fingers over the fabric.

"Nice, isn't it?" Carter grinned. "We call this room the abbey. Remember the old TV show, *Aristocratic British Family*?"

Angela nodded. Carter probably knew she had never watched TV in camp, and she was reading Angela's responses, so she sat still with an enigmatic expression.

"Angela, you appear surprisingly fit, all considered."

Angela's lips set in a straight line, waiting for it.

Carter opened her notebook and read from it: "You have difficulty forming emotional bonds with people." She gave a disapproving shake of her head.

*She read my juvenile psychological evaluation*, Angela mused. *Who hasn't?* She waited for the deputy director to continue, but when she didn't, she gazed at her flatly.

"Sorry, what was the question?"

"I was thinking when people around you become—incapacitated— you lack empathy. You showed no remorse for little Lucy or now for Isabella. You do know Isabella is in the box?" Angela shrugged but imagined reaching out to strangle Carter with her bare hands. A sudden stillness filled the room as each woman judged her opponent.

Carter's lips pursed. Angela reflected on Carter's egocentrism; it was innate. How strange it must be to judge the world by how it affected you personally.

Carter fumbled through loose documents in her journal, retrieving a photo. She waved it at Angela like a warning flag. "Speaking of unlawful…"

Angela looked with disinterest at the photo of her and Isabella kissing at the Lincoln Memorial.

"You flaunt your perversity in public. Did you want Isabella to get caught?" Angela gave Carter a doubtful look.

"What is your point? Isabella and I are together, and it's not against the law anymore."

"Because you knew she was undocumented?"

"No. Isabella is not a Luman."

A hint of smugness graced Carter's flawless complexion. "I thought you'd be a better liar. Look at the photo's date stamp."

Angela didn't look. She remembered the kiss. True. They broke code that night, but not if Isabella was a Solo.

"Freewill has a retroactive ameliorative clause, prohibiting prosecution, Alice."

"Not equivocally," Carter said with a smirk. "Maybe to humans but not to robots in love."

Angela raised her chin slightly in this standoff of wills. Carter turned the page of her notebook and studied it. "Isabella's a Solo and a spy and you know it. That makes you a coconspirator, but we can look past that if you help us," Carter reassured her. "This is your only chance to negotiate your release."

"My release! All I've heard are general assumptions and prejudiced remarks. What do you have on Isabella that proves she's a Solo?"

Carter leaned back, not willing to show her cards.

Angela sipped her brandy. "This is nice." She swirled the golden-brown liquid in her glass, staring at it for a long moment, then set the glass on the table, letting her fingers fall away from it but never letting her impassive expression falter.

"Carter, is this as good as it gets for your kind—leveraging power over those different from yourself? Unlike the Lumans, you seem to feel a need to judge everyone by age, gender, sexuality, race, intellect… Should I go on?"

"Oh, please do enlighten me, Angela." Carter crossed her arms.

"I thought the Freewill Bill would bring our society together. Congress voted and agreed to it. It is easy to convince yourself something is possible when you want it badly enough, I guess." Angela scrutinized Carter like a piece in a chess match.

A smile split Carter's thin lips. She inched closer to the edge of her seat with excitement. "Rest assured, Angela, I haven't simply been blinded by my desire to prove Isabella is a Luman." Carter's voice raised as she stood. "I have all the evidence I need sitting in the box." She pointed to the floor. "Enough evidence to crush the Guardians. And once I have extracted all of Isabella's memories, well, it's hard to say what will happen to your kind."

Angela had her on the defensive. She stood, matching Carter's stance while masking her dread. "So, right now, you don't have any evidence, except for Lieutenant Goodwin's accusation, am I right? Let me guess, she told you she confronted me? By the way, she calls herself Raven because she's a Luman—now."

Carter's eyes widened.

"I see Director Herschel Hill and Secretary General Erivan Owen kept you in the dark about that. And here you were, so quick to believe a Chip. Wait till they find out you placed an innocent human in the box, ignoring the international and US law against torture. Talk about history repeating itself. How many Control inquisitors have mercilessly killed innocent humans, suspecting them to be Luman? Hmm? Are you ready to be the next one to kill a human?"

Reading the doubt on Carter's face, Angela knew her bluff had hit its mark. It mattered to Carter how people perceived her.

"We had lots of evidence on Isabella before she went into the box."

"Lots of evidence? She's not a Luman, so what kind of evidence could you possibly have?" Angela folded her arms across her chest and stared through Carter. "I think we are through."

Carter shook her head. "No, we are not. The government will not stand for any militia activity. Tell us what you know about the Guardians for Isabella's sake."

Angela scoffed. "You cannot hold me. I have rights." She moved toward the door.

"You seem to forget who I am. I can put you in the box right now."

Angela stopped in her tracks as the moment swelled and anxiety built in her. Carter needed to be in control, even if it meant twisting the facts. She'd never be free, not with people like Carter subverting the rules while policing the nation. She turned to face her. Fear was raging through her veins, but she'd be damned if she'd let Carter see it.

"I've seen it before. She calls herself Raven, not Lieutenant Goodwin, because her personality has split." She sold her lie by including a morsel of truth. The beauty of uncertainty, doubt, was her weapon of choice. "It happens when they transplant neural implants in an adult. The brain never adapts, and the previous donor's memories resurrect to some degree." In a mocking gesture, she pursed her lips. "Your scientists really don't understand the power of our neural chips."

She shook her head. "You should ask yourself how a Luman like Goodwin got on the MindControl board." She paused to let Carter respond. When she didn't, when she couldn't utter one single, coherent syllable, Angela told her why it had happened. "An unlawful segment of the government, a very powerful one, is working to transform soldiers into Lumans. Director Herschel Hill and Secretary General Erivan Owen might have kept you out of the loop because they judged you incompetent. Maybe they thought you're an older woman, befuddled easily, who knows? But, Alice, now you know something about Raven that they don't. Raven is suffering from a disruption of identity. In other words, she is a soldier with borderline personality disorder."

Deflated, Carter sat down and took a long drink of brandy, thinking over everything. Angela just knocked over the queen.

"I'd like my phone call now, please." She let the corners of her mouth curve up slightly.

# CHAPTER FIFTY-SIX

## *The Ghost in the Machinery*

Isabella hung upside down, half conscious.

Inside the control room, computer commands scrolled down the screen as Bob's fingers fluttered across the keyboard, guiding the system as it scanned and downloaded into Isabella's brain the personal photographs that David had retrieved from her apartment.

The probe withdrew from Isabella's skull and retracted to its hiding place. The chair swung around, setting her in the upright position. Images of her life passed before her eyes: Lorraine, Frank, Gin opening gifts at Christmas, Gin on the beach, Lorraine and Frank's wedding.

Carter watched Isabella's emotionless face and turned to Bob. "These images will prompt her subconscious to think about other things besides Noah's death." She spoke into the mic. "Isabella, tell me how you escaped the camps."

Isabella's body hung silently with no peripheral awareness, her eyes staring blankly into space.

Carter sighed. Bob gave her an encouraging smile. They had been at this for hours with little response from Isabella.

"Why are the drugs no longer working?" she moaned. She needed to find hard evidence that Isabella was a Solo. Angela's father had arrived in response to her phone call and had negotiated her release.

She had no leverage with Angela unless and until she retrieved evidence from Isabella's memories. "Everyone breaks," she told Bob, the tension in her voice obvious. When Isabella broke, she'd get her, and she'd get Angela too.

"Isabella, what is your birth name?"

Bob studied Isabella on the monitor. "She's unresponsive to external stimuli. How is that possible?"

Carter rubbed her forehead and sighed, having gone thirty hours without sleep. "She is torturing me." She tapped the toggle switch, and the camera zoomed in on Isabella's bloodshot eyes. On close inspection, it was clear that her face was devoid of fear. "She's not feeling anything." Carter looked at Bob in bewilderment.

Humiliation blasted across Carter's face as she realized Angela had somehow interfered with Isabella's interrogation. "She tricked me." She pounded her fist on the table, remembering the secretive and often misunderstood nature of Luman communication abilities. "Angela must have been communicating with Isabella telepathically."

"How did she know Isabella was here?" Bob asked.

Carter didn't know how; she just knew Angela was to blame. "That woman cannot be trusted. I should have held her without a phone call. *Ugh!*" She turned on the mic. "Isabella!"

Isabella's expression gave back nothing.

"Angela worked out a plea deal." She had the chair slowly spin Isabella around. "She told us what you are. Go ahead. Try to contact her. You can't because I let her go. She's free, but you are not. We all know, Isabella, so just say it."

Carter's strident voice vibrated the incandescent lights in the box, making it look like the walls were speaking to Isabella. "Tell me your true identity, and this stops. Say it out loud."

Isabella's eyes were vacant.

"If you do not willfully give me the information I seek, I will take it from you." Carter turned to Bob. "Juice her again."

Bob raised an eyebrow. "But…that's over the permitted limit."

"Let me worry about that."

Serum filled a thin tube that ran from the chair, feeding into Isabella's neck. The drug jolted her physical brain into a frenzy of activity and Isabella's digital mind rushed back into her neural implant.

"Her EEG activity is increasing," Bob reported.

Carter stared into the monitor. She watched Isabella's fingers tremble and twitch. "Come on, Isabella, say it." She turned to Bob. "More. Give her another dose."

"No!" Isabella screamed with every bit of the air left in her lungs as she tried to stay conscious.

"Download the photos again. I want her whole life to flash before her."

The inversion chair flipped her into position as the probe penetrated Isabella's skull. Within minutes, images of Lorraine, Frank, and Gin with Isabella standing in front of her F1 race car occupied her thoughts.

"No." Her voice was barely audible.

"Go to sleep, Isabella. It's easier that way."

* * *

Racing photo after racing photo displayed in Isabella's mind and she heard the engine's throaty sound idling, waiting to run free:

She and Gin were racing in the dog days of summer. It was early morning at the Detroit Grand Prix and the temperature on the street circuit track had already reached 100 degrees. The smell of hot asphalt and exhaust mixed with the sulfur odor rolling off the Detroit River; surreal and dreamlike, an orange mist rose off the black water. Isabella sat inside the F1's cockpit while Gin straddled the narrow front chassis and locked Isabella into her seven-point harness, securing her inside the machine. Gin's red hair blew like flames licking at the wind.

They went over Isabella's racing checklist but they were not here just to race. Gin used the event to pass intel to the Detroit Guardians during the winner's ceremony. Gin gave her a final pat on the side of her helmet.

"Find your way free." It was their saying right before a race. And then Gin undulated into the distance, like a desert mirage, evaporating in waves of heat, lost to Isabella.

It was time. Isabella glared at the red lights as they extinguished one at a time. There were five, now four, three, two. Her Formula 1 car rocketed off the line, the track ahead blurred and bent as she jetted down a long straightaway, warming up her tires, correctly aligning her head and steering wheel to take the first right-hander. She was in the inside lane coming out of the curve, and she was running parallel to the river. As she accelerated, she glued her tires to the track's inside edge, maximizing her corner entry into the next turn. She ripped through the gears on a long backstretch as the G-force flattened her to the seat. She hit 196 mph, then plucked the clutch, diving into a banked corner and riding the middle lane; she was now a lap ahead of the other racers.

The track ahead looked like rush hour on the expressway. Maneuvering to the outside lane against the wall, she passed the pack of cars like they were standing still.

Lighting flashed and flickered in her eyes, disturbing the edges of her reality, and suddenly she was back in the box. The robotic chair spun her around quickly, like a Scrambler theme park ride.

"Isabella, tell me how the Guardians transmitted communiqués during your race events." Carter's words exploded through Isabella's mind.

"No," she screamed in desperation, realizing she had been dreaming. In a flash, she was back inside the F1 cockpit, but she also felt something beyond her dream—she felt Carter watching her. She knew she needed to stop the race, create a different ending—so the Guardians stayed safe.

She was on the straightaway again, riding next to the river, glancing in her rearview mirror, marking the cars she passed. As she returned her focus on the road, her roadster entered a hairpin. She swerved purposely onto the shoulder and into the marbles, the discarded tire rubber that flew off car wheels during a race. She couldn't control the car as it violently shimmied and slid through the marbles, bouncing her body around the cockpit. Her hands flew off the steering wheel— the car broke through the racetrack barrier and she headed straight for the river. Gin's voice echoed in Isabella's mind, *"This isn't a dream. You are dying."*

Flashing red lights and alarms blared in the box's control room. Carter and Bob watched Isabella convulse. Her right arm broke free from its straps and flailed violently, ripping out the electrodes, and blood splattered across the sterile white walls.

"Her vitals are crashing." Bob's voice raised an octave. "She's overdosing."

"Calm down and call the paramedic." Carter dashed out of the door. She launched herself onto Isabella, trying to restrain her jerking body.

The F1 roadster impacted the river water as Isabella imagined her escape from the cockpit. Traveling through the engine, surging into the carburetor, and then snaking down the inlet valves and into the cylinder where her spirit and fuel mixed and ignited, forcing down the piston, driving up the crankshaft, she escaped through the exhaust pipe and into the water, into the electric river of white light—she was safe in the light again.

Carter made a reluctant noise as she watched them working on Isabella. She hadn't meant to give Isabella a lethal dose. Maybe she had been a little too ambitious, but you had to push the subject to the brink to break them, she rationalized.

A paramedic straddled Isabella, strapped to a gurney, as she performed CPR. Isabella's eyes rolled back into deep blackened sockets, and blood erupted from her mouth, covering the inside of the air mask.

"We're losing her," the medic said. "Move it, move it!" They entered the military hospital as Carter trotted behind them. Dr. Austin and two nurses met the gurney and ran alongside as the medics communicated what they'd learned—"Patient X is in shock hemorrhaging, suspected overdose"—and pushed her faster to the ER.

The nurses removed the sheet covering Isabella and stared at her body, emaciated from being in the box. They rolled her onto her stomach as Carter watched. One of the nurses gasped as the puncture wounds on her shaved head and her body were revealed. It was clear that an obscene amount of cruelty had been bestowed on a body stripped bare of its dignity. Dr. Austin looked at Carter, and she met his judgmental gaze with her own look of contempt.

*  *  *

Hours later, Dr. Austin pushed through the emergency door, sweat saturating his cap. He removed his mask and gloves, dropping them into the trash. Frustrated, he looked around until Carter stepped wearily forward.

"I'm Deputy Director Carter," she said.

Dr. Austin observed the blood now dried and dark red on her outfit. "Her seizures are under control, but she remains in a coma."

Carter sighed. "Will she recover?"

"We will know more if she makes it through the next twenty-four hours."

Carter signaled two agents to enter the emergency room and guard Isabella. They handcuffed her to the bed. When he protested, Carter said, "She is a Solo."

"She is still a person," he retorted, setting Carter back on her heels.

# CHAPTER FIFTY-SEVEN

## *Cannibal*

Angela opened the apartment door and eased into the darkness. A flip of the light switch provided no illumination. She felt her way in through a darkness relieved marginally by weak light fighting its way through closed blinds. After a few steps, she let her purse fall to the floor, bringing her hands to her face. Every inch of their apartment had been pillaged and searched. The place felt foreign. She wandered through the wreckage, without purpose.

While Carter was questioning her, Control agents had been in her home, knocking over lamps, overturning the leather sofa, and ripping off its backing. Every drawer had been ripped open, and its contents dumped onto the ground.

And now, Carter was trying to ransack Isabella's mind. As Angela figured it, Carter had no incriminating evidence against Isabella or else Angela wouldn't be out on bond. She'd be in jail or, worse, in the box herself. Instead, after negotiating her freedom, her father had driven her home. To this.

As she made her way through the room in the faint gray light of morning, her foot bumped against something solid. Glancing down, she saw a photo album lying open at her feet. She tried the table lamp in the living room, but it was broken. She found a candle in the mess on the floor and lit it, its arc of brilliant gold light casting warmth over the room's disarray. Drained of adrenaline, she knelt amongst the clutter and cradled the photo album in her arms. They had taken Isabella's photos. Longing to be with her, Angela began paging through what was left. Paper memories were common for Solos, ensuring a low digital profile. The only photo that Angela owned was actually a postcard that Sister Margot had given her on her tenth birthday. It featured the sunflower fields of Arles, France. Worried suddenly that the agents had taken it too, she rummaged around, finally finding it amid her new outfits scattered on the floor of the guest bedroom.

Obviously the agents had deemed it inconsequential, but the simple present was her only sacred memento. Most of the children in the camp lived in their heads, dreaming that someday, somehow, something would happen to make everything better. *Poof, you're free.* She held the postcard up to the candlelight. The rolling hills were full of sunflowers angling toward the sun.

Angela couldn't live on false hope, but knowing that there were places like Arles out there gave her something to dream about. During the worst of times, this small memento fought its way through her darkness to bring a sparkle of joy.

She resumed looking through Isabella's album, thinking of her. They had a rare connection, one that took her muted emotions and made them sparkle. She wished their pairing could stretch for miles, and she could be with her now, but it didn't work that way. Even the Lumans had limitations.

Overwhelmed by a need to talk to Isabella, Angela found a pen lying amidst the clutter of papers. She flipped the postcard over and jotted a note. Chances were Isabella would never read it—Carter would stop at nothing to prove Isabella was a Solo, including imprisoning and torturing her indefinitely—but somehow writing the words brought her comfort.

\* \* \*

Angela awakened with a gasp, discovering herself on the floor curled in a tight ball with the photo album and postcard lying by her side. The candle had long since snuffed itself out, and the sun's late afternoon rays were filtering in through the west windows.

Her sleep had been steeped in bad dreams, dreams that Carter had put there. Seized with panic, she rushed to the bedroom only to stop short at the sight of the mattress, empty and off-kilter on the bedframe, and Isabella's leather jacket tossed messily on the floor. She picked the jacket up and pressed it to her cheek, inhaling her scent. She laid it carefully on the dresser, then turned her focus to the heavy armoire. Its contents were now littering the floor, but it was still flush with the wall. With great effort, she moved it enough to slide behind it. After fiddling with a hidden panel and the safe's keypad, she pulled out Isabella's emergency escape backpack, clutching it to her chest, eager for what was inside.

She pulled out the oblong GPS tracker terminator and set it carefully on the bathroom countertop. Inside it, she knew, was a computer chip. On the outside was a blue button, her button to freedom. *Or death*, she thought, her optimism wavering. Recalling Isabella's instructions on how to short-circuit her GPS tracker, she unwound the red wire coiled around the chip's silicone base. Using a hand mirror, she secured it inside her tracker, wiggling it until she felt it snap into place. Without hesitating, she squeezed her eyes shut and pushed the blue button.

An electrical shock sent her stumbling backward against the wall and black sun dots floated across her vision. She glanced at herself in the bathroom mirror. She half expected to look different now that she was liberated, but she looked the same. Had it worked? She would know soon enough, she thought, plucking the pliers from the backpack and staring at them. Sister Agnes's imperious tone played in her mind: *"Don't even think about removing the tracker. It will fry your brain."*

Angela reached behind her neck, placed the plier's jaws around the rim of the metal tracker, and yanked hard. She screamed—the pain was so intense she had to stop. Using the mirror, she checked her progress. It hadn't budged.

"How was that possible?" she said to the mirror. "Come on, Angela, this is easy. Pull the tracker out, and you're free." Taking an alternative approach, she pinched the tracker between her finger and thumb, wiggling it like a loose tooth. And then, with all her might, she pulled on it while twisting it, screaming, tugging, groaning. A final hard yank—and finally, it was out.

She held it up to the light; its head was no wider than a dime and a half-inch thick. Protruding from the blood-stained head was a wiry filament tail. Which swiveled about and bent with the energy of an unearthed worm. She yelped, dropping it in the toilet. "Ugh…it's still alive."

She flushed it, then placed a cloth bandage over the hole left in her neck. It was time to get moving. By now, the GPS tracking system would have alerted Control that her signal was offline.

* * *

Tiffany's message had been short and to the point: "Tonight at six-thirty, Wellworth Hotel, Room 804. Good luck." So here Angela was, ready to speak with the woman she had admired, then loathed, and now didn't know how she felt about, besides desperate for her help.

The Wellworth Hotel, the largest convention and hotel complex in D.C., was a hub of activity day and night. Angela stepped into the crowded lobby and sliced through the swarm of guests with a scalpel's efficiency, feeling eyes following her as she sauntered along, her long, dark hair swaying in a steady rhythm to her hips. With one gloved hand she grasped the strap of her Bulgari overnight bag; the other pulled a carry-on suitcase. Her tailored, backless, sequined red dress shimmered with each calculated step, and a stunning black scarf draped around her neck hid her recent…termination. It was an elegant disguise.

She placed her purse on the reception counter and adjusted her Givenchy red eyeglasses. Without looking up, the receptionist muttered, "Name?"

"Tiffany London."

He glanced up and smiled at her, then referred to the computer's screen, clicking and scrolling. Thanks to her parents' money, Angela's Primitive persona was a mishmash of designer brands in fake lashes and giant hoop earrings—all the things she could never afford as a Luman.

The receptionist handed Angela a keycard for Room 389. She frowned and whined, "Oh poo. When I made my reservation, I requested something on the eighth floor. I heard the view of downtown there is to die for."

The receptionist sighed and returned to his computer screen. Minutes later, he handed her a keycard for Room 807. "Here you go, Ms. London."

Angela smiled and took the envelope in her gloved hand. "Thanks, sugar." *How convenient*, she thought as she moved toward the elevators.

"Oh, wait. Don't forget this." The receptionist handed an envelope to her: *Tiffany London* was written on it. She grinned, already knowing what it was.

On the eighth floor, her eyes swept the hallway checking for exits, amenities, and, of course, security cameras. There were probably some cameras in the stairwells, but she didn't spot any in the hallway. She opened her hotel room door and left her suitcase in the foyer. Retreating to the powder room, she checked her hair and makeup, applying another layer of lip-gloss. She tried to push down her welling dread for Isabella, knowing it would distract her. She needed to be focused on dealing with Janet.

This was not just for Isabella—all their lives depended on stopping Corpus—but Angela's thoughts kept defaulting to Isabella. The more she thought about her in the box, the more desperate she became. She took a deep breath and cleared her mind. Negotiating with Janet when she felt so vulnerable could cloud her judgment.

"Here goes nothing," she said in a sultry whisper. She opened the letter addressed to Tiffany and retrieved the keycard for Room 804.

Angela casually walked the short distance to Room 804. Slowly, she slid the keycard into the slot and, hearing the door unlock, slipped into the darkened foyer. Spotting Janet's briefcase on the foyer table as she passed, she tiptoed down a short hallway that opened into a small entertainment area with the bedroom off to the right. Dropping her overnight bag on a chair, she studied the suite: classic yet modern, a step up from the Wonderland Hotel. The bathroom door was closed, and she heard muted conversation coming from inside. It was twilight and Angela's eyes were drawn to dinner for two set by candlelight and overlooking the D.C. skyline. *How romantic*, she thought, and lifted the metal cover on the heated dinner plate and touched her chest. "Mmmm, filet mignon."

Janet's voice grew louder and the light shining from beneath the bathroom door was interrupted by the shadow of someone marching back and forth. *Wonder who is riling Senator Abrams up this time*, Angela thought. She turned to the wet bar and mixed two whisky sours; her back was to the bathroom when Janet stepped out.

"Tiffany, you gorgeous thing." Angela could feel Janet's eyes appraising her in the backless dress as she strolled over. The senator dropped her phone on the dinner table, then reached an arm around Angela's midsection, and pressed her jutting breasts against her bare back. "Hey, playmate."

Angela's heart raced. She twisted toward Janet, leaning in until her cheek caressed Janet's. Their lips met and for an instant, it was July again.

Angela stiffened when a sharp blade pressed against her flesh and the warm sweet and sour taste of Janet burnt like poison on her lips. Janet held the steak knife against Angela's belly, letting the serrated steel stretch the dress fibers. As they pulled back from their embrace, Angela didn't flinch under the weight of Janet's glare. Instead, she batted her long false lashes, whispered, "Surprise," and raised the drinks in her hands, adding a sheepish grin.

"God. You never cease to amaze me," Janet said and took another step backward. Angela took her in. She was dressed in a silky blue blouse and tailored pants, her bare feet stuffed into fluffy hotel slippers. She was just as Angela remembered.

Janet ran her manicured hands through ebony hair that fell loosely on her shoulders, plainly affected by Angela's scrutiny. "Well, you have my attention. What do you want?" she asked, letting her gaze wander over Angela's Tiffany disguise.

"Janet, don't ask questions you already know the answer to," Angela said, handing a drink to her. She kept her velvet voice indifferent, though her desperation was building. *Janet knows how I needed her. Christ, she made sure I did*, Angela thought.

Janet smirked. "You screwed the pooch, toots. I'm done with you." She moved to the table and a hunger flashed in her eyes. "I'm famished. Care to join me for dinner?" She removed the cover from her dinner plate and sat with a huff.

Angela looked pointedly at her, then shrugged. "Why not? Thank you."

Janet returned the knife to its proper place, then grabbed her napkin, shook it out, and placed it over her lap. "I have to admit, I would have loved to see your expression when you read the Solo tracking provision added to the Freewill Law," she said.

Angela glanced out the window. A canopy of fog had settled over the city as the haloed glow of streetlights and headlights popped on. She had known Emma would tell Janet of her plan to disguise herself as Tiffany to meet with her; it was the only time Janet released her security detail. Still, she hadn't expected Janet to be so cool and aloof. This Janet was foreign; it was their estrangement in all its painful pleasantries and suspicion.

Why had it been so easy to manipulate Janet into coercing Senator Green? That question had tormented Angela since the vote.

"Outstanding view." Janet's comment brought Angela out of her thoughts.

Janet's perfect pair of lips tightened as she sliced through her filet like butter, and juices flooded onto the porcelain plate. She watched as Janet took a bite of steak and washed it down with her drink, impassive.

"The night sky always looks ominous and pissed off to me."

"Aw, are you projecting? Feeling a little desperate?" Janet said in a cloying tone. She was obviously enjoying herself immensely and wanted to play, Angela thought.

"Hmm…your lovemaking was always a bit desperate." Angela gave her a sexy grin.

Janet waggled her fork as she chewed a piece of steak. "Your lovemaking"—she paused, wiping her mouth with the napkin as if trying to remember—"was like being devoured by a cannibal." Her eyes gave away her pleasure. "You are a killer."

They broke into laughter, then Janet's phone rang, breaking the moment. She turned it off and swallowed the last of her drink. Angela took the empty glass from her hand, letting her gloved finger brush against Janet's before she freshened both their drinks.

"Here you go, Madam President. Hey, that sounds fitting, doesn't it?" Angela said as she handed over Janet's drink. "The Freewill Law would have been the perfect platform for you to run on. It demonstrates how you reached across the aisle and rallied both parties in the House and Senate. At the helm, you inspired Congress to invest in technology that will end disease and resource scarcity, reduce poverty, help children born with life-threatening disabilities, and free the Lumans from decades of oppression. We have not experienced such ambitious initiatives and dominating leadership since President Lyndon B. Johnson's vision of The Great Society."

She shook her head, sad and mad in equal parts. "Now, regretfully, the Freewill Law will fail and be revoked. It is a real loss: for you, your legacy, but most importantly, for the Lumans. You were our hero." She glowered at Janet.

Janet's eyes flared at the insult. "So here we go. You use everything in your being—imagination, sexuality, and intelligence—to unscrupulously manipulate every situation. You are a hurricane of lies, leaving politicians' reputations in tatters."

"Only," Angela interrupted, "to push narrow-minded people in the right moral direction. It is my necessary evil."

"You cannot coerce politicians without there being blowback." Janet jabbed her fork into the filet, her irritation increasing. "You forced me into your web of lies. You betrayed me. You…didn't earn your freedom. You stole it."

"We both know that isn't true." Angela's tone was brittle.

There was a sharp rap at the door.

"I live in a different world from you. If you want a Great Society"—Janet pointed her knife at Angela—"you must prove you're worthy of living in it. Get the Solos onboard with the tracking."

The knocking became more urgent.

"To do that, I need Agent Dodge out of the box." Angela crossed her arms.

Janet gave her a pathetic sneer. "It's too late for Agent Dodge. Find another country bumpkin."

"You appointed her task force leader. You put her in the box. Why? To hurt me?"

"I didn't know she was a Solo."

"*Janet regrets you.*" Tiffany's word resurfaced and suddenly Angela realized why it had been so easy to talk Janet into coercing Senator Green. She was afraid of Angela. If her lies about Mort got out, it would reveal Janet's true involvement in Corpus.

"Mmm-hmm, so you didn't send Corpus's first success, Lieutenant Renae Goodwin, to threaten me either?"

Janet looked nonplussed by the unexpected question.

Angela was gaining confidence by the minute. "The Guardians know about Corpus. They plan to storm the White House and tell the world about Corpus unless Congress revokes the Solo tracking provision. And we both know your scent is all over Corpus. And what about Dar Preston? How could you, Janet? You changed sides."

The knocking on the hotel door turned to pounding.

Janet rolled the drink around in her glass and snorted out a laugh. "I can't believe you. Citing Lyndon Johnson's presidency when it was mediocre at best. This gambit of yours makes me question your intelligence. Your story is full of holes."

Angela caught Janet's hand in hers and pressed into it a piece of paper containing Donovan's contact information.

"Get Isabella transferred out of the box, and I promise you I will stop asking questions about Preston. I will do whatever you need. Run your presidential campaign, manipulate your opponents, get your jackass of a husband off your back. *I will do anything.* I can make sure you win the presidency—nobody else can make that promise."

Janet looked askance at Angela, then withdrew her hand from beneath Angela's and placed the note in her jacket pocket. "I haven't changed sides; I've changed my priorities."

Angela could tell Janet was warming to the idea, but she didn't want to push her too hard. The most important thing was to get Isabella out of the box. Once Isabella was out, they could regroup and go after Corpus. One disaster at a time.

There was yelling and battering on the door.

Irritated by the disruption, Janet tossed her napkin onto her plate, pointed her steak knife at Angela, and in a low resolute voice warned, "Stay here," then marched toward the door. Angela followed but stopped at the end of the hallway and listened.

"I told you I would deal with this," Janet hissed. Angela could see Janet pointing what she thought was her fork at someone, but she couldn't tell who. It was dark and Janet was blocking the light.

A voice raged in a strangled whisper, "You lose your objectivity around her. Listen to me. Go now or risk losing everything."

Their voices become incoherent and strained for a moment, and then, "Wait here. I need to grab my things." Janet grabbed her briefcase off the foyer table and slipped back into her high heels.

She returned to Angela, and inches from her face she whispered, "I'll get Agent Dodge moved." Angela wanted to believe her, but she was wary of how Janet's convictions had relaxed and shifted in the past. She added, "But *you* better start living up to your end of the deal," and Angela knew that this is not about a promise at all.

Janet placed the steak knife into Angela's gloved hand. Her face expressionless, she turned around, and Angela watched the distance widen between them until the only thing left standing in the hallway light was Mort's menacing profile. As he closed the door and moved closer, Angela's heart seized. His pleasant smile contrasted sharply with the evil lurking behind his eyes, robbing her of breath.

"I was hoping Emma was wrong. That you would not be foolish enough to try to slither you way back into Janet's good graces."

Angela staggered backward, her resolve vanishing. Mort growled, "But here you are." Angela bumped against the chair, then against the bar, as Mort moved around the room, sizing her up. Recoiling in fear, she felt the steak knife's jagged edge against her gloved palm. She realized if there had been a chance to leave it was gone now.

Mort exploded into a tornado of swinging fists, landing multiple blows to her jaw, another to her head. His final blow, an uppercut to the ribs, knocked the wind out of her. She collapsed into him, and he pushed her onto the bed. Gasping for breath, she tried to crawl away, but he was on top of her, pressing her face so hard into the bed she couldn't scream. She paled in size to him; his blocky brick form pinned her down with ease. Knowing what was coming next, she focused on the innermost depths of her chip, left her body, and became one with the light.

Mort flipped her over, letting her catch her breath. Angela stared at him blankly, feeling no fear. He leered at her in disbelief, and his sausage fingers encircled her throat, cutting off her airway. He laughed, then cursed when she didn't respond.

But Angela heard nothing save for the swish of the blade as she plunged it deep into his neck. As her consciousness returned, she realized she was still holding the steak knife. And that Mort had stopped choking her. She watched as his face contorted, eyes bulging in disbelief as a slight trickle of blood moved over his Adam's apple, traveling down his neck. A demented sound escaped her lips as she watched the blood form into a droplet and release, landing on her chest. She gasped for air as his fingers slackened around her neck and he fell onto his side. As air filled her lungs, she wrestled her way out from under him. He uttered a strangled moan as he lay on his side, paralyzed, the knife buried so deep in his lower neck that only its stylish curved handle protruded.

She wanted to scream, but instead she gripped the hilt of the knife. Mort's eyes swiveled, staring at her in shock as she yanked on it. It didn't budge. His watery eyes pleaded for mercy. Her lips set with determination, she used both hands, giving the handle another jerk, this time pulling it out clean. Blood gushed from the jagged wound, and Angela gaped as it flooded the white bedspread, turning it into crimson silk.

An awful, guttural sucking sound was released from his wound, but she was unable to turn away. He looked like a beached whale, walleyed with fear, as he lay across the bed. As if the tide had drained away and left him aground. His discordant voice faded in and out, but there were no words. The sounds unlocked something dark in her. For a moment she wished her heart had remained sealed shut and she could go back to feeling nothing again.

Angela scrubbed Mort's blood from her body. A drop of blood had dripped onto her painted toenails; a whoosh of water washed it down the shower's drain. Twisting pain in her ribs, where his fists had battered her, doubled her over in misery. But it didn't stop her. She scoured her skin raw, ensuring every cell and platelet, all the smell of him, was washed away. Only then did she collapse into a heap on the shower's tile floor. Rocking back and forth, she went deep inside her mind again, letting the silvery-white light surround her as she left her body to heal. This time she planned never to return. But in the light's divination, she learned that leaving this body would not release her from recalling what he did to her—it would only intensify her memory of his hate. And she thought of Raymond and then of Mort's lifeless body in the next room. She wondered if Janet knew Mort had planned to kill her. There was no misunderstanding of Mort's message, but was it Janet's message as well? *Was this always her plan or had Mort taken it too far?*

Rising slowly, Angela wiped steam from the bathroom mirror and studied the agony etched on the face reflected there. Her time in the light had revitalized her body, but it could not erase the marks that had been left on it.

"Christ, he really did a number on me," she uttered in disgust. She got the concealer out of her makeup bag and began covering the bruises that were already forming. Pink blush blended with the red marks left from Mort's fist. She pulled clean undergarments and a new little black dress out of her overnight bag and put them on, reaffixing her Tiffany wig and large dangling earrings.

She stared in desperation at Mort's body, twisted and pale, and felt afraid for herself. Afraid *of* herself. Panic surged through her body, her mind frantically assessing and reassessing things. "A setback," she whimpered, exhausted, fearing that her injuries might be worse than she imagined.

*"You are a killer."* Janet's voice was so clear in her head her scalp tingled. She'd never planned to kill him. There were other ways of getting rid of Mort; he had made it easy for her to accumulate enough evidence to send him away for years.

She scrutinized the room. She had on gloves, so there were no fingerprints, and she cleaned her bar glass, stacking it with the clean ones on the bar. Her DNA was all over the bedspread; that couldn't be helped. She decided to let Janet deal with covering that up. After all, she reminded herself, it was Janet who had put her in this life-or-death situation. "This was not the deal," she moaned, grabbing her side in pain.

She straightened, taking a last look around the room. Spotting the knife on the bed, she cleaned it and wrapped it neatly in a hand towel, putting it in her bag along with her bloody dress. Gritting her teeth, she lifted the bag and slipped its strap over her shoulder. As she walked back to her room the pain in her ribs progressed to the point that it was almost impossible to walk naturally. She was going to have to change her plan. There was no way she could make it to the train station in this condition. Inside her room, she checked her appearance once more, then made a phone call.

\* \* \*

*Just keep going,* Angela told herself as she walked unsteadily through the Wellworth's lobby, pulling her suitcase, makeup masking most of her bruises, hair hanging in her face, and eyeglasses helping to cover the swelling around her eyes.

Everything was steeped in darkness as she exited the hotel. It felt like she had been in the hotel for days, when in fact only three hours had passed. The street was teeming with young professionals enjoying the nightlife, and she momentarily got swept up in a swarm of them that was buzzing with chatter and laughter. She was alone, though, when she reached the corner at 19th Street. She searched up and down the road, finally spotting the SUV. She stumbled up to it and waved at the tinted passenger window. It rolled down.

"Margot, it's me, Angela."

Margot's eyebrows narrowed with suspicion until she recognized Angela behind the Tiffany disguise and realized her distressed state.

"Praise be, child." Margot rushed out of the car to help Angela. Her concerned eyes washed over her. "Oh dear, girl, what have you gotten yourself into?"

"More than I planned for." Angela's voice shook.

"You're hurt. Let's get you to the hospital."

"No hospital, just…drive. Please get me away from here." Angela leaned her head against the headrest and imagined the sunflower fields of Arles. Margot put the car into Drive and Angela contemplated the eighth floor as they passed by the Wellworth. More than ever before, she wanted to rid herself of the darkness she felt, but tonight, the best she could do was to rise above it.

# CHAPTER FIFTY-EIGHT

## *The Business of Killing*

Carter returned from the military hospital and collapsed into the big, comfy Queen Anne chair in the abbey interrogation room. It had become a home away from home since Isabella's betrayal, a thought that triggered a throbbing pain in her head. Her trembling fingers brought a snifter of whiskey to her lips, and she downed it in one long quaff, resting the empty glass on the table. Noticing a red lipstick mark on it, she took her thumb to wipe it clean.

Now on her third day with little sleep, she needed the abbey's quiet to be able to reflect and craft a detailed report on Isabella's accidental overdose. To justify her actions. She shivered. *Justify.* The word made her queasy, made her question what she'd done before she dismissed her self-doubt. "The Mindhunter has still got it. I'm not some dried-up old prune," she muttered, half asleep.

"You look tired." The rumble of a baritone voice caused her to stir. Director Hill and Raven were leaning over her.

"Not too bad. More relieved than anything." Carter looked at her watch—it was 4:30 a.m. She must have dozed off. How long had he been standing there, watching? Unnerved and confused, she snatched at her notebook. Holding dear her private thoughts, it had slipped between her thigh and the arm of the chair.

"You remember Lieutenant Raven Goodwin," Herschel Hill said. "She will replace Agent Dodge on MindControl, so get her up to speed."

Carter, recalling what Angela had suggested about Raven's mental state, grew suspicious. "There's no time. My interrogation is not complete, and we need more information about the Guardians. All I learned from Agent Dodge were outdated protocols. I want to get members' names and locations. Frankly, I don't have time to do that and brief Lieutenant Goodwin fully. I want the Guardian leader. We need Isabella back in the box."

"Is Control in the business of killing?" Janet entered Interrogation One in a swift, austere stride. "Your methods were illicit. We need to make this legal and fast."

Bob must have briefed everyone on Isabella's condition, Carter realized. *Typical Bob, trying to save his ass.*

Hill cast his eyes down at Carter. "Senator Abrams wants to move Agent Dodge when she's stable."

She stood. "For what reason?"

"D.C. has suspended capital punishment. Senator Abrams wants to transfer Agent Dodge to Baton Rouge. Dodge is connected to Angela Mathers and that is Angela's hometown. It's also a place where they hate Lumans," he replied.

Carter looked from Janet to Hill. "Director Hill, if we keep her here we will learn so much more. She was a member of the Guardians."

Senator Abrams cleared her throat. "I want to charge her with espionage. Agent Dodge leaked national security information to the Guardians—known terrorists. We want the death penalty—and it's legal and current practice in Louisiana."

"You did your job, Carter, but now it's time to let the prosecutors do theirs. They will find out her true identity," Director Hill said softly.

"And now that it's filed under the Espionage Act, we can detain Ms. Mathers," Raven said, her ebony eyes brightening with excitement.

Director Hill patted Raven's shoulder. "The lieutenant here is our secret weapon, Carter. Her IQ rivals that of any Luman."

Carter's hands shook. Even though she had known about Raven, the director's confirmation made it hurt all the more that he hadn't trusted her with the information sooner.

"Wait, just...everyone, hold on." She had heard enough. She paused and glanced from Director Hill to Senator Abrams. "I need to speak with you privately," she said to the senator.

After Hill and Raven left, Carter paced, gathering her thoughts while Abrams crossed her arms and watched. "We can't trust Raven," Carter whispered. "I've been monitoring her. Something's not right with her—she's not of sound mind to run MindControl."

Senator Abrams dropped her arms to her side and stiffened. "I've heard she wants to reopen the Lewis case. You think it needs to stay sealed?"

Carter nodded.

"Out of extreme precaution then, perhaps Raven should report to the military hospital for observation. Do you agree, Deputy Carter?"

Pleased that her allegations were going unchallenged, she said, "Yes. I concur. You can never be too careful with those tin heads."

"Deputy Carter, we as a society need to stop thinking of the Lumans as machines. They are not. All the Lumans need to be free, the documented and the undocumented. We can't have Solos incarcerated and the documented free. Do you understand what I'm saying?"

"But the provision requires us to track Solos. You helped to draft that, Senator."

Abrams's tone was guarded. "Not because it was the right thing to do, but because it was the only way to pass the bill. We don't need to enforce it. Control's execution of it using MindControl will divide our nation."

"Nobody wants that," Carter lied. She sat, relaxing into the leather chair. Why would Abrams want the death penalty for Isabella or care if the Lewis case was reopened? Had someone gotten under the senator's skin?

"We need to end MindControl," Abrams said. "I will address this very matter with Congress in the near future."

Director Hill reappeared at the door. His face was grim, his shoulders hunched, aging him. "Janet, I need to speak with you on an urgent matter. There's terrible news."

Abrams stiffened. Lips pursed, she gazed for a moment at her hands, then raised resolute eyes to Hill's.

# CHAPTER FIFTY-NINE

*Venom*

"We need to reopen the Lewis case. and find out where Jonathan Riley's body is."

When Carter opened her eyes, Raven's ebony ones were only inches from her face.

Carter responded tersely, "The case went cold, lieutenant. We never found his body. It's time to move past it." She stood. "Tell me, Raven. How did you know Isabella was a Solo?"

Raven stepped backward. "Well, it was obvious."

"How was it obvious?"

"There was just something fake about that Southern drawl of hers. I could tell she wouldn't know the difference between a hoe and a hoedown."

"How?"

Raven stared at the carpet. "It was a gut feeling, and I was right." She retreated to the fireplace, which had gone cold, added a log, and turned on the gas starter.

"You accused her without facts."

*Something's wrong with us,* Warren thought.

"I am fine," Raven reassured herself.

"No, I don't think you are," Carter said.

*She's got a point. You shouldn't be here; it should just be me in your mind,* Warren warned.

Raven looked at the poker next to the fireplace, then picked it up and poked at the firewood, stirring the ashes. "Huh, I could say the same," she said under her breath. "I evened it up. She took away Jon and I took away Isabella."

*You're talking aloud again. Stop it,* Warren thought.

The wood caught flame. It was pleasant, and the warmth felt good against Raven's skin. She wasn't sure if the chill in the air was from Carter or the weather.

"Raven, who are you talking to?" Carter was standing next to her. She ignored the older woman and busied herself with poking at the logs, watching the flames jump.

"Raven, I just learned you are a Luman."

"Yes, I am." Raven couldn't hide the pride in her voice.

"And I learned about Corpus, the initiative that reprograms neural implants with a sense of loyalty to humans, similar to a dog's loyalty to its owner. Learned that Dr. Austin created you to care about people like me and protect all humans. It's gratifying to have you on my team."

Raven laughed out loud. "That's good."

Carter returned to the leather chair and sat down.

*She's just pushing your buttons, Raven,* Warren thought.

"Who are you calling a lap dog?" Raven said to the poker.

Ignoring her, Carter rubbed the back of her neck. "I'll handle MindControl. I need you to go to the military hospital and manage Agent Dodge's transfer to Louisiana. Find Dr. Austin. Forget about the Lewis case—Jonathan Riley is irrelevant."

Raven was mesmerized by the well-behaved flames as she listened to Carter babble on. "…after Agent Dodge's defection, all Lumans are under additional review."

Raven held the poker in the gas flame until the tip turned dark red, matching the searing fury boiling inside her. "There are no orders unless I give the orders," she hissed.

*Calm down, Raven. This is just Carter's modus operandi,* Warren thought.

Raven said to the ceiling, "Shut up, Warren. I'm not part of your poor, sad children from Camp I/O tale. I've been a human all my life."

Carter appeared startled by Raven's outburst.

Raven tilted her head to Carter. "Is this a test?" In a flash, she was now before Carter. "If they coded me for loyalty, then I'm above suspicion."

Raven's unnatural speed did not frazzle Carter as Raven had expected it to.

A coy smile played on Carter's face. "No Luman is above suspicion."

Raven didn't feel like a Luman. She was more of a viper coiled in the grass, biding her time, overriding her programing to strike without warning. Raven, wrongly chosen for a neural implant, watched Carter now and smiled.

*Raven, if you fight back, you lose.*

She just hissed at him. As Warren felt his emotional tether to Raven begin to shred and unravel, Raven tapped the shaft of the hot poker on her palm, feeling its reassuring weight.

# CHAPTER SIXTY

## *Madwoman*

A buttermilk-colored cat jumped onto the bed, and Angela jackknifed awake with a cry.

"Nancy, get off of her," Margot scolded the cat as she entered the small bedroom carrying a tray. After leaving the Wellworth Hotel, she had brought Angela to her home.

"What time is it?" Angela hoarsely asked as she blinked away the sleep.

"It's early, hon."

"I have a flight at noon." With a groan, she swung her feet off the side of the bed. A burning pain shot from her abdomen into her lower back, and she cried out.

"Flight? You're not going anywhere!" Gently, Margot maneuvered Angela back to the bed, pulling the sheets over her. "Easy does it. There could be internal bleeding and bruising of your organs."

"Am I…going to be okay?"

"Honey, you'll be fine. The body is very resilient. But you have to rest. You've been through too much. There are bruises all over you." She patted Angela on the upper arm, a small show of affection. Lingering rules from the Codes were still ingrained in their relationship.

"When we went shopping the other day, I thought you were up to something. Some of the outfits you bought just didn't seem your style." Margot's questioning glance met Angela's swollen eyes. "What have you gotten into, young lady?" A slight smile promised Angela that she wouldn't judge.

A sharp shudder of air escaped Angela. It was impossible to hide the torment of her failings. "I have been trying to salvage the Freewill Bill. They added a provision designed to take away the very freedom it bestowed."

"Who's 'they'? The person who did this to you?"

"I don't want to involve you, not after what happened in camp. It's not fair to do that to you again," Angela said, remembering the night Sister Agnes had found them in a chaste embrace and Margot had been excommunicated for it.

"Dear, I'm already involved. Besides, getting away from the church allowed me to go to nursing school. I'm much happier now."

Angela reluctantly told Margot about the whole sordid mess with Janet and Mort, all of it. "If the police figure out it was me…" The rest of her words died in her throat. "I have to run, you see. Will you please help me get ready for my flight?"

"You need to stay put. It was self-defense. The police and the courts will see that."

"I'm a Luman. And someone accused before of murder. The truth didn't matter then and won't now. I'll be assumed to be guilty."

"But Freewill is the law."

"The law is not ours, not really. The humans own it—they can change it. You can't imagine what it's like to waste your entire life for an idea that could never happen. Our freedom relies on our opposition's ideals and beliefs changing, and that will never happen. The Freewill Law is a ruse."

"Hush, you stop that talk." Margot gave Angela a sad smile. "Freedom takes time, but that's why it's so important. People are far more tolerant of the Lumans now, and you, my dear, had a hand in making that happen."

"I don't want tolerance. I want acceptance."

Angela had analyzed it from every perspective, but even with her giant intellect, she could not understand the humans' distrust of Lumans. It was part of the burden that came with being the first of a kind, she guessed.

"You need to be patient." Margot patted her hand lovingly. "And you need to rest, honey. You can't travel—you're too weak." Ever the nurse, she studied Angela's eyes, flesh tone, her trembling hands. Angela knew she could not stay. It was too risky. She had learned the hard way about Janet's unpredictability. Mort's death brought possible damage to her run for president. If it was Janet's plan all along to have her kill Mort, then she was already spinning things in her favor, covering up the real facts of Mort's death.

"Come with me!" Angela's dull stare sparkled at the thought. "You can take care of me. I have the money, and we always talked about traveling together."

"I don't know…I mean, what would I do with Nancy?" They glanced at the furry ball at the end of the bed as she groomed herself. Nancy stopped mid-lick and stared back at them.

\* \* \*

The ticket agent reached down to hand Charlie the airline ticket. The older man gave her a crooked smile from under his 49ers baseball cap and placed the ticket on top of the kitty kennel in his lap. Then she stamped another ticket and handed it over the counter to Margot. "Bless you," Margot said as she took her ticket. She leaned down and whispered to Angela, "Ready?"

Sister Margot, clad in her old habit, pushed the wheelchair with elderly Charlie Hopkins in it toward the airport security area. Angela-Charlie's fake face, made by Donovan's father as part of their deal, hid the bruising and dark shadows under her eyes. They were a harmless-looking pair.

Margot handed the security guard their passports. He scrutinized every line of Charlie's passport, eyeing Angela suspiciously, before handing both of the passports back. They sat in the gate area, watching a swath of travelers pouring off the plane when a news alert grabbed their attention. Mort Abrams's and Tiffany London's images were displayed over the newscaster's shoulder.

"Mort Abrams, a well-known business executive and husband of Senator Janet Abrams, was found dead in a Wellworth Hotel room early this morning. Tiffany London, shown here, is wanted in connection with his death. If you have seen this woman, the D.C. police ask you to call the number below." Snapshots of the real Tiffany London and a video of Angela disguised as Tiffany repeated endlessly on the monitor.

Confused, Margot turned to Angela with a stern tone. "You never said you were impersonating a real person. That poor lady. Why did you wear a disguise in the first place? What were you planning?"

"Shhh, calm down, Margot."

"This will ruin her. You have to tell the police the truth."

Angela observed the news of Mort's death scrolling across the TV monitor. The horror of the previous night churned endlessly in her mind. The painkillers Margot had given her were taking the edge off her pain, but it still vibrated like fear coursing through her body. She couldn't come unglued, not while Control was searching for her and security cameras were watching.

"Janet Abrams will handle it; she'll make it all go away." Angela hoped.

"What? She's devastated. Her husband just died."

Angela gazed at Margot, detached. "Janet has wanted Mort dead for years. It wouldn't surprise me if she planned this whole thing."

Margot wrung her hands. "How could she know you'd get away and have the strength to fight him off?"

Angela shrugged. "In either case, she rids herself of a problem." She dropped her head to hide the emotional storm battering her inside. She hoped Margot would let the topic rest. But of course, she could not.

"My Lord, the Devil just changed its disguise."

The Devil was just a very old word for a madman. Angela didn't want to believe that about Janet any more than she wanted to believe it when people had said it about her. Then again when Janet promised her freedom, she had fallen for it, ignoring all the signs when Janet had started to waver. She had underestimated the depths of Janet's obsession with power. Or was it a kind of madness? It was hard to tell what Janet would do next, now that everyone she cared about was gone—her child, her husband, and Angela.

Over the airline speaker, they heard, "We will begin boarding Flight 103 to Nice, beginning with those passengers needing extra time."

"Here we go." Placing Nancy's cage on Charles's lap, Sister Margot pushed the wheelchair down the ramp to the plane. As she did, Angela reflected on something Janet had once told her, that those who are most adaptable survive. She and Janet were still bonded by their secrets, something that could make the darkest of things powerful and turn allies into enemies. She was sure they would meet again, but Angela would be ready for Janet next time. She would cultivate her own power, and she prayed Janet had kept her promise and gotten Isabella out of the box. She tried not to think about what she would do to Janet if she hadn't.

Finally, the D.C. Compound rolled past Angela's airplane window, and, as the plane broke through the steely haze, she watched the

National Mall disappear. She smiled as she soared free in an expanse of blue, her old life getting smaller and smaller until it vanished under the cloud bank. Where she was going, she would be free, wholly. America was the only country that segregated Lumans from society. She tried to imagine herself experiencing that in the future with Isabella. She reflected on the note she had left in their apartment, praying that someday Isabella would have the chance to read it.

# CHAPTER SIXTY-ONE

## *She is Risen*

Patient X's chart hung off the ICU bed holding Isabella's empty shell, tubes and IV lines, a life-support machine, and the resuscitation mask bringing oxygen into her system, keeping her body alive. On the EEG monitor, green wavy lines blipped across the screen, showing limited electrical brain activity.

*I could live here without gravity on the green edge with you*, Isabella thought.

Gin's voice echoed through the light. *You can't stay here. Find your way free.*

From a million miles away, billions of ethereal atoms of knowledge, memories, dreams, and love filled Isabella's virtual heart with an incandescent glow. A sudden burst of brain activity sprang across the EEG monitor as her digital consciousness surged back into her neural implant. Memories and dreams flooded into her biological brain—making Isabella who she was again. Her vitals improved instantly, a sweeping force bringing her out of her coma. Her eyes flitted under her eyelids, then suddenly opened. She gasped for more air, arms reaching for her mask. An ICU nurse rushed to remove the resuscitation mask and Isabella's lungs filled with fresh, warm air. She sat straight up, grabbing hold of the nurse's hand.

"Help me," she cried, not knowing where she was.

As the nurse guided Isabella gently back down onto the bed, she was inundated with memories, called down to the river.

There was chanting and singing as the pastor's hands gently dipped four-year-old Mazzy deep into the river water. She squirted out of his hands like a born-again tadpole. Looking up, she watched the sun's rays break through the water prism, refracting God's light down on her. She was safe, her immaterial soul cleansed by the water.

Hands reached for her, finding her, pulling her out of the water. A younger version of her father greeted her. "You are loved, sweet Mazzy." There was singing, welcoming her home as Lorraine gathered Mazzy into her arms, walking her out of the river, removing the fabric belt around her wet baptismal gown.

When Isabella opened her eyes, the river and her parents were but jagged flashes, fading as she struggled to understand the chaos unfolding: the guard untying her leg restraints and stripping away her blanket, the men who were haphazardly ripping the tubes and IV lines from her body before lifting the sheet underneath her and roughly casting her down onto a gurney. Her head hit the stretcher, a lightning bolt screeched through her skull, and she slipped into unconsciousness again.

# CHAPTER SIXTY-TWO

*Corpus*

Janet gazed into the eerie dark military hospital lab. In the center of the room, in a hospital bed, a thin sheet draped the silhouette of a young man, barely discernable. She often thought about Jason when it was dark, like now. Remembering when her son left her body, the emptiness she felt at first turning into sloping waves of euphoria at hearing his first cry. Remembering her heartache when, six years later, done fighting, he left her to survive her despair alone.

She heard loud voices and the lights flickered on, bleaching the man lying in the bed with light. Dr. Austin entered, and Raven followed, waving a sheet of paper at him. This was a private conversation—their body language made that obvious—but Janet could not turn away. She watched them shamelessly from behind the one-way mirror.

Dr. Austin grabbed the paper from Raven's hand and read it. "You want to take her to Baton Rouge? No way. No goddamn way, Raven! She'll never make it."

"Well, I guess that will be Agent Dodge's choice. Sign it, Doc." Raven glowered at him.

"This isn't you, Raven. Please, this is crazy."

"I'm doing my job. Isn't this what you programmed me to do? To be man's best friend?"

Austin paused, looking stunned, then took hold of Raven. "I don't know what you've been told, but that isn't true."

"Sign it."

Looking desperate, he announced, "I found him."

Raven searched his eyes. "Jonathan? Where?"

Austin turned around and pointed at the man lying in the hospital bed. Janet pressed her face to the glass to hear better.

"Jonathan?" Raven's eyes softened as she approached the bed. Dr. Austin stood next to her as they gazed at the man. In his late thirties, he was handsome with a cleft chin and dark curly hair. Raven's lips curved into the slightest smile as she touched his hand. "I found you."

"He's in an induced coma," Dr. Austin said.

"Jonathan, it's me, Warren. I'm waiting for you."

Dr. Austin glanced at the one-way mirror, then stabbed a one-hit syringe into Raven's arm, injecting tranquilizer into her system. She whipped around in disbelief as he gazed at her, full of regret.

"It will be okay. You're going to sleep now so I can fix you."

In a ragged breath, Raven said, "But I'm not broken." Her legs buckled, and she fell into his embrace.

Cradling her, Dr. Austin lifted her and lovingly placed her on an exam table beside Jonathan's bed. He covered her body with a blanket and kissed her softly on the lips, then considered the one-way mirror again, remembering, no doubt, that Janet was observing them.

"You will be safe here," he whispered as he swept her hair from her forehead and attached a heart monitor to her finger.

Janet Abrams slipped into the lab and stared glumly at Raven. "What's wrong with her?"

The doctor jumped. "Senator Abrams, you startled me. Nothing. She just needs some minor memory modifications." He faced Janet. "I heard about your husband. I'm so very sorry for your loss."

Janet winced. *I'm not*, she thought. She was concerned for Angela, however, and what she likely had suffered at Mort's hands. "Thank you."

"I need to modify some of Lieutenant Goodwin's more aggressive tendencies."

"'Tendencies'? Good God, she branded Deputy Carter with a hot poker. On. The. Face. She needs more than reprogramming. Her personality has split."

They stared at each other until Janet's anger was replaced with curiosity. She looked at the man in the hospital bed. "Is he in the last stage of recovery?"

Ryan's grimace turned to a grin. They walked over to the patient. "I know you were hoping for that woman's neural implant, but I think you will find this one to be more than adequate." He gestured toward the bed. "Senator Abrams, may I introduce you to Darwin Preston, your running mate and the next vice president of the United States."

Janet leaned in and studied Darwin's face and broad shoulders. Her eyes brimming with tears, she whispered, "And here you are." He would be her shimmering moon, her new Jason. "The secretary general and Director Hill know nothing of this?"

"I told them Jonathan Riley's chip disappeared." He shrugged. "There are no other viable neural implants available. I've had to put Corpus on hold." He frowned. The senator knew he was not happy about being coerced into this decision.

"And what happened to Lieutenant Goodwin cannot happen to Darwin?"

Dr. Austin cleared his throat. "No, that was a fluke. Dar won't remember who he was. He has been programmed to your specific needs."

She nodded and said dryly, "In due time you will continue your work, I guarantee it. But heed my advice. In the future, don't become romantically involved with one of them." She took Dar's hand, but it felt involuntary. Having lost the opportunity to have Angela by her side in the White House was still unbearable.

A nurse stood at the doorway and cleared his throat. "Dr. Austin, they are taking Patient X."

Austin's judgmental eyes flayed Janet.

"It was beyond my control, Ryan."

# CHAPTER SIXTY-THREE

*Sworn Enemies*

The guards marched Isabella's stretcher down the hall. The hard thunk of her gurney hitting the double door jolted her awake to a world of bright fluorescent lights, hurried footsteps, and elongated bodies towering over her. They were moving her so fast that her body quivered from the sheer speed, like a loose wheel rattling beneath a cart. Through another set of double doors, her world changed again; she was swept out into the cool night air and the biting smell of exhaust fumes. She turned her head, watching the hospital's loading dock move into view, and an undercurrent of panic scored her already raw skin.

The guards propelled Isabella into an ambulance. Its metallic interior contained operational equipment, monitors, and shelves stocked with supplies. An awaiting paramedic locked the gurney's wheels into place as the harsh interior light dimmed and the ambulance's engine roared to life. Two guards entered after her and slammed the doors shut. One spoke into his walkie. "What's Lieutenant Goodwin's ETA? We are ready to roll."

The static-drenched response blared, "Lieutenant Goodwin is offline. Go without her." Isabella was cognizant enough to know these men were military, and fear thrummed through her. She tried to break free, pulling and thrashing her body against the restraints that bound her, crying, "I'm not going back."

A shadowy figure appeared in her line of sight, a man with high cheekbones and stubbly cheeks; a red jacket covered his white paramedic uniform. His voice, barely above a raspy growl, blew in her ear. "Calm down." He stared at her with a mixture of pity and anger.

Those eyes! Isabella knew them well. They were the eyes of her sworn enemy. She stiffened, struck by a thunderbolt of certainty—it was Donovan in disguise.

As the ambulance sped down the road, sirens wailing, Donovan studied the guards sitting on either side of the rear door, then returned his gaze to Isabella's gaunt face. Isabella felt her head lolling back and forth uncontrollably from the motion. She was helpless and terrified. Donovan reached out to hold her head still. The warmth of his palm pressing against her forehead brought tears to her eyes.

She didn't understand why he, of all people, was here. She silent-messaged him, *They sent you to kill me?*

Busy monitoring her vitals, Donovan didn't answer her at first.

Then, with a sideways glance, he messaged, *Relax. If the Guardians wanted you dead, you'd already be dead. I'm here to rescue you.* He peered up at the guards again, assessing them.

*But why you?*

*Gin would have wanted it that way.* His eyes said it all; he knew Gin was in the light. He was fighting for her now—he had something to live for again.

*What about my parents? How's my mom?*

*They're safe out of the country. No contact. You know the rules.*

*What about Angela?*

*She has forsaken you.* The tone of his message was patronizing.

*I wouldn't be alive without Angela.*

Her silent-message garnered Donovan's attention, but he had no words to comfort her. *No one knows where she is. Her tracker went offline two days ago.*

Loneliness swallowed Isabella. Surviving without the people who loved her was just another kind of death. *Save yourself, let me die.*

The ambulance screeched to a halt, fishtailing, and without warning, Donovan pulled a gun from inside his jacket and shot twice. When Isabella's flash blindness settled, she saw that both guards were down, slumped on the floor.

"Shit just got real. You run or die...what's it gonna be?" Donovan asked as an explosion outside rocked the ambulance. He braced himself against the gurney as bandages and rolls of tape rained down on them. There were screams from the ambulance's front cabin. Isabella jumped, as more gunfire erupted. Her eyes shifted frantically from side to side, as she tried to understand where the enemy was.

"We are getting you out alive." Donovan kicked open the ambulance doors and pushed the guards' bodies out of the way. As they toppled to the ground, he yelled, "Move." Two shadowy figures emerged out of the darkness. Isabella recognized them: Donovan's dad, Bill, and his buddy Johnny. Donovan pushed Isabella's gurney out of the ambulance, delivering her into Bill and Johnny's arms. A hail of bullets rained down on them from every direction.

"It's an ambush. Get back in the ambulance!" Bill screamed.

Donovan hovered over Isabella, shielding her as Bill and Johnny pushed her gurney back into the ambulance. The doors slammed shut and Isabella heard bullets riddle the vehicle's exterior.

"Get us out of here!" Donovan yelled, and Johnny and Bill jumped in the ambulance's front seat. Gravel crunched under the spinning tires of the vehicle as it roared to life, sirens howling. Isabella's pulse raced as Don took out a pocketknife, then feverishly cut through the restraints across her chest and hips. A drop of blood landed on her cheek.

"You're hit," she said.

He glanced down to inspect the wound in his chest; the fabric of his white shirt was drenched in blood from the affected area. "It's nothing," he said.

Isabella pushed herself up on her elbows. "We have to stop the bleeding."

Donovan was not listening to her. "Roll over, Isabella." When her movements were too slow for his impatient nature, he flipped her onto her stomach.

"Shit, I should have checked for that." She could hear him searching a shelf and from the corner of her eye, saw him pull down a portable defibrillator.

"What? What's wrong?" Isabella asked while he fumbled with the defibrillator wire leads. As the bus sped down a straightaway, Johnny cut the lights and sirens; they rode in heavy silence.

Isabella, still on her stomach, couldn't see Donovan; she only heard his ragged breathing.

"You don't sound good."

A sudden humming began, one that Isabella didn't understand. Donovan stood over her, defibrillator in hand, and she felt something snap into her neck. The hum turned to a loud buzzing.

It dawned on Isabella. "Jesus. They put a GPS tracker in me?"

"Hold on to your ass." Isabella turned far enough to see Donovan press the red button on the defibrillator. It fired off a charge, Isabella's body spasmed, and she blacked out.

The next time she woke, she was on her back and four men were pushing the gurney she was on. It was the dead of night and stars lit the night sky. They were out of the city, she guessed. Her breath plumed in the night air as she breathed in the river's earthy smell.

"We got you, Isabella." She didn't recognize the man.

Isabella searched, but the ambulance was gone. "Where's Donovan?" she asked but no one answered.

"Donovan," she whispered.

# CHAPTER SIXTY-FOUR

## *I'm Back*

The ambulance wailed down the back roads, the long glow of headlights showing the way. Donovan had lost consciousness, and his vitals were unstable. Bill braced himself against the stretcher as the vehicle swayed around turns. He cut away his son's face mask with a pair of surgical scissors, revealing a pale, expressionless face and eyes that were dark and unresponsive. Ripping open the blood-soaked shirt he was wearing, Bill placed a bandage over the wound in his chest, just above his heart, and applied pressure to it. With his other hand he felt Donovan's neck for a pulse—it was weak but steady, and his hope surged.

Familiar with the equipment that was still functioning in the ambulance, he swiftly hooked up a heart monitor to Donovan. The beats came slowly and irregularly. The vehicle merged onto the highway, picking up speed and heading for the nearest hospital outside the D.C. Compound.

Bill yelled above the sirens, "How much longer, Johnny?"

"We are crossing the Anacostia River now—it won't be too much longer."

Donovan's eyes fluttered open, and he tried to tell his father something.

"Shut it off. Shut off the siren," Bill cried.

He leaned in his ear close to his son's lips, and Donovan breathed out, "It's okay. Let me go, Dad."

The heart monitor stopped. Bill checked Donovan's pulse, but it too had slipped away to nothing. He clutched Don's wrist tighter— still no pulse. "No, boy, it's not your time." A guttural rasp exited Donovan's throat. Bill pounded on his chest, trying to restart his heart. "The defibrillator! Where is it?" He searched, but it was nowhere to be found, so he started CPR while the heart monitor's piercing alarm sang.

Minutes later, Bill collapsed onto his son, stopping the CPR. As he leaned back, he studied his bloody hands. He remembered his Don, sitting at his computer, typing away deep into the night. Coding was the only thing that interested him. Other activities and friends barely kept his interest. The programs he wrote, the code he hacked, were in his DNA. It wasn't until years later, when Donovan met Gin, that he had developed an interest in something else. He had chased after her for years until he finally won her heart.

Bill watched his son's lifeless body and did something he never thought he would do—he prayed. He startled when the heart monitor began beeping slowly and Donovan jackknifed, sitting straight up as breath flooded into his lungs. The heart monitor progressed into a steady regular rhythm. Shocked, Bill reached for his son's hand, felt it warming in his. Donovan turned to him—and his dark eyes were filled with Gin's emerald resilience.

"I'm back." His voice came as a whisper. But it was true. As her shapelessness permeated his shell, Gin felt her heart beating faster, felt gravity holding her tightly. Glancing down, she saw the familiar body that once had held her close. She now possessed it—she was now Donovan.

# CHAPTER SIXTY-FIVE

## *When November Goes*

Her rescuers lifted Isabella's stretcher onto a large fishing cruiser and carried her under the covered cockpit and then downstairs, bumping her like a pinball along the narrow stairwell into the main cabin. A friendly face leaned over her and reassured her. "You're safe. Get some rest."

"What about Donovan?" she asked as their eyes caught, but the man grunted a meaningless reply. He locked down the gurney's wheels and left.

An outboard motor revved to life, and over her head, the boat's wooden deck creaked and moaned as people moved about, their voices flowing and ebbing. The darkness closed itself around her, pressing down tight like a coffin. There was no distinction between her and the darkness, and though she was no longer restrained, she lay motionless. She was frozen, as if something inside her was inhibiting her movement, as if she were malignant, a strain of something foreign to herself. Her left eye pulsed as it scanned her surroundings: a galley with a table and booth seating was at one end and at the other was a door, leading, she assumed, to sleeping quarters. She was alone, so very alone.

How long had Carter held her in the box? Hours? Days? She had lost track of time. What information did Carter get from her? Did she take her secrets, her memories? Isabella listened to the engine's hum and the waves rushing against the bow and, eventually, drifted into the blackness of sleep.

"Who are you?" Carter screamed, jolting Isabella awake. Her eyes swiveled frantically, hunting for the evil lurking near her, talking to her. *It was only a nightmare*, she assured herself. The boat's motor throttled down and then cut out. She was immobile, afraid to breathe, blinking the dark away. She heard the sound of hurried feet crisscrossing the deck overhead, deep voices too muffled to understand. The footsteps grew closer. What was happening? The hatch opened, and flashlights and bodies rushed down the stairs. Isabella pulled her blanket tighter to her and squeezed her eyes shut.

A lantern switched on, its pale yellow glow encouraging her to open her eyes a crack. It filled the room, changing its very nature. There was a muffled cry, and Isabella squinted against the light, barely distinguishing a haloed shape—a woman?—hunched over her. Pulling at her face, tugging and stretching, she struggled to remove her skin. Isabella recoiled from the nightmare unfolding. The fake face at last came off, accompanied by an odd sucking sound. Isabella jerked away, her heart trying to burst through her chest.

"It's me, it's me!" her stepmother cried. Her face was moist with perspiration, a smear of baby powder covered her cheeks, and when she smiled, Isabella wept uncontrollably.

Her father appeared on the other side of Isabella and through his tears, choked out, "You're safe." But any other reassurances were lost to his anguish. Isabella could see reflected in his eyes her own fear and her emaciated frame. He gathered her into his arms and squeezed her tight to his chest; she felt his warmth transfuse her. She was alive again.

Her parents helped her to a bed in the sleeping quarters.

"There's not much time. The doctor needs to check you out," Lorraine said.

Isabella shrank into the covers as a stranger in fishing apparel approached her bedside carrying a tackle box.

"It's okay. He's a doctor," Frank said.

"I'm here to make you more comfortable," the man said. After quickly examining her, he hooked her up to an IV drip. "Once we get some fluids in you, you'll start feeling better."

After the doctor left and the fishing cruiser stole off into the night, Lorraine opened an overnight bag. "Let's get some decent clothes on you to keep you warm." Frank busied himself bringing down suitcases and straightening Isabella's covers.

"I'm afraid something bad has happened to Angela," Isabella said as Lorraine placed a stocking cap over Isabella's bald head. "Have you heard anything?"

"No, honey, we dropped off the grid when you were captured." Lorraine patted her leg. "You need to focus on getting better. The doctor gave us some medication for you. He says you'll be just fine."

Isabella could read the concern in her parents' eyes. Her voice hoarse with fatigue, she said, "Dad, I'm not fine. Just tell me the truth."

"You're mending from your physical punishment, but the doctor is concerned about your mental state. There's a small hole in the back of your skull." Frank's tone was calm as he reached out to take her hand.

"I don't remember what they did or what I told them." Isabella looked away, hiding her shame and anger. "They took things from me?"

"It's okay. The doctor couldn't say for sure, but what they did might cause some hallucinations or mental instability for a little while. Don't worry. The worst is over. We are here with you."

"We'll get through this together." Lorraine put an arm around her.

"How did you know where I was?" Isabella propped herself up higher in bed.

Frank sat on the bed next to her. "Donovan struck a deal with Senator Abrams. She could not authorize your release, not formally, but she texted Donovan the name of the hospital where we could find you. In return, she ordered the Guardians to stand down. No attacks or hacks."

"Donovan, is he okay? He got shot." In the dim light of the bedroom, Frank and Lorraine's eyes met.

Lorraine gently cupped Isabella's cheek with her palm. "There have been no updates, honey." Frank kissed Isabella's forehead and went topside.

Lorraine wiped a tear as it streaked down Isabella's cheek. "By morning, we'll be in the North Atlantic and on our way to Nova Scotia. Everything will feel better in the light of day."

Lorraine handed Isabella a turkey sandwich. She gave her a wry smile. "It's Thanksgiving today."

Isabella studied Lorraine's deepening worry lines, and the cast on her arm. "I'm so sorry, Mom. I should have never visited you that day."

"Hush, you."

"How are you feeling?" Isabella asked.

"I feel thankful," Lorraine said. "Don't you worry about me. I got a lot of good left in my good years."

Isabella took a couple of bites of the sandwich, then set it on the nightstand and said, "Come lie down with me. You need to rest too."

Lorraine cuddled next to Isabella and began humming a favorite Nancy Wilson tune. Her soothing voice carried Isabella away. But no amount of sleep brought relief to Isabella's questions about what had happened in the box. As she faded in and out of slumber, the question remained.

Isabella sat up, suddenly remembering a fragment of her time in the box. "Angela told Carter I was a Solo."

Lorraine's eyes opened as she surfaced from sleep and focused on Isabella next to her. "Honey, you've got to trust what's in your heart. They were trying to make you talk." Isabella lay back down. "We stopped by your apartment and picked up a few things, clothes, racing trophies, and an old photo album."

"I'm worried about Angela. I need to know she's okay."

"Honey, Angela's resilient. She'll be just fine. Do you want to look through the album? There are some cute photos of you and Gin." Lorraine draped an arm around her, teetering on the edge of sleep.

"I don't know," Isabella mumbled half to herself. She pondered what Donovan had meant when he said Angela's tracker had gone offline. Had Angela removed her GPS tracker or, worse, was she dead?

"It's my fault I got caught," Isabella confessed, dropping her face into her palms at the sudden realization. "An encrypted document in Angela's Dark file proved her innocence. She wrote it right before they took her into custody. I broke the code the other day and read it. Control must have traced it back to me. I knew it was illegal to access the file, but I did it anyway. Mom, the government was hiding Angela's innocence on purpose, putting doubt in society's mind about us, making Angela the scapegoat."

Hearing nothing in response, she gazed at her mother, who was sleeping soundly. The guilt Isabella had unburdened was swallowed up in the silence.

Isabella watched Lorraine sleep for a while, then, overcome with restlessness, she unhooked the IV and stumbled to her feet. She wandered the small quarters, working through the motions to move her limbs. Glancing through the stuff from her apartment, she found her favorite leather jacket. She was happy her parents were able to salvage it.

When Isabella emerged from below deck, clutching the stair handrail and weak from the brief journey top side, Frank spotted her and rushed to her side.

"You should be resting," he insisted.

"I'm fine. I need some air." The wind was cold off the river—it felt so good. Her time in the light had reenergized her mind, providing her with the strength to deal with her battered body. Already the ache in her bones was fading. She turned her face to the night sky, catching mist off the bow. Frank regarded his daughter. His expression grew sad at the sight of her, but Isabella believed his concern was mainly for Lorraine.

"Mom's asleep. She's worn out. Dad, you shouldn't have let her come. She's missing her chemo and it's reckless; the cancer cells will grow and become resistant."

"Honey, I know, but there was no stopping her. Being here with you gives her the strength to fight her cancer."

"Donovan told me you two had left the country and that I shouldn't try to contact you."

Frank studied the city lights on the horizon. "I broke a promise, something I don't take lightly. I promised to leave, but we heard about the escape plan and the doctor's rendezvous location. The skipper resisted letting us on the boat at first, but Lorraine convinced him." Isabella and Frank both smiled at the thought of Lorraine sweet-talking the man.

"The Guardians may never forgive me. We broke an important Guardian rule—family members never travel together."

"We are better together," Isabella said.

"Yes, and just like when you were young, the river will flow us out to the sea—to safety."

Frank guided their ambling across the deck toward the boat's portside railing. As the wind pushed against them, the distance seemed insurmountable, but they made it. The sharp smell of the water's shifting salinity filled her senses. She could tell they were nearing the river's mouth, where the tide met the stream and fresh and saltwater fused, becoming a transitional mixture. Like the brackish water they were riding on, Isabella felt herself shifting and evolving. She reflected on Donovan, her parents, Gin, Angela. It was apparent no one got through these times unchanged.

"You know, you can start over again." Her father pulled Isabella out of her thoughts. "You have a second chance, kiddo. You can still be whoever you want to be. Where we're going, you will be free. You won't have to hide you're a Luman."

She smiled at him. "Right now, all I want is an extra-large pizza with lots of cheese and pepperoni."

Frank chuckled, probably for the first time since he had learned Isabella was burned. "Knowing your momma, I'm sure she brought some of your favorite snacks. Let's go check."

"I want to stay here. I'll be fine." She held tight to the railing.

"Okay, I'll be right back." He glanced back once, and Isabella caught the familiar look of concern in his eyes, and then he disappeared below deck.

She felt something simmering, marinating deep inside of her, too deep to name it really. A kind of rage. She sensed it in her dad as well. About what they had done to her and why was unfathomable. It was best to leave it buried, at least for now. And then she heard Lorraine telling her, "If you don't forgive and move past it—they win." And Isabella thought, *They do not get to win. Not this time.*

Isabella stood rigid against the wind as it ruffled her upturned collar. It was Thanksgiving, and she was thankful that her parents were now with her. The fishing cruiser snaked past the last bend in the river as the dense forest at Cape Charles gave way to a spangle of moonlight across the dark ocean. Ancient navigators called it the glitter path.

Watchmen had long used the moon's reflection off the sea's surface to read the water and avoid the shallows. Isabella studied the rippling water, seeing it turning choppy as they entered the North Atlantic. The glitter path bulged, and refractions of moonlight were distorted— there would be rougher seas ahead.

For Isabella, escaping was not as hard as remembering. Who was she now? A spy, an unwilling informant? Was she mentally unstable or completely sane? Her words pushed against the wind. "If only I could remember what happened in the box, then I'd know the damage I've become."

She contemplated the stars fading into a silver dusting scattered across the sky, and reminisced about Angela. To win Angela's heart, or at least get a foot in the door leading to that, she had put together an outing that would fill Angela with a sense of freedom. Angela had driven a car for the first time, and they'd journeyed beyond the stifling smog out to the last fringes of wilderness left in the compound—the river. While stargazing, they had dared to dream of a future together. A future in which they were free. It had seemed so radical.

Isabella recalled the look of wonder on Angela's face as she peered up at the stars. Had sensed her freedom. What that might entail. There had been an inkling, a stirring of something just out of reach, something not unlike magic. Isabella had felt it too. She remembered it all, every bitter and sweet moment. She shoved her hands in the pockets of her jacket, tilting her head slightly as she felt thick card stock in the right one. She pulled it out, confused at first by the sunflowers of Arles postcard. Flipping it over, she saw a message, addressed to her. In Angela's handwriting. She took a deep breath, fighting back tears, and read it.

*Dear Isabella,*

*When you think of me—after your trust in me falters, and it will—please know I loved you, impossibly so. This note is my untold truth. Beyond my beating heart, there has always been a deafening silence. A dull, dark place where I feel little to nothing. But you, Isabella, changed that. You changed me. With you, I can now feel things that before I only pretended to feel. You gave me what was missing. Loving you put me in orbit, there to experience a wonderful yet terrifying gravitational pull toward you. Many times my navigation from my world to yours has wavered. Still, it has never ended, at least not for me.*

*I hope someday you will understand that what I've done is not a betrayal but an act of self-preservation. For you are headed somewhere else, and our worlds move on, our fates uncertain. So, in your reminiscence, try to be happy. Don't let my darkness complicate your heart or stop you from believing in a world of possibilities. If not for possibilities, why else would we shimmer like diamonds?*

*Love, A~*

Isabella breathed in the depth of Angela's words and knew in time the note's meaning would take shape in her, for better or worse. Having exceptional visual perception provided Isabella with no clues about Angela's darkness. It was the only time her two views of the world merged as one. There was no difference between Luman and human regarding matters of the heart.

In the remains of the night, an image of Angela came to her, undulating out of the clouds like an approaching storm. Her form rolled in and over her, a Day-Glo tempest. She shuddered against the warmth of Angela's lips pressing against hers. This wasn't a repercussion of being in the box, she was sure of it. It was Angela, her being, reaching through the distance, letting Isabella know she was okay. Theirs was a tale of survival. In a world of uncertainty, Isabella wanted to believe in possibilities.

*Angela was a lost star but one worth finding. Some day, some way, they'd be together again.*